RIVERSMEET

RICHARD BRADBURY

Riversmeet

[handwritten inscription]

The Muswell Press

First Published in Great Britain 2007
This paperback edition published 2007

The moral right of the author has been asserted
A CIP catalogue record for this book is available from the
British Library

ISBN 978-0-9547959-3-1

10 9 8 7 6

Printed in Great Britain by
Short Run Press Ltd.
Bittern Road, Sowton Industrial Estate,
Exeter EX2 7LW
tel 01392 211909
www.shortrunpress.co.uk

The author would like to thank Ruth Boswell and Jan Woolf,
without whom this wouldn't exist and certainly not in this form.

THE MUSWELL PRESS
129 Rosebery Road, London N10 2LD
www.muswellpress.co.uk

Design: Ralph Kinnear

To Deirdre, Gabriel, Aidan, Àine and, most of all, Maureen, because they lived with the writing of this, and - much more difficult task - they continue to live with me.

CONTENTS

PART ONE	1
PART TWO	47
PART THREE	67
PART FOUR	91
PART FIVE	93
PART SIX	113
PART SEVEN	119
PART EIGHT	155
PART NINE	157
PART TEN	207
PART ELEVEN	211
PART TWELVE	281
PART THIRTEEN	285

PART ONE

AUTUMN, 1830

A young boy creeps out of his father's house where he is made to sleep on the floor among the dogs and runs through the trees that surround the plantation house until he reaches the slave quarters. As quietly as he can, he lifts the latch of the third shed in the middle row and steps inside. On an ancient strawstuffed mattress a woman sleeps on her back with a young girl drawn in under her arm. The boy stands looking at her in the semi-darkness, and watches the tiredness drool slowly from the woman's half-open mouth. Then he steps back out again, into the darkness and stands for a while looking up at the sky, looking for the North Star. When he finds it he whispers very quietly as though telling a secret, "I will go; I will run away".

So far away that the boy would think it another planet, Eamonn MacDonagh, a young man in his early twenties stands in the thin darkness before dawn with his arms full. What he is holding looks like small logs in the gloom, but they are not. They are more of the place; slices of turf cut from the bog and stacked to dry all summer and into the autumn, to keep the home warm and the potatoes cooked the winter through. The mist stirs over the low ground running away behind the cottage and he sees motion within it. It is not the mist itself moving, it is being moved. He cannot make out, though, what is causing the movement and does not want to think what it might be that he thinks he sees. Does not want to believe that he can hear it, now that it has more definite shape. He clutches the turfs tightly to his chest, as if to protect them. Until a lick of the mist runs towards him and he knows that it wants the turf returned. So he throws one back into the bog, but the mist licks again and the sound within it but not of it echoes again. Now he knows it is not angry with him, not angry with him and his family, even though he knows that the mist and the presence within the mist are angry. It is not angry with him, It is warning him. Warning that something has gone wrong. No, he listens more carefully; that something will go wrong, terribly, irreversibly wrong.

Badhbh chaointe

Bean sí

Somehow he knows that when he remembers this moment, he will have to translate it: from early adulthood awash with promise to an angry middle age, from gróigín, an ghaoth aniar imeacht, ionnarbadh…

Before he can do that, though, he will need to leave. This place, this tongue. He will have to translate himself.

Banshee

FREDERICK DOUGLASS
SUMMER, 1837

Dust hangs in the still air. The motes float through the shafts of sun cutting across The air is heavy, smells of horses.

When the door opens, he looks round with something between anticipation and fear on his face and in his blood. He braces himself when he sees who has entered.

Covey and two of his men holding ropes and a whip

He takes half a step back, and then two forward, bracing his feet on the floor.

Covey advances

He lifts one hand towards the advancing figure, keeps the other clenched behind his back. He bends his knees very slightly, so that any coming shock won't make him stagger.

"This is for you. Do you know what it is?"

It is a whip, coiled and dragging the floor

like a thin evil snake

Before the man can come any closer he starts forward, still keeping his right hand behind his back.

Steps inside Covey's outstretched arm
Grips Covey's right hand with his left
And punches Covey hard as he can on the nose

It shatters into brittle redness.

His hands move fast now, doing what they must.

Throwing more punches, holding tight
to the slavebreaker's arm
"I don't want to beat you, boy just let me go and I'll stop
now and we'll say no more"

He lets go and the slavebreaker falls to the floor scattering droplets from his nose and mouth

*"I let you go: I let **you** go.*
You raise your hand to me again, I'll beat
you again and I will say more"

<hr />

EAMONN MACDONAGH
SUMMER, 1837

Yes, yes you're doing very well
What is this yes?
It means, it means

What a thin language, Eamonn thinks, that uses just one word when a full sentence would serve the purpose. I am not sure that I am doing right, to be here among the thin lipped, thin mouthed people. Yet what choice do I have?

You're doing very well, Edmund
Edmund?
I'm sorry, I thought
Oh, yes, yes. Edmund

Edmund Brown. That's who I have become. But before that, one last time. One last sentence. To myself, quietly, under my breath. Under my tongue and behind my teeth, I will say my name. Eamonn MacDonagh. The name that I have, it means the same in both worlds. Only they don't know it, the ignorant pigs. They step on the earth and they don't know the name of the place under their boots. They use names like trinkets. One day, one day, I will show them the meaning of my name: it means blessed protector, the one who wouldn't share his land with the invader.

Miss Fry, I want to thank you for your help.
That sounds as though you are think-
ing of leaving us, Edmund.
Oh, no, Miss Fry. I was wondering, would you teach
me to read, to read and to write in English?

They both know now they will have to run. Change their identities and hide from the past, lest the past reach up into the present and drag them back again. They both need anonymity, to re-establish their lives. So they start to run, away from here and off to some place where no-one in the past will think to look for them. And there they will hide, until they are ready.

Where else to hide but a big city? So they go, in their different directions, towards different big cities. They learn new skills that will help them conceal themselves until the moment comes. Neither of them, though, will know when the moment has come until it does.

And then it does. And then they do.

JUNE 17, 1845
A SHORT EXTRACT FROM THE "LIBERATOR"
NEWSPAPER EDITORIAL PAGE

On the glory of the coming day and on the occasion of the publication of your life's narrative and its account of the bestialities of human slavery, I salute you, the dearest and bravest friend of the struggle for abolition in North America. Frederick Douglass, you are a beacon shining in the darkness of ignorance and oppression. Your very existence gives the lie to the slavers' claims that blackness means less than wholly human. Your narrative is, as Wendell Phillips's introductory letter to that volume has it, "the roar of the lion come to drive the lies of the slavers from the field." Every friend of the struggle to end slavery should read your words, and should tell their friends to read them also. For truly, your writing demonstrates that the pen is mightier than the chains of slavery. You have broken those chains, as this slim volume tells, and have come to claim your birthright as a citizen of this nation that was founded on the premise that all men are created equal; a premise most grievously abused by those who imprison their fellow human beings in the shackles of chattel bondage.

I salute you, Frederick Douglass, fellow citizen and friend of liberty.

I commend the narrative of your life to all the friends of liberty and urge them to buy and read this marvellously brief, yet mighty, work.

Signed,
William Lloyd Garrison, editor

<hr />

AUGUST 4, 1845
WILLIAM LLOYD GARRISON'S LETTER
TO FREDERICK DOUGLASS

My dear Douglass,

I do hope the attached statement reaches your hand before your departure for Europe. I thought it unwise to mention the European tour in the "Liberator" until you were safely away, so that we might avoid any further attempt by the enemies of liberty to prevent your embarkation. The slavers, our secret friends in the South tell us, have been gathering their plans to seize you and return you to Thomas Auld the man-stealer. Better then, that no news leaks until you are away. I wish you good fortune and success on your mission. With truth as our sword, we cannot but prevail in our efforts to bring down slavery and so end the scourge of the modern world.

Your friend,
William Lloyd Garrison

My dear sister Harriet,

It is a great comfort to me, to know that yourself and the good Jeremiah Sanderson are now installed at the house with Anna, and that the two of you will stay until my return. My plan, and indeed the plan agreed by my friends within the movement for abolition, is that I should write to you enclosing letters to my Dear Anna. These I would entreat that you read to her over and over again until Dear Anna fully understands their contents and that you shall then pass the letters to my friends and sponsors Mr. William Lloyd Garrison and Mr. Wendell Phillips for use in "The Liberator", if they think that these letters are useful in spreading the news of our efforts here.

I thank you now for all your kindness both past and to come,

Your brother
Frederick

My dearest wife,

I am now safely arrived in Dublin after the most extraordinary events during the voyage. Mister James Buffum, it is clear to me, wished to avoid any controversy during our time aboard even after the insult of our being refused by the shore crew at Boston the cabins we had reserved and so having to take steerage passages. But, poor James, it was not to be! There were too many British aboard for that to be possible, too many who wished to speak and sit with me. Too many to whom I sold copies of the "Narrative" and whom, on reading in it, wished to talk with me further about the crimes of slavery and slavers. It is astonishing, their apparent absence of hatred for the colour of our skin among these people. They came and took their seats by me on the deck, and conversed with a man who was their equal, looking through the skin to the heart and soul beneath. They had an excellent heedlessness to the muttered insults of several of the passing American passengers. Eventually, by delegations, they prevailed upon the captain to have me speak to the passengers as a whole and, despite the efforts of a few Southerners, a time and place were agreed.

The night of 27 August on the *Cambria's* promenade deck, the crowd was dense and as soon as I rose to speak those Southern gentlemen - those who had not gone below in protest at my presence - attempted with catcalls and cries of "that's a lie!" and "take down the nigger!" to prevent me from going ahead with my speech. Now, you know that your husband is not a man easily set aside, but even so it was hard going until Mr. Hutchinson settled the crowd by starting an abolitionist anthem in which many joined, albeit uncertainly for a lack of the exact words. Even so, as soon as I began to speak again, a cry of "I wish I had you in Cuba" and "I wish I had you in Savannah" came from identifiably Southern throats and the melee started over. I sat down until the intervention of Captain Judkins and another gentleman whose name I later learned was Thurlow Weed. Together they held the slaveholders' mob at bay until I was finished, Mr Weed offering to put the interrupters over the side and the Captain showing them the irons they could expect to wear for the rest of the voyage unless they were quiet. Fond as they are of the irons they put on others, they were not so ready to wear them themselves and they fell silent until I concluded. However immodest it may sound I feel that the evening was a great success and it gave me heart for this venture, having left behind so much that is familiar and necessary to my being.

I also feel a great burden of responsibility towards our people, for much depends on my success this next while. It is, then, doubly strange to be given such responsibility for the collective and then to find one's self separated from all those to whom one can turn without hesitation to say, "how goes it? Am I proceeding as you would wish?". However close to Buffum I feel, there are still the subtleties of color difference between us which express themselves most in his unwillingness to speak directly to me of any problems that he sees with my way of proceeding. He is, in short, altogether too polite.

I wonder if it might be that Buffum, even against his will and strength, has been somehow infected by the hatred for our color that fills every corner of American society. That hatred draws its strength from our enslavement but its infection spreads much further, so that even such a good-meaning man as Buffum cannot overcome the barriers it has erected even before his birth. The problem seems rooted in the fact of living in a world where one is told repeatedly, this person here, that person there, they are not wholly human by virtue of the color of their skin. And so he finds himself, I feel, infected by that idea in the strange way that means he cannot argue with me as he would a white man with whom he disagrees. There is, ever, a gap between us as there is a gap between even the kindest master and his favourite dog.

This absence of genuine friendliness is entirely different from that I have experienced from strangers since we arrived in Liverpool and now Dublin, from where I am writing. Here, I feel, an Irishman can take me by the hand and almost not notice the color of that hand.

This sensation was at its most intense just yesterday, when I visited the prison in which Daniel O'Connell was jailed some years ago and spoke to a group of the inmates. Here were men robbed of their liberty and so they said they had some sense of what it was to be a chattel. Yet, they continued, they had the consolation of parole or release whilst in the Southern states a slave was ever a slave and the whole state is a prison. Beside that, their own imprisonment was as the merest trifle. I was much moved by this meeting.

Becoming now more settled, I will write and send my letters as often as I may. And so, even though the voice of Sister Harriet must stand in for mine until I return, be assured that when I write it shall be as though we are alone and together in the room where you are now seated.

Your
Frederick.

My dear wife,

Forgive me for not having written again until now but these last two weeks have been taken up enormously with establishing myself with Dublin friends and with a round of meetings and occasions. Almost as soon as we were arrived we began our work, and it has been a great success to this point. The Irish have an almost natural affinity with our cause, for they know what it is to be hated for being what you were born without the chance to show what you are. They turn out, often in the thousands, to hear me speak. To hear me speak! What a strong savour those four words have for me. Especially when it is to the Friends' meeting house that I am invited and I am ushered through the front door. No voice cries, "niggers ain't allowed", as I step through the portal. No raised hand insists that I must go round to the back door. Tomorrow, they tell me, will be the biggest yet, when I go to a place that holds upward of three thousand persons.

I have also made good use of my time in other ways. I have to tell you, and I know the news will be pleasing to your heart, that I am seriously preparing myself to take the Pledge. I have seen here the detriment drink can wreak and find myself all the more opposed to the weakness it represents. I feel most strongly that I am on this earth to perform a mission and that whatsoever prevents me from that must be set aside.

I am aided in that purpose by the simple fact that among the people here I have encountered none of that special American condition, the virulent hatred for all members of our race that precedes any knowledge of particular individuals. I have spent the last two weeks in a state of anticipation, awaiting the first insult and only now do I feel that I have relaxed slightly, beginning slowly to believe that it will not come.

At the same time I am sickened to the depth of my heart by the news from Lexington. In Cassius Clay, we had a true friend whose voice rang out in protest against the crime of slavery and the loss of his press is a blow. More terrible, though, is the blow that has robbed us of his intelligence and energy. At the same time, yet, I am strengthened by the thought that it is only mob violence that can silence our arguments, only a hooligan's hand overturning a tray of type that can stop the flow of our words and arguments. Our enemies are too afraid to debate with us in public, but must come like thieves in the night to burn our houses and offices. They are knaves and cowards, who would only strike against such a man by darkness.

I trust that both your good self and the children are well.

Your
Frederick

SEPTEMBER 29, 1845
DOUGLASS'S LETTER TO ANNA

My dear wife,

It continues to be astonishing to me how different here is the place of a man with my color of skin. I am not shunned from public places, but welcomed in. I am not ignored by those who would claim to be allies, but taken into their confidence. I am not ordered to the gallery, but invited to a seat on the platform. Just this last evening, for example, I went to hear Daniel O'Connell the Liberator speak. He is a great man! He is a great orator, the best I have heard in the four years since I first climbed onto a platform and said my piece.

When he had finished his speech and sat down, I was invited to the platform. Nervous as I was, I managed to say a few words before returning hurriedly to my seat. After which and at the end of the gathering, O'Connell came and sat beside me and we talked for several minutes. In that time he showed no sign whatsoever of the color hatred. All this has put my head in a spin, such that there are nights when I can barely sleep and instead sit at the window looking out at the streets of Dublin. In the seven years since we ran from Baltimore, because I was driven by my need for liberty and by your love for me; in those seven years how far have we come, you and I. The runaway slave now takes his seat beside the most famous Irishman in the world! How I long to see master Thomas Auld's face, as he reads of the doings of his chattel!

In the next few days we leave for a tour of the west of this country, and so I do not know if it will be possible for me to write before I return here again to this magnificent city.

I have included with this letter two newspaper cuttings, which report the meeting. One tells what O'Connell said after I had spoken, whilst the other reports my words with an accuracy I have long since come to expect from only our own papers. It is quite astonishing to me to see my name beside his.

Your
Frederick

Mr O'Connell followed the eloquent young American with these words: I have been assailed for attacking the American institution, as it is called – Negro slavery. I am not ashamed of that attack. I do not shrink from it. I am the advocate of civil and religious liberty, all over the globe, and wherever tyranny exists, I am the foe of the tyrant; wherever oppression shows itself, I am the foe of the oppressor; wherever slavery rears its head, I am the enemy of the system, or the institution, call it by what name you will. I am the friend of liberty in every clime, class and colour. My sympathy with distress is not confined within the narrow bounds of my own green island. No – it extends itself to every corner of the earth. My heart walks abroad, and wherever the miserable are to be succoured, or the slave to be set free, there my spirit is at home, and I delight to dwell.

We were very struck by the words of the young American, who showed no signs of trepidation or nerves before he began his speech, a small part of which we reproduce here:

"I am the representative of three millions of bleeding slaves. I have felt the lash myself; my back is scarred with it; I know what they suffer, and I implore you to bring the weight of that powerful public opinion which you can make so effective, to bear on the hearts and consciences of the slaveholders of my country. Tell them they must give up their vile practices, or continue to be held in contempt by the whole civilised world."

<hr />

SEPTEMBER 30TH, 1845
CAPTAIN JUDKINS' REPORT

I am a working man, plying my trade as best as I can, and the only difference between myself and another manager is that my working place is the Atlantic Ocean and my office is the deck of a ship. I spend more of my days afloat than on land and have done so now for so long that this seems to me the natural order. My owners, the owners of the ships I captain I should say, inform me by periods of the ships I will take on the North Atlantic run. This is the route for which I have volunteered, for here I make the acquaintance of more varied and interesting persons than I could ever essay in other manner. Mostly frequently I work two ships, the *Cambria* and the *Hibernia*.

My owners, the owners of the ships I captain I should say, issue me with instructions both general and specific to each voyage. Combine speed with safety they write in each communication, as though I were likely to endanger my own life in order to ensure their reputation as the fastest passage. After the recent events on board, caused in so small part by my belief that I was acting in accordance with the company's wishes in denying a black man a cabin, I found myself the recipient of a letter from the owners pointing out the bad publicity and the potentially damaging effect this disturbance onboard might have on their trade. I was, therefore, advised to ensure there was no repetition of such events. That is what I shall do.

<hr />

OCTOBER 8TH
DOUGLASS'S LETTER TO ANNA

My dear wife Anna,

I have now been one hectic week in Dublin, the capital of Ireland, and I find myself fêted even more than in England. I have learned, also, to make this distinction as so many I meet here insist upon it. Not the English, to be sure, but everyone else is clear that this is, this should be, that this will be one day another country, this place that I have crossed into. The common language, I might say, conceals the difference, but then that is also the case with the two sides of the Atlantic. So much difference is concealed by the surface similarity of language.

Most obviously, the difference consists in religion. For there are many of the Popish persuasion here. I have learned, very quickly, that if I am to make friends then the word Papist will not be my friend but I find the term Roman Catholic too unfamiliar to me to be sure of its easy production in public. This I must practice though, for I am to go on a tour to the west where the English presence is still more tenuous than here. If I am to speak, and to speak and write defines me, then I must find a way to make the priests and their powerful laity my companions.

Beyond that I find Dublin a city very much to my liking, with the many white buildings which line the city center streets a great contrast to the greyness of New England's industrial towns. Whatever its quiet backwardness, this is still the home place of the good Sheridan from whose writings I first began to learn the art of reading, without which skill I would still be classed a beast of burden.

It is apt, then, that we have also come here to make arrangements with the publisher Richard Webb for a British edition of my *Narrative*, which he will arrange to have printed and then delivered to the towns and cities at which I shall speak, so that the people may read of the horrors of slavery as well as hear my expostulations. Webb himself is a man of great intelligence and knowledge. As well as being a great supporter of our cause, he is a profoundly well-read man and we talk much of both politics and literature. He also holds strong opinions close to my own on temperance and also on the end of warfare through the spread of rational intelligence. I have spent several very pleasant evenings at his house, when we have talked and discussed much.

By God, though, the smell of the river and the privy - and the two are nearly one - pervades the streets so much that I find myself wishing to be away from here when the stench wakes me in the night if the wind changes. My hosts tell me that I will pine for Dublin when I am in the country and they make many jokes about what I will meet there, and they use a language filled with words of uncertain meaning. I have no idea what a "gombeen" might be, and whenever I enquire they laugh mightily at their own wit. I am ready for the trip to the south and west.

Your,
Frederick

_____

OCTOBER 13TH
DOUGLASS'S LETTER TO ANNA

My dearest wife Anna,

I am now arrived in the town of Wexford and I must plead your indulgence for writing twice in one week but I have so much to tell of the dreadful and shocking journey here, and of my preparations for tomorrow.

Buffum obtained a coach for our transport and we departed Dublin early in the morning. Within a short while we were "beyond the pale", which I now understand means that we are into the real Ireland, the land not wholly dominated by the English presence.

This real Ireland, my dear, is country strange to my eyes for it is such a densely populated place. The number of people abroad strikes a visitor from the Americas, such as myself, very forcibly. That general observation is made more striking still when one considers the smallness of the plots of land these people work. Some have as little as a half- or even a quarter-acre to provide for themselves and their families – which are, I must say, often considerably larger than would by many be considered usual. At every small village we approached, and they are numerous indeed along the road, almost blurring one into the next, the fields were alive with several generations of the same family at work. The men digging, the women collecting the largest of the crop and the children coming along behind scrabbling in the soil for the smaller potatoes missed by the scrutiny of their elders. All wrapped with whatever covering they can find, but all still filthy and plastered with thick mud so that they seem almost creatures sprung from the earth rather than people working upon it.

We made slow progress, for the conditions of the roads beyond the confines of Dublin are very poor, much potholed and clearly more used to the passage of feet than of wheels. Our companion and guide, a Mr. Ennis from Cork, told us that the situation of the roads was worsened still more by the persistent rains that have fallen since the end of June. Indeed, the clouds lowered around us all day and the light was so feeble that we barely noticed the passage of the day.

Yet, shaken and battered as we were by the passage, Mr. Ennis was most delighted at our progress for by nightfall we had reached Arklow, a small town on the coast, and here we rested at a hotel of sorts, which was the house of some distant relative of his.

The next day, we had little reason to celebrate the morning for the rain greeted us when we rose and then stayed with us throughout the whole day. By reason of this, our progress was much slowed as we slithered rather than bumped along our way. Just as I had become resigned to the discomfort of this form of travel, we came to a complete halt. Mr Ennis, sitting with the window cracked so as to give himself some air, had banged upon the roof demanding that the driver stop. Buffum and I waited for some minutes within the coach after Ennis had descended, but as we received no intelligence from him we both climbed out into the drizzle. We could not at once see the reason for Ennis's silence, for he was standing some distance from the road deep in conversation with another man. He seemed so utterly still that after we had watched for some time we decided to approach and try to discover what was the matter.

As we approached our nostrils were assailed by the most truly dreadful stench, worse I would say even than that of putrefying human flesh, and we stopped short of the pair.

When we could bear to approach, with our handkerchiefs pressed to our faces, we were better able to apprehend what was the matter. The two men were standing looking down into a pit about twelve feet across and perhaps three at its deepest, but it was hard to tell the exact depth for the whole was filled with a huge mess of almost liquid rottenness from which the appalling smell rose. It was, we understood from Mr. Ennis's translation, the first diggings of the man's potato crop, which had been sound when first lifted but which had now rotted. The same was true, we also understood, for many of his neighbours.

Not knowing what to say to a fellow creature faced by destitution but divided from me by language, I stood in silence. After a few moments, though, Buffum asked if the foliage had first turned black before the tubers had been lifted and when the question and the answer had been translated, he told that indeed this was the case. He nodded and turned away. I followed and we returned to the coach to wait for Mr. Ennis, who returned after a few minutes with a look of some considerable concern on his face. He was, he said, most anxious to know the import of Buffum's question but my travelling companion was very tight-lipped, saying that he did not wish to spread rumour where he was not sure of his case. Nothing could persuade him to change his mind and even after we had continued on our way for some time he was immovable.

At this Mr. Ennis became very cold towards him and engaged exclusively myself in conversation. From him I gathered that he was entirely at a loss to explain what was happening to the crop. Failures he had seen before but this was entirely new and he was most anxious to know what was afoot. At the first opportunity, when we were changing horses at a small town the name of which I now forget, I questioned Buffum and he expressed the opinion, very quietly and under his breath, that the crop was affected by the blight that had attacked the potatoes in America this last few years. The rottenness and the blackening of the foliage convinced him, but he was not prepared to speak for fear of the consequences. Also, he said, the awfulness of the stench was not something he had encountered before and thus he was not sure of his case. Better to wait and be sure, than to cause a needless panic, he said.

What possible consequence could there be, I asked, from telling the truth in any situation. To which he replied that I should think of the impact that the intelligence of the possible complete loss of the staple crop would have on an already impoverished population. You have seen, he said, how whole families, generations of the same family living piled one on top of another, depend upon the potato. Think what would happen if the one source of food within the country vanished. The flight into the towns, the strain placed upon an already strained provision for the poor, the speculation in other foodstuffs. I was moved to agree but now felt caught into the conspiracy of silence against Mr. Ennis. I avoided this by engaging him in vigorous conversation about the route we were taking, the conditions of the people along the way and the history of the places through which we were passing and in consequence learned a great deal of the Irish and their history. I was much taken by his tales of the myths and legends of the past, the heroes that bestrode this landscape in the distant past.

That second night we reached Enniscorthy, where we again

stayed in a house owned by associates of Mr. Ennis, though this night we were not left to our devices and our beds, but after we had eaten the conversation turned to our mission in Ireland and to much discussion of the life of a chattel slave. Several people wished to make a comparison between the Irish peasant tenant farmer and my previous condition but I argued at great length that the certain knowledge of the permanent loss of liberty was worse than any other form of bondage. One of our hosts then turned to Buffum and enquired after his observations on our journey and while he was as much struck by myself by the poverty he also wished to agree with me that there was a difference of kind between the slave and the worker. At this, one man who had not yet contributed to the debate, opined that the freedom of the peasant here was the freedom to starve, as he was sure Mr. Buffum had seen that day. Buffum enquired what was meant by that comment, to which the man replied that Buffum had knowledge of what was amiss with the potato crop and would not tell.

At this I was most angry with Mr. Ennis, and told him so, to have betrayed our private exchanges. Niceties, the previous speaker said in a quiet but very firm tone, were as nothing when starvation stared the populace in the face. We should tell everything we knew, he thought. Then, of a sudden, he stepped very close to us, his voice dropped to a whisper and he implored us that, if we knew what was rotting the potatoes, we should tell.

This comment was followed by a long silence as we all turned to Buffum, as the source of the intelligence. I could see that he was torn as to whether or not to speak, with his head lowered to his chest to avoid the eyes of all present. When he made up his mind, he raised his head a little and said simply, it is the blight.

Rarely, if ever, have I seen four short words do such damage. I saw grown men start suddenly pale and shake, and others with tears in their eyes. The silence that had preceded Buffum's words was as nothing to that which came after. It seemed to me that lives were draining away there in that room.

Then the dam was breached and the men began to pour with questions. What treatment was there, to which the answer was that there is none. What could be done, we were asked but that did not seem to be a question we could answer. Indeed, I offered that my business here was other than this and said I must go to my bed. I left them talking, and they barely noticed my departure.

When I woke it appeared that Buffum had not slept at all the previous night, with talking and arguing, and he seemed very tired. He was also somewhat distressed to think that he had chosen the wrong path the night before and that he now considered that silence would have been a better policy. I said again that truth can never be harmful, and that he had spoken well.

My faith, though, was a little shaken when we left the establishment and set off again on our journey south. For the streets, the alleys rather, of this little town were filled with the news of the night before. Buffum was several times taken by the hand by people of all ages who were most distressed by the news that had spread so swiftly from his lips to, it seemed, every ear in the town. All, it seemed, wished to know what cures for the blight he knew and their distress was much deepened when they were told by Buffum that he knew of no cure save burning the crop and not replanting the same ground with potatoes for several years. Indeed, we were greeted with much disbelief at the extremity of this measure but as our questioners saw that Buffum was serious, their dismay grew immensely more until it seemed to me that we two were Moses and his flock parting a way through a Red Sea of weeping and protestation. We were greatly relieved when we reached the stables of our coach and could proceed out of this lamentation.

We had not travelled very far upon the road when we realised that we were followed by a group of horsemen whose intent, it became clear, was to intercept our journey. As it was obvious to all that we could not outrun them, we continued at our usual pace until we were overcome and stopped.

One of our pursuers introduced himself as an officer in the British Army, a Captain Holland, and also one of Mr Peel's Scientific Commissioners. His task, he informed us, was to request that we desist from spreading alarm among the people of Ireland by disseminating tales of ruin. I took with him the same tack that I had employed with Buffum and enquired what damage the truth could ever do, to which he replied very shortly that I should not consider his request as a request made by my equal but as an order being given by a Crown official. I again enquired what he meant by this, to which he replied that I was a damned insolent nigger and he would like nothing better than to take his whip to me but that I was already too notorious among meddlers and do-gooders and that I should know that naught but my fame kept me from a flogging.

I was so shocked by this - for as I have told you several times before the great relief of being here was the absence of color prejudice - that I was speechless even as he rode away, and remained so for the rest of the day's travel. I noted, though, as we travelled this day that the stench receded and was replaced by another smell. When I enquired of Mr. Ennis what it might be, for I had never smelled anything quite like its dark smokiness, he told me that it was the turf fires. At my blankness, he explained that the people here, where they have the opportunity, use the bog turf dried as fuel for their cooking and heating. It is plentiful and cheap, he continued hurriedly, and for himself he preferred coal or wood.

The rest of our journey was uneventful. We arrived here in Wexford by mid-afternoon and I prepared myself for tonight's gathering by putting as much of the last two days' events out of my mind as I could, for I feel that my purpose while I am here is to speak for the cause of the abolition of slavery. That is my only purpose, from which I will not be distracted. I am to address an audience of local notables, mostly Quakers, and then tomorrow we will continue on to Waterford where I will speak again. After that, we will go on the larger town, city almost I am told, of Cork.

I will endeavour to write again as soon as we are settled here, but cannot now tell how long this may be.

Your,
Frederick

────────

Most alarming accounts of the failure of the staple crop of the Irish poor in the county of Cork - the Yorkshire of Ireland - have appeared in recent numbers of the local papers. So long as there was room to hope that these statements were exaggerated, we shall forbear from alluding to the subject; but from the multiplicity of corroborating testimony, in the shape of letters, some bearing the signatures of gentlemen of skill and experience in such matters, which have since been published, it is greatly to be feared that the calamity will be much more severely felt than was at first supposed.

"Ennis!"
"Not now, not now!"
"Ashamed to be seen in my company?
Bad for your reputation?"
"We have agreed…"
"Indeed we have, so I will be brief."
…
"The American."
"?"
"Douglass."
"Oh. Yes?"
"The American."
"Enough."
"I want to meet him."

────

"So do many others. Attend one of the meetings."

"Ennis."

"Very well. My house. Tomorrow."

"Is mise…"

"Enough of that!"

"Tomorrow."

"Tomorrow."

OCTOBER 24TH
DOUGLASS'S LETTER TO ANNA

My dear wife Anna,

These last ten days here in Cork - or Corcaigh, as I would wish to call it in all but the most public communication - have been a great success for our cause. I have addressed twelve meetings, the smallest of which had well over one hundred people present, and have been able to address the respectability of this part of Ireland to great effect. We have raised a good deal of subscriptions to both "The Liberator" and also to the British movement, and Buffum tells me that my speeches noticeably move members of the audience. I wish I could believe that this were the case, but know myself too ill-trained in the art of public speaking to be wholly convinced of this. The amount of practice I am gaining, though, does lead me to believe that my skills could improve as the weeks and months pass.

I have discovered that it is simply too tiring to make a different address every night and so I have, under the guidance of some of our friends here, been rehearsing a number of passages so that I may have a little polish to some parts of my lectures. This I began at the suggestion of a Mr. MacDonagh, an associate of Mr. Ennis. The great advantage I have gained from this activity is that it has allowed me to concentrate my thoughts onto certain parts of my speeches because I am relieved of worrying what I must say next, and this has given much clarity to my previously somewhat muddled thinking. For example, I have begun to see ever more clearly how slavery corrupts as a whole American society and religion.

Its effects on the slaves themselves and also upon the slave-holders have always been clear to me but as I have discussed with friends here I have begun to see how bondage spreads its influence through the whole body politic of America. To touch pitch is to be defiled by it, and even those who argue against slavery but continue to have dealings with slaveholders are touching the evil. I would despair that they cannot see this, were it not that I have but lately come to see this for myself.

I was in conversation with Mr. MacDonagh but two days ago and having said how much moved and stirred by Mr. O'Connell I had been, when we came to this subject he moved his face close to me and said that there were some here in Ireland who thought of O'Connell as a toucher of pitch in his dealings with the English Commons, but then he as quickly withdrew and I could see that this would not be an easy point of discussion.

I have, as though innocently, offered his ideas as my own sup-position to a number of other people in conversation and, after the merest hesitation of embarrassment on the part of my lis-teners, have been told that this was a very eccentric idea held by only the smallest group of the most extreme thinkers. The majority opinion is that the way forward is through negotiation with the British, such as may find some way of increasing the influence of the Irish themselves in their affairs. Thrown into a confusion by my own ideas and by my ignorance of the history of this country, I have not repeated this experiment.

As I have written before, the question of temperance has be-come a subject very close to my heart since I have been here and I am happy to tell you that I have been afforded the opportu-nity of speaking on this subject several times. I have made what I think are some sound points about the connection between the bestiality of slave-holding and the equal bestiality caused by drunkenness.

That the route away from both is through application and a sense of one's worth as a human person is my firm judgement.

I very much like the people here, but I have to report that there have been a number of occasions when I have seen some of the lower sort exceedingly drunk in the street in the middle of the day. I can understand why this might be, with the poverty so grinding upon those who have little or no work, but I cannot sympathise. Such levels of drunkenness were rare in the slave quarters through which I passed, and most often found in those places where the master himself supplied the drink as a sedative for his slaves.

Religion, of various sorts, was our consolation and I have talked much on this with a Catholic priest whose acquaintance I have made here through the auspices of the temperance movement. Father Theobald Mathew - that is his title and I would call any man by the name he chose for himself whatever my opinion of his beliefs - has told me of his concerns for the poor here if one-tenth of what is feared for the potato crop comes to pass. He has also told me that, if I were prepared so to do, he would be happy to prepare me for taking the Pledge while I am here in Ireland. I would beg you, my dear wife, not to think ill of me for having taken such a decision without consulting you first - for I have already consented to the good priest's offer - but there seems no mechanism through which you could tell me what you think of this proposal. Perhaps Harriet could teach you your letters, and then you could make replies to my questions that would come to me unfiltered.

I fear I must stop now, for Mr. Ennis yesterday brought me a copy of Charles Lyell's "Travels in North America", recently published here to much noise and I must set to work reading it so as to be better able to refute his arguments. I find it strange that a man who can be so profound in his thinking in the field of the science of the natural world can be so wrong-headed in his opinions on the social existence of some of his fellow human creatures. This task, I fear, will be a stiff challenge for this work of tight reading is not something I have had to come to previously but I can see much of it before me if my arguments for our great cause are to stand up against opponents such as the famous Lyell.

So, I take myself to my bed with Lyell's words as my cold companion.

Your,
Frederick

NOVEMBER 2ND
DOUGLASS'S LETTER TO ANNA

My dearest wife,

My visit to Ireland is now going forward with quite remarkable success, and the crowds to which I am invited to speak seem to grow every day ever larger until I often have to repeat myself to a second overflow audience once the first has left. Part of the attraction, I feel, flows from a passing remark I made in my lecture a few days ago. I turned, extempore, to my thoughts on Lyell's book which I mentioned in my last letter. Having read this arrant nonsense through, I found myself compelled to say that I have rarely encountered such willed foolery in such an intelligent man. To which one of my auditors loudly replied for all in the room to hear that Englishmen were often thus, hearing and seeing in others only what they already wished to see and hear. I responded that I had much sympathy with such a view, and I saw the Irishman and the Negro as both being under the thrall of another's boot. The cheers from the crowd at this were quite remarkable, for as soon as the words were out my mouth I remembered several occasions at home when such a parallel had brought much wrath from the audience of whites, to hear themselves placed in parallel to a "nigger" and his treatment. But here the prejudice towards color seems entirely absent, and my words are heard for what they are without the blinkers of hatred placed around them.

That is, of course, until some of the less gentle of the crowd have taken drink and then, it seems to me, I see the sparks of a familiar hatred glowing at the back of their eyes. This has determined me still more in my course as I outlined in my last correspondence, and in two days' time I will do that which I never thought to do in order to do that which I wish. To whit, I will cross the threshold of a Catholic church in order to sign the Pledge.

Since the departure of Buffum back to Dublin, I have spent much time at the home of the inestimable Jennings family who have made me welcome indeed. They are an outstanding example of that absence of color prejudice I have remarked before, and they have welcomed me into their bustling home - as well as the parents, there are eight children present - and have made me feel their friend. The smallest of the boys, Alexander, has taken to me very strongly and enjoys nothing more than sitting upon my knee and chuckling happily for hours at a time. For all the difference in coloring, he reminds me of our own little Frederick and I am glad for the sake of this little Alexander that he will never suffer the cruel separation from his father that has been imposed upon my child.

I must bring this to the mail now, for Mr MacDonagh stands at the door, pressing an urgent claim upon my attention.

I am, as ever, your
Frederick

THE POLE COMES ASHORE

What better night for it? They celebrate killing one of ours, we'll bring in the instruments for killing some of theirs. Senseless murder, they'll call it. Revenge, is what it is. I see that. I have seen it ever since I started to understand the larger picture. This is not just about me. There are many, thousands, like me all across the country, the continent, the world. We just have to find each other.

The sky is darkness, the land a deeper darkness still. They creep along. For all the winter storms and bad winds, this is still a good time. The nights are long, dark. Good for concealment.

After following the line of the cliffs, listening to the surf and feeling the boat's movement, there is it. The push of the river. He starts to turn the bow inwards, and the sail catches and flaps. Then it is tight again and the boat surges, even though they can feel the contrary push of the current. Less sail, less speed. Sudden muttered exchanges about the hour, equally sudden replies about the rocks at the mouth of the estuary. The smaller man retreats to sit in the lee of the cabin, while the others steer carefully in. Past the first rocks, then more, almost an island. And when they clear that, ahead is the city. Darkness lit by bonfires that seem to encircle where the city is, hidden in the night.

Not the crew need any light, for they can steer as much by memory as sight, sound and touch. They know where the turn will be, so that they can come ashore at the quiet wharfs, away from the bustle of the commercial heart. They turn.

Later, the boat glides in. It is almost morning. The thinnest grey infiltrates, to see the early fishermen to their boats. They pass the night boat with an occasional gesture: any luck, only a little, we'll go again later, good luck. Then they wait, until the fishermen have gone away to the far end of the quay. He waits, too, in the alley between two of the sheds until they have gone. Then hurries out, gestures to the boat. But he has to wait, for the small man has fallen asleep tucked in between the spare sails and the unused lobster pots.

When he is awake, he is instantly fully awake. He reminds MacDonagh of a cat that lived in his parents' cottage. The tom would sleep all day before the hearth but the instant a mouse stirred it would be awake and on it, snapping its neck before exhaling the first waking breath.

MacDonagh steps forward, trying to remember the words he has been taught as a greeting to this man. But they have slipped away, for they are not even distant cousins of anything he knows. He has to use *that* instead.

"*You're here.*"

"Indeed. I have arrived."

My dear sister Harriet,

Notwithstanding my previous requests, I would urge you not to pass on the enclosed letter to Phillips or Garrison until I give you explicit permission so to do. Indeed, I would think it a great service if you were to read it through for yourself beforehand then decide whether or not you think it appropriate that Anna should see it.

Your brother,
Frederick

NOVEMBER 7TH

DOUGLASS'S LETTER TO ANNA

My dearest Anna,

It was done and for a few brief hours I felt like the lamb with its wool white as the driven snow. I was new again.

I went with Fr. Theobald these two days past to the largest church in the town to sign my name publicly upon the Pledge and to make a brief speech on the rightness of temperance. We then, I and the other signers, made a brief procession in the streets calling on others who were of like mind to step forth and join us. To little avail, I must say, but my spirits were not lowered.

Not lowered, that is, until I reached my rooms again to discover within the secretive and, it is true, slightly drunk Mr MacDonagh returned to press his claim of the previous night. For I had pleaded tiredness before and tried to turn him aside with a promise that we would meet the next day.

He was, he told me, come for me; that he had friends in the town he wished me to meet and that we must hurry.

I responded that I did not wish, on the very day that I had signed for temperance, to be seen walking the streets with a man with the smell of strong drink about him. Then we will not be seen, he said, and gripped me very tightly by the elbow.

Even though he had been drinking, I could easily see that beneath the alcohol there was some urgent purpose and so, taking up my coat, I went with him into the street behind the hotel. Here he had a small carriage that he had evidently brought with the express purpose of conveying me through the town with the minimum of observation. Off we went, and at his urgings I kept my eyes turned from the window so that I could not tell, even had I wished, where we went.

Our destination, though, I could tell before I saw it for the smell of the quaysides was all around us for the last few minutes of our journey. I heard a large door scraping open before us and we entered in, carriage and all, before Mr MacDonagh would allow me to dismount or even to look out.

When we did step out, it was into the gloomy interior of one of the quayside sheds. Sheds they are called, but in truth they are immense stores into which much can be gathered. And gathered here were several men, all either with their hats pulled low or their scarves up about their eyes, so that I could not be sure of the identity of a single one of them.

When I asked the purpose of this gathering, Mr MacDonagh told me that he and his associates wished to make clear to me that there were here in Ireland men who held the example of my brother in slavery, the insurrectionist Nathaniel Turner, close in their bosoms. These were men, he said, who understood that serpents must sometimes of a necessity be struck with a heavy hand steered by a righteous heart, at which there was much muttered agreement.

I protested against this small tide of nods and whispers that this was not the route I believed, that the only way to bring down evil was through an appeal to the goodness in men's hearts. We needed, I continued, to hold close to our belief that our God had made us with a capacity for both good and ill, and that we must show men that to act in the light of goodness was to stand closer to God. At this, the men around made no answer and I thought for a brief moment that I had persuaded them of their error with the smallest effort. Then, from the darkness further back into the great warehouse, a figure emerged. A man with no scarf or hat to obscure his face, but only a heavy cloak of an unfamiliar design drawn up onto his shoulders. He had the most striking brown eyes and hair swept back in waves from his forehead, but the centre of his face was marked by the signs of a healed harelip. As soon as he spoke, I knew he was neither Irish nor English or American for his words and the structure of his sentences were too precise, too carefully chosen and arranged.

He asked me whether I would still hold to my belief if it could be proved that there was not even the merest trace of goodness in the hearts of some men. For he knew, yes he knew, that he could demonstrate this proposition to me.

As he spoke, he came to stand so close to me that I could see that not only was English not his first language but that the harelip was the merest sign that he had also overcome the obstacle of a repaired but still clearly visible cleft palate. This coming so close was a quite extraordinary gesture, for he stood now so close that I could feel his breath on my face as he looked up at me and I did not know for a moment what I should say. The directness of his gaze, and a deepness behind the eyes, showed something I could not comprehend. Its power in this small man, though, was clear to me. I stepped back and looked, spluttering something to the effect that I could not believe this to be true.

He replied that it must be my bible which gives me this hope, to which I assented, and then he gripped me by the elbow, turned to Mr MacDonagh and asked that he and I be allowed to walk alone a while in the night air. MacDonagh assented and the small man led me out through a small door set into the much larger entrance to the shed.

As soon as we emerged, he indicated that we should turn to

the left and away from the harbour proper. We walked briskly, his grip never leaving my elbow until we reached a set of large wrought iron gates in a high wall, which he opened and led me through into the most extraordinary garden. When I asked what this place was, he replied that it was an arboretum recently begun by a local business man and that he wished to take me to a place deep in beneath the more mature trees where we could speak. How he knew of this place I cannot tell, for not even natives of the town have remarked upon it to me when I have asked what places I could visit in the hours when I was not speaking. He hurried me along at such a pace that I feared several times for my footing on the slick grass until we evidently reached the spot he intended.

Here, he set me back against the tree and for the first time I felt fear of this unarmed and smaller man. His energy seemed to glow before me and, as I still could not divine his purpose, my imaginings turned to the hurt he might wish to visit on me. He seemed to know this even as I did, and drew back apologising for his hasty purpose and saying that he could understand my fear for many of his friends and compatriots had been taken in similar fashion into the darkness beneath the trees. Yet, he exclaimed, he felt safe beneath the canopy of the branches, a dark place for the telling of dark business but also a place to hide one's self. He said he thought I would know the value of a place to hide when one is running.

I agreed.

Then he turned to his business. He came, he said from a country that is not a country and therefore its people had no alternative but to turn to themselves for aid. Most immediately, though, he wished to tell me that my moral suasion would founder on the evil within men's hearts and that I should - if I wished to be true to myself - steel my resolve for battle. He knew this, he said, because of what he had seen in the place he called his motherland.

I protested again, but he silenced me by beginning a catalogue of the crimes against the human body he himself had either seen actually committed or of which he had seen the aftermath.

My dearest Anna, what that young man told me not merely turned my stomach but, as he persisted despite my protests that I had heard enough, was so wicked that - I fear I must tell you - it shook my very faith in God. For the crimes were so vile that they made all that we have seen within the bowels of slavery seem slight. Furthermore, he said, all this he had seen done not only from the hands of Russian heretics or wild pagans from further to the east but also from those who styled themselves his Austrian co-religionists. Those who claimed to stand at the heart of European civilisation, he told me, seemed most steeped in savagery.

In the course of one grotesquerie, I heard him catch his breath and was about to enquire for his welfare when all at once we heard a great shouting and running from the direction of the harbour. We hurried to the gates to look out but, thankfully, before we came out completely from under the cover of the trees MacDonagh appeared at the gates and shouted into the park that we were surprised, that he would lead the chase away, and then he turned and ran off. Moments later, several soldiers ran past and we heard a few shots before the night's quiet returned.

The young man enquired, astonishingly calmly it seemed to me for my own heart was racing as though I were pursued by a slaver's bloodhounds, if I thought that I could find my way to my hotel. I said I thought that I did, and he said that this was good for it was not to my advantage to be seen in public with him. When I protested that any man who suffered at the hands of the enemies of liberty and who struggled for his freedom was my friend, he stilled me by insisting that I know and be clear be that he was not merely a fighter for freedom, not merely a past murderer but also that he was proud of the fact that he intended murder again. The English authorities, he said, whilst no friends to his enemies were not keen to have him here in Ireland among men who shared his views on force as the tool of liberty.

He knew I was his friend, he said, and that was why he had prevailed upon MacDonagh to arrange the meeting but I should also know that any talk with MacDonagh about what had passed between us was out of the question. It must be as if this had never happened. With that, he pushed me towards the gates and when I looked back from the road, he had already withdrawn into the darkness. He had vanished as though he had never been there, and I stood alone beneath the trees. That wooded darkness that I had always before thought of as a place to which I could run and hide from the public cruelties of slavery and in which I could be safe, now seemed to me a concealment for the most dreadful crimes.

I walked back to my hotel, deeply troubled by the young man's words. For they challenged every precept that I have pursued in discussions with Phillips and Garrison. Yet I did begin to wonder whether it was not the fact of their safe whiteness that led them to eschew the extremities of resistance that this young man had defended to me.

Much confused, and deeply tired, I finally reached the hotel to find the whole place and everyone within it in, thankfully, a profound sleep. Something which eludes me still.

I must impress upon you, dearest Anna, the importance of not showing this letter to Phillips or Garrison, for until I know clearly what I should make of this last night's events I would not share these thoughts with anyone beyond those most close to me. By which I mean just yourself and Harriet.

I remain, your troubled but still
loving
Frederick

I had thought to sleep after completing my letter to Anna and eventually I did, but only very fitfully and finally came completely awake in the deepest pit of the night. So dark that I could pass my hand before my face and still not see but only feel the movement. Pushing back the bed-curtains, though, I could see the faintest light beneath the door and taking the extinguished candle from my bedside made my way into the hallway to obtain light. For the dreams, the wraiths, which had pursued my slumber, were of such terrible nature that I knew I would sleep no longer that night and needed light in the room to keep the visions at bay.

Not since the darkest hours of my captivity and enslavement at the hands of the brutal slave-breaker Covey have I been so sorely troubled. Indeed, this is worse. For when I was under Covey's power I knew that I could act to change my situation and knew what it was that I faced in my extremity.

But these dreams are populated by the young man's whispered words, the words I could not tell even to my wife or closest friends. For he told me how Christians hunted Christians like wild beasts. He told how he had seen his people fleeing from their villages into the forests for safety's sake. This, he said, was an act they had performed for many centuries and that the forest had come to occupy a similar place to the church as a sanctuary. But that then the Austrians, the civilised Catholic Austrian soldiers, had pursued the people. First into the churches and when those were dead into the forest. And then they had committed the most appalling outrages in the gloom. Indeed, it seemed as if even they wished to hide their acts from the light of day.

For they disembowelled pregnant women, and hung the babies from branches by the cord. They cut off men's hands and feet and then propped them against trees to watch while they raped wives and children with fists and muskets. They inserted muskets into men's anuses and then fired them. These things, and much more I cannot bring myself to write even here. The memory of his words, spoken quietly and evenly as though he was telling me of a country walk. The catalogue of horror went on and on as I sat in dumb shock beneath the trees in the park, and even though I have seen with my own eyes the barbarism of the slave trader, I could not recall crimes to match these. This was not the jealous rage of my master when he thrashed my aunt, all the while crying out that she was a damned bitch for talking to Ned. This was a calculation, that those who saw what had been done would be broken by it.

More, for when I slept, dreams of another kind passed before me. Never having seen such atrocious acts I could not dream them but I did begin to dream what I can only think are more primitive dreams, filled with the animals of the dark woods - the bison and the wolf, the bear - who hunted in a fashion more human than that employed by the human beings of whom the young man had told me. For they ripped flesh for food, and not to serve some other appetite.

At this thought I came clean awake, for if this were true then what price my faith as a Christian and believer in the word of God? If the line between the animals and ourselves is so blurred, then should we not turn aside from some people and try instead to convert the beasts of the fields? For when has even a fox done what these Austrian soldiers have done? I was, and am, sorely troubled by this thought and am helped to a conclusion not at all by the last words the young man hissed to me before the up-roar on the quayside interrupted us. He said, if I remember his words right, that when dealing with such wild beasts, argument was superfluous for all they understood was force and violence. Better, then, that the blow come first and swift.

The dawn is beginning to move on the windows, back from which I pulled the curtains long since so that the light of day should come to me as soon as possible. I look to it as some consolation.

My dearest Anna,

I am now arrived and settled in Limerick, a bustling and busy town to the north-west of Cork, where last night I converted my hasty thoughts on Lyell's writings into a more considered attack. This I did before a large audience of the town's notables and they seemed well pleased with what I had to say.

I said that Lyell was, as I understand the situation, a man of great intelligence when it came to geology. A man who understood rocks in all their complexity. And not just a geologist, but also a lawyer of some note. A man who understood the laws of England. But he appears to have left his wits at home when he crossed the Atlantic, for what he has written about the existence of slavery in the United States is the most arrant nonsense. It is as sensible, I said, as anything I might write about geology; for my ignorance of rocks is equal to his ignorance of the realities of slavery. The difference is, I admit my ignorance and do not claim a knowledge of rocks based on my questioning of the trees that cling to them whereas he claims to understand the enslaved after talking with their enslavers. My audience seemed much amused by this, and applauded me long and with good humor at the end of the evening.

I came here in the company of Mr Jennings alone, Mr Ennis having returned to Dublin to prepare the northern stage of my journey through this country and Mr MacDonagh having not returned after that night in the Cork docks. On the way through the country, I began to see again and more definitely the effects of the failure of the potato crop spreading further into the west. Children already rendered to scraps, with the eyes of their mothers and fathers filled with a sorrow and pain grown from the hunger of their babies. Once, we stopped at a mud-walled, windowless hut with a board on a box for a table, rags on straw for a bed and a picture of the crucifixion on the wall. I could not but think how these people were themselves the victims of a slow and awful crucifixion of starvation. Beside the hut, the potato clamp was no more than a pit half-filled with green scum and filth. I see here much to remind me of my former conditions and I confess I should be ashamed to lift my voice against American slavery when such as this is happening at the very doorstep of the houses in which I stay, but that I begin to feel that the cause of humanity is one the world over and that it may be possible to draw parallels from one to another.

Yet even though those who come to hear me speak against American slavery often enter the hall by stepping over their own hungry and starving, I do not know how I speak to them of that. I feel somewhat that it would be an offence to my hosts to upbraid them for their greater interest in affairs across the Atlantic than in their own lands, especially so when my express and chosen purpose in being here is exactly to win their interest in the cause of abolition. Yet, when I took one of the children in my arms and could feel her every bone through the loose flesh, the tears started into my eyes at the thought that this free child faced a worse lot than any slave-child I could remember.

I wish I had a companion here with me who could understand my feelings and with whom I could discuss these matters, but Mr Jennings was in a hurry to return to his beloved family.

Hold me in your thoughts, I pray,

Your,
Frederick

NOVEMBER 15TH
DOUGLASS'S LETTER TO HARRIET BAILEY

My dearest sister Harriet,

I must ask again that you keep this letter from Garrison. I think you will see why when you have read it through, which I would suggest you do before deciding whether or not to read it to Dearest Anna.

Your brother
Frederick

DOUGLAS'S LETTER TO ANNA

My dearest Anna,

Since last I wrote I have been witness, I think, to the most troubling sequence of events. But, let me begin the story from its beginning.

Having completed the last of my scheduled speeches in Limerick, after which there was the most extravagant reception at which I had the opportunity to converse with many of the more notable members of the community who had been present there, I elected to walk to my hotel alone and through the streets. I needed, I told my hosts, to clear my head before I slept and needed also to prepare myself for the long journey back to Dublin. I was strolling through the town centre towards the hotel when, to my extreme surprise, Mr MacDonagh stepped from a doorway and greeted me as casually as though we had parted from each other's company but earlier that day. To all my enquiries he gave no answer, but insisted that his sole purpose was to see me to my hotel.

When we arrived there, though, he did say that he had a proposition for me that he thought would be of interest. As I had never been to Athlone, he said, it would be his pleasure and privilege to accompany me there and show me the historical sights of the town and the castle. I was very agreeable to this proposal and so the next morning, after informing my comrades in the struggle for abolition in Limerick of my small change in intentions, we set out to hire a small carriage for the journey. Which we secured very easily and agreed to set out that very afternoon as the driver was amenable to our plan.

The land to the north of Limerick was even to the first glance very much more badly affected by the blight than anything I had hitherto seen. Indeed, occasionally, I saw what I thought were corpses lying by the wayside and was sickened by the idea that these poor wretches were now in so desperate a state that they had not even friends to bury their mortal remains.

Mr. MacDonagh, though, seemed darkly distant from what we saw as we travelled. He neither turned his gaze away from the sights nor remarked upon them, but his face seemed darker and his eyes deeper than I had seen before. I said so at one point, and received the most surprising response; that his darkness of skin was because he came from what was called a "Phoenician" family. As soon as the words were from his mouth, I was most amazed by the resemblance I could detect between his features and those pictures I had seen of Levants. An olive skin, certainly, but even more strikingly his high cheek bones, a hooked nose, swept black hair rising off the face and a beard more carved than grown. Yet until the descriptive word he chose had been placed before me he had seemed entirely a part with the rest of the populace.

Indeed, he continued, this subject of the Phoenicians' place in the history of these islands has exercised some of the more interesting minds among the English. Opening a leather folder he took from the bag he always carried with him, he withdrew some sheets of paper clearly torn from a journal of some sort and read to me some speculations on the visits of the ancient Phoenicians to both Ireland and Britain. The author of this piece, though, admitted himself that his evidence was at best circumstantial but when I pointed this out, MacDonagh snorted and replied that circumstantial evidence seemed frequently good enough for the English when dealing with the Irish. He recovered himself instantly from this moment, though, and continued by saying that he found the idea of a history which lay beyond the narrow boundaries of official versions, or rather touched the edges of those accounts, a most fascinating conjecture. We can never know everything, he said, so why should we not admit that this is the case and then construct our pasts and therefore our present, as best we can? What if the author of this article, who is now as I understand it thoroughly obscure, were to become one of the great men of letters? How would we then read these speculations in the years to come? These questions

Mr MacDonagh asked me, and several more besides, but when I said that I could make no good answer to any one of them, he subsided in his seat and stared a while out of the window.

Not, he continued suddenly after a long pause, that he thought he was indeed descended from the ancient Phoenicians traders who had sailed past the barbarous English to exchange with the Irish and their close keltic relatives in Cornwall, so much as from Spanish sailors wrecked off the coast of Ireland during the Armada of 1588. There were, he said, legends aplenty of sailors washed ashore and concealed from the English by the people of the west coast and also of treasure wrecks still unexplored off the coast. Yet, here and there among the ancient ruins of the west there were signs of a people who used patterns and designs entirely different from those more familiar, great swirling circular displays. The possibility that these were indeed "Phoenician", he was willing to concede. For, after all, many Europeans had come to these parts long before the English brought their barbarities.

I remarked that this was all new history to me, and he replied that the trade in tin, gold, artefacts and horses stretched back before the birth of Christ. Roman emperors, he said, had sent their envoys to buy horses at the great horse fair. I knew, did I not, of the great horse fair? Where all of Europe had come for many centuries to trade horses, where Romanies from every corner of the continent came together to speak in that language only they understood?

When I admitted my ignorance, he suggested with great excitement that we take a brief detour on our journey to visit the town of Ballinasloe - it is spelled this way but pronounced Ban-la-sloe - where this great fair was held; an idea to which I agreed readily. This arrangement was made with the driver when we next paused for water, and shortly thereafter we turned off the direct road to Athlone to make our way to this town of which previously I had never heard. As we journeyed along, MacDonagh pointed away to the east, saying that the ruins of the great monastery of Clonmacnoise lay in that direction. When I again expressed my ignorance of this place he explained that it was here that much Christian lore and faith had been preserved in the face of the pagan invasions sweeping the rest of Europe, and that it was to these monks in large part that we owed the preservation of our faith when elsewhere - Rome, Avignon, York, and so on - surrender before barbarism was the order of the day.

He concluded this lecture by muttering that it was indeed the case that history was written by those who commanded power and that the great revenge of the English upon the Irish was the ways in which they had expunged the mighty contribution made by Ireland to the civilisation of Europe. Then he said little else, until we reached our destination.

Which was, at first sight, a small and unimpressive town with but one major street which eventually forked. It being late in the afternoon, MacDonagh suggested that we rest for the night at the only decent hotel in the town; an idea with which I readily agreed and we took ourselves there. The man at the desk seemed entirely unamazed by both our entry and our appearance, and once we had secured beds I took myself to my room and slept soundly the whole night.

At breakfast the next morning, the owner of the hotel introduced himself to us, saying that my reputation had preceded me among the better class of citizen in the town and that he was honoured to have me as his guest and refused the notion that we pay for our accommodation. A son of liberty such as myself, he said, was a child of the great traditions of Wolfe Tone. Once again, my ignorance of Irish history was shown and immediately our host offered to accompany me to the house where Wolfe Tone had stayed in the town. As we sat at the table my host insisted on explaining the great man's history, and I must say that I was much delighted by the story of a man who could step beyond his own origins to defend the rights of those who - his culture told him - were his enemies. For here was a Protestant who stepped past the prejudices of religion, which here operates in a way similar to that occupied by color in our own homeland, to press the case of justice for all. At which point in this history lesson MacDonagh interrupted, saying that we must be on our way to see the horse grounds. Indeed, he insisted with such vigor that our host withdrew.

We stepped out from the hotel and within a very few minutes had reached, at the edge of the town's heart, a huge open field which was, MacDonagh said, the place where men had come from all over Europe for over two thousand years to trade horses. He much enjoyed coming here, even though now the size of the fair was much reduced, because he could feel that he was walking in the footprints of history and could feel close to his brothers from across the national boundaries drawn by his and their enemies. We walked around the field for some time and I must admit that I too could feel the weight of the past beneath my feet.

At one point we were standing side by side at the centre of the great field, with the whole place to ourselves, when he turned to me and welcomed me to his homeland. When I said that this was not necessary, such sentiments having been expressed by both himself and others many times before, he raised his finger to his lips and, having obtained my silence, continued by repeating the same sentiments - so he told me when he was finished his litany - in a flurry of different languages. Some, I could guess at from the sounds of the words but others were no more comprehensible to me than noises. When he had finished, he smiled.

After which we turned back towards the town and came again to the fork of the road. The main street seemed reasonably busy, with numbers of people walking the whole width of the road. Then suddenly the whole crowd seemed to draw back, as though flinching from something profoundly distasteful in its midst. "It is the English agent", MacDonagh said to me in explanation, "the man who puts the starving from their houses for not paying the rent". The man was making his way diagonally across the street towards the other fork of the road and was no more than twenty yards distant from us when, from a doorway to our left, a man ran out and directly up to the agent. The small man placed a pistol between the other's eyes. I was so close that I could see the sudden utter terror in the man's eyes as he tried to look away, tried to find some way of disbelieving what was so obviously, horribly true. Then the other man shot him. The instantly lifeless body was thrown backwards, and blood and brain splattered over those near at hand.

Even though I have seen runaways shot in such fashion, the sight still made me wretched in my stomach. Pieces of the man's brain were scattered in the street, much of his scalp was blown away, and his body had fallen directly to the ground almost as though still in the act of walking. His assassin stood over him momentarily, and placed a foot on his chest, before walking briskly but calmly back in the direction from which he come and then disappearing down an alleyway. I was still rooted to the spot by my surprise and horror, but several of the other people in the street took the moment to kick the corpse where it lay before walking calmly away. Then a whistle blew somewhere in the distance and the sound of running feet coming nearer scattered the crowd. MacDonagh pulled at my sleeve, insisting that we must go and quickly.

He dragged me away, repeatedly insisting that if I should be caught there, the English would simply and automatically assume that I was involved. We must get to the carriage and away as quickly as possible. I was so shocked that I allowed myself to be guided by him, and so it was that in less than an hour we were on the road to Athlone and moving quickly. I sat staring from the window, and then had to demand that we stop immediately for I needed to be sick, my gorge having risen into my mouth with a suddenness that I could not explain until I was bent over by the road. My sickness, I realised, was caused by the fact that I knew the killer. It was the European man I had met in Cork but a few days previously, in MacDonagh's company. I looked across the carriage at him, but he avoided my gaze and closed his eyes. He remained thus, as if sleeping, for the rest of the time we were seated in the carriage.

We completed the rest of our journey to Athlone in silence and once here I insisted that we find lodgings at once, for I felt unwell and needed to rest. It is from these rooms that I write this letter, as an attempt to unburden my confusions and doubts as to what has happened.

Your,
Frederick.

———————

NOVEMBER 17

DOUGLASS'S LETTER TO ANNA

My dear Anna,

My state of mind is no better now than it was when last I wrote, for the last two days have been an utter confusion. No sooner was my last to you completed when, despite my agitation, I was overcome with a profound fatigue and went directly to my bed where I slept, strangely, very well and soundly until Mr MacDonagh came to wake me in the morning. He proposed, he said, to take me to see the old castle and to tell me of the siege which all but ended Catholic resistance in the west in the days of James Stuart. The man's calmness served only to agitate me once again, but when I said so he merely commanded - yes, commanded - that I be calm for there was nothing for me to be worried by. When I hissed back that I knew the identity of the killer, he seemed surprised and asked me his name. When I admitted that I did not know, he asked further how then I could then identify this person if asked.

To which I was silent, for of course he knew that my only answer could be that the connection would have to be made through him.

We continued in silence until we reached the castle, through which he led me and demonstrated a great knowledge of his own people's history and also how it fitted into the larger story of European history. I was moved to ask, during this, if he did not think that the struggle then had been a useless one given the forces ranged against them. To which he replied, that these rebels have their place in history and memory assured in ways that cowards and runaways will never achieve. Then he remarked that he thought this was something I especially would understand, given what I had written about my fight with Covey the slavebreaker: "Covey seemed now to think that he had me, and could do what he pleased; but at this moment - from whence came the spirit I don't know - I resolved to fight". Then he asked, gently, if I had known at the onset of that fight, its outcome?

I was struck dumb by this; not simply by the nature of the question but also that MacDonagh could quote my own work to me with such facility. I simply agreed that I had not and again fell silent.

We continued to walk through the streets and at last returned to the hotel, where we parted as MacDonagh said he had business elsewhere in the town and then would return to accompany me to the coach to Dublin. I entered the hotel, preparing to pack my belongings for the journey, but was approached in the lobby by two men who asked if I had been in Ballinasloe two days earlier. I said I had, there seeming to be no purpose to denying it. I must have been very noticeable, as the only black man in the whole town. They replied that as this was the case they had business with me and wished to discuss what I had seen while I was there.

I immediately said, the killing. Yes, I saw it.

To which they asked, did you see who fired the shot?

To which I answered, that I had but the briefest glance at the man before he fled the scene.

They asked if I would recognise him again, to which I replied that I would not. To which they asked, not even if there were a substantial reward? I replied angrily that money was not the consequence of my ability, at which one of them shrugged in the most offensive manner and turned away. The other adopted what seemed to me a slightly apologetic stance, and said that the landowner for whom the murdered agent had worked was very keen to bring his killer to justice and had therefore offered a reward for information. To which I replied that this was a strange form of justice, which could be purchased, and then asked if they had other business with me for I was in haste to take the Dublin coach.

They said that they were finished, but as they went out the door the offensive one looked back and said that if he were me, he would be careful of the company I kept. To which I replied that I was glad that this was not the case and turned on my heel for the stairs, but not before I detected a muttered insult. I ignored it, but noted that on the very few occasions I have been abused for my race in this country the abuser has been a servant of the Crown.

Within the hour, MacDonagh had led me to the coach. He gestured that I should enter the carriage first but when I had mounted, he closed the door abruptly, saying he hoped that we would meet again. Before I could answer he was striding away and I was aboard and heading for Dublin, from where I shall post this letter and make my preparations for the journey to Belfast.

Your,
Frederick

PART TWO

THE STORY OF EAMONN MACDONAGH

Only way to be away was to move. Only direction was west. Even if it hadn't been the way I was going, it would have been the right way. When the ancient heroes knew it was their time, they went west, walked into the setting sun. Odysseus. His last voyage. Only it rains too much here ever to be sure where the sun sets, unless you already knew. I knew. It was easy finding people, people with horses and carts, to speed me along. Further towards the city I went, the smaller the fields became, the bigger the stone walls hedging them round.

I talked to everyone who took me a few miles but I felt as though I'd held my breath all the way to, and then beyond, Galway. Not true, for I'd wanted to breathe in the smoke. It was the smell of my life, all of it. How could I not draw it in.

Yet even when I heard the words, casual in the street, the words bearing part of life like cooking, I still held my breath tight. Drew in a little more.

Not until I was past the city that used to mark the edge of my world, my known world, did I let out the air. Stood on the bridge between is and was and, as I stepped across, my chest loosened and the small whisper that sits under words slipped out. And then, on the recoil inbreath, the sudden gasp, caught all the flavours of my childhood into my mouth. Words had their real taste again.

Smoke, peat threaded into potatoes, tang of salt when the wind comes from the south, fire and water laced together.

Best part of two days that lasted. From Galway to Maam. Squeaking reeds, stopping to sit on a stone by the side of the road in Oughterard to talk to a woman who could have been my mother, for the ease of the gossip. Then, outside the house at the big crossroads, the reek of their words was in the air. A dog farts in a small room and then slinks out, but leaves its smell behind. My chest tightened with the need of breathing again. Then there they were, just past the big house, sat on a wall and gassing. Without even breaking stride, I stepped off the road and onto the land. Stepped off their intrusion and back into my place.

Walking in off the road, it was slow going. Looking for the too-green shine and skirting it. If want to get to there, this isn't the place to be starting from. But no place is the place to be starting from, for no route goes from here to there without visiting this, that. This is no place for straight lines, and Euclid .. Euclid .. was wrong. The shortest path between any two points isn't a straight line, not if time is your measure. We have learned how to take the long way round, to go where we want to be.

It gave my face time to get used to the shapes of the words under my tongue again. Every push of the jaw at every slainté out here, and there were many of them for I met many people taking the quick way of the winding paths through the bogs, every one of them left a small ache in my throat.

And then it was easy, one night sitting before a cottage. I didn't have to reach for the words any more, they came to me. I relaxed into language and felt my years out in their world peel away.

That's the word. They didn't wash off in an easy cleaning. Stripped away. If I'd listened more closely I would have known the words for what they were. A premonition. A moan of the future. Banshee words.

But I was too busy anxious for home.

An Clochan. The Stone. As though any one of the stones in this place was more remarkable than any other. Except, of course, this one was. Is. It is the rock upon which I built the foundations of my life. Given how the sea slides off and leaves no mark or sign of wear, this rock, this stone stinks of my life.

I'd been on the coast road half a day, feeling safer with every step. It's slow going if you expect that road to take you from A to B. So I went from B to S, K to E, from sineadh to fadha.

Came to a crossroads that, had I not been there every day of my childhood, would have seemed no crossroad at all. For those with eyes to see...

No choice. Off with the shoes, into the bóithrín.

So it was that I came in by a side way. Saw them before they saw me and, seeing them, stood stock steady still until their eyes had swept over me like any other fragment of the landscape. Miss Fry, she taught me so many words. Autochthonous. Then let myself down into the grass, the heather. I could wait. I did wait, for my moment. It came, I took it, and now I could wait again. Knowing that my moment would come again.

They, those who do not know how to wait, went. It only took four, less than five, hours. Barely got comfortable and then they, bored with looking at the things that grow out of the soil, were gone.

And I went home.

Slipped over a last wall and down onto the road into the village. Hadn't taken more than ten steps before the deserted doorways were peopled. Saw my aunt and asked

"Auntie, who were the brits after?"

"Don't auntie me, just because you've
a beard and think you can."

"I apologise Mrs Swiney. I should have known better.
How is your son Aodhan? Is he too busy with the
fishing now to be making bodhrans any more? And
now Auntie, tell me, who were the brits after?"

Managed to get my hand onto her wrist before she flicked her apron up over her face, just in case anyone who shouldn't be watching at all was watching too closely. And whispered fast

> *"Auntie, tell me now and tell me quick,*
>   *who were the brits after?"*

Not me at all. How could they be, for they didn't know anything except what they did know. And little enough of that would be any use to them. Routine patrols, my aunt said. There's no Irish for that phrase.

Waiting. Waiting for what. All the years have the same large rhythm, but every year is different because every year is. There is always this lull at the end of the summer, start of the autumn. Before we lift the spuds. Sometimes I wonder what happened before the spuds but I can't imagine it. Always this moment when everything is done except the harvest of the year's labour. No point in any more weeding, any more carrying of seaweed to stack between the rows. So we just wait.

———

They weren't doing anything in particular, they said. Just looking. One of them, though, had sticks. One of the sticks had a thing on it. And he kept looking through it, and then writing in a book. Then they'd walk, and look. And he wrote in his book some more. Reminded auntie of the men who changed the names of all the villages and rivers from our words to theirs. But they couldn't be going to change the names back again, could they?

I walked on, through the village. This thin strip of people between the sea and the bog. Thought again how the sea and the bog had defined me for so long, the bog especially because the sea had always scared me. Stories of drowning and mermen. Never liked a story or a place where my feet didn't touch the bottom. So I'd stand on the new quay when it was finished, stand on it with the others of the village and listen to the men talking and not know what they were saying. Their words, the words of the sea. My words, the words of the land. But I wouldn't go too near the edge. A good boy.

I walked on, past the church quiet in the middle of the day. The priest would be asleep in his chair, or out visiting in the parish. Up the slope away from the new quay, up to the rise where the houses clustered and then on along the rise. The houses began to thin out and I could have closed my eyes now and still found my way.

I came so quiet, she was still kneading the bread when I stepped over the hearth. This time of the day, the doorway away from the sun cast no shadows into the room. I stood there, in the doorway and listened to her. Talking quietly to herself and squashing the flour and the water into each other. She'd never liked dogs. Had given away the father's dog soon as he died. What use are they, she'd said, except for making a noise and chasing the rats, and I can do both of them for myself.

She did, slowly. As she turned she was ready to chase a rat. Flour in one hand and the knife in the other. Ready to throw one of them, and then use the other. I raised my hands, so that they she would see they were empty. Took a step back, into the doorway to tell that I would go back out if she wished. She looked at me. I nodded. She stepped forward. I stepped forward. And she threw the flour at my face, but I ducked. My hair greyed and I took her wrist with my hand as she swung. Guided the knife past my stomach and said,

"*Mammy, it's me*"

Later, when I'd brushed enough of the flour out of my hair to wash it through without getting sticky lumps clinging to my scalp, we sat on the door step facing down into the village. We weren't mother and son, because she couldn't forgive me the days, weeks spent looking for me along the shoreline, across the bog and in the sinkholes, questioning everyone in the village again and again until one by one they melted away and she was left looking for me on her own. Always the strange one in the village even before, what was she like just the one child didn't she know what happened even if she didn't lose that one. Step by step, she stopped.

Now, she was just waiting. Waiting for the roof to fall in. That would be the start, a puddle in the middle of the room and knowing she couldn't climb up to stuff the hole even if she could find it. Then winter days when it was warmer and only just as damp outdoors as in. Then coughing. She knew.

We weren't mother and son, but neither were we strangers entirely. We knew the stories we shared. I hadn't forgotten them and she had never set them aside. So we talked. The world beyond Galway, beyond Maam, past the bend in the road across the bay. How many fish in the sea, how many spuds in the field. I held my tongue once we got that close. Held my tongue.

Aodhan, he's a good lad. Brings me silver darlings whenever he has some. His mother, though. Only speaks in the church, and then only the briefest. Always wanting to be dancing at the priest's skirts. Worse, even, since Pat died. Barking up the wrong tree, there; though God forgive me even for the thought. And her even older than me. Let go of your tongue. I'm an old woman now. I know it, and so should you. The goats have made a difference. Biteen of milk whenever I can lay a hand on them and some meat for a few weeks… …Then, one day when I was sat here watching the tide come in, would you know it, I saw coffins floating up on the rising. Like boats coming for the peat. One behind the other. Lining up to pull into the quayside for their cargo. That's strange, I thought, because there's no-one died in the village for months so why would they pull in here. I can understand why there'd always be business for them at Clifden, what with the fever hospital. Perhaps that's where they going. Then one of the goats came and butted softly at my back, that was strange because usually they're keener to run away. I turned around to push her away and when I turned back what do you know. The coffins had all gone, sailed away fast as you like. Or perhaps they all sank, and they're sitting at the bottom of the channel, waiting. After all, this is a good place to wait.

Once I'd managed to ease the idea that the brits would come any moment, I'd be walking down through the village and bang there they'd be and that would be that, once the idea had eased itself away because slowly slowly I came to see that what we'd done had caused consternation in Ballinasloe but the ripples died fast before they reached the banks of the county even let alone the whole country. What was needed was to take a real big one in the streets of Dublin, on his morning walk in the park perhaps. Make the bastards afraid to step out of their doors. But for now I could walk down the main street of the village in which I was born and have people greet me and call me by my own name, and nothing happened.

So I could wait awhile and while I waited I could put mammy's place straight for her. She's looking her age, like she didn't when I left.

Every one of the village people looking their age and then a few years more besides, for the sheer effort of clinging to this landscape.

So it was that early one morning I was up before her, up before the goats needed milking and off up the boíthrín to her tatties. They looked fine, the smelt fine when I lifted the first few. Beautiful great opals erupting from the dark almost black soil. Smell of the earth when I got down on my hands and knees to rummage through the ground for any little ones I'd missed with the spade. Then back to my feet, knocking the earth from my hands by clapping my legs and then in with the spade again. More treasures from the ground. After the first row with my head down, I straightened up to ease the pull in my back and looked around just to be sure there were no local lads near enough to see that I'd gone soft having to check my back after only a few minutes' digging. But I had the place to myself. It was deadly quiet. This far back from the water I could see the waves' motion on the shore but they were a silent breaking. No birds.

I bent slowly from the knees, trying to make it seem I was going for another close search beneath a lifted plant and its haulm. Actually, making myself less of an easy target, up there against the skyline. On hands and knees, crawled a few yards to the edge of the plot and then rolled into the heather and the long grass away at the side of the potato field. Still no birds. A fox perhaps but strange that one be that bold this far past the darkness.

I lay and I listened, gripping the handle of the spade until my fingers ached. Tried to ease my hold and everyone of the fingers creaked under the strain on top of the hard work. I could feel a blister coming, at the base of my left little finger. Years in the city, getting hard in the mind had made my hands go soft. It only takes the slightest pressure of a soft hand to pull a trigger. The Pole had soft hands. Noticed that, the time I shook him a welcome.

No fiery shredding of my flesh by a bullet warning of the sound's arrival, no rifle crack, no boots coming through the grass to kick my head. I waited another five minutes into sudden boredom and then stood up.

And there was nothing. No people, no abrupt appearance of a brit shouting fenian bastard get on your knees before I blow your brains to kingdom come – strange phrase – just the earth and the sky and the sea moving in the near distance. That was it, I realised. There was nothing. The place was empty.

Told myself, for the next few days, that it was the contrast with the bustle of the cities I'd occupied for the last few years. The gold of people, to airy thinness beaten. A stroll to Raftery's, that would settle the problem. I told mammy and, though she looked down her nose at me, she said nothing against the idea.

You're the old man's spit now, Eamonn, said Raftery when I pushed the door open that evening. I'd have know you the second I saw you. I hope not, I replied. Ah but go on now. And Raftery was keen to talk. It took me a while to realise only that he lacked company. So desperate for a wag of the chin that he came and sat and raised a small glass with me. His poitín had singed my throat whenever I was sick as a child and if I had thought that I had grown out of its burning power, that first sip proved me wrong. With all the colour of the bog distilled away, this water of life stood nearer to the fire. Fire and water.

So when he asked what I'd been about all these years I told him.

We sat, all evening, him getting up for the bottle until he found it easier to bring the bottle and sit and we talked. I'd always thought of him as much older than me, but gradually realised there was but four years between us but he'd grown fast after his father died and he'd turned to the family business early.

Woke up when my head jerked sideways off the chair back and I was up and ready to go before the floor moved. The road rippled all the way back to my mother's through that darkness thinned by the closeness of the sea.

A few more days, and then Aodhan came to ask if I would go fishing with him. Told him no, that I'd never been close to the water. It'll get us away from the smell, he said. And when I looked at him as though I didn't understand, he growled at me and said he wasn't daft even if he'd never strayed far from home and did I think that living the city ways meant I could have the airs and graces to pretend that my old schoolmates were .. tick. Their word, he said, jerking his thumb at the barracks by the pier head. They use it a lot. What does it mean? I told him, and he spat in the direction of the barracks, only you're not saying it right. It's THick not Tick. I don't fecking care how you say it, Aodhan said, the next one calls me it will be feeling my thick fist on his scrawny face.

We went fishing. From the boat we could see the fields alive with people hoeing and weeding and pushing the last perilous additions to the earth heaped around the potato plants. To encourage them to grow tall. It's the perfect plant for us, for here, my father had told me. Little enough land to spread out across, so better to grow plants that grow upwards, and he showed me how to bury the seed deep so that the haulm grew tall and there was plenty of growth for the potatoes to gather above the seed but below the ground. He was a master of the teetering hills of earth gathered up around the plants and our family never lacked for the potatoes through the winter or the following

—
55

spring. Even when there was little enough else, there was always plenty of spuds. Enough for us, and a few left over for the passing tinkers or the village widows still dazed from the death of the man, too stunned to have worked their fields that year.

The boat rocked, and Aodhan started pulling gently on one of the lines he'd cast to trail in the water behind us. Hmm, he sighed gently, big one. Salmon, if we're lucky; pike, if we're not. We weren't, that time. But later, when the tide turned and started to drop, the salmon found it harder going to swim past so easily and we took a couple by line and another by net. Four feet long and solid enough to bruise my knuckles when I held them to punch them senseless. One for Aodhan, one for me, and the pike for the priest. We'll tell him there was only pike and a few bass. He doesn't like bass, for some reason. And the other one; we'll see, said Aodhan and tapped his nose.

We rowed back to the beach beyond the pier head and, as we splashed ashore carrying the four hefty fish, three of the constables came along the sand. Not towards us, but they arrived at the same point at the same time.

"What's your name?"

He asked in English, so I shrugged my shoulders and stepped past him. His hand came up quickly and gripped my elbow. His thumb jammed into the soft flesh and the spasm that ran down my arm flexed my fingers and I dropped the fish.

"Oops."

"What's your name?"

The other two shifted their weight onto their front feet, so that they were ready. Just in case. I shrugged again.

"I … don't … know … what…"

"Thick fucking paddies."

I turned my head sideways and glared at Aodhan. Not now.

Then, while the other two oohed and aahed, he mutilated our words and asked again.

"Aodhan Coneelly," I answered straight away.

"On you go then."

I picked up the fish, now dusty and stuck with grit, and we walked away.

"You took a chance, there", Aodhan hissed at me.

"No. No I didn't. They look at each one of
us and all they see is a paddy. You and me,
we're interchangeable in their eyes."

So it went on for the next few weeks. We fished while the others waited on the potato harvest being ready. We drank Raftery's poitín in the evenings and after Sunday mass, and gradually I got used to its fiery burn and noticed it less and the taste of the peat under the fire and the water more. Then at last there was the sudden lifting of the spuds. Everyone seemed to have waited on someone to start, not wanting to be first. Then suddenly the spades were flailing into the ground from first light right through until the last gleams of the sun faded over the sea. Everyone joined in, digging and wiping off, and loading into baskets and carrying to the clamps. In four days, the work of the summer was lifted and stored. Then we all seemed to pause for breath, waiting for the last threads of summer to wear away into autumn laced with winter.

I learned the hours that the constables did their rounds, for they were simple creatures of habit mostly, and so I could avoid them much of the time. The softness of the city began to go out of my hands and my feet remembered how to walk over uneven ground without my having to keep looking down. The English went out of my mouth, slowly. Best of all, the volume of the world around me lowered until the occasional yell of a seagull could startle me if I hadn't seen the bird beforehand.

That's why the banshee only had to whisper to wake me up the night she came. The quiet insistent muttering pulled me into the moonlight. Both in the room and out of it, calling me to come outside even as it was there beside me in the room. I followed it out even as I left it behind in the room. The yard in front of the house and the fields beyond were silvered grey and

I walked on past. Following the call. It led me down through the village towards the pier head. All the lights were out in the barracks but at a command from the banshee's voice the gate opened. Then out of the gateway, one by one, began to slide coffins. Out onto the pier head, where they arranged in neat rows. Every time I tried to step forward or tried to move away, the banshee's voice, ordered me to stand still. Look, it said, look at the coffins. Look at them. And as I looked the lids began to open. I closed my eyes, but it seemed as though my eyelids had become transparent and even with my eyes closed I could still see. Still see as the coffins lifted slowly into the air until they hung level with my face. And as they hung there I realised I could smell it. Then they began to rise higher into the air and started to drift out over the edge of the pier, to hang above the sea below. Then, slowly at first, they began to float out to sea. Slowly, at first, but then they accelerated until they were rushing away and disappearing out to sea. And as they rushed away I counted them; one, two, three, five, seven, nine, twelve, fifteen, eighteen, twenty-two, twenty-six, thirty, thirty-five, forty, forty-five, fifty-one, fifty-seven. On and on, faster and faster, until I had counted to three hundred and eighty seven and then, now breathless and gasping for air, I sat up in bed. Panting, sweating, and counting. Aodhan Coneelly, his mother Mary and father Pat, two sisters can't remember their names: the Healeys, James and Finola, sons Simon and Brian, his brother Pat and his wife, can't remember her name, and their children Finbar, Jarleth and Dara, the other brother Gerry and his Bernadette and the son Niall and the sweet little lad. Counting everyone in the village. Three hundred and eighty seven.

It made no sense to me. I knew I had counted the coffins and, having retraced through every house in the village and counted up the people, I knew I had the right numbers. One more time I counted the village through, and then I realised. Three hundred and eighty four, and three peelers.

Then the smell.

Barely by the time the sun was up, that morning, the reek filled the village. It seemed to bubble out of the ground. It was there even in the brisk wind at the highest point of the land above the houses, tainting the bright scents of the bog and the heather. And as I walked down into the still air of the village, it welled up until before I'd even made it as far as Raftery's door I was gagging and pressing my handkerchief to my mouth.

In the east it had been different. The blight had crept from village to village, clamp to clamp, like a ripple of corruption. But here, in my own place, it had descended in one mighty sweep. Overnight every clamp in the village had turned from a winter store of vegetables to a swilling pit of awful stench. I saw men who had dragged unflinching the drowned and bloated corpses of friends from the sea, grey bags that had burst open on the sand in a grim rush, I saw these men heaving and staggering from the thick oily belch. Yet they needed, it seemed, to slice every pit open. Whether from some dull hope that something could be saved, or from some need to know that all hope was gone, I could not tell. I could only stand and watch as they went from clamp to clamp, clutching their spades and their scarves. It looked to me, even then, like a funeral procession winding through the village streets. A funeral procession without a coffin, though. And I gasped quietly, when I realised that I had seen the coffins. I knew what was to come.

That evening, the priest sent word that we should all gather at the church. Within the hour, the whole village was assembled. The church held more people than I could ever remember seeing within its walls; not even Seanín's wedding had pulled in such a crowd. I was there, though I'd not set foot in a church for years. As the church filled with families, they went to their usual pews, the several generations together. Padraig Colohan, with his nine children before him and his wife's mother and father behind, arrived early. He sat with his hands pressed between his knees until Mikey tapped him on the shoulder and beckoned him out to join a clutch of the younger fathers drawn together by the font. At first, his in-laws sat and watched over the children but then first he and then, after, she were drawn away to stand with the older men and the older women in different places within the church. I watched awhile the children sit quietly, and then a twitch ran through them. A brother tweaked a sister pinched one of the twins who yelped. And most of the adults looked round at them, pausing in mid-muttered sentence while Padraig hissed at them and they settled. The conversations began again, until another twitch as the twin had revenge for the pinch and the sister flounced out of the pew to join a bevy of young women with their backs to the wall so they could keep an eye on the young men who were trying to look older than they were by forgetting that they'd puked on their trousers earlier.

Padraig was three strides across the church with his hand at his belt buckle when the priest's voice pulled him up.

"Not in the House of the Lord!"

And then more quietly,

"Padraig, leave them be; they have the tribulations
of the world before them. Leave them be."

Padraig retreated towards the group of his peers, while the priest turned and began to speak to the whole assembled village.

"There have been rumours aplenty circulating for some
while now. And, it seems, some of them are proved to be
true. The plague has come upon us, like the plagues that
descended upon the house of Egypt in ancient times."

I cleared my throat and the priest glanced round at me, and then very deliberately looked away again and continued.

"In those dark days the Israelites turned to God
for protection while the Egyptians held fast to their
idolatry and refused the way of the one true God. For
which they were punished. And when the children
of God were led out of wickedness it was only the
wife of Lot who looked back who was punished."

I cleared my throat again, louder this time.

"That's a bad chest you have, Eamonn. Must be all the dust
and dirt you inhaled in the city while you were away."
"My lungs are fine, thank you, father. It's
my memory that's playing up."
"Is that so? Dear, dear."
"Yes, father."

I took a deep breath, because I knew the possible consequences
of what I was about to say.

"You see, when I took Bible class with you when I was
just a wee lad I thought the Egyptians were punished for
what they had done or not done, and not for what others
had done to them. And I thought that Lot's wife was
punished for what she had done, not for what others had
done to her. But I must be wrong, because you seem to be
telling us that somehow we are the cause of the blight."

The air in the church seemed to thicken, both with the gathering dusk but also with a blend of hostility, questioning and
disbelief.

"No, no, Eamonn. I'm telling you" he gestured round the
church, to show that the "you" was all of us, "that now more
than ever we will need the power of prayer and faith. Now,
in our hour of greatest need, we need God's guidance."

"What we need, father, what we will need in the coming
months is food."

"Man cannot live by bread alone."

"I agree, but without bread we do not live at all. I have
been in the east recently, and I have seen villages like this
one where the blight has hit. I know what's coming."

"And what is that? Tell us, Eamonn,
tell us all what awaits us."

And as I looked at him, across the church, I knew he'd got me
where he wanted me. For if I told people here, in my own place,
what I'd seen elsewhere, how I'd seen whole villages torn apart
and the people scattered before the wind of a terrible change,
if I told my own people death by starvation or destruction of

their lives stood before them, no-one would thank me. I'd be as welcome as those daft protestant vicars that passed through sometimes telling us all we were doomed and that only immediate repentance would save us. I wanted to give my people the strength to stand and fight, and I couldn't do that with a message of despair.

"We're all waiting."

People were looking towards me now.

"I just, just want to say, to say that we need to be ready for whatever the future brings. That we can stand together, or we will all fall separately."

There was a silence, a pause of disappointment, and I knew that the priest had won. He knew it, too, and turned his back on me.

"Let us pray"

As everyone else knelt, I walked slowly from the church. Outside, the three officers from the barracks were standing among the gravestones. I stopped, glared at them, daring them to approach, hoping that a confrontation with them might bring the villagers back. They glanced at me, almost indifferently and without hostility.

I knew then that being ignored is worse than being beaten.

It took a few weeks. The villagers had their rent money and used it to send a few of the village men into Clifden to try and buy some food. They were gone for three days and when they came back, they had a few sacks and little else. The price of flour had already doubled and they were, they said, lucky to get what they had. With the money gone, and the days getting shorter, people spent more time indoors. I walked the bounds of my homeplace at least once a day, and it became more and more usual to see no-one the whole length of the walk. I was gone to the foreshore one afternoon, looking for some wrack to boil and chew. The silence was becoming ever more unbearable. I could feel the whole place slipping. Sat on a rock, looking out across the water,

I thought for the first time about going. Leaving. Finding some way to go, to America or to England. I sat there the whole time the tide turned and began to fall away. The sharp clear smell of the sea turned slowly to the dank odour of wet sand and mud. The drying seaweed I'd collected, slowly ceased to smell like something I could eat and started to reek.

As the tide fell, the wind shifted and slowly slowly I became aware of another scent in the air. The smell of burning turf, so much the smell of home for me, still trailed in the air from time to time but this was a coarser thicker smell of burning. Wood, perhaps. But no-one burned wood here; it was too precious to be burned. We only ever used wood for building, for rafters if ever we found a piece long enough. But wood it was, I knew that smell.

By the time I got to the village, three roofs were already down and the bailiffs were at two more. When I reached the door of the first of these two, I saw the bailiff punch and kick Maire Donnelly to loosen her grip from his knees. And, having shucked her loose, he went back to smashing the door off its hinges and throwing the pieces into the already burning interior of the cottage. Maire sat in a heap, wailing and wiping the blood off her face with her shawl. No-one in the little crowd moved. They just stood and watched, so I stepped up and helped her to her feet. With my back turned to the bailiff and his men, because I knew I couldn't hold myself if I looked at them, I asked who would take her in. Just for the night, just for a few days while she sorted herself.

No-one spoke, until a voice quietly said, "look to your own, Eamonn, look to your mammy."

I was running and got to the house ahead of the bailiffs. Told her to lock the door and push whatever she could up against it from the inside. There I was when they came along the lane, the smell of smoke clinging to their clothes and preceding them like crows before an army as it marches.

"We've come for the rent." He had a Connemara tongue in his head. I stared at him. Then he spoke again, in Irish. "We've come for the rent" and then, to the others with him, "bog-trotters. I'd make 'em all learn English."

"*You have no need to make me learn it.*"

He stared at me a while.

"*Then pay your fucking rent, and pay it now.*"

I stared back. He stepped closer, until there was about four feet between us. We looked deep into each other's faces for a long while.

Then very quietly he muttered, in Irish "when they have as many words for us as we have for shit we've lost and when there's a choice between winning and losing I knew where I want to be" and then louder, in English, "this one's finished". Then he began to turn away.

I looked past him, to see where his men were, what move they would make and as I did, he span on his heel turning back towards me and caught me full across the neck with his stick.

———————

My throat was thick and choked when I woke up. My head throbbed and pulsed. I was lying almost where I had fallen, unconscious before my face hit the wall of the house. Almost where I had fallen. My arms were numb, tied behind my back and I'd been lying on them. My back ached because it had been arched for so long and when I tried to move my legs they were tied also. Tied together and tied to what felt like a stake. I couldn't tell, because a flour sack was over my head. My nose was caked shut with blood, snot and flour and my lips were dry and cracking. It was still daylight, though, and I could feel a little warm sunlight. On all of my body except my legs below the knees. My feet and calves were cold. For a moment I thought perhaps my spine was damaged but I could wriggle my toes. So, no. Just cold, clammy almost.

When they pulled the sack off my head the following morning and threw water over me and hauled me into a sitting posi-

tion, I could see why even with one eye swollen shut. I was teth-
ered to a charred rafter that had been buried into the bottom of
our potato clamp. There was no smell anymore, but the pit still
swilled with a viscous liquid. They must have tied my legs to
the rafter and then hammered it into place, because I was sub-
merged up to the knees. Slung over the edge of the clamp.

Then the English and their man had wandered away. Laughing
and joking about who they'd fucked in the village. One said, as
he walked away, "I can't decide whether I like it more when
these cunts beg me for it or when I have to make them take it"
and they'd laughed and then they were gone.

I lay there nearly all day. Trying to forget how to speak their
language.

They were gone.

I thought at first that the whole village was gone but then I
could hear human-made noises in the distance.

I called out but no-one came.

I lay there all day, and all the next night.

I was relieved when my nose began to run because I could
sniff the snot into my burning throat for some little comfort.

Then, at last, late on the third day Joe Donnelly came up and
pulled me out and cut the ropes and said he wanted to thank
me for trying to help Maire and he was sorry that he hadn't
come before but he was worried that the bailiff would come
back and someone, anyone, would tell that it was him that had
cut me loose. He was sorry, he said, but I could see how it was.
Could smell how it was, his eyes said, as he backed away from
me as I hauled myself out of the clamp. I looked down. The
trousers, that I couldn't feel, were slimy-thick and soaked. I
knew I couldn't feel them because I could see that they were
clinging to my legs. So, it wasn't the trousers I couldn't feel but
my legs. That's all right, I thought, it'll be like when you've slept
on your arm and the feeling is gone when you wake up but it
comes back soon in a tingling slide and everything returns. It
starts from the bone and works out. So, if the bones are still

there it'll be all right. I moved my toes. Or rather, I told my toes to move but nothing happened. I put my hands onto my thighs and I could feel the skin in both my hands and my thighs. I moved my hands lower but as soon as the edge of my little fingers touched the slime that clung I flinched away. Just like Joe, who had retreated several strides away. Stood watching me as though I were some circus act he hadn't seen before and didn't like.

"*Joe, I need your help*".

He didn't move.

"*Joe*"

"*Eamonn*"

"*I need your help*"

There was a long pause.

"*Joe*"

"*Eamonn*"

Then he came back.

As he helped me up he gagged a couple of times. He tried hard to hide it, but I could hear the gasping in his throat. It was good of him not to vomit over me. Good of him.

When he'd got me upright, he looked into my eyes, nodded, let go of me and stepped back. My legs crumpled beneath me.

"*I'll need help, Eamonn*".

Then he was gone, walking swiftly towards the houses.

Leaving me lying, stinking and sprawled on the heather of the place I had thought of as home since the day I could think.

PART THREE

My dear Phillips,

The first part of the tour of Britain has gone remarkably well. The Irish have been most receptive to our arguments on the abolition of chattel slavery, and have turned out for our meetings in large numbers. Indeed, it has been most enheartening to see members of all classes and parties so eager to hear what I have to say. With only a very few exceptions, I have been accepted into society both as a spokesman for our cause and also from genuine kindness. My travels have been repeatedly marked by invitations to take up brief residence in the houses of those I have met at meetings. So marked has this been that I have been moved on occasion to remark on the contrast in behaviour between those who are subjects of a crown and those who claim to be citizens of a free, independent republic committed to "life, liberty and the pursuit of happiness".

With the tour of the west of Ireland now complete, I am preparing for the journey to Belfast and will depart from Dublin in the next few days. I shall be sad to leave behind our good friends here, especially Mr Webb who has done such fine work in printing and distributing the edition of my *Narrative* for the British audience. Equally well, though, I am delighted to be reunited with James Buffum. He has been hard at work making plans and arrangements for the tour of Scotland and tells me that once I have completed the itinerary for Belfast, he will meet me in Glasgow for the meetings already planned for there and more besides he hopes. I have great hopes and expectations for our work and success here.

I remain, your
Frederick Douglass

My dearest Harriet,

Once more I must ask your indulgence not to show the attached letter to Phillips or Garrison. I hope and pray that this will be the last time I need resort to this, which feels like deception of men who have done so much for me.

Your,
Frederick

My dearest Anna,

My allegiance to myself led me to promise that never again would I dissemble before another man, but would always speak my truth. That, I told myself was a marker of the difference between the slave and the free man. The slave lives in a world where he must lie if he is to survive, for the slaver's absolute power makes him capricious in his actions towards the slave. I followed my path to freedom, and it has brought me here, removing myself from the reach of Master Thomas Auld. He can now identify my new identity and whereabouts from my *Narrative* but cannot seek to reclaim his "property".

I came here to Ireland to speak the truth about slavery, to say my piece and open people's eyes. That I have done, and our cause is much strengthened.

Yet, at the same time, I found myself in situations where my allegiance to others has cut across my allegiance to myself. I saw a man who touched me deeply with his fervour for freedom, shoot another man dead in the street, and when asked his identity said I knew him not. Does this make me a wise man or a fool? A good friend or a Simon Peter on the night between Maundy Thursday and Good Friday, denying that he knew his friend? I feel as though I was set a test that I did not know how to pass.

My thoughts have not been helped by the fact that the instant our train arrived in Dublin, Mr MacDonagh laid his hand upon my wrist, bade me farewell for the while, and disappeared into the crowd so adroitly that the waiting Buffum did not notice his presence.

This also further strengthened my impression that the Ireland I have seen divides between Dublin and the rest, between that within and that beyond the Pale. The former seems familiar to me; the latter, very strange indeed.

Your,
Frederick

DECEMBER 4TH
DOUGLASS'S LETTER TO ANNA

My dearest Anna,

After several diversions, excursions and delays, I am now arrived in Belfast. My departure from Dublin was initially prevented by the most unusual, unexpected and violent snowstorm, which brought the whole city to a grinding halt. This made me laugh a good deal, as the snow was very minor compared to that which we have seen in Massachusetts, until I realised that they city was so ill-prepared for even such small extremities that a number of the less fortunate poor of the streets had died of the cold. My amusement shrivelled in my throat.

When at last we did depart, the Reverend Samuel Hanna, whose meetinghouse is one of the venues planned for me in that city, accompanied me on the train to Belfast. The good reverend had journeyed down to Dublin to collect me, and his demeanour on the first part of our journey seemed most peculiar. He seemed nervous in the extreme and for a while I wondered whether it was my color which disturbed him, but as he seemed to calm as we journeyed further north it seemed to me that this could not be the cause and, much intrigued, I was moved to ask if there was something which had worried him during the first part of our meeting. He replied that indeed there was, and that it was being in that house of the ungodly, Dublin.

I answered that I found the people of the city nothing save charming, friendly and committed to our cause. To which he replied that it was a city ruled by the idolatry of papist priests and lashed to a frenzy by the mad dog O'Connell. I demurred that idolatry was not much to my liking either, but that I believed every man had a right to make his peace with God in whatever fashion he felt was proper for him. He was about to reply to that, but I continued to a defence of O'Connell who, I said, I found to be the most eloquent of speakers and the speaker of the truth.

He had by now turned a color close to puce, so I thought it best to try and turn this difference aside, lest our disagreements interfere with our larger purpose. I said so, and with rather ill grace I thought he agreed and then turned to look out of the window for some considerable time.

Indeed, thereafter, even when he spoke to me again it was only in the briefest and most formal terms. So my entry into the city of Belfast, late that evening, was unmarked by any guidance as to what I was seeing as the train arrived at the city centre.

Here, we were met by a party of reverend gentlemen come to accompany me to the house of one of their elders, where I was to stay. With them, although now with Reverend Hanna withdrawn into the general company, I walked to an area of the city named Donegal Place. Here there are a large number of meetinghouses and churches all gathered close, and it was here they said that I would speak. Their plan, they said, was to have series of meetings at the meetinghouses and churches, all building towards one final gathering at a large hall called the Commercial Rooms before my departure to Scotland. In this manner they hoped to build a momentum among the people of Belfast for the cause of abolition.

We had by now reached the house at which I was to stay and I bade them all a good night. I shook Reverend Hanna by the hand and thanked him for his help in bringing me here, but he avoided looking me in the eye and made only the most formal of responses.

So, I am now embarked upon the next part of my mission and have many expectations of the trials and possibilities before me.

Your,
Frederick

DECEMBER 6TH
DOUGLASS'S LETTER TO ANNA

My dearest Anna,

The city of Belfast reminds me, strange to tell, of Baltimore. Both are port cities into which the surrounding country bustles to do its business with the rest of the world, and both are much involved with the trade in textiles. This impression that I was somehow returning home, has lingered these last two days despite the fact that Belfast is much more the smaller place. For, small though it is - not much larger than the city of Cork far to the south - it seems to have that spirit of expansion that is so much a part of American cities and not something I have seen much in this island.

The difference that stands clearest to me is that the textile trade here centres on the production of linen. Large factories devoted to the weaving of linen dominate much of the city nearest the port. This is a recent development, since the flight of the cotton trade across the water to Lancashire. From the pictures I have been shown of the fields where the flax for the making of the linen is grown, I suspect I would also see none of the irony of the cotton boll's blazing whiteness in black hands but rather great swathes of the gentlest blue-grey reaching up from the banks of streams and rivers. I do regret that I will not have the opportunity to see this for myself, for at this time and for the time I am here - I am told - the fields are stripped bare and readied for the spring planting.

I am also in the presence of some of the very sternest

Protestantism I ever encountered, which makes the loving-kindness of our Massachusetts friends seem very thin theological water indeed and makes my own commitment to temperance seem lax in the extreme. These are men who believe in the manifest power of God, and feel themselves visited with a vocation to spread far and wide the word of that God.

Yet if they are stern in this fashion, they are also deeply wedded to our cause and yesterday evening I spoke to one of the firmest audiences I have yet encountered. There were none present there with foolish questions about the simple childishness of blacks and their consequent need for mastery. These were men who knew slavery for an abomination in the eyes of God. For all our differences of color, creed and origin, they took me by the arm and called me their brother in the cause of the end of enslavement.

Indeed, at one point after I had told the story of my life as a slave, which I now have quite well rehearsed, members of the congregation called to hear the tale of the events aboard the Cambria. They greeted my account with much amusement and almost universal cries of approbation, and I myself was warmed by the remembrance of a frightening event now turned amusing by the passage of time.

Lastly, I am very happy to tell you that the sales of the Narrative have been so great that I have had to write to Mr Webb asking that he send me more copies as a matter of urgency. I feel myself more profoundly optimistic for my mission here than I have felt up until this point.

Your,
Frederick

DOUGLASS'S LETTER TO ANNA

My dearest Anna,

I am sending, with this letter, some gifts that I hope will make some compensation for my absence at this Christmas, and I send you also the hope that I will be returned by Christmas next.

I speak here every evening, and spend the days in conversation with those who have the time and will to talk with me. This has led, I feel, despite our continued success and popularity, to a number of exchanges when I have seen other currents swirling beneath the main course. The first was with a young and most intensely religious man associated with one of the Donegal churches, who approached me as I walked from my hotel towards the port in search of some sea air. He had, he said, been somewhat perturbed to note the apparent distance between myself and the Reverend Hanna, especially as he had been told that the latter was my host. I was not a little astonished by the young man's directness and at first attempted to turn the conversation to other matters. But he persisted, and then, again with astonishing directness, said that he thought the root of the difficulty lay in our differing opinions as to Mr O'Connell. I was now most astonished, and asked how he could know such a thing, this being our first meeting. To which he replied, that he could and did read the newspapers and had seen reports not only of my voyage to these lands but also of my meeting with O'Connell in Dublin. I demurred, not wishing to provoke any divisions within our cause, but he again persisted and said that he thought the Reverend Hanna would do well to know his history of Ireland as well as he knew his Bible.

Despite the fact that I now began to feel that the young man had gone altogether too far and too directly, I was also intrigued and - almost entirely forgetting all those years of learning to dissemble and disguise before the white man - I asked what he could mean. To which he said that Wolfe Tone, the founder of the United Irishmen, had been a Protestant of a persuasion close to the Reverend's heart and that his army had been very strong among the Protestants of this very city before being beaten underfoot by British soldiers. That, he hoped but did not think, would persuade the Reverend that the cause of Irish liberty was not the cause of popery.

When I asked why he held so little stock in the power of truth, he laughed and gestured around him. Then, just as abruptly as he had begun this line of conversation, he tried to turn the tack of the conversation to my immediate plans and when I said I had very few, he asked if he might be permitted to arrange for myself to meet and visit some of his associates. They wished, he said, to discuss what I had said the previous night about the difference between the condition of the American slave and that of the oppressed Irishman.

To which suggestion I was very hesitant, but replied that I would be delighted to meet his companions and suggested that he arrange a meeting for one luncheon time a few days hence, so that we could gather and talk in a way that would not interfere with the already planned schedule of meetings. He said he would be delighted so to do and, turning on his heel, strode off in the direction from which he had approached me.

I, still not a little confused by his demeanour, continued my walk in the direction of the docks and there eventually found myself seated on a bollard looking out to the various vessels drawn up along the quays.

Where I remembered those days when I first lived in freedom after our flight from Thomas Auld's tyranny, and my work as a caulker in the shipyards, and I wondered at the distance I, a black man born a slave, had come. I reminded myself that all were for naught if I forgot for one moment what it was that had brought me here, namely the freedom of all my still imprisoned brothers and sisters.

Soon after, snow began to flurry down and I was forced to hurry through the streets to my accommodations, at which I now write this letter.

Your,
Frederick

———————

My dearest sister,

I fear that I must break my recent promise and ask you to conceal, again, the arrival of this letter from Phillips and Garrison. My mind is in such turmoil that I feel I must write these letters to those closest to my heart, even if they can offer little advice, support or help. It is a burden lifted from my mind to know that I have shared these worries with my family and very closest friends, and that knowledge stands in the place normally taken by the other half of the conversation.

So it seems that your communication, which eventually reached me here in Belfast, detailing Anna's refusal even to contemplate the effort of learning her letters, brought with it a concealed blessing. For it means that you can continue to act as intermediary and indeed some sort of censor between my conscience and my wife. Yet I would still have you continue to urge her to turn to her learning.

Your brother,
Frederick

———————

My dearest Anna,

Much has happened since last I wrote to place some boundaries around the unbounded optimism I then expressed. As I told at the end of my previous note, I had agreed to meet with the young man and his friends and we agreed that the dining room of my hotel for lunch would be a good place. This much relieved my worries, for I have grown very wary of the prospect of private gatherings these last few weeks.

In due course the young man and his friends arrived, and I was surprised but not displeased to note the number of women, obviously poor, in the company. The hotel manager, though, was less happy at their presence and was about to put them out of the door until I intervened, indicating that they were my guests and I would be grateful that he accommodated them. He agreed, but only if we sat at the far end of the dining room, away from the entrance doors.

As we all sat down, I remarked that I was very happy to be sharing time and conversation with all the people of Belfast. This comment, though, seemed to produce some sharp response from one of the company, who asked very quickly why it was that I drew such clear distinctions between the condition of the American slave and the Irish citizen. I am afraid to say that I matched his sharpness with my own, replying that if he had ever been another man's chattel then he would not need to ask such a question; that to be a chattel was to be at the absolute command of another's whim. The young man's gaze, though, remained steadfast as he asked me if I did not think that a man's use of his language was a part of his humanness. To which I replied, of course. He said he knew this would be my answer, for I had written such in my Narrative, and that therefore did I not believe that to deprive a man of his language was to deprive him of his manhood in some degree and that therefore did I not believe that the English destruction of Irish language was a slavery. To which I said that, whilst I understood his anger, I wished to make two replies and then perhaps we could sit down. First, that I was grateful to the English language for having given me not only the power to speak and write my thoughts but also the ability to read and take heart from the words of others. Second, that I thought it was indeed a slavery to be robbed of one's language but not a slavery to be compared to that which I had endured in which I was robbed of all that made me human.

The young man seemed extremely unhappy and was about to vacate the room, when one of the women, grasping him by the wrist all the while, asked me if then if the difference were a matter of degree rather than an absolute.

To which I answered that I needed to think longer on that subject; that I knew this answer was unsatisfactory but that I promised I would consider much on that point. I sat down not a little confused.

But again she asked me in the same quiet voice employed before, whether she could show to me some matters that might affect my judgement. She had, she said, heard much of my belief in the power of truth and all she wished to do was show me things which might contribute to my sense of truth. I could not but agree. She thanked me for being in Ireland with my truth and then said she must excuse herself as she had other matters needing her attention. At her departure there was a ripple of muttered farewells, or so I deem it for they were made in words I did recognise. I realised in a moment that they were speaking Irish and, assuming that this was a point being made to myself, I said no more about it.

Thereafter, the conversation became a very cordial discussion of the progress of the cause of abolition both here and in Britain (a distinction my guests were persistent to make) and many good wishes for our success were expressed around the table. There came a point, though, when it became clear that the whole party needed to depart and, with many good wishes and farewells made this time in English, they left in a group.

I was still sitting at the table some few minutes later when the manager of the hotel entered, came directly to the table and standing before me requested in a low but brisk tone of voice that I not invite such people to his establishment again. The alacrity with which he turned on his heel having said his piece made the exact nature of the "request" clear to me.

Yet the exact nature of the consequences of this meeting did not become clarified until the next day, when a small delegation of local Presbyterian ministers came to speak with me, they said, on a matter of some urgency. They were concerned, they said, to hear that I had had a meeting with some undesirable people, to which I replied I had not. They said again, that they had heard that I met with a number of notorious Fenians the day before, to which again I replied that although this was not a term with which I was familiar I did not make it my business to ask people their religion or their politics before agreeing to speak with them, that I believed that we are all God's creatures and that was the main root of my hatred for chattel slavery and also, I believed, that this was their belief as well.

To which one of their number said, in a tone I thought somewhat condescending in manner, that the matter was not as simple as this and that I needed to be mindful of my hosts' sensibilities. I asked him directly if he was saying that they wished to control my activities by circumscribing the list of those with whom I could speak, at which he seemed to fluster a little and said that this was by no means his meaning but that I needed to be circumspect in my dealings with those less scrupulous than myself. I agreed, and commended him on his ability to determine the motives of others. At which his face seemed to darken a little and he turned away. One of the others quickly intervened, to say that all they wished was to assure themselves that those with whom I had met the previous day did not intend to attend any of the meetings planned for the immediate future, to which I replied that I had no sense of their intentions but that we had parted on good terms as friends in the cause of abolition. He pressed the point, though, and again I was moved to tell him that I was not the keeper of those with whom I had met the day before and could not tell their intended movements.

This seemed barely to satisfy the company, but they agreed that little was to be gained by prolonging the conversation further and they left as abruptly as they had arrived. I must say that I find my impressions of their stiffness before God to be extending to a feeling of their stiffness before their fellow man.

I had no more visitors of any sort until one of the ministers came to accompany me to my second lecture in the city the next evening. When we reached the hall, the stewards were caught in a small scuffle at the door but I was hurried inside with such alacrity that I had no time to ask what was afoot before I was on the stage and the audience were applauding my presence and I was obliged to begin my address. As by now I have some sections of the speech well rehearsed, my attention was not wholly engaged with my words and so I was increasingly aware that the disturbance at the door was continuing. It was at the point at which I heard one of the stewards say, "you shall not enter", that I stopped and said directly to him over the heads of the audience that as a man who had been prevented from entering many halls I was not prepared to see others stopped from hearing and debating me, for I assumed that those at the door were supporters of slavery. The steward did not move until I repeated my statement in somewhat firmer tones, at which he stood aside. I realised my mistake at once, if mistake it be, for the small group who now entered the hall were some of those I had met two days earlier and others who were clearly with them. By now, much of the audience was looking round and, on seeing them, were much agitated. I turned to Mr Mulholland, the chair of this meeting as well as the last at which I had spoken, and asked him to call for quiet. Eventually he prevailed by means of beating with his gavel on the table and calling loudly for order. When peace was achieved, he warned those at the back of the hall that they should stay where they were and be quiet and asked those in the body of the hall to give indulgence to this most unusual state of affairs.

Thinking that this was the best state of affairs to be achieved in a situation I did not entirely, if at all, understand, I continued with my speech and the evening seemed to conclude well. Yet the reception after was rather less well attended than usual, and those who were there seemed ill at ease.

This is a state of affairs with which I needs must wrestle but I find myself wrestling in a darkness I cannot fathom how to penetrate.

Your,
Frederick

THE CAPTAIN OF THE FERRY TELLS WHAT HE SAW

The wind is frequently this fresh westerly in December and into the New Year, and the Stranraer ferry is often late on the crossing. Rarely if ever completely stopped, but sometimes. Tonight, the wind was bucketing the sea and throwing waves onto the quayside, where they crashed and shattered over the boxes stacked ready to be loaded. What was to be the evening sailing was already becoming, at best, a night voyage.

I remember my first night crossing like it was this week, because I thought I'd never come back from it. I'd been out in worse, but always before I could see what was before and around me. That night, I could only hear and feel the rage of the waters. One of the passengers puked into his hands and, staggering to shake himself over the side, slipped and smashed his ribs against the rail. Even through the scream of the night storm, I could hear his wailing all the way to Scotland. The captain slapped my shoulder once and said that anyone making that much noise must be a Fenian terrified of being made go to Protestant Scotland. Then the human noise stopped. We reached Stranraer was the dawn was thinning the night over the harbour.

Tonight, though, it was just a bad blow. Just bad enough to discourage all but the hardiest, or neediest, passengers. No more than a dozen left by midnight. The rest gave up and went back into the town for a bed. Then this one. Arrived on the coach from Belfast and sat in the booking office bolt upright and reading a book. Didn't even seem to notice when one of the others inched away from him and glanced at the others waiting.

Just kept reading his book, apart from when he suddenly got up and walked over to the desk to buy a ticket.

Even when the ferry finally arrived, he only glanced up and then back to his book until all the others were moving out of the door and across the quay to the gangplank. Then he followed, stepping from the warm light of the office into the wild dark outside. Strangest thing, then. Half way across the yard, clutching his ticket and seeming to follow the other passengers, he looked around. Thought no-one was watching, and then hurried off into the dark. Disappeared into the darkness.

DECEMBER 22ND
DOUGLASS'S LETTER TO HARRIET

My dearest Harriet,

I fear that once more, and I pray that it will be but this once more, I must ask you to keep this letter from Phillips and Garrison. For I have now determined that the secrets and deceit to which I have led myself this last two weeks are something I must now set behind me if I am to feel in any way that I can speak a truth in which I believe.

Your brother,
Frederick

DECEMBER 22ND
DOUGLASS'S LETTER TO ANNA

My dearest Anna,

After the events described in my last letter had come to a conclusion, I felt that there had grown up a certain distance between myself and certain of my hosts. They and I became unhappier still when, at the next meeting I was scheduled to give, the audience seemed considerably reduced from previous occasions. When I asked the Reverend Hanna why he thought this was, he replied that there was growing among the influential people of the city a feeling that the language I and others of the cause of abolition used was too stern and uncompromising. He also said that, frankly, there were those who thought I was up to mischief when I spoke of emancipation rather than the end of slavery. I thanked him for his frankness and stated again that I spoke my truth and that I was here for one cause, the end of slavery, but that did not mean that I would not talk of other matters with people of all persuasions if the moment arose.

He continued that there were those among the cause that believed also that it would be better if I did not speak in the city for a while, so that other tensions might be allowed to cool and be forgotten. Shocked as I was by this, I told him that I would consider this proposal.

The truth of his words became apparent as I was leaving the hall, for several people turned their backs or in other wise refused to acknowledge my departure.

The next morning, as I sat reading in my hotel room, there was a knock on the door and when I called for the person to enter, I saw that it was the young man I had come to think of as the root cause of my present problems. I told him so, to which he replied that the truth of situations often lies buried deeper than the surface, like gold in the ground. I asked him what he meant, to which he answered that the events of the last few days were one small outcrop of the history of the last three hundred years, with the tensions between the Protestants and Catholics spun into a tight web of conflict when common interest pointed to another way. I said that this was of little interest to myself, as I was here to argue the cause of the end of American slavery and nothing else. To which he replied, in most extraordinary terms, that it was not possible to separate one form of slavery from others; that the robbery of freedom took many forms but that it always remained the theft of liberty.

I hear, he continued, that you have been asked to cease your speaking duties here for a while and so I have a proposal to make. Give me ten days of your time, so that I may show you the lineaments of my argument and I will show you how you might pull the fragments of the cause back together here in Belfast.

I agreed that this would be a good bargain if it might be achieved, but that I could not see how it could be done. To which he replied that I should tell Hanna I had received news from Buffum that he needed my presence urgently in England, to discuss matters of importance and that I proposed to take ship from Larne as soon as was possible to cross to Scotland. He would, he said, meet me at Larne so that I might make my half of the bargain. I could then pantomime a return from Scotland, and resume the list of meetings planned.

This seemed to me a plan that had the merits of relieving the tensions that had built up between myself and my hosts in Belfast that, even though it involved trickery, I was prepared to try.

The Reverend Hanna was clearly so relieved at the prospect of my absence from the city for a few days that he did not question what seems to me, in retrospect, the frail tissue of the story I had told him. We agreed that an announcement of my urgent visit to England and the consequent cancellation of my next meeting in the city would be circulated to the newspapers and the Reverend gentleman bade me farewell with barely concealed relief. So, I set off for the small fishing port of Larne, where the young man and also the woman with whom I had spoken at length in the Victoria hotel met me. They proposed, they said, to take me to Londonderry, simply to see the lives the people lived there. They regretted that we must travel in a closed carriage for my presence would surely be noted with great interest along the way if I were seen.

So, for two whole days, I sat, dozed and slumped within the confined space of a darkened coach. Constantly shaken, I barely slept during the night and barely woke during the day. When at last we stopped and they announced that we were within sight of Londonderry, I insisted that I must dismount and stretch my battered body. Bleary-eyed and extremely weak in the legs,

I climbed out into a grey and drizzle-ridden late afternoon to look down over a small town huddled around what seemed to be a castle of some considerable size that overlooked the whole mass of houses from its high walls. We then continued down into the town until, by darkness, we were moving slowly through the streets and arrived at a stable where we dismounted and I was led quickly through the now dark lanes and alleys to a house into which I was ushered with all due speed.

The house itself seemed familiar to me, for its smallness and cramped conditions reminded me strongly of the slave quarters in which I had lived with my grandmother in Tuckahoe. Not least because the activities of the house moved around the two adult women present and they seemed to orchestrate all that happened here. This, despite the presence of a man in his early forties seated silent and immobile in a corner. When we entered, the women instantly beckoned us to be seated at the table and whisked the children away onto the floor before the fire. Despite the obvious poverty of the household, I followed my guides' example and accepted the generous offers of food and drink, realising that refusal would be a clear insult.

No-one within the household, neither adult nor child, seemed to show the slightest surprise at my presence and indeed within a very few minutes one of the children had entirely recovered her confidence to the extent that she came and sat on my knee. I refuted any claim that she would be a nuisance or distraction as we turned to the business of my visit. All that they wished to do, my guides said, was to introduce me to some of the people of this town and have them tell me of their lives.

And so, with all due effort to be clandestine, I spent the next few days resting in the generosity of the poor people of the city of Londonderry. As they told me of their lives and asked me questions of mine, I think I began to see the purpose for my guides of this expedition. As the people talked, I heard parallels between their existence and my own previous life as a slave. They were paid for their labor, which to be sure is a difference, but they had no control over the amount of payment and if they rebelled against the level of their wages they were swiftly reminded that they were others aplenty who would take their places in the sewing of collars and cuffs for shipping to Belfast. The clear result was a poverty very close to that suffered by the plantation slaves of Maryland. They had no political voice in the affairs of the city, and yet were taxed. So, in at least two directions, their masters took their money and spent it on themselves and on edifices to their glory. I could not but agree that this was a heinous state of affairs. The absence of any decent - indeed, any - sanitation within the areas I saw of the city cannot be described as anything other than a crime against the dignity of these people. Indeed, I agreed at almost every turn that their lot was a heavy one and should not be theirs.

I also thought, but did not say, that it seemed to me that there is a difference in kind between being paid however badly for one's labor and having that labor stolen wholesale and openly. However bad the conditions of work are and were for these people they could, and some did, refuse the burden. That seems to me in major contrast to my memories of Covey's whip.

Also, it is clear to me from the discussions I have had with the citizens here that they can and do take themselves to church to worship in whatever manner they see fit and no-one tells them that this is not their right as free people. Their employers do not come and stand at the back of the church to see that they approve the doctrine being preached. At the same time, though, we have talked of the nature of the services and I can see and hear a parallel between some of the psalms we sang as slaves, which told of our true wishes in ciphers, and some of the hymns I heard here. The consolations and exhortations of the testaments are clear in both cases, though they are also obscured in the Catholic services by the inclusion of much else which is later doctrine and elaboration.

In short, I could see the purpose of the invitation to the city. But I was, and one night towards the end of my visit I said that

I was, less sure of the reasons for the secrecy in which the journey was shrouded. To which my guides replied that many of those who were my hosts and strongest supporters in Belfast were also men with major investment in the businesses of this city and they assumed that these men would not thank them for showing me the sources of the money which paid for the hire of the halls and the printing of the leaflets that had made my meetings in Belfast so successful. At which I was considerably incensed and said that I was not in the least concerned for the source of the money which strengthened the cause of abolition, as long as that money came freely and without conditions - which was the case, as far as I could tell. I continued that I found this presumption that I could not grasp the complexities of modern finance and politics extremely condescending and indeed even insulting. My vehemence was such that the assembled company seemed somewhat abashed and even a little ill at ease at my outburst, and the evening ended in some confusion.

The next morning, I found myself alone at the table of the first house to which I had come, having slept there the night before. In many ways, I was unsurprised by the absence of my two guides after my strictures of the previous evening. As the morning progressed, though, I did become a little concerned that they had not reappeared from wherever it was they went to sleep. When I expressed my slight anxiety to my hostess, she merely shrugged and said that she had no idea of their whereabouts and indeed had learned that it was as well to know no more than she needed, and this was intelligence she need not have.

Despite the bad terms on which we had parted the previous evening, I have to admit that after this response I was now more than a little worried, not least because the two had been previously extremely punctual in the mornings. I suggested to my hostess that I could go in search of them but she rightly replied that not only would I have no notion of where to look but also that my appearance in the streets, after the care that had been taken with my concealment until now, would jeopardise those under whose roofs I had stayed. The best thing I could do was wait, she said and then she took herself off to the tasks of running her household.

After barely two hours of this waiting, I have to admit that I was becoming almost frantic with concern for my guides and when, of a sudden, they appeared at the back door of the house, I greeted them almost as long-lost closest friends and withdrew unreservedly my harsh words of the previous evening. They were as unreserved in their apologies for their tardiness that morning but, they said, a sudden piece of urgent business elsewhere in the city had prevented both their arrival at the house and also any chance of sending word.

They also proposed, without further ado, my swift return to Belfast via, of course, the village of Larne so as to maintain the fiction of my visit to England. Indeed, they urged as immediate a departure as I could possibly make. Even though I felt, shall I say, bustled by this sudden change in plan, I could also see the wisdom of their argument for, having been drawn into this fiction, I could see no profit in allowing its demise.

So it was, then, that within barely two hours I found myself back on the road to Belfast only this time without their company. I was left alone with my thoughts of what I had seen and heard during my visit. As I considered, it became clear to me that the purpose for my guides of this visit was to persuade me of the parallels between the condition of our people and the condition of the Catholic Irish, but I remain convinced that there is a major difference - which is chattel slavery, for which I see no like among free people. Indeed, by the time I was arrived at Larne I was more than a little annoyed by the transparency of their actions and their assumption that I could not come myself to an understanding of their motives. I determined then, that this last fiction I would maintain but that I would do my best to distance myself from these people, with their love of intrigue and subterfuge.

Thus it was that I returned to Belfast with invented tales of my trip to meet with Buffum, and prepared to fulfil my obligations in that city. The days away seemed to have repaired any rift that may have occurred as a result of my naiveté, and I prepared to deliver the last of my Belfast lectures. In the course of which I could not resist making some less than creditable references to the actions of so-called Catholics from Mexico in the Texan war, which raised the spirits of my Protestant audience a good deal and returned me to their favor to such an extent that I was invited to stay until after the New Year. Short of funds as I am, I accepted this offer with ease and thus will remain here until I have fulfilled that obligation and then I will take myself to Glasgow. Where I will, in truth, meet with Buffum and prepare the next leg of the great tour.

Until I am in Scotland, then, I will not write again for I have much to settle in my own mind and much to prepare for the offensive there. The opposition to our cause among some Scots is, my friends here tell me, stiff and well-organised.

That this letter will not reach you until after Christmas, I am well aware, but nevertheless it bears my greetings and affection.

Your,
Frederick

DECEMBER 25TH
DOUGLASS'S LETTER TO WENDELL PHILLIPS

My dear Phillips,

I write to you on this Christmas day with my greetings and felicitations for the New Year. Let us hope that by this time a year hence I will be returned home again, and as a truly free man, rather than a man merely licensed to freedom by my own actions and still caught within the tangle of laws by which our country ensnares the so-called defenders of freedom into an alliance with slavery.

I have great hopes for our coming mission through to Scotland and England, where I hope Buffum and I will repeat our Irish successes. I know, though, from intelligence from our Belfast friends, that the opposition will be stiff. Yet I have the courage born of knowing we are right.

I remain your ally and, I hope, your friend,

Frederick Douglass

<hr>

DECEMBER 31ST
BUFFUM'S LETTER TO GARRISON

My dear William,

The plans for the tour of Scotland are now well advanced, though I have not advised Douglass of the probable extent and nature of the opposition we can expect. The Free Church, it is now clear, is in some areas dependent upon slavers' money for its continued workings and so we can predict some open battles. I will make every effort to prepare Douglass for those, and have got ready for him some papers that will be of assistance.

This coming confrontation with the pious men of the Free Church does not worry me as much as some of the rumours I hear from Belfast. That Douglass has not been as wise as he might have been in some of his associations, it is clear, and he seems to have been somewhat swayed by arguments linking all aspects of reform one to another. As must be clear to you, this has not helped our cause among some of the Belfast clergy and merchants, who do not want to hear of O'Connell and his arguments.

I have also had the strangest intelligence that Douglass paid a visit to Scotland, to meet with myself. But no such visit has taken place, and I am most concerned what this presages. I would, dear friend and fellow in arms, welcome your advice and words on this peculiar matter.

Your,
Buffum.

PART FOUR

THE STORY OF EAMONN
MACDONAGH, CONTINUED

Joe wasn't gone long, I suppose. An hour, perhaps a little more. I lay there, looking at the familiar places of my childhood from an angle from which I'd not looked before. One cheek pressed to the heather, the world tipped on its edge. That seemed about right.

When he came back, he'd got Jimmy and Pat and Proinsias to come with him, though they looked like cats scared by a dog. The four stood and looked at me, as though I were a problem they had no way of solving.

"What's the problem, lads?"

"We're trying to work out how .."

"How?"

"How to pick you up."

"One at each corner. Oh. Ah."

Another silence.

"Have you got a knife, Pat?"

When, at last, we reached my mother's cottage, me mammy's threshold, she was standing there in the doorway with her shawl hitched up about her shoulders. When she saw me, she lifted the shawl higher until it covered her head. And she began to wail

Bean sí

That was how it was, then. I sat by the door, looking out over the village and the inlet beyond, towards the sea, as the autumn went away and the winter coldness came down from the north. When she had ceased sobbing and crying, she continued to wail as she moved around. Even when she was quiet, even when she was asleep, my mother wailed for what had happened to me.

It took some weeks. Before I could even contemplate it. At the beginning, all I needed was water and the odd cup of tea. Then one day she looked down at me as I sat by the door.

"*You need to eat.*"

Needed to, to be sure. But couldn't. The smell of the cabbage and tiny bit of bacon, the boiled potato, brought the smell of the clamp pouring back into my nostrils, my mouth, my throat, until I was gagging bile and a little watery tea-coloured liquid into my lap.

"*I can't. I can't.*"

———

PART FIVE

THE CAPTAIN OF THE FERRY, AGAIN

T he oddest thing, that I should see him again on the quayside and so soon after his peculiar visit. This time, though, he arrived for the morning sailing and in the company of numerous Belfast worthies. There was a great deal of hand-shaking and speech-making, and then he was aboard the ferry and gone. Only then did the smiles fade from the faces, and there was much muttering before the worthies strode off to their carriages and away.

I watched the ferry disappear down the loch and I thought, I will not see his like again.

JANUARY 9TH, 1846
DOUGLASS'S DIARY

I have now completed my crossing from Ireland to Scotland, after a difficult last few days in Belfast, during which I felt that several of my hosts had grown quite cold towards myself. They seemed to have forgotten that I was no mere cypher of the cause but a man with opinions on many topics that I had thought upon, developed and felt obliged to express. As soon as I strayed the merest jot from my appointed mission, my judgements were seen as ill-informed, hastily made and always wrong. Indeed, I may be being too quick to see prejudice where it does not exist, but this thought about my ideas seemed governed by the second thought that no man of my color could hold an opinion of their situation which was both considered and contrary to their truths of themselves.

It may be, though, that any man of any color who found himself in disagreement, however small, with these men who are so sure of themselves and their beliefs would feel as I feel now.

These difficulties, though, are as nothing compared to my problems of conscience. For I have already been moved to sins of both omission and commission on this journey, I have lied both by silence and by active misdirection of those who would be my friends; to whit the inestimable Buffum. Irritant he may be, with his insistent wish to never offend me, but he is a man of good heart. I was mightily glad of the awful weather and conditions of our drive here from Stranraer, for it permitted me to a silence which, whilst still evasive and therefore omissive, prevented his questions.

It allowed me, further, to explore within myself my reasons for having come here. Reasons, that is, beyond the obvious expediency of flight. As I considered, I did ask myself whether or not the decision to join in the cause of abolition in the ways I did were not some strange effort at attracting the attention of Thomas Auld to myself. I answered this within my mind by replying that thinking thus was to continue to allow that man to rule my life, even my thinking, and I reaffirmed that my task here was to alert a civilised nation to the savagery and atrocity being committed within a few days' journey of their shores. The abolition of slavery within the British Empire was the first mighty step that the people of this nation have taken, but now they must see the mutuality of their relations with the United States and the moral pressure that they could exert against their American friends.

Rehearsing these arguments within my mind pushed the shade of Thomas Auld back again into the darkness it so richly deserves to occupy in my life.

A day's rest has been prescribed for me by my hosts here in the city of Glasgow, for I am tired from the journey. Indeed, tired to the point of sleep now.

Yours
Frederick

My dearest Anna,

I have been already one week and more in the city of Glasgow and only last night gave my first full lecture here. This is not because of any reluctance on my part to speak, or on the part of the supporters of the cause here to hear but rather because on the journey from Ireland I caught the most awful cold, the like of which I have not before experienced, and have had to take to my bed for nearly a whole week. I was on the first day here, my host's wife tells me, the very picture of a caged lion for I wished to be about my business.

I tried, the day after I reached the city, to speak to a small audience of the Emancipation Society but was so overcome by the effects of my cold that I had to finish as quickly as I could and then excuse myself. From the small hall I went as fast as I could to my bed and remained there a full week, heeding the advice of the good lady. Her words gained in resonance as the fever spread from my head to my limbs and I was taken for two or three days by the shakes and sweats.

Yesterday, though, fully recovered, I made my first speech in Scotland. This is of the greatest personal importance to me, having taken the name Douglass from one of the poems of the national poet and novelist of this country. My new friends here in Glasgow tell me, though, that Walter Scott is a man of the south and east of the country and that here the land lies differently. So, it seems I will have to wait until I cross to Edinburgh to make my thanks to the writer whose work made me who I am today.

With Buffum on one side and the Reverend Jeffrey at the other, I found myself seated before a substantial audience - perhaps fifty people - drawn from the best elements of the population of the city. After Jeffrey's introduction, which included Henry Wright's letter of endorsement for myself, I described the conditions of the slaves in America and then went on to tell the story of my own voyage across the Atlantic. This drew much laughter from the audience, at the tales of the discomfitures of those who find themselves uneasy at the prospect of calling themselves my countrymen. After I had finished, the good Buffum made an excellent short speech explaining the importance of British public opinion to our cause, even though the suffering slaves were separated from this land by the Atlantic Ocean. This has been the most excellent start to our campaign here, for we seem to have attracted a group of the very best of the citizens of Glasgow to our cause at one stroke.

Indeed, my temper is hugely improved since the day of my arrival in Scotland and I am looking forward to carrying our message still further through these islands. I stand convinced that the good hearts of the men and women I meet can be prevailed upon by the simple words of the truth I tell.

I remain ever yours,
Frederick

DOUGLASS'S DIARY

Even as I listened to Buffum talk this evening, I began to feel more well disposed towards him for he spoke with an eloquence and passion which eludes him in his private discourse. Yet, I also found myself in the most profound disagreement with his argument. I do not feel separated from my brethren just because there is water between us. The ocean does not cut us off from one another, but rather is the bridge across which we may pass. By coming here I do not feel that I have left people behind but rather that I have expanded the circle of my acquaintance to draw in ever more of the friends of abolition. It is men like Lyell, who willingly blind themselves to the truths of slavery, who also feel that the ocean is a barrier between men.

BUFFUM'S LETTER TO GARRISON

My dear Garrison,

I have tried, without success thus far, to talk with Douglass concerning the mysterious trip here before his public arrival. He passes the matter off, though, as if it were nothing and will not discuss it with me. True, he has been ill the last few days with a bad cold but now he is recovered I feel I must pursue the matter with him with some more vigour. I hope that there is nothing in his conduct that will damage our cause.

What news of your own visit here, which you mentioned in your last letter? It would boost our cause inestimably to have your voice added to those we already have to hand.

Yours,
James Buffum

JANUARY 20, 1846
DOUGLASS'S LETTER TO HARRIET

My dearest Harriet,

I fear I must ask your indulgence once more and make a request to which you may find very hard to respond in a positive manner, for I need to plead that if needs be you lie for me to Garrison and Phillips regarding receipt of letters from me. I would ask that you deny the existence of all those I marked not for transmission onwards. You know of my business here, and the complications into which I have fallen these last few months. But I would impress upon you the importance of not telling the white men of my complexities and supplementary activities and doubts. These are things of which they do not need to know, just as there was much about our thoughts and actions while in slavery that we have kept - and keep still - from them.

I am moving in their world now, and I must needs have all my wits about me.

I would not wish that they knew any more than they need, and the whole of the tangled tale of my days in Ireland is something of which they do not need to know. I have a version for them which will serve them adequately, but I need to ask for your support.

I know, dear sister, that this is a hard thing to ask of such an honest and upright woman as yourself, but I ask you to consider the consequences for him who thinks of himself as your brother and friend.

This comes to you with a letter for Anna, which can well be passed along. In this way I hope to disguise somewhat our communication.

Your loving brother,
Frederick

───

DOUGLASS'S LETTER TO ANNA

My dearest Anna,

Since my last, I have spoken at another three gatherings in this mighty city, each at least the size of that first about which I was so jubilant. The people of Scotland have a thirst for liberty which does not stop at their own doors but flows out to embrace all those who struggle for their freedom. At every turn the men and women of quality in this city are turning to our cause and, if I was moved by our progress and success in Ireland, I am the more enheartened by the obvious prospect of success here.

We are beginning to command an influence among those who have the power to influence others, and also the money to help our cause still further. This combination of the ears and the purses of the influential is most important to us. Without either one we are most probably turned to voices crying in a wilderness, speaking our truth but unheard by any other; without both we are utterly overthrown. I think of this not as touching the pitch of mammon and thus being defiled, but rather gathering the finance necessary to continue our truth-telling in ways that can, that will, be heard.

I am further heartened by the ecumenical nature of our influence here, for men and women of all cloths and persuasions come to hear our lectures and then invite us to their houses. In the last week, since that tremendous debut occasion, Buffum and I have taken lunch or tea or dinner in a procession of houses until I feel that we have made the acquaintance of every minister in the city. The Reverend Jeffrey, a Presbyterian, in particular has made us welcome and we have been to his house several times and met many of his family and his congregation. On every occasion we are greeted with great friendship, though there have been a few times when some of those present have expressed surprise that I am not darker than I am and in this I can see an ignorance about the nature of slavery as it exists in America. I am also at a loss as to how to correct this without offending the sensibilities of those with whom I am speaking, for to tell how my skin came to be this way would be to speak of fornication and rapine before an audience I would not wish to distress in this way. The moment may come, though, when there is no other way to show the real face of the slaver. His impress is upon me in a fashion all can see, save those who would deny what is so manifestly before their eyes, and we need to tell this in order to show the depths to which the peculiar institution drags all who come into contact with it willingly.

As well as the good Buffum, I have always by my side these days the indefatigable Henry Wright, who has been on the stump in Europe for nearly four years already. Together, we are making ready for a journey to Dundee for a series of lectures for which we have great hopes of success.

Your,
Frederick

DOUGLASS'S DIARY
JANUARY 25, 1846

I am much distressed by a letter I have received from Reverend Stanfield in Belfast, in which he tells me of the aftermath of my time there. He has been moved, he tells me with some pride, to rebuke another minister - a man of the Free Church - for his

—
99

criticisms of myself during my stay there. Whilst I am always pleased to see a white man coming to my aid when he himself is unthreatened, it does tell me that beneath the surface of that seeming success there, I have left behind other depths which I have muddied rather than cleared. I cannot tell, though, whether or not this is the nature of the enterprise in which I am engaged, that it is impossible to pull one weed from a pond without disturbing the silt around the roots of others.

Whatever the case may be, I can see no course for myself other than to continue as I have, speaking my truths to whomsoever will hear me out. This conviction is stronger within me now than it has been before, partly from the successes we have had and also because of the great obstacle I can see before me. For the second part of Reverend Stanfield's letter tells me of the money the Free Church has been raising in the slave states in order to finance its Christian activities elsewhere. These religious men are at one remove from those pious whip and shackle wielders who quoted the Bible as they sold our living flesh, but they are cut from the same cloth and I will say that it is so.

Canting hypocrites that they are, they will tell their congregations that the source of the money does not matter an ell. What is of the moment only is the good it does elsewhere, spreading the word of God among those benighted enough not yet to have heard the word of the Free Church. I will tell them that you cannot dip a brush in pitch and expect it to whitewash a fence.

JANUARY 26, 1846
BUFFUM'S LETTER TO GARRISON

My dear Garrison, though there is nothing you can do at the remove of the Atlantic Ocean, I should tell you of the developments here, that you are forewarned and thus forearmed. Yesterday evening, Douglass and Wright came to my hotel room to tell me that they plan to attack the Free Church of Scotland for its fund-raising activities among the Southern states. No matter that I argued the danger of such tactics, as having the potential to lose us many powerful and influential friends here in Scotland, they are determined, they say, to begin this attack at the great meeting called in Dundee for two days hence. So, unless I can prevail upon them beforehand, by the time you receive this letter it will have happened and there will be nothing you can do. But I thought you should know of this move.

The idea for this comes from Douglass, I have no doubt, for even though Wright was the more vehement in his denunciations of the Free Churchmen in my presence, it was Douglass who stood firm in the face of my objections. I will continue to argue with Wright, for I believe he can be swayed, but my experience of Douglass is that there are few people who have influence with him once his mind is settled and I am sure that I am not among that number.

I look for news of your departure from Boston, and even better your arrival here, every week for I know we need firm guidance at this point if the successes we have had are not to be lost by an act of foolishness.

My best wishes,
James Buffum

═══════════

JANUARY 29, 1846
DOUGLASS'S LETTER TO ANNA

My dearest Anna,

We have taken Dundee by storm! The first two nights we spoke here, the small chapel engaged for our employment was so tightly packed, and with many standing in the street outside, that it became necessary to issue tickets for tonight's meeting and then the final meeting tomorrow.

At the same time as we have had these evening successes, gathering to ourselves the very best of the society of the banks of the Tay, we have also made many friends during the day. There has been, though, one interesting turn in the reaction of the Scottish to myself. Remember before how I remarked on their surprise at the lightness of my skin, and my preparations for a speech to explain such a thing. Well, I have also found that though I am hardly black enough for British taste, by keeping my hair as woolly as possible I make out to pass at least for half a Negro, which sets aside many objections and persuades the more sceptical to hear me out. This stratagem, whilst I have many doubts about it, is no more than a theatrical show to catch the attention of others. My other powers, I begin to feel, can hold them with me once I have made that first connection.

Walking from last evening's success to our hotel, Buffum tried once more to dissuade me from my determination to strike at the Free Church tomorrow. He cannot see, he says, either the wisdom of the tactic or the force of the principle. We may well lose more influence than we gain by so openly attacking the institution to which many of our supporters adhere in their Sunday worship. Further, he does not hear my argument about the proximity of America to Britain; he sees the empty ocean between rather the myriads of people crossing it with their words, their minds, and their bodies. Last, he asked if I would refuse money for our cause from a factory owner here in Scotland.

I asked what he meant by this question, and he replied that there were some who saw a close parallel between the chattel slavery of the Southern states and the wage slavery of the North. At which I balked and replied that if there were such fools as could not see the difference in kind between slavery and work then I would be happy to explain to them that being imprisoned in the clasp of another man and always at his whim is of a very different water to being able to walk from the workplace gate at the end of every day.

Buffum replied that he was of the same mind as myself, but that there were many who were not and who would be prepared, happy even, to criticise my taking monies from such a source. And, he continued, not merely eccentrics like Bronson Allcott, that young friend of Emerson's who has set himself up in a one-man republic in the Connecticut woods and calls down wrath on the heads of those not as pure as himself in their dealings with but also men of the world who could hold the ear of many another. To which, again, I said that I would be happy to debate such matters with those of different opinion to myself and that I had a firm faith in the rightness of my distinction between slavery and what some called slavery.

Further, I continued, that Buffum had no experience of the use of the Bible as a justification for the enslavement of my fellows, had never heard the recitation of texts accompanied by the crack of a cow-hide whip across some poor wretch's back or, worse, seen some child felled for insolence with a blow from a heavy leather-bound copy of the Good Book itself. These are no Christians, Mr Buffum, I said and I will expose both them and their friends who claim the light of God but take their sustenance from the darkness of slavery.

My voice having risen to quite a pitch by this time, Buffum pleaded that we stop this conversation for we were attracting the attention of those we passed in the street while we were engaged in argument. I saw then that he was not prepared to pursue this further at that time and that the impetus was now with me. I agreed then that we should end the discussion and took myself happily to the hotel to make my preparations for tomorrow night with Wright's assistance.

I found Wright in his room and intent on the writing of his speech for the morrow, he not having been here these last three days and not scheduled to speak with us tonight. When I told him of Buffum's objections he snorted and called them "abjections". Together we marshalled the evidence we would need for tomorrow and then planned our strategy. I will speak first, and open the campaign against the hypocrites in general terms, while Wright will follow up with the more detailed evidence. He has agreed that, in fairness to Buffum, we will need to tread carefully and speak with measured tones so as not to drive away those who might use any intemperance of manner to deny the substance of our arguments.

Your,

Frederick

JANUARY 30, 1846

Today, I will take a great stride forward if I can bring myself to the point. For until now all I have had to do was rise before an audience and tell them of my life, of the life of my brothers and sisters in bondage, show them the tools of wickedness and they would come to our cause by numbers because they were convinced by my presence. I know this, I have known since that first day in New Bedford that God had given me the power and the strength to be a leader of my people and I came to know that it would be a sin to set that talent aside.

I knew also that it would be a sin further than that to turn away from my brethren when I had my own freedom. For I knew that my freedom was dependent upon theirs, that I would not be released from bondage until all were released. Every day since I have thanked God for the existence of men such as Wendell Phillips and William Garrison, that they showed me the path to tread in search of that over-arching freedom and showed me also that not every white man and woman was my enemy.

Tonight, though, I will step beyond the bounds of the man they appointed as my guardian whilst here. For Buffum is against the plan to upbraid the Free Church and, I warrant, has reported this to Garrison and Phillips. I will have to do more than simply show myself. I will need an argument that will convince even in the face of opposition that we, that I am right.

DOUGLASS'S LETTER TO ANNA

My dearest Anna,

Last night brought success and controversy pointing toward failure in almost equal measure.

When we arrived at the hall, just as we had on the previous three evenings, Buffum was all of a twitch with the sight he had of the many members of the Free Church present in the room and attempted once more, but this time in a strained undertone, to dissuade me from my course. I indicated, though, that I would not be moved. With my arguments and my quotations marshalled before me upon the table, I began by telling the audience that I had no quarrel with the Free Church as a church, that I had no opinion on their existence as a church. I continued that I knew the Free Church was not alone in its sanction of slavery; there were also the Episcopalians, the Roman Catholics, the Presbyterians and the Congregationalists. My quarrel, then, was not with the Free Church alone but with all Churches that, instead of offering succour to the fleeing slave, take the money of the slaveholder. Perhaps the edge of my quarrel was with a church that did this and did this in Scotland, the inhabitants of which are distinguished for their love of liberty, and still calls itself "free". At this the audience laughed, and I felt them come slightly to my side.

My quarrel, I continued, was with the actions of such of their ministers as had taken money from the slaveholders to finance the church here in Scotland and then represented the view of the slaveholders on slavery as the view of the congregations of the Free Church. Was this the case, I asked, did this view accord with the view of the audience here before me? No!, they cried and, emboldened by this, I named the Reverend George Lewis as the friend of slavery.

The reaction of the audience to this was most extraordinary, for sections hissed me for the naming of names. They can, it seems, live with the general argument but when it is specified and individuals are pointed out in their hypocrisy this is against their belief. I dropped the tone and volume of my voice a moment, and welcomed the hissing as the sound made by the cool voice of truth falling into the burning vortex of falsehood. Those who hissed, I suggested, love sect more than truth, Church more than God. What had I said that was falsehood? Had not the Reverend Lewis travelled to the United States, had he not been received by the slavers and received in turn their monies and brought them home again? If I lied, and he was present, let the good brother speak up and debate me.

I waited a moment, then a moment more, but he was not present and neither was any man or woman who would speak for him.

I knew, then, that I had them and went onto the offensive. I read from *Isaiah*, "your hands are full of blood", and threw that down as a challenge to the Free Church ministers. I said that if the congregations reflected that the chapels in which they sat were built with slave money, they would cry with me "send back the blood stained money, send back the money".

Then, again at quieter pitch, I went on to refute the arguments of the Free Church ministers one by one. The religious education of slaves, of which they are so fond, I said, consisted of but one quotation from Paul - "Servants obey your masters". Four words, in all the great tide of wisdom that is the Good Book. Four words! This, I suggested was the text used to tell the enslaved that their happiness depended upon obedience, that their gratitude was expected for having been saved from what might have been in the heathen hinterlands of Africa, that obedience was the recognition of their being adapted to their present condition. This was the religious education offered to the enslaved; a sophistry designed to hold them in bondage in the belief that it was God's wish that it be so.

Then I brought up from the table before me a copy of the resolutions of the South Carolina Presbytery, as an example of the quality of the religious education offered to the enslaved, and quoted a passage concerning those "good old slaveholding patriarchs Abraham, Isaac and Jacob". These were the brethren to whom the Reverend Lewis was so attached. Then I quoted from a New Orleans newspaper, which ran side by side a eulogy for a Free Church minister and a series of advertisements searching for escaped slaves; and if that same minister asked how he had come by this eulogy, I would reply, I said, that he had clapped hands with the slaver, that he had taken their blood-stained dollar. That was the reason for his eulogy, he need look no further than that.

That was why, I concluded, that I wished the people of Scotland to tell that the Free Church's view of slavery was not their view, that they wished no more compact with the slavers; that they wished for the Free Church to send back the blood-stained dollars, to send back the money of slavery.

Amid a great applause I took my seat, rising only again to nod my appreciation at the applause and acceptance of my arguments. I had, I felt, taken an audience shot through with the lukewarm and even the hostile and turned it to my side by the power of argument. For not once had I referred to my own story. I had contended with ideas, and with ideas had won these people to my side.

Then came the disaster, and I wish now that we could have closed the meeting with my final words. Instead, the good Henry Wright rose in my aftermath and sought to continue the argument. Or so I thought, but all our contentions about moderation and care seemed to have deserted him and instead of argument he followed with assault. He said some foolish things: he made no distinction between Church and ministers, thus making those whom I had separated from the ministers fall back to their side; he called several well-known ministers drunkards, when I had been at pains to keep my remarks only to their attitudes to slavery and thus not muddy the waters of the arguments, and that brought down cat-calls and hissing. Worse still, he seemed not to notice that he was chilling the audience and instead of stopping when he could, continued on until Buffum felt forced to intervene and quiet him.

With the meeting now in confusion, Buffum brought the evening to an abrupt end despite my protestations that I felt I could return the audience to our side again.

All this, of course, has further convinced Buffum that the tactic itself was wrong and he refuses almost absolutely to attend further meetings unless I will give him assurance to turn away from attacking the link between the Free Church and slavery's monies.

Yet I cannot believe that this is so, for the audience tonight were turned by careful argument from one position to another, and then were turned again by intemperate argument. I believe that I am right in my attacks upon the finances of the Free Church, in my belief that all of a man's doings are connected one to another and that a veil cannot be drawn between some and others. So, I will determine to carry on with this.

Your,
Frederick

———

FEBRUARY 2, 1846
DOUGLASS'S DIARY

It has been the hardest matter I have had to hand thus far in my career as a man of the cause. I could see that, in one respect, Buffum was right. It was the intemperate words of the good Henry Wright which lost us the Dundee audience, and that intemperance repeated could damage our larger cause by driving an unnecessary wedge between us and sections of our support. And so, despite my great feeling for him and despite my lesser affection for Buffum, I agreed that I would break from Wright in return for Buffum's agreement that he would continue to support meetings at which I cautiously, temperately and with great care raised the question of the Free Church and its monies.

Which left to me the portion of speaking with the good Henry. Two days after that disaster in Dundee, just yesterday, when we had moved on to the house of a good friend on the outskirts of Dundee, I drew Henry aside in the garden walk. I asked how he thought the recent meetings had been and he waxed lyrical on the success of the occasion, but as he spoke I could tell that his definition of success was that of a sectarian, for he spoke of how he had placed the unvarnished truth before the audience and that for many it was too strong a medicine. Yet, he continued, he had not balked from his task and mission, and had continued to the end.

I tried to ask if he had seen how that meeting had turned against us, but he was blind to it. Which made the task of severance both easier and much harder. Easier, for I could see all too clearly how he could harm the cause but much harder for he could not be led to any comprehension of that harm.

In the end, we parted on bad terms, he turning his head for Edinburgh while I set my course for completing the cycle of meetings here before moving on to Arbroath.

While I know I have done the right thing in this, in setting the larger cause before the needs of the one man, I feel that I have shed an ally and a friend at the moment when I will need such people close beside me. For already the winds of opposition are blowing and the Free Church journals are in full array against us.

<hr />

FEBRUARY 10, 1846
DOUGLASS'S LETTER TO ANNA

My dearest Anna,

After a series of successful meetings continuing on through the first days of the month, James Buffum and I have begun to win many friends to the general cause of the end of bondage and also to the more specific cause of cutting the knot binding the Free Church of Scotland to the slavers by chains forged with the dollars of the latter. A current of popular opinion begins to move with us, that would say that it is hypocrisy for a church to claim the word of freedom in a hall built with the blood money of slavery.

Today we are arrived in Arbroath, and ready to beard the lion of the Free Church in one of its dens.

My confidence in our cause is high, and I feel as though I were carried here on a tide of the good will of the people of this noble land.

> *Your,*
> *Frederick*

FEBRUARY 11, 1846
DOUGLASS'S LETTER TO ANNA

My dearest Anna,

Would that the confidence of my last had been fulfilled but I find that the Free Church has been here before us, with rumor that we are paid by other churches to calumnise their good name. With the result that the pulpit we had been promised for yesterday evening was locked against us and we had to go into the street at once to seek other premises. The only place we could find was the workingman's Trades Hall, which has the advantage of being able to accommodate a large crowd. Which was as well, for we had an exceptional turn-out. One friend, a machinist from a small factory in the town, told us that this was for the simple reason that many came who would not by any means enter a church for lack of belief that they could share anything with their employer, not even a God.

Be that as it may, it was an exceptional audience for what is quite a small town. There were also, though, it seems to me an audience not much moved by my refutations of the claims of the Free Church. I felt that I needed to lay aside the accusations that that Church has laid at our feet before I could say anything else. I needed, I felt, to make matters clear. But they seemed little interested. They had come to see what I have begun to think of as the dog and pony show, where I perform the pitiful slave and make no arguments of my own. From this stolid crowd I was rescued by Mr Anderson, who rose to thank me for my speech in one of the small pauses and offered the use of the church for which he is a lay preacher for my subsequent meetings here in Arbroath.

I continued on with the theme that the Free Church should send back the money and managed, at least, to raise a small cheer with that slogan. The collection at the door for our cause was also disappointing and I have returned here to my hotel a little dispirited.

My consolation in telling all to you revives me, though, for when I put my pen to paper I feel that we are almost in communication and the gap between us seems closed a little when I tell you of my difficulties. With my sense of your closeness, I know that I and the cause will prevail.

Your,
Frederick

FEBRUARY 14, 1846
DOUGLASS'S LETTER TO ANNA

My dearest Anna,

With the assistance of Mr Anderson, who has been a terror in our cause in Arbroath, we have prevailed here among the best people of the town. After the quietness of our first meeting, the latter three have been the most explicit triumph and we have turned a corner. The Free Church has retreated from the untruths it had spread about our funding, and has taken up residence on the ground of slanderous remarks about our characters, which cannot of course be so easily refuted but merely rebuffed in the short time available to us. Indeed, I have not felt especially the need even for this rebuttal and have told Buffum several times that such moves by our opponents are signs of weakness, not strength.

I feel the power of our cause when I meet with the quality of the town and one says to me, with a smile "send back the money" indeed, indeed. A slogan, it seems, carries the weight of a dozen complex arguments. Even Buffum's doubts seem to have withdrawn somewhat and once or twice he has been moved to remark that it would appear that we are more popular than we were. It is not appearance, it is a reality!

I will go from here on to a grand tour of Scotland, now all planned and arranged, to gather still more to our general and specific cause. First, though, I have a small matter of my own to attend in Glasgow, for I have been invited to address the Scottish Temperance League alongside many of the great men of temperance in these islands. I feel the honor of being at their side already, brought there not as the escaped body of a slave but as an orator for the movement to temperance. As a man who can speak his own ideas and thoughts, in his own right as an intelligence.

Your,
Frederick

PART SIX

THE STORY OF EAMONN
MACDONAGH, CONTINUED

That was how it was, for the winter. I gagged at the smell of food, every time she tried to get me to eat. Sometimes I kept a little down, for a few minutes at least, before spewing it back again when I lost the fight with my churning body as the smell, the stink of the clamp gushed over me. So I ate at the door, else the house would have reeked.

The rub was, that from the doorway I could see the houses of the village.

I could see the people coming from the houses of the village. Could see, in their glances in my direction, that they would have sent their children to lick up what I vomited, for the want of a little food. For my mother and I were fortunate. We had, compared to others, enough money to buy food. Little enough though it was, there was some.

THEN, JANUARY 7TH 1846.

Bean sí

Sound sharp as the blade of the knife rippled from the Donnelly's house. Rippled, and sucked in the women of the village one by one. While the men just stood, every one of them with his hands clasped before his groin. Each trying to hold on to his manhood, in the face of this.

They were powerless, though. As the children died one by one, they saw that.

The Donnellys were lucky that their child died first. Because he got a coffin. Nothing special, right enough. A few old bits of planks hammered into a box. But at least a box. By the middle of February, they were carrying the children to the graveyard wrapped in a sheet, by the end of the month in their arms.

Then, by the second week of March, for the first time a father had to open the grave of a child he had already buried. Because there was no more room in the graveyard. I sat and watched him first peel back the little turf that had re-grown on the small mound and then ease his spade into the earth. Slowly, slowly before I saw him jump back and I knew, if I'd been nearer, that I would have heard the chink of iron on bone. Watched him stand there, panting but not with the effort of the little digging he'd done, looking off across the water and then down at his feet. Trying to avoid seeing what was between him and the sea; his child's open grave. Then, when he had his breathing under control, he started again to dig, only this time barely spooning the soil aside. He paused and, for no reason I could discern, glanced up in my direction. And kept his gaze on me.

I suddenly felt ashamed that I should sit there and watch a father do what a father should never have to do. Not just bury a child, not just that. But bury a child and then re-open that child's grave and bury another within it.

I went into the house, slowly and all the while I moved I could feel his gaze on me.

Thereafter, I always had mother go to the door and look to see who was abroad before I went out to sit. Which was little barrier, for by now there were few enough in the village who had the strength to do anything save that which kept them alive. So, for much of the early spring I could still sit out except when there was burying to be done. It came harder to tell when that was, though, for there were not many left with the power in their hearts or lungs to call out loudly at the mere death of a child.

Hunger is a stiff broom, that sweeps the street tidy. Chickens were long gone, and even the grass that had grown up along the centre of the road through the village had been plucked for a thin soup – for we are not great eaters of salad, and would not change our patterns now. The cottages that had been turned out by the bailiff were now picked clean of any rafter wood or scraps of furniture. Just as the people, so the untidiness of life was slowly being cleared away.

March 27th, in the early morning it was drizzling. A heavy mist that kept me sat within the doorway. Even so, I could see a black sack that had been dropped half-way between the church and the parish house. It was early, so I wasn't that surprised that its contents hadn't yet been scooped up and disappeared. But I was surprised that it had been dropped in the first place. The drovers coming from the west had stopped travelling at night, they were robbed so much and in the quietness that filled the land now I would have heard them in the night.

For hunger is a stiff broom, that sweeps away the need for much sleep.

Slowly, one by one, the few women strong enough to venture out came to look at the sack. And stayed to stand looking. Slowly, one by one, the men came out to stand with them. Mammy understood before me and went down to join them. I counted and, as far as I could tell, by now every living adult in the village was standing in a tight circle around the black sack. Just standing in the rain, as though the effort of walking back indoors was too much.

The rain settled in heavier as the day went on, until the small colours of spring had bleached into grey. Patches of darker grey and brown against the lighter grey of the wall that ran between the church and the parish house. The wall of the graveyard, of the holy ground.

I sat in the doorway and watched as they stood in the rain, and I sat in the doorway and watched as – eventually, but not until late in the afternoon when they were all soaked and nothing had happened, no-one had come, and nothing had happened – watched as they drifted away. Mammy came back up to the house and stepped past into the gloom, without a word.

Only when it was dark did I move. Slowly. Much of the shortening night to stumble my way down the slope steeper than I remembered, and carefully enough not to fall. For to fall would end this journey, because I had not re-learned the art of standing unaided. As the last definite threads of darkness were wearing away with the rub of the dawn, I reached the black sack and took up my position. To stand next to it. I knew why, but I had no comprehension what I would do if anyone came to move it. For now, all I knew was that I would stand there beside it. The black sack had a white collar and feet and hands and a head that once had been the priest's head but now was the black sack's head.

So when the men first came and saw me standing there beside it, they went away without speaking. And came back again an hour later with a cart and long-handled turf spades.

"This is it, then."

"It is."

"Shall we?"

"We shall."

"We will."

"Not."

"Eamonn, step aside."

"Not."

"He was nothing to you, Eamonn."

"Not. True. Not true. We defined each other."

"What?"

So we stood a while, 'til the agent rode up. He sat on his horse at a distance for a while, and then urged the horse nearer and spoke.

"you .. needs .. him .. go .. make ..Do .. worthing .. I .. went .. for the money .."

Paddy Jack giggled and the agent seemed to know where the laughter came from, because he urged his horse nearer and began to raise his whip. I was distracted by this, took my eye off the long handled spade in Proinsias's loose confident grip.

All he did was poke me in the chest, but it was enough. I went over, and Proinsias was in, talking loudly, calling to Paddy Jack to give him a hand and then turning to the agent once he was between Paddy Jack and the whip.

"We are, thank you sir, ready for the task in hand
and completed it will be within the day."

The agent looked as though one of his dogs had starting asking to be fed. Then,

"Good. Good. And him, move him."

But they didn't. They took the black bag with the white collar and feet and hands and a head that once had been the priest's head but now was the black sack's head. But they left me where I was. It took a while to get back standing but once I was up again, I took my place – his place – and stood on the dark patch beside the wall. The dark patch left by the black sack when they took it away.

It first happened three days later. It must have happened when I was asleep, because those first few days I needed to sleep and so lay against the wall for a while every night. There, before me on the road, was a cup with water and a bowl of porridge, already cold. So, they didn't understand. Still saw me as outsider, even though I had grown here.

I drank the water. A dog came and started to sniff at the bowl. I chased him off a few times but then realised I had to let him eat it, to make the point. I watched, tears on my face, as the dog ate the porridge and then looked around to make sure someone else had seen. Couldn't be sure. Couldn't be sure that I had made my point in such a profligate fashion, as to let a dog eat a bowl of porridge, a whole bowl of porridge.

But the next time, it was just the cup of water. Then I was sure.

———

PART SEVEN

My dearest Anna,

In my last I spoke of being invited to the meeting of the Scottish Temperance League but when I did so I had but little idea of the complete nature of that honor. I had imagined a small gathering, but on arriving at the city hall - a most impressive building situated at one of the city's main square. I found that there were people there not merely from all over Scotland but from England as well. There were gathered in the hall that day many of the most famous friends of the cause of temperance in the country, by whose company I felt deeply honoured. So that before it came time for me to speak that my throat became extremely tight and for the first occasion in my time as a public speaker I felt afflicted by my nerves.

That is, until two things occurred to me. First, that my position was considerably better than that of Buffum who on the way to the meeting had somehow lost the bag in which he had been carrying his notes and who was, as the others began their speeches, gathering his thoughts into note form as best he could whilst at the same time attempting to appear engaged with the proceedings on the floor. Second, that I had some considerable time to recover myself due to the fact that I was the last but one speaker. In the end, I had nearly three and one half hours during which I had the honor to hear some of the finest advocates of temperance in these islands. Indeed I was applauding one speaker with such aplomb that little did I remember that I was to be the next to speak until the chairman laid his hand upon my wrist.

This gesture, clear to all the audience, caused much good humor and I could feel that I began with them already at my side. This moved me to begin with a little joke about Buffum's loss of his green bag with his notes and my own greenness as a speaker, the laughter at the end of which convinced me that I had little to fear from this audience even though what I had to say seemed to me to be little connected with much already said. Even despite my doubts, though, my comments on the connection between chattel slavery and the slavery induced by drink drew many appreciative comments from the audience. I reminded myself, again, that these are audiences who have heard little of the realities of slavery and are often shocked by details of life which I regard only with a heart-weariness from my familiarity.

"So it is with the practice of distributing so much liquor to slaves on a Saturday that they spend the following Sabbath day in a state more like that of an animal than a human being. It is clear to me that if liquor enslaves, then the drunken slave is still more enslaved, degraded to the point where he is incapacitated from freedom. This is, of course, the argument much made by the advocates of slavery - that the degraded state in which so many of our people live renders them unfit to live with whites on the same basis - but this condition is made and not a natural state, and made moreover in large part by the use of drink."

I concluded by turning to my own past as an intemperate. To many of those present, I think, an understanding of power and effects of drink are entirely unknown and I felt moved to tell them of my own experiences and finished my words that afternoon by recounting the story my old and dear friend Sandy Jenkins told of the man who felt like the president whenever he had a drink but that the truth of his life was revealed when he woke one morning to discover that he was president of a pig sty - that being the place where he had slept the night before.

The memory of Sandy made me wish that he were with me now, that he might see the heights to which a black man unimpeded by the chains and heavy weights of slavery might climb. At that moment I took my seat again, with my feelings mixed between pride in myself that I had done well in my speech and great sadness at the thought of my long-lost companion.

Though it is very strange, the man who rose to close the meeting, one Henry Vincent, reminded me of Sandy in his demeanour and bearing, even though one was very dark and the other is almost pallid. A slight figure with few prepossessing features, he nevertheless commanded his audience's attention from the very first. He spoke a quiet truth, so it seemed to me, about the connectedness of the reasons for our being gathered here today and all the other campaigns for justice and reform that held the liberal mind of the country at this hour. I had, he said, shown the inevitable and ineluctable connection between slavery of the body and slavery of the mind to drink, and had shown also the connection between slaveries of many sorts.

I was about to applaud this sentiment when I realised that it had raised many hackles in the audience, many of whom seemed steadfastly determined not to applaud or support such ideas. Mr Vincent, too, seemed to sense this mood and gently changed the line of his argument such that he moved towards points on which all could agree and brought the meeting to a most satisfactory end.

Or so I thought, until I was leaving the hall some time later after having spoken with many of the good people present and received many remarks of encouragement and support. As I made for the door, intending to walk a little by the river before taking dinner, I was met by Buffum, whose demeanour was that of a man who was badly disappointed and angry. He made it clear very quickly that he had little truck with the ideas of Mr Vincent and was, he said, dismayed that the same seemed not the case for myself. His argument was an argument for concentration, for taking our tasks one step at a time and only then when we were in agreement with all. I replied that I was of a different opinion, and that he knew this to be the case and that I could not see the cause of his anger for I had done nothing to disturb the unity of the top table and indeed neither had Mr Vincent.

Buffum continued that I should know that Vincent was "a damned Chartist" and, if anything, a worse friend to us than Henry Wright, for whilst the latter spoke from an intemperance of mind the former took his positions from a belief in the need for a fundamental alteration to the patterns of British society. Again, I insisted that while I did not know this, it made little difference to me for I had seen Vincent as a friend of two causes close to my heart and that was enough for me.

"Enough for you to feel the need to insult me as well, I fear", he burst out.

At this I was most amazed, for I could not recall any occasion, or indeed any wish, to insult Buffum. Other than in my letters to you, I have kept my criticisms and misgivings to myself. And so I enquired what he could possibly mean, to which he replied that he took my jests about greenness and the loss of his notes very hard. I was beside myself at such news, not knowing whether to laugh at the man's sensitivity, to apologise profusely even though I could see no insult and certainly had intended none, or to be angry that he had let his emotions intrude upon his judgement of an event a good deal more important than his bruised feelings. I stood there before him, dumbstruck with my own confusion. Which, it quickly became clear, he interpreted as further insult and was telling me in a rising tone that he took such things ill when he considered the lengths he had been put to in my cause. At this last phrase, my own anger which had until now lain dormant was stirred, that he could so belittle the great crusade of our times so as to see as some foible on my part, and I replied very sharply that he was a fool to see an insult behind innocent words.

His wrath was roused still more and he seemed close to striking out at me, and was certainly roaring now, when Mr Vincent emerged from the door of the hall behind Buffum and, on seeing the two of us engaged in such an exchange, hurried over and stepping between us, urged us both to moderation. All in a quiet and almost untroubled voice. The effect of the sound of his voice was certainly with great power over my own emotions and I could see that the same or similar was true for Buffum, even despite the opinions he had expressed in the very recent past about the man. Vincent's next turn was to take us both by the arm and to insist that we walk awhile with him, that we might resolve this dispute.

The upshot of his intervention was that, within a very few minutes, Buffum and I were at least reconciled to each other through Mr Vincent's good offices. I admitted that I had been intemperate in my words and Buffum in turn agreed that his anger towards myself stood on no good ground. He then said he wished to return with all speed to the hotel at which we were both lodged and left me in the company of Mr Vincent.

Who asked if I wished to take a turn with him along the river side and I agreed very readily, having been deeply impressed by his calmness and his ability to bring both myself and Buffum to our senses. As we walked through the now-darkening streets, I told him that I found myself in much agreement with what he had had to say that evening, even if many another present had seemed less enthusiastic. He replied that he was pleased by my reaction and not surprised by that of others. The effort of education, he said, is always a mighty one and he knew that new knowledge came hard to many and that he must be patient in his role as teacher.

We continued our talk, which was mostly concerned with the conditions under which our enslaved brethren are imprisoned. He said, on several occasions, after I had told him of a particular detail of atrocity, that he thought himself well-versed in the crimes of men until he had listened to me but also that such things existed to test the extent of his ability to forgive his fellow creatures without surrendering his own convictions that they were in the wrong. The enslavement of his fellow men, be it by drink, the whip or the wage, was the greatest of crimes and against which he had vowed to speak and educate for the rest of his days. He had also, he said, sworn that he would endeavor not to descend into the pit of hatred but always to attempt to see in his adversaries the concealed light of humanity.

"You have written the same or similar, have you not, Mr Douglass", he continued, "when you argued that even in the slave reduced to the edge of bestiality there was still a glimmer of humanity. I take my present lead from you."

Against which I protested, saying that if anything such an inexperienced campaigner as myself, especially one so easily moved to anger, should think of himself as always learning from the likes of Henry Vincent.

By now it was quite dark and becoming cold and, seeing that I wore no topcoat, Mr Vincent was concerned that we reach my hotel as quickly as was possible and so we hurried through the streets almost without speaking until we reached our destination. At which he made his farewells and said that he hoped to meet and speak with me again in the nearest future.

I do feel, my dearest Anna, that I have been this afternoon in the presence of a man who approaches as close to being a saint on this earth as it is possible for living flesh to come. With such men in our camp, how can we fail?

Your,
Frederick

My dear Garrison,

I wait, I have to say, with ever-growing anticipation for news of your departure from Boston bound for these shores. For whilst our cause goes from strength to strength among the English, this is not without problems and difficulties.

Today for example, I excused myself from our work to speak on a Temperance platform. You know how close to my heart this is and I am sure you will not begrudge me one day away from my duties to the war against slavery. As well as Douglass, the platform party also contained one Henry Vincent, a member of the Chartist party of some notoriety and only included in the speakers this day by virtue of his long dedication to sobriety. Indeed, I am glad to say that this band of agitators and stirrers-up of the lower orders have declined a great deal in recent times. The jailing and transportation of many of the leaders three years ago does seem to have snipped off most of that particular hydra's heads. They do still linger on, though, at the margins of our movement with their squeakings for the extension of democracy and the rights of workers. Whatever small argument they might have is drowned out by the harshness of their voices and their urging of social change to a point which I would call anarchy.

But I do fear that Vincent has taken some influence over Douglass, who seems much taken with his radical ideas - even though I have pointed out to Douglass that they have little if any relevance to our activities and seem to all here who are more sophisticated in their thinking to be a very out-dated set of ideas. Indeed, when I spoke with Douglass about the ill-advisedness of being seen so close to such as Vincent, the very same interrupted us and took Douglass away for some private confabulation.

I am much worried that Douglass being seen so close to such as Henry Vincent will harm our cause, but I know that I have little influence with Douglass these days and I feel that we need you here to set him back onto the right path again.

I know that there is much to keep you in America at this time, but I would implore you if you can to endeavour to join us here and see if you cannot turn matters back to our side again before we lose all that we have gained this last six months.

> Your,
> James Buffum

My dear Garrison,

I must apologise, it seems, for any offence I may have given to you for my description of Henry Vincent in an earlier letter which I hope by now my sister Harriet has passed to you. My sense of Vincent was based entirely upon my perceptions of the man as he stood before me, and in no way reflected an agreement with his ideas. Indeed, I have told him clearly that I hold it ill that he has chosen to attack your good self in the past, for your moral positions and refusal to engage the dirty politics of government. I applaud you in this and have in recent days been sure to remind my audiences of the dirt that clings to any who do partake in such politics.

I would not wish, my friend, to have given you any offence. I am all too aware of my debt to yourself and I would wish that we remain companions and fellows in the cause of the end of slavery.

Your,
Frederick Douglass

My dearest Anna,

At every turn we are moving forward. Where once we commanded audiences of 100, now we can draw crowds of 1,000 to our meetings. Where once we had to search for halls in which to speak, now we are offered churches and public places of all kinds to preach of our cause for the abolition of slavery within America. Where once the passed hat raised little more than our expenses to travel on to the next meeting, now we collect such sums that we can send monies to the cause at home.

I grow more confident of our victory every day and look forward to that day when all our people can join hands to sing together, "free at last, free at last, good God almighty we are free at last".

Your,
Frederick

My dearest Anna,

It is all true. We do grow in strength at every turn and the people come in ever-larger numbers to hear and support us. Yet rather than being cheered by this, Buffum my constant companion seems more downcast by each large crowd. After every success he returns to his themes that attacking the Free Church so directly is a mistake for which we will pay one day, but not as high a price as we will pay for being seen to be associated with such men as Wright and Vincent. After every smaller meeting, or a larger one where the basket is not so well filled, he seizes upon the "proof" of our failure.

This has been made easier by the absence from Scotland for some time now of both Wright and Vincent, who are both gone to London for meetings with the British and Foreign Anti-Slavery Society. This has hardened Buffum still further against them, for this party is known to be opposed to Garrison's refusal to become involved with daily politics and he calls them "an anti-Garrisonian bloc". By my genuine ignorance of such things, and my refusal to learn and thus be drawn into factional arguments, I have avoided any open conflict with Buffum thus far.

It is, I realise, fully six months that I have now been gone from the bosom of my family and whilst I know that the work I do is the work of the righteous I could not continue without my constant thoughts of my family, my wellspring and support. Though it is hard to know when I can return home, with Master Auld ever breathing fire and brimstone to have me back in his grasp, I wish you all to know that it is my constant and steady wish for us to be re-united even if that be on this side of the Atlantic rather than on the shores of home.

It pains me a little, then, to know that you will hear these words through the mouth of another, even though that other is my beloved sister Harriet, and I would urge you once more to consider learning your letters, that you may hear my words directly and for yourself.

Your,
Frederick

DOUGLASS'S LETTER TO ANNA
MARCH 18, 1846

My dearest Anna,

After our capture of the North, we are arrived in Paisley. We are in truth going from strength to strength, for we have been given the use of one of the very largest churches in the town and our meetings here are already over-subscribed for the next three evenings. The town itself ranks nearly alongside Glasgow in importance in the area, by virtue of its large concentration of textile mills which draw in large numbers of workers from all around and turn out large quantities of wealth, much of which has been used to make the public buildings of the town monuments to the wonders of cloth-making and the men who command its manufacture. Carry Paisley, our friends here tell us, and we will have Scotland entirely within our camp.

The journey back from Dundee and Aberdeen to here brought us via Glasgow, from the beauties of the wilds of the northern part of this country with its heather moorlands the like of which I have not seen before, to the grimy air of the industrial city. It is, indeed, the air which marks the difference for as soon as one steps out into the streets of the city, one is assailed by the stench of sweated labour and humanity packed into tiny spaces. This is a mighty shock after the sweetness of the wind in the north.

While we were here, we had news that Wright and Vincent had returned from London and I was determined, despite

Buffum's protestations, to have news of the progress of the cause in England. Whilst Wright was little more than cordial, which I can understand, Vincent was most exercised to see me again and questioned me at great length about our successes in the north of Scotland, by which he was much excited and proclaimed that it seemed to him that the hour was coming again when the people would rise against injustice in all its forms and throw off the yoke. When I asked what root this great optimism had, he replied that it was at the meeting of the British and Foreign Anti-Slavery Society that he had seen the beginnings of the coming-together of the forces opposed to slavery in all its forms. I replied that I had knowledge of but one form and that my single purpose was to bring that American variety to an end.

At which he asked if I could not see the similarity between the slavery under which my brothers toiled and the slavery his endured. To which I replied that I indeed I could not, and challenged him to prove to me that any such similarity existed. Slavery, he said, was the condition in which if a man did not work he did not eat. Slaves were tied to that necessity; either by the bonds of being a chattel or by the bonds of needing to be paid. To which I replied, shortly, that if that was his opinion he knew nothing of the condition of the enslaved in America but that I would be willing to enlighten him. By this point, indeed, I was so hot under the collar that whether or not he wished to hear more from me, that this was what happened.

I lectured him for several minutes on the precise and detailed nature of the life of the slave in America, the laws and the whips used to hold our brothers and sisters as goods of their enslavers. I reminded him that no man in this country, after leaving his job for another, was arrested for theft of his employer's property, as happens to fleeing slaves. I reminded him of the anguish of mothers when their children are taken from them to be sold, of husbands and wives when their marriages are declared concluded because one or the other is to be sold, of children who see their parents flogged for placing the needs of their offspring above the needs of a master's beasts. Was there anything in the nature of slavery in this country to compare with that? With this question still ringing in both our sets of ears, I turned on my heel and strode off.

My rage was such that even by yesterday evening I was still not calmed and when we reached Paisley that evening I could not sit still in my seat but paced the stage before I spoke that night. My anger with Vincent filtered into my speech and I found myself conducting the argument with him again, only this time from a public platform and in his absence. The effect of this was only to bemuse the audience.

Buffum was in high good humor all through the train journey back to Glasgow and as we walked to our hotel, began to sing the praises of the campaign against the Free Church. By which I was much surprised but also much pleased, and I was moved to admit to him that his moderate tones had seemingly had much effect. To which he answered that he thought that, whilst my reasons for such words may have seemed obscure to the audience that evening, my description of the nature of slavery was of the most convincing sort and that as a result anyone could see the need for its end. He also thought that my closing remarks, in praise of British liberties, had been taken very well by our listeners. In all, we arrived back at the hotel in good humor and feeling very much more friendly towards each other than has been the case for some time.

Your
Frederick

DOUGLASS'S DIARY

MARCH 19, 1846

A most odd and almost disturbing incident this evening, during the latest of our Paisley meetings. I had just asked of my audience a rhetorical question concerning the fact that slave rebellions are such rare occasions, and asked why that was. In answer to myself, I replied that a rebellion with the absence of weapons would bring down slaughter when a voice in the hall called out, "Like the slaughter of the helpless Poles by Russian and Austrian brutes". The sharpness of this interjection, so loud in a quiet room, quite threw me from my stride and for a few seconds I fumbled with my words whilst at the same time trying to ascertain the source of these words. Unable to identify the speaker, I began again with the same question and this time managed to complete my argument, which was that whilst slaves have no weapons and we do not wish to wield weapons of war, we have the great weapon of morality and moral purpose on our side and that it was incumbent upon the British people to use this weapon in the cause of freeing my brothers and sisters in bondage.

Still distracted, I concluded my address by turning to the well-used phrases of my attacks on the Free Church and then turned the platform over to Buffum.

In the melee which often ensues after such meetings, when all wish to meet with and shake the hands of the speakers, a voice I recognised as the young man I had met in Cork and then seen again in Ballinasloe when he murdered the land agent whispered close at my shoulder; "But it is real weapons that we need, for it is real deaths that we are suffering". Even despite the speed with which I turned I could not identify the speaker, and for the rest of the evening was much distracted and departed the hall as soon as I could.

I am now seated at my hotel room desk, having been woken from my sleep by the return of the awful visions of murder and abuse which haunted me after my encounter with that man, visions that seem to lurk at the very depths of my soul and have risen unbidden to my mind. It is very dark in the streets beyond and I feel most strongly the need to keep the candle alight until the dawn.

My dearest Anna,

Paisley is ours! No, the whole of Scotland, for on all sides - with exception of the sectarians of the Free Church - it is now accepted that dollars stained with the blood of slavery cannot be washed clean by passage across the Atlantic waves; that the argument that slavery and the enslaver can be separated one from another is as specious as is the separation of the sin from the sinner, or of adultery from the adulterer. Yesterday, indeed, I took the bold step of announcing that I saw the actions of the Free Church in taking money from slavers as a sin and, calling on my recent readings in Wesley, reminded my listeners that the great man himself has called slavery "the vilest sin that ever saw the sun" and that he who touches pitch will be defiled.

I was emboldened to this point by the fact that before me, Buffum had risen to speak and had begun by announcing bluntly that the object of his speech that evening would be the Free Church and its associations with the slavers, and that he was not afraid to give offence to any who would defend such actions.

With such victories in hand, we have accepted an invitation to a few days' rest in Ayrshire at the home of the Reverend Renwick, a great supporter of our cause in that area. I am much excited by the prospect of this visit, for it will not only give my inflamed throat a chance to recover before the busy days of April but also because it will afford us the opportunity to visit some of the sites of a poet whom Buffum holds in the highest esteem, one Robert Burns. His excitement at this prospect has reached to myself, though I know little of this man and his writing.

Your
Frederick

My dear Garrison,

Whilst the need for a visit from yourself to this country is still great, it does seem that the crisis with Douglass is somewhat abated for he has had a great falling-out with that pest Henry Vincent and in a way I could hardly have planned. Vincent had been to a meeting of the British and Foreign Anti-Slavery Society in London and when he returned was full of Chartist nonsense about the different slaveries. Which, in his excitement at having been with his good friends for several days, he repeated to Douglass. And repeated it, I have no doubt, in that supercilious tone he so often adopts when he feels the need to educate those around himself to the points which are so obvious to him and yet thoroughly concealed from them by their lack of learning and consideration.

This was the red rag to Douglass, who was in a furious state for days and, as a result, came firmly and publicly back to our side by pouring scorn on the idea of slavery's existence in this country before a large audience of the best sort in Paisley. For which he was well praised and applauded.

At the same time, I have come to see that a well-moderated critique of the Free Church may carry our cause forward; as, indeed it already has in some towns. To this end, I have endeavoured to temper Douglass on the subject whilst prefacing him as often as I can with words of my own that make it clear that the object of our anger is the institution of the Free Church and no-one especial within it.

We have a few more meetings to complete in the west of Scotland before our assault upon that great bastion of rectitude in the east which, our friends here tell me, will erect some great barriers of objection to the tone with which Douglass has spoken of the Free Church, barriers which will obscure the content of his words unless we are extremely prudent in our behaviour. I will continue to prevail upon him in the cause of caution, but I know that a few words from you - or even better your arrival on these shores - will have a great effect on him.

Your,
James Buffum

DOUGLASS'S LETTER TO ANNA
MARCH 29, 1846

My dearest Anna,

This last week has been, after two highly successful and large meetings at which we spoke in Ayr, a time of recuperation for both myself and Buffum. Indeed, so well rested are we that much of our previous rancour with each other might almost be traced to the simple fact of exhaustion. We are agreed, moreover, that Ayrshire and the area to its south known as Dumfries and Galloway are an ideal location in which to take one's leisure, even despite the weather which has been mostly cold, damp and raining and has contributed much to the continuation of the bad head cold from which I have been suffering for some time now. Without the recourse to liquor as a solution to the soreness of my throat which this has occasioned, moreover, I am at a loss to know what can be done.

Nevertheless, on the two or three days when the rain has held off, we have been afforded the opportunity to walk through some of the most delightful country I have yet seen in this country. The Lowlands, as they are known, share much of their vegetation with the Highlands and at this time of year the great swathes of gorse are beginning to scent the hillsides and higher valleys, while in the lower ground many greener plants set off a contrast which only the dullest mind could miss. Buffum says that he can see why this landscape would have been such an inspiration to the poet Burns. Many of the valleys have at their bottom fast flowing streams and rivers which, swollen still with the heavy rains of the winter, fill the air with the sound of running water. This swift movement of the stream and the sounds that it generates, so unfamiliar to an ear born and raised in Maryland, lifts my spirits each time I have the chance to linger a while at its side.

The Reverend Renwick has entertained us and made us welcome in his house while we have been here. We have spent a most pleasant time in his company, even though it took my ear a little time to adjust to the sound of his voice, for he speaks in a manner which he later told me is called "Lallans" (that is my nearest approximation to the word) which is also the word for "Lowlands". Similar such adjustments of sound fill his speech which, whilst always melodious, was on several occasions robbed of its meaning for me by the sound of the words as spoken. When I remarked to Buffum on this, he replied that he thought it a deliberate posture on the reverend doctor's part, for he knew him to have a well-developed education in theology gained from the university in Glasgow.

One morning, I enquired of the reverend doctor whether or not he possessed any volumes of the poetry of Burns. To which he made excited answer that he had in his ownership copies of every volume the poet produced, and even four inscribed by the poet himself. I was welcome, he said, to read any of them that I wished.

So it was that I armed with a copy of some of Burns's poems and determined to shake away the effects of my head cold by inhaling the sweet and chill air, I settled myself at the edge of the beach at Ayr late the next morning and, taking some deal of delight in the pleasure of a day to myself and away from the hurly-burly of the tour, commenced to read. But within a very few minutes found myself almost entirely frustrated by the language of the poems for, not being able to reproduce either in my mind or by whispering aloud, I could make but little sense of any of them and was left with but a very loose sense of the meaning of any of the poems before me. After perhaps two hours of fruitless wrestling with the book, I admitted defeat and in some ill humor returned to the presbytery for lunch. The sum total effect of the morning was to have made my nose stream and my head feel as though it were packed solid with cotton waste.

Buffum being absent on some business, I took the opportunity to question the reverend doctor further on this problem I had encountered. His solution was to propose that he take me into the villages of Dumfries and Galloway to hear the language of the poems being spoken for that was the only way in which he thought I might come to an understanding of the poems that was thorough and well-rooted in the words themselves. I agreed to this proposal with alacrity and, on Buffum's return he agreed that this was an excellent plan and agreed to accompany us.

So it was that, once our meetings were concluded, that we departed from Ayr for a brief tour of the sites familiar to the poet.

On our journey we passed through many villages which seemed to me almost as poor as some of those I had seen whilst in Ireland, with the singular difference that here at least there was food, albeit that it consisted mostly of a thin gruel called porridge which the people here seem to eat in as great quantities as they can acquire. Beyond that, though, the face of extreme poverty looked very familiar to me. In the larger towns matters seemed rather less desperate, with some signs that there are here at least some folk who are managing to survive the crisis that is sweeping others to ruin.

At length we arrived in Dumfries, the birthplace and burial ground of the great poet. It is a delightful small town straddling a fast-running small river. On several occasions as our business was made plain by the good reverend, we made the acquaintance of ordinary townspeople who referred to "Rabbie" - for this is how they call him here - as though he were a close friend and living still. Reverend Renwick had arranged for us to stay at the house of his fellow-minister in that town and to this house we eventually came and were introduced.

There was a considerable party of the congregation gathered at the house, at which Reverend Renwick was somewhat annoyed for he had seen this trip as a chance for rest for myself and Buffum. We, though, were happy to speak with this little gathering and to make our apologies that we were unable to address a larger gathering. During the soiree afterwards, I was in the process of telling one small group of our reasons for coming here, when he expressed his reservation very clearly to me, saying that if we wished to become acquainted with the poetry of the islands we would do better to become acquainted the continuing work of Mr Wordsworth or another such. For these were men, he said, who at least had the virtue of writing in plain English and on decent subjects.

I begged to differ, but was reluctant to be drawn into a discussion at this point in our travels, feeling very strongly the need for the days' rest before us. A short while later, I withdrew to my room and slept with a soundness born of the great tiredness I was feeling and also the profound quiet of this little town.

The next day, Renwick proposed a walk on the surrounding moorland followed by a meeting with some of the older folk of the town who, he said, were prepared and happy to recite some of Burns's work for us. Despite the beauty of the country, then, I was too distracted by the prospect of really hearing the poetry for the first time to be fully aware of the sights through which we passed as we walked and made little contribution to the discussion between Renwick and Buffum. At length we were returned to the town and on our way to the gathering.

The evening coming on fast, we hurried through the rain-wet streets to a large hall which, Renwick told us, was called the Mechanics' Institute and it was here that the working people and poor of the town met together to read and discuss. For, the reverend continued, the tradition of autodidacticism is very strong among his people. When we entered the room, indeed, there was a small group assembled in a corner by a stove who were I gradually understood engaged in a deep discussion of a play by Shakespeare whilst in another corner a reading class was taking place. I stood at the back of the latter group to listen for a while, until the teacher - a young man barely past his youth - became so embarrassed by my presence that he was unable to continue his class. In the presence of such greatness, he said, it was not right that he should speak and that I should be silent. I demurred, and said that I was greatly pleased to see people hard at work in the study of words and explained how such pursuits were unavailable to our people in bondage.

The teacher then asked if I would tell the story of how I had come to a knowledge of letters myself and I was glad to tell again of my stolen possession of "The Columbian Orator" and of how I had persuaded arrogant free whites to show me, all unwitting of my purpose hidden behind my pose of stupidity, how to form words and numbers until I had hidden within myself the power of language. At which point the teacher stepped forward, grasped me by the hand and proclaimed that it was the highest honor to have made my acquaintance and asked what was my business here.

When I told him that it was my wish and purpose to hear the poems of Robert Burns read aloud or recited in the fashion of his writing, he replied that it would be his pleasure and his class's, so to do for me. At once, one of the younger rose and recited from memory "My love is like a red, red rose". Which was followed almost immediately by "Who is that at my bower door" and many others besides, until the whole class together recited "Scots wha hae" and "Auld lang syne". It was wonderful indeed to hear words which before had lain upon the page almost as barriers to my understanding now become alive and filled with the joy of the tongues for which they had been written. And I saw again how it was that power of language is its ability to lift a person from where they are to a better place, albeit only for a moment. That gives the power to continue, even in the face of the most awful conditions.

I thanked the class profoundly, and turned back to my companions who had been stood all this time at a distance, watching and listening. As we turned to the door, the young teacher again took me by the elbow and drew me aside. He wished to know if I was familiar with the tradition of singing Burns's works, to which I answered that I was not for this very evening was the first time that I had heard the works aloud and had not had to wrestle with each and every word. He asked further then if I would wish to hear such a thing and I replied that I would. He then bade me meet him the following evening at the town square and he would meanwhile arrange it for me.

So it was that we spent the next day tramping the hills and returned to the town for our supper. After which I declared my intention of going out to hear some of Burns's songs sung aloud. I was most surprised at this point, that the Reverend Renwick tried most strenuously to persuade against such a course of action, citing the possibility that such an event might take place in what he called a "bothy", which he explained to be an illegal drinking house. I was, though, firm in my intention, even though I knew it to cut across the minister's view of proper behavior. I reminded him that I was not only an abolitionist but also a temperance man who believed in absolute abstinence, and that I could resist the temptations to drink that such an event might entail. Even so, Buffum declared his intention to accompany me and I saw no purpose in resisting such an arrangement.

We set off for the square, where we met the young teacher of the previous evening. He led us through the streets and across the river, until we came to an area of the town which I could see was considerably less prosperous than the part in which we were lodged. Eventually we came to a house slightly larger than its neighbours and set back a little from the road. He knocked on the door and we were admitted instantly to a large parlour already crowded.

Here, we were given a great welcome and the young teacher made a short speech of introduction in which he revealed a good knowledge of the cause of abolition and the reasons why Scots should stand behind any movement against tyranny. We were come, he said in conclusion, to hear the songs of the great "Rabbie" sung and so he would be obliged if the company would sing, which they did. They sang all together or in little groups. All were clearly well practised and rehearsed, and I could see the great comfort these people took from their singing, despite what the local ministers might have to say. All, I say, but one elderly man sat a little apart from the company with his head turned slightly to one side and seemingly listening intently all the while. In some ways, the whole performance reminded more of our own church gatherings than of any music hall of the fears of the minister.

The whole matter must have consumed upwards of a two hours, during which time there were a number of short breaks for members of the crowd to take a drink and to engage both myself and Buffum in talk about the cause of abolition and in particular the campaign against the Free Church. The evening was drawing clearly to a close when all rose and sang a delightful version of "Auld Lang Syne", in which both I and Buffum joined even though we were not entirely sure of the words. Then, as all were applauding and shaking hands and preparing to depart, the old man rose with a loud scraping of his chair and stood with his hand resting on the sideboard which filled one wall of the room. Once the chair had scraped, he simply stood until all had turned and become quiet.

He said, in a very quiet voice for which one had to strain even though the room was now silent, that he was pleased we had come here to this small town to honor the memory of the great poet. He was pleased, also, that we were men in the cause of freedom for he had thought many times in recent years that that candle had been quite blown out. He wished, he said, to sing one last song for us, to which many of the company murmured their assent.

What he sang, I have not heard before but it is clear to me that it was a song from the pen of Burns because I questioned the young teacher later and he was glad to confirm my sense. I set the words down here as best I can for you to hear, for it is a very fine piece.

These are the words the old man sang, in a voice surprisingly powerful after his quietness of speech, as best as I can remember them.

Is there, for honest poverty,
That hangs its head, and a' that?
The coward-slave, we pass him by,
We dare be poor for a' that,
For a' that, and a' that,
Our toils obscure and a' that;
The rank is but a guinea stamp;
The man's the gowd for a' that

After the first verse, I could not hear so much but only snatches such as

The man of independent man,
He looks and laughs at a' that
The pith of sense, and pride o' worth,
Are higher rank than a' that

Then came the last verse, with which all joined in until the "bothy" near shook with the singing voices.

Then let us pray that come it may,
As come it will for a' that;
That sense and worth, o'er a' the earth,
May bear the green, and a' that.
For a' that and a' that,
It's coming yet, For a' that,
That man to man the warld o'er
Shall brothers be for a' that

I was very much struck by the sentiments of this piece and asked if it were indeed one of Burns's poems, for I had not heard it before. To which the young teacher replied that he was not surprised for there were many abroad in the world who knew that they would profit more from the people being kept in ignorance of such sentiments.

As we returned to the minister's house across the river, Buffum was at pains to express his opinion that, while he had much enjoyed the evening, the final song was a forgery that could not be attributed to Burns. When I replied that the young teacher had been equally adamant that it was indeed of the poet's hand, Buffum began upon a long discourse on the folly of youth and how it was tempered by time into the maturity and reason of age. He quoted me the example of Mr Wordsworth, all afire for the French revolution but now more sensible of the need for order and reason. I asked was this the same Wordsworth who had written his praises for my brother Toussaint L'Ouverture, to which Buffum huffed a reply and was ill-tempered the rest of the evening and for much of the rest of our stay in the little town.

We are called back to Paisley tomorrow for a great meeting on temperance and slavery and I have asked the young teacher, Mr Gordon Phillip, if he felt able to accompany us. To which he replied that a temperance meeting a good distance off was not much to his liking and that he would in any ways find it hard to be gone from his work for even the two days a trip of that sort would take. So we parted on somewhat distant terms.

I am much refreshed by this visit, and my throat feels almost entirely recovered to its former strength. I am girded for the fray, both by my rest and by the wise words of that great man and poet, Robert Burns, to whom I shall hereafter always refer in my mind as "Rabbie".

Your,
Frederick

My dearest sister Harriet,

I would entreat to reverse the conduct for which I have pleaded in the past, and would request that you make especially sure that this letter comes into the possession of William Lloyd Garrison as swiftly as will allow you first to read it to my dearest Anna.

How ever grateful I am for your efforts in transmitting my letters to my beloved Anna, I would have you impress upon her the frustration I feel at her obduracy in refusing to learn to read. The loneliness which sometimes comes over me here is compounded by the knowledge that I cannot speak direct to my own wife.

Your brother,
Frederick

My dearest Anna,

We have made great progress in our mission since the return from Ayr, and I have spoken at seven meetings in seven days each larger than its predecessor. The day we returned I plunged directly back into the fray, addressing a Temperance and anti-slavery gathering of some of the finest folk in Paisley. I found my words affected by my contact with the words of the great poet Burns, by his sentiment of connection with all the good people and I said that "I am a temperance man because I am an anti-slavery man; and I am an anti-slavery man because I love my fellow men".

I am able to quote this verbatim not because I remember my own words but because the local newspapers have now begun to report our activities in great detail, often sending reporters to copy down our every word and then to reproduce them on their most prominent pages. It is a very strange matter indeed, for a man born into chattel slavery to see his words carefully written down by freemen and then read in the best houses of a town, and then to be congratulated in the street by people who were not present at the original gathering, for the finest of my words! The power of the written word is indeed a marvellous thing to feel.

I am less sure, though, that Buffum entirely approves of my words, especially now that he has had an opportunity to re-discover and explore them in the finest detail. He said of that speech that he found my language infected by the sentiment of "that song" and that he was not at all sure that these were the sort of expressions the good people of Paisley wished to hear. I replied that they seemed to have little or no difficulty with what I said, if the reaction I felt in the streets was anything to go by, to which he answered that the street was hardly the best place to judge the effect of our campaign. I said that I for one was greatly pleased by the story I had heard that our words, "Send Back The Money", had been painted up on a wall. The Free Church hired a woman to wash them off, but still they could be seen. So the Free Church hired a mason to chisel them out, but still the words could be seen cut into the very fabric of the wall, for all who passed in the street. That, I said, was a tale by which I was greatly pleased even if he thought it rabble rousing.

He was still more greatly displeased by what I said last night, when he claims that I reviled the United States publicly and be-fore an audience of foreigners. I answered him that I thought Garrison would not be as chary of the feelings of the Unionists and that he had often called the Union a union with slavery, and also that I had been careful not to revile the United States but to refuse to speak well of a state which held to slavery. Indeed, I quoted my words to him, having carefully prepared the speech beforehand and then asked the reporter present straightaway at the end of the evening for a copy of his report. So, I could show Buffum that I had actually said that: "I think I may boldly tell you that I am a republican, but not an American republican.

Aside from slavery I regard America as a brilliant example to the world: only wash from her escutcheon the bloody stain of slavery, and she will stand forth as a noble example for others to follow. But as long as the tears of my sisters and brothers continue to run down her streams unheeded into the vast ocean of human misery, my tongue shall cleave to the roof of my mouth ere I speak well of such a nation".

That, I think, is a clear expression of my views and entirely in accord with anything other on this subject which the leading figures of our movement have said. I find Buffum altogether too cautious on occasions, too attentive to the feelings of figures more imaginary than actual. I am very glad that we go forward in our enterprise, for then he has little with which to make his arguments that we should adopt another course. But if we should falter, he will return I am sure to his great theme of caution and compromise with renewed vigor.

We now have meetings planned that we will carry us from here in Paisley, down to the coast town of Greenock, then back here for one last great push before we return to Glasgow and then on to Edinburgh. We aim to be in Edinburgh no later than the twenty-fifth day of this month, so that we may have several days to pull that stiff-necked city to our side.

I feel myself ablaze with the cause these days, and look forward to every occasion when I can speak for it. Every day, I thank the Lord my God that he put Wendell Phillips and William Lloyd Garrison in my path, that they could show me the way to the service of my people.

> Your
> Frederick

My dearest Anna,

I am greatly pleased, even elated, by the last two weeks. For if my life was busy before, these few days I have been awhirl with activity. I am saddened that this has left me no time to write before now, but today I can sit at one of the writing-desks in the lobby of the hotel and take my time, for all I have to do is acknowledge the passers-by who nod their approbation and support for our mission. We have now carried the whole of the west of Scotland before us, and everywhere people cry out that the Free Church must break its links with the slaveholders and "Send Back The Money".

For this last great push, we have been fortunate indeed to have the services of those two great pillars of the cause of abolition, Wright and Thompson. Their opinions for the tactics and strategy of this final stage have influenced Buffum, for I believe that their status weighs more heavily with him than any of my arguments. Whatever, we have now completely carried all the best of Paisley before us and no small part of that has been the combined force of the oratory of the four of us. For we each have a different manner of public speaking, so that between us we cover the tastes of the whole audience.

The presence of Wright and Thompson emboldened me to such a point that I found myself able to say what has become rooted in my heart these last few weeks, for I still hear the old man's singing in my head. I rose to speak before a great crowd of the intelligence and respectability of Paisley in the wake of the two great men and thus had no work to do bringing the audience to my side. I could speak more openly of my wider views of the cause of abolition without feeling this night that I must rehearse again the arguments against the Free Church, for this was already done. I felt that I could take the audience to new places, new ideas. Thus, I said "I am a man before I am an American. To be a human being is above being an American.

To be a human being is to have claims above all the chains of nationality". So enthusiastic was the applause from Wright and Thompson that I felt able to go still further and to say that "God had made of one blood all nations of the earth, and he had commanded them to loose the bonds of wickedness, to undo the heavy burdens, and to let the oppressed go free." At this Thompson was on his feet, throwing his arms about my shoulders and with tears in his eyes calling for the end of slavery now, this moment. The respectable citizens of Paisley were for a few moments released from the burdens of respectability and found themselves able to stand and stamp their feet, calling for more, calling for the end of enslavement. It was a very fine hour, and such was its effect that we are forced to delay our departure for Edinburgh, to speak one last time to Paisley audiences. Buffum complains that this will mean we will arrive in Edinburgh around the first of May, but I do not understand this objection and the other two have cast it aside in favour of the chance to raise still more funds for the cause from a willing audience and at the same time attempt to relive the glories of that evening passed.

From Paisley we travelled into Glasgow to complete the rout of our enemies. So cowardly are they now that they will only attempt attacks on myself from the floor of the gatherings, thinking that I am the weakest of the speakers because of the color of my skin. Thompson has proposed that an invitation to Garrison to come and tour Britain for the cause, and received not only approval for this notion but also sufficient funds so that we can pay for the great man to travel here. What a boost this will give to the movement, and we are all already looking for his arrival even though we know it cannot be for several months.

Your
Frederick

My dearest Anna,

Such is our momentum that even what seemed at first a set-back has been turned to our favor. Let me tell you how it was. When we returned to Paisley we found that the last bastion of the Free Church in the town, one Macnaughton (I will not call him reverend), had used his influence to have the doors of the hall we had proposed to use closed against us and we found ourselves with the prospect of an audience and nowhere to put them. For a whole day our friends here scattered into the town in every direction to search for a hall to accommodate us, with the result that by the early evening we faced the problem of having not one but two venues, both already advertised throughout the town, such was the vigor of our supporters. We overcame the dilemma when I suggested that we hold two meetings simultaneously, dividing the platform between the meetings and then having them change about half way through.

This was agreed, and we commenced to speak to two audiences, each as big as the whole we had expected for the evening and every member of the gatherings paying at least a penny to be present. I was so incensed by Macnaughton's behavior that I spent much of my speeches attacking him in terms that I am sure Buffum would not approve. I was safe, though, having been put on the platforms together with Thompson who thoroughly approved my saying that Macnaughton was a man "whose pockets are lined with the gold with which I should have been educated, and yet who has the gall to charge me with ignorance and poverty". Led by Thompson's applause, the whole room cheered this description.

As we passed through the streets, on our way to the second meeting and after we had passed Buffum and Wright with high humor from all four of us at this meeting, Thompson told me that he had been invited to the annual convention of the British and Foreign Anti-Slavery Society and wished to know whether

I would accompany him to London for what promised to be a great gathering. I accepted his offer with alacrity, for London is the great fortress which we must carry if we are to have a lasting success here.

So clear was I that this is a necessary move, that even Buffum's protests that the British and Foreign Anti-Slavery Society's *Reporter* had carried a number of critical commentaries and attacks upon Garrison could not sway me. Indeed, I did tell Buffum that I thought I was capable of judging for myself where the loyalties of any person or organisation lay and did not need a guardian. Furthermore, I told him that I thought it my duty to speak wherever, whenever and to whomsoever I could in order to continue the work of exposing slavery's bloody mark.

So it is that when we are done in Edinburgh, our little band will separate for a while and I will go to London with Thompson.

Your
Frederick

DOUGLASS'S LETTER TO ANNA
MAY 4, 1846

My dearest Anna,

I am writing to you from the railroad tracks which stretch from Edinburgh to London. Thompson is asleep across the carriage from me, and we have the compartment to ourselves. So it is that I can settle with pen and paper, to tell you what had passed since my last letter.

All the news we had had beforehand of the difficulties of Edinburgh was confounded by the reception we received when we arrived there, for we were feted through the streets and in the houses of the very best supporters of our cause. I took my chance to see the monument to Scott, for then I could stand before the image of the man from whose works I had taken the name I now bear, when I cast off the slave-name given me by

Thomas Auld.

Below the castle walls, on the afternoon of May Day, we spoke in the Music Hall to an audience of above two thousand people, all of whom had paid sixpence - sixpence! - to hear us. Used as I was now to not having to make the basic case against the man-stealers and their friends in Scotland, I took as my theme the rebellion of Maddison Washington and his escape from American slavery into the arms of British freedom, which my listeners much appreciated. They were especially taken, I thought, by my suggestion that the defenders of American liberty had a deal of hypocrisy when they defended as an honor and a glory their own white seizure of freedom, yet saw Maddison Washington's acts as an outrage on the part of a black man. All round, the afternoon was a great success except for Buffum's carping at myself for having taken a violent insurrectionist as my theme for the day.

A carping which continued and indeed increased as we passed out into the street, where a festival appeared to have begun whilst we were engaged indoors. Much dancing and singing was taking place which we discovered, when we asked, was a celebration of the may, both the month itself and also the hawthorn blossom which with its white and pink flowers marks the real beginning of spring here. Buffum took himself off away from the revelry with a great show of disapproval, and Wright and Thompson declared themselves both too old and too tired for such work and so I was left alone in the midst of the street-dancing and celebrations.

The people I met during the next few hours - for I stayed and much enjoyed myself for some considerable time - were of a very different sort to those in whose company I have spent so much time during this barn-storming of Scotland. For whilst they showed no prejudice to the color of my skin, neither had very many of them heard of our mission here. Indeed, several expressed quite strong opinions about the activities of our supporters, one man in particular saying that he thought they would do well to consider the parable of the mote and the plank and when I asked what he meant he went on to say that there were many in the city who found the cruelties of poverty and enslavement the more repulsive the further they were from the city of Edinburgh. But before I could question him further, the dance whirled us apart. Several times I was offered strong drink and was looked at a little askance when I refused, but neither was I pressed to take liquor. I did, though, see several people, both men and women, very much the worse for drink and I thanked my Lord God again that I had taken the pledge and was safe from such abuse of my self and soul.

There was, though, overall a great feeling of companionship and pleasantness in this huge company of ordinary folk taking their pleasure, and when I eventually parted from them there were offered on both sides many sincere good wishes for the future.

Later, I was confronted by a most sour Buffum who made great play of sniffing at the air until I more than a little sharply told him that if there was an odor about me, it was no more than the sweat of honest folk. He apologised but went on to say that he had come, one last time, to attempt to persuade me against the trip to London. When I told him I was steadfast, we parted on cool terms and he went off into the night air without even one backward glance.

So it is that I find myself bound for London. Treading in the footsteps of all those who have seen that place as the place of their aspirations and dreams. When first I began to read the works of Sheridan, I was struck by his excitement at his first visit to this great city. Imagine, then, how I must feel as one from far below Sheridan's position who now has the opportunity to visit this city grown more huge and magnificent since he last walked its streets. Behind all such thoughts also hang those childish stories I also read, those mythologies of such as Richard Whittington, for whom London was the heart of all.

Even though it is now an hour well advanced, and I am writing this as best I can by the light of my own small candle held at the edge of my portable writing desk, I am too much caught up in anticipation to sleep. So, I shall sit and look at the passing dark and think of how far I have come in the years we have known each other. Even though we be far apart now, I would have you be sure in the knowledge that you are always at the centre of my innermost thoughts. That is why I would have you learn to read, so that I might speak to you directly of all that I hold within me.

Your loving husband
Frederick

DOUGLASS'S DIARY
MAY 5, 1846

Then, after I had retired and fallen into a deep and restful sleep, I cannot tell if I dreamed or if I was woken. I prefer to think, I hope, it was the former. For the young man I last saw in Ballinasloe was standing at the foot of my bed in the darkness, with a curl to his lip made more cruelly pronounced by the deformation. It gave his face an expression of utter contempt, which he turned from me to the man he had brought with him.

And after all the words and the arguments, the stories and the illustrations, what if they still turn their gaze in your direction and shake their heads as if you were some foolish child who has asked why nightime comes every day? What then? Will you argue still? Will you wait for them to be persuaded? How long will you wait?

And then he drew a pistol from beneath his coat and placed it to the forehead of the other. And pulled the trigger. I was in an instant wide awake and crying out, though I had heard and seen – yes seen – that the hammer had fallen on an empty barrel.

The maid came running with a candle, for I had made such a noise as to waken several other guests. I assured her, and them, that all was well and they left me. With the candle lit, though, I found the floor at the foot of my bed lightly crusted with pine needles that subtly scented the air. I knew then that I could never again sleep in that room.

═══════

PART EIGHT

THE STORY OF EAMONN
MACDONAGH, CONTINUED

My stomach growled for a while, once deprived of even the little it had been receiving, but after a few days that stopped. The empty aching in my gut slowly stopped also, and was replaced first by an awful farting that lasted long enough to bring comments from one or two of the bolder people who came to stand with me from time to time. I did come to believe for a while that they came to hear me fart, for once it stopped they seemed to come no more.

But then another came, and when I asked, she said

"They've gone."

By the time of the warm air of spring, I could stand most of the night as well as most of the day. A paradox, I know, and one I cannot explain. I would stand in the darkness, and recite my verbs, quietly, to the stones of the wall I now knew so well. I was addressing one near the top of the wall, slightly loose and therefore in need of a gentle tap back into place but who was here to do it? I'd seen the agent stand by a wall once and notice a loose stone. He'd shoved it back, and the whole wall had collapsed into the field beyond. Always a man for big gestures.

"Not any more."

I looked around, surprised shocked even that the Pole would be here for he should have been long gone across the water. He was.

*"Not once I had him in my sight. I always aim for
the head. Not just because of the smell. But also
because I think of it as a gesture, a mark. Destroy the
head, the rest dies also. And I do love the smell."*

"The smell?"

The question was off my lips before I could halt it.

*"The smell of the two ends of human life. Shit. They
always shit themselves when they get shot in the head.
And brains scattered in the breeze. It's the chemistry,
because the two alone are pretty awful but when
mixed together … it is the smell of my victory."*

Another night, my mother climbed over the wall. With tears
in her eyes, starting telling me I must eat something, just a little something, I'd have a cup of tea, just a little cup of tea surely,
that was nothing, that wouldn't matter would it. And what was
this all about any way? Didn't I know it wouldn't do any good.
Didn't I?

I threw a piece of turf at her and it went straight down her
throat and stopped her from talking. She climbed back down
off the wall and went back to her bed.

Then I saw the desperate men and the desperate women carry
a child, no more than baby, into a house. I knew them all and
I knew whose house it was. As they went into the house, the
desperate men and the desperate women, they were all crying.
Men I had never seen cry before, not even at their mothers' fu-
nerals, were crying now as they carried the baby into the house.
Women I had never seen cry before, not even at their fathers' fu-
nerals, were crying now as they carried the baby into the house.
Then they closed the door tight and for many hours none of
them came out. When they did come back out again, the desperate men and the desperate women, none of them were crying anymore. None of them.

I cried the next day, such as I could, but there was little enough
left in me now for tears.

PART NINE

My dearest Anna,

I have now been domiciled in the great city of London for just over one week and I feel as though my mind has been through a series of mighty revolutions. Before, I remembered Baltimore as a huge city; now, I see it as a place of no great distinction. Before, New York was the finest bustle through which I had ever passed; now, it is a quiet almost sleepy village. Before, I thought myself a man of the world; now, I have met the most cosmopolitan crew in the shortest time.

Thompson and I have taken lodgings in an area called Aldwych which, although very full of theatres and places of entertainment, is also close to many of the great halls and gathering places of the movements for social reform. Of these there are so many that my head is a whirl with names, groups of initials, and the differences between the various organisations which seem to me all in pursuit of the same goal. We hurry from one meeting to the next; a lunchtime gathering with a few friends of our brethren, a soiree with advocates of temperance, an evening with those who would have the common man educated so that he might wield the suffrage. One after another, the events crowd around me so that, by night, I feel my head loaded with ideas almost to the point of bursting and even though I am thoroughly exhausted with talking and walking, I can barely sleep. Not the least cause of this effect is that the streets glow all night from the new gas lights installed in large numbers throughout the city, so that even the dead of night seems almost daylight. Without the thorough darkness to which I am used, it seems almost that I cannot sleep as well or deeply as I would wish.

I feel that this would be the case even if I were but a general visitor to this capital city, for it is always a-bustle with noise and activity. From the early morning, as the boys deliver fresh milk to doorsteps, through the rush of the business day, to the late evening as another cohort of boys sell tomorrow's newspapers. All the time I feel the presence of other people around me, and this runs like a pulse of energy in the streets even when they are deserted.

So, you can tell from this that even if this were not London, this city in which I am at present quartered would be a source of great excitement to me. For it is alive in ways that surpass with ease even New York and Boston. That it is indeed London - the city of the world as I have heard it called several times by people who live here - only serves to heighten my expectations of awe and surprise, for Thompson has insisted on taking me, whenever we have the opportunity, on sight-seeing walks through the streets and parks of the city centre. Thus it is that I have come to see much of the great history that is accumulated here; it is the presence of a past which stretches back into antiquity which is impossible to find anywhere in our country. Imagine, just within perhaps no more than two miles of the door of the house in which we are temporarily resident one can find the Tower, where there has been a castle of some sort for at least two thousand years, and the tower bridge which is an extraordinary feature of the river. Closer to us is the mighty St Paul's cathedral, through which Thompson conducted me with many comments on both the grandeur of the architecture and the laxity of its occupants' moral and religious sensibilities. An opinion he expressed so loudly at one point that a man in a black cassock stared at us and then followed until we left the building.

Thompson has also been an invaluable guide to the people of the city, introducing me to many that it would otherwise have taken me weeks, perhaps even months or years, to seek out on my own. Yet even while I appreciate his kindness and assistance, I know that he introduces me to the circles of his associates and allies. I have already on more than one occasion had to set the record straight, that I am politically in the company of Thompson but not always necessarily with him in all things.

It is also a great contrast to me that this city of liberty should be so loaded with the symbols of monarchy, for it is a great article of faith with the man-stealers that they tore themselves loose from the grip of a king's tyranny over their freedom.

Further east again along the river is the Parliament. The whole area around the House of Parliament, itself a new and most impressive building, is undergoing much reconstruction in a more or less uniform style which lends the area some considerable grandeur. This 'cradle of liberty' marks the farthest end of my evening walk, which I take alone after Thompson, who is not altogether well, retires for the night. It is a most uplifting experience, to be able to walk the streets of a city without being constantly halted and interrogated about my business by men who feel their superiority over me by the mere virtue of the color of their skin. Even now, after more than six months in this country, I await the stranger's rude hand on my shoulder and every day I exult in its absence. Indeed, it is my American accent which gives me greater fear, as there are enough hotheads abroad in the city anxious and even hungry for war over Oregon, that I have learned to keep my words to myself when abroad alone lest I face assault for being a "Yank". What irony, that I should be thrown in with all that I despise for the sound of my voice!

Today, with Thompson otherwise engaged elsewhere, I took myself to the British Museum to admire the splendour of the building and its extraordinary contents. I wandered through the rooms for several hours, amazed by the assembly of the fruits of human creativity. From there, to see Charles Dickens's house. Here, I found myself part of a small crowd hoping to catch a glimpse of the great man, but we were all disappointed for he did not show himself at all. If only you would get your letters, Anna, then you would be able to read his books. For he is a great friend to our people and has written well of the hypocrisy of the slavers.

The city itself is divided by a river, south of which I have not yet ventured for all the people who I wish to meet and who wish to meet with me, live on the northern bank. Here, at what seems to me to be the heart of the city and within sight of the river, stands the great network of law courts and lawyers' offices called collectively the Temple and at the heart of this is the Crown and Anchor Inn. This place, although called a drinking house, is much more than simply a house of carousel. For here, the great friends of liberty and the great wits and writers have gathered for perhaps a hundred years to meet with each other. Thompson told me of its history and indeed said that more than one of the meetings I have been invited to attend will take place in this house. This has given me a great sense of my historical responsibilities, and I feel a little humbled to be stepping in the footmarks of so many great men.

This is especially in my mind, for my days of easy leisure in this city will soon be over. Tomorrow I begin a tight schedule of meetings of all sorts, and will I feel be busy beyond my previous experience until the day of our return to Scotland for a final mighty assault on the hypocrites of the Free Church. I will, if I can, write again before that journey north yet my mind, already whirling with new experiences, faces many severe tests these next few days as I set myself before the powerful political minds of one of the greatest cities on the planet.

Your
Frederick

DOUGLASS'S LETTER TO ANNA

MAY 21, 1846

My dearest Anna,

I write early in the morning, for today I go to the Exeter Hall, to address the anniversary meeting of the National Temperance Society, to make clear to my audience the connection between the slavery of man-stealers and the slavery of the mind imposed by liquor.

My first two visits onto a London platform proceeded, I feel, with some considerable success. Certainly, the annual convention of the British and Foreign Anti-Slavery Society held in the grand surroundings of the Freemasons' Hall, at which Thompson and I spoke to a small but most enthusiastic audience, was extremely welcoming. Even after Thompson's lengthy introduction, during which he lambasted the Free Church, I was allowed - indeed even encouraged - to speak at great length and detail about my life as a slave, for a London audience (I was told) has been waiting my arrival. For many, it is the first time that they have had the opportunity to hear a fugitive speak, for even when Charles Remond was here some six years ago and speaking with great authority on slavery, he could not express the experience of having been a slave.

So, for more than two hours I was given my head by the chairman, and even when I turned to the subject of slavery as an American institution I was let free from the usual constraints of time-keeping to make as many unbridled attacks on the "land of the free and the home of the brave" as I cared. It was only when I turned to a new topic, that of the place and condition of freemen in the north, that John Howard Hinton, chairman of the meeting and editor of the *Anti-Slavery Reporter*, felt that he should stop me and propose another meeting for this specific topic. I stepped down to great applause and was met after by many requests from among my auditors to sign copies of the "Narrative", which has been produced in a new edition for this stage of the tour. By the close of the evening, my hand and wrist ached from so much hand-shaking and book-signing.

Yesterday evening, I had been invited to address a meeting of the London Peace Society, for there are many abroad in this city who talk openly of their pleasure at the prospect of teaching the ex-colonies a lesson. Indeed, as I arrived for the meeting there was a small crowd at the door who attempted to prevent our entrance to the hall until we pushed our way through. I had barely time to set myself straight before the meeting began and I was on my feet. I had thought that this would be a hard meeting for myself to address, for I have never spoken on this subject previously but as soon as I began I found my convictions again and from my heart made it plain that if the choice was emancipation through the shedding of blood or continued servitude, then slavery was my choice. At the close of the meeting many approached to say that there were greatly moved by my commitment to peace being greater than considerations directed towards my own being. But how can it be otherwise, for I cannot free myself at the cost of another's liberty. I could not sell my own children, to buy my own freedom. Neither will I strip another man of that greatest freedom, life, nor will I advocate that others should, so that I may be "free". What freedom would there be in this, that I would be ever imprisoned in the knowledge that others had suffered for my liberty?

It was also at this meeting that I strengthened my connection with Joseph Sturge, a great reformer of all sorts and especially prominent in the Complete Suffrage Association, for whom I spoke yesterday evening. This quiet man from Birmingham is the finest advocate of peaceful reform that I have yet met, for he holds hard in all circumstances to his argument that education is the key to all. In the years since the failure of the last petition to parliament for the extension of the suffrage here, he has worked with unceasing vigor to build a great alliance of all people to urge the extension of the vote. At the same time he has sought an improvement in the quality of the lower orders such that they may be given the power of the vote with confidence that they will not abuse this right. Sturge approached me at the conclusion of the British and Foreign Anti-Slavery Society meeting to express his (unnecessary) regrets that the meeting was so small and to request that he take it upon himself to organise another such gathering in the nearest future.

At his meeting last night, I spoke of the power of education and urged support for Sturge's cause, even in the face of some interruptions from the body of the meeting. Yet even then, Sturge did not raise his voice to this rudeness and maintained the order of the hall.

I must stop now, for I must prepare for this great day.

Your
Frederick

<hr />

DOUGLASS'S DIARY
MAY 21, 1846

The unease I feel at having dissembled to my own wife nagged me to the point at which I felt I had to abandon with some abruptness my latest letter to her. Yet I knew, still, that the letter must be mailed for the expectations at home of regular news are such that any significant silence would be suspect. And so I lie to my wife. If not lying, then at the very least I do not tell the whole truth to her. I know I have before been economical with my audience at home, when I have felt that certain thoughts and actions of mine might not do the best for my brethren as a whole, if seen by the eyes of whites. That habit of dissembling before whites comes easily, but to do the same to my own wife…

… and yet I do not know why I should feel so uneasy, for the whole of the incident was that whilst I was on the platform of Sturge's meeting there was an interruption from the floor, just as I have told in my letter home.

But I did not tell that the heckler was a black man, short and very black with no trace of the slaver's blood about him. He spoke with such force and speed that I could not altogether catch his words, and then the moment was passed, for as soon as he paused for breath, the men sitting in the row before him rose in a group and thus obscured him from the rest of the hall and at the same moment Sturge moved the resolution and brought the whole meeting to an end.

Who he was, none could (or would) tell, and by the time I had made my way to the hall floor, he was gone. No longer in the room.

———

DOUGLASS'S LETTER TO ANNA
JUNE 6, 1846

My dearest Anna,

Since my last letter, I have spoken to the two very largest meetings I have yet addressed and then rushed the length of Britain to press home the attack on the Free Church and then returned to London. For two long weeks, the hurly-burly has been such that I feel as though I have not slept but a few hours and those in a railroad carriage or station.

The great news is that we have the hypocrites of the Free Church rocking from our blows. They tried, at their convention, to prevent all talk of the money that flows to them from the man-stealers. We counter-attacked with public meetings where we demanded again and again before ever -growing audiences that they "Send Back The Money" until the whole of Edinburgh echoed with our words. With those voices ringing in our ears, Thompson and I returned to London.

Before that great journey, though, I had the greatest pleasure of addressing the single largest gathering of the followers of temperance that I have yet seen, at which I again made plain my commitment to being teetotal because I would free myself and the rest of my people from the slavery into which they have been cast by men and liquor. Indeed, I made it plain that I thought that the end of the rule of the man-stealers would not be the end of slavery itself for one freedom would need to be followed by labour towards another freedom. After the body is set free, the mind too will need to be liberated if a new slavery is not to come to pass. I look around me in this great city and I can see the signs of so many held in thrall by the slavery of liquor, that I know we will have mighty labors to perform.

It is a great sign of the enthusiasm of the audiences here that, even though I spoke near the end of a meeting which lasted upwards of five hours, there were none who left and at the end there was a great applause.

The next night I went with Sturge to the meeting he had promised and was most surprised and deeply moved to discover an audience of perhaps three thousand people packed into the Finsbury chapel despite the closeness of the night. On the way there I had remarked to Sturge that I was beginning to feel that I could not remain much longer in these islands without my wife or children and was beginning to think of a return home to the bosom of my family, no matter what the dangers of such a course of action might be. I was, then greatly moved when Sturge began the meeting by rising to his feet to apprise the audience of the possibility of my imminent departure from Britain, if the money were not raised to bring yourself and our children here, and he called therefore for a collection for your travel. Which within a few minutes, and over my protests, had brought in over ninety pounds sterling.

I was, I said when I finally rose to speak, most deeply grateful to my English friends for such a gesture of great companionship. With this feeling within me, I spoke I think as well as I ever have done and it was perhaps one of the most effective and satisfactory meetings which I have attended since landing on these shores. Indeed, the emotion helped shaped my speech such that I made some formulations with which I am most happy. For example, I said that while the southern states are the slave-holding states, the northern states were the slavery-upholding states. This is a phrase, I think, which says very clearly and shortly what I feel, even while I find it extraordinary that I can arrive at such statements without preparation. When I think how, even but two years ago I needed every word written down beforehand before I could feel confident with my audience, I can see the distance I have come.

One of the journeys I have made is that I can now see with great clarity the connections between slavery in America and interests elsewhere, such that slavery must be a concern not merely within the boundaries of the American nation but throughout the world. When the price of cotton gets up in the market in England, the price of human flesh gets up in the United States. Slavery, then, pervades the world with the smell of its corruption and it will take a movement the whole world over to put its stink aside.

Yet I wanted also to be clear that the fashion here for calling all manner of injustice slavery, does not help the cause of the slave. I have met a few too many people here who would blur the line between the slave and the worker, and I also wanted my attachment to Mr Sturge's ideas on this matter to be clear. For he is a man who sees that the various threads of reform, while connected, must be held in parallel rather than in a tangle.

The meeting ended in a great acclaim and Thompson and I left for Scotland, to complete the rout of the hypocrites to which I have already made reference.

Your
Frederick

POST SCRIPTUM

I have returned from my evening walk in a state of great distress, for whilst I strolled by the river I was approached by a group of young men who, without a word, suddenly attacked me, striking me several time around the head and tearing my jacket very badly. All this happened without warning and ended equally abruptly when one of my assailants suddenly cried out "it ain't him, it ain't the nigger" and they all in a group ran off.

A passing gentleman came swiftly to my aid, escorting me back to my lodgings and apologising for the crudity of his fellow Londoners at every step. So much so, that by the time we arrived here I felt somewhat recovered and wished that you would know if you hear of this incident from any other source that I have sustained no injury that will leave any mark by the end of a week.

My hosts, on seeing the condition in which I returned to their house six nights ago, were most concerned and angry at the treatment I had received, and they were insistent that such things only happened from the hands of the lower orders. Indeed, I agreed with them that the most shocking thing about the whole incident was, ironically, its isolated character and I assured them further that I felt no ill-will towards any English person other than those by whom I had been assaulted and very little even towards them, given the slightness of its consequences.

They suggested, moreover, that they pay for the repairs to my clothing, saying that they thought that this was the very least any self-respecting English person could do. I readily agreed, seeing their anxiety to make reparations for the behaviour of their anonymous countrymen, even though I could see no reason why they should feel guilty for the actions of others with whom they had never had any contact. The next morning, nevertheless, I handed my clothes over into the care of their maid, who left the room saying that her mistress had informed her that she was to take the items to a well-known master tailor for repair.

I thought no more of the incident, as anything other than a passing and now passed irritation, until two days later my hosts informed me as we were dining that during the day a note had come from the master tailor that he would need an appointment with me, to re-fit the clothes and that he would be grateful if I could attend at his shop the following afternoon at about five o'clock. Having discovered the address of the shop and a route by which I could arrive at it, the next day I set out. My journey took me, for the first time since arriving here, across the Thames and into South London. That I had not been here before was largely due to the absence of reason, for there are no monuments of any great interest to compare with those north of the river, and none of my hosts or companions seemed ever to have business in this "deep south". Eventually, after a walk of some three miles into these southern regions, I found the street and then the shop for which I was searching. I knocked on the door at exactly five o'clock and then entered in answer to a called invitation.

I was entirely unprepared for the sight that greeted me, for rising to greet me from his seat behind the shop's counter was a small black man. He was certainly no more than five feet tall, with a head almost completely bald and features that were as determined in their expression as they were diminutive in scale. For as he rose, I could see him compose himself to the extent that he slipped his left hand into the top of his waistcoat as he stepped forward to greet me.

It was with strangely mixed emotions that I grasped the hand of the first black man I had met and spoken with since arriving in this country.

"Good day to you, Mr Douglass. I am extremely pleased that you could honour my shop with your presence, for your fame as a friend of freedom has gone before you."

At this point my feelings became still more confused for the combination of the man's appearance and the sound of his voice seemed to remind me that we had met before, though I could not tell where.

"And I am extremely glad to make your acquaintance, sir. I am most grateful that you have undertaken the repair of my clothes and I am pleased to have met you, for there are but few of our people in this country and I do feel the need of company on occasion."

"Indeed sir? I had thought you were very happy in the company of such fine men as John Hinton and Joseph Sturge. You seem so."

"Yes I am, for they are as you say very fine men who are dedicated to the cause of the slave's freedom."

"The American slave's freedom, yes."

I could not wholly grasþ the meaning of this, and so after a slightly awkward pause I asked,

"Forgive me, sir, that I have not asked your name. My hosts here in London referred to you only as the master tailor."

" My name is Cuffay, Mr Douglass, William Cuffay. And I am not surprised that your hosts know me only as a master tailor."

"Indeed, sir? I think you are mistaken, for they were at pains to distance themselves from my attackers. And I have encountered while I have been in this country none of the color prejudice rife in my own. Other than, of course, from those by whom I was assaulted."

"Then you are fortunate indeed, Mr Douglass. Yet I did not mean necessarily that they were prejudiced against the colour of my skin. They did, after all, direct your clothes to me in their hour of distress."

"Indeed they did sir."

"No Mr Douglass, I meant more that they would see me as a master tailor rather than as William Cuffay. The colour of my skin would only have led them to me in particular; the black master tailor."

"I am not sure I entirely grasþ your meaning, sir."

"Call me Cuffay, or William, if you will, for
I have no liking for that other word."

"Very well, Mr Cuffay. But I am still not sure that I grasþ your meaning."

For answer, he turned away and reached down my jacket from a hanger behind the counter and with an expert flick of the wrist presented it to me to put on. I slipped off my other coat and turned away to slip my arms into the sleeves, but found that I could not for the jacket seemed to be in very slight but nevertheless constant motion. I turned around to enquire what was afoot, and saw that as I turned Cuffay had raised a finger in the air, as if to prevent my speaking.

"That's the ease of it, Mr Douglass. How easy it is to slip another person into a place of servitude, and your face betrays your annoyance even now that I have not done as you expected."

"Then I would see this as an ill-mannered trick, Mr Cuffay."

"There are many in this land who see all my behaviour as ill-mannered, Mr Douglass, and I have come not to worry at the thoughts of those who I know stand at a very different point to myself and my friends.

"And am I one of these people, sir? For if I am, there seems to be little reason for my remaining here. I will take my coat and go."

"I do not know what your thoughts might be, Mr Douglass, on any but the questions I have heard you address and they are but a limited range of subjects when there is so much about which we might have conversation."

"But how would you know my opinions on anything, for although your face is familiar to me I do not think that we have met before. Indeed, I do think that I would remember having met one of my brethren in this country."

"*Your brethren?*"

"A black man, Mr Cuffay."

"We share a colour of skin, Mr Douglass. There would need to be more connection before I would know whether or no I could call you brother. Indeed, that is why I have taken this serendipity of your torn coat to have this conversation. For your coat, as you can see, is already repaired and ready for you."

And he now helped me into my jacket, which fitted as well now as it had before the attack. Then, stepping round before me so that he was now between myself and the door of the shop he fixed me with a steady look.

"You may go if you wish, Mr Douglass. I will not prevent you. But I have heard that you are not a man who is entirely of one party. Indeed, I have heard that your coming to London with

George Thompson has ruffled a few feathers among those who thought they had you entirely under their wing."

"No man holds me under his wing, as you put it, and never has since I first felled the slave breaker, Covey, in Maryland. I came here to this country to do whatever I could to end the slavery of my brothers and sisters who are yet held in bondage in America, and I will speak on whatever platform I can to further that cause."

"And I say, good to you for that. But slavery has not been your only theme while you have been here."

"Indeed, no. I have spoken also in the cause of temperance for I have seen the slavery of the mind produced by drink and I have spoken against the preparations for war between this country and mine because I am a Christian. Slavery, though, the slavery of America has been my main theme."

"How strange, then, that your "brothers and sisters in the cause" here should be so concerned at your behaviour when you take even the smallest step beyond their supervision."

At this I felt some considerable concern, believing that somehow this man had come to know of my activities in Ireland. But then he continued,

"Strange, indeed, that they are also so keen in their appreciation when you draw such clear distinctions between the slavery of America and the slavery of wages in this country."

"You are of that camp, are you, Mr Cuffay? Then I tell you, sir, that if you are of that mind then you are sorely ignorant of the condition under which slavers suffer in America!"

"And you, Mr Douglass, may be somewhat less knowledgeable than you think about the lives lived by many in this country."

"I have seen the awful poverty of the Irish for myself, and still I know that they do not live in bondage!"

"Indeed, Mr Douglass, are you so sure of that? And since you came here to Scotland and England, I have not heard that you have been abroad a great deal in the slums and poverty-racked districts. Indeed, for all I know this may be your first journey south of the Thames, away from the finery and plenty."

"It is true, Mr Cuffay," I admitted in a quieter tone, "that this is my first journey across the river. But I have been excessively busy with my own work."

"And excessively directed to a particular
sort of busy-ness, I would say."

"I hope, Mr Cuffay, that you are not speaking ill of my companions. For I have received nothing but kindness from men like Joseph Sturge, who has shown great kindness to both myself and my family. He has contributed most generously to a fund to bring my wife and children to this country, that we will be separated no longer."

"A cause to which I will contribute my fee for your tailoring, Mr Douglass, with the wish that I could be as generous as Joseph Sturge and amusement at the thought that he and I are one in this enterprise. A thought that amuses me more than, I think, it will amuse him."

And then I knew where I had seen this man before, for he was the heckler at Sturge's Complete Suffrage Union meeting.

"I know you now, Mr Cuffay. You attempted the disruption of Joseph Sturge's meeting in support of the extension of the suffrage to all people in this country. A strange position for one such as yourself to take, indeed! I will not stay here another minute."

"Very well, Mr Douglass. I will not prevent your departure, but I will leave you with one question. How comes Joseph Sturge by the means to his financial generosity to you, a generosity I freely admit I cannot match?"

"What do you mean?"

"No, Mr Douglass, I will not detain you further. Please
be sure and close the door behind you when you leave."

And with that he withdrew very quickly into a room behind the counter, letting the door swing shut in his wake. I was left alone in the small shop, not knowing what to make of the question, nor even knowing what I should do next.

The decision was made, in part, for me by the fact that the outer door now opened to admit a tall and extraordinarily thin white man who was well, but shabbily, dressed and who, on seeing me, seemed a little perturbed and whose eyes were never still on one object for more than the briefest moment but moved incessantly, looking around even while his head remained still.

"Mr Douglass? What a surprise to meet you here, for I did not expect, no I did not .. yet it is a great honour to make your acquaintance, indeed it is. Is William here, yes of course he must be for you would not be standing in the middle of his premises without that he is here. Yet he is not here, is he, for he is not here with you. So perhaps you have just this moment arrived and are awaiting his appearance but that cannot be so for I did not see you in the street ahead of me. What can be afoot here, then, what .."

"I was, sir, about to depart."

"Indeed, Mr Douglass? Yet we have had no opportunity to talk, to discuss your impressions of London and suchlike. And there is much on which I would like to hear your opinion, for all I have of you thus far is William's description and very accurate he was too and what I have read in the news sheets and what they have to say is all too often tosh of a major order when it is not outright lies so I am grateful to have the chance to hear you yourself on subjects of mutual interest which when we consider would well include about every possible aspect of the movement for reform and social justice. I hear you are against the coming war between America and here and that is good for the warmongers are only about lining their own pockets for half of them own the armaments industry and the other half own land in Canada or have friends who do but I also hear that you are against war of all kind even a war for freedom."

"Indeed, sir, I am for I am a Christian."

*"Indeed you are Mr Douglass, you
have told us that already."*

Cuffay had re-entered the room without my noticing, so over-whelmed was I by the outpourings of this man before me.

"I wonder, though, how your opposition to war of all kinds squares with your assertion in your narrative that you beat the slave-breaker Covey until he could no longer beat you? That was war of a sort, was it not?"

"And a war of a very necessary kind."

"So you are opposed only to war of an unnecessary kind? I am sure we are agreed that the war over the Oregon border will be a war of the most unnecessary sort and I am equally sure that we are agreed that your war to be free was a war of the most necessary sort."

"Indeed, Mr Douglass," the tall white man began again, "most necessary for there is no other way I think to remove the slave-holders' yoke from the black people of the Americas. Our own lords and masters had their minds concentrated for them by the Jamaica rebellion and concluded that it was better to rule less completely than to attempt and fail in the effort of ruling in the old ways. We take our example from those who have seen that reason is insufficient in itself to overcome self-interest and have taken the world by the throat to bring change to it."

"Indeed, sir", I replied in some confusion, "then we are agreed that it is very well for the slave to take into his own hands the means of his liberation. In the past I have argued merely that I would not have another take up arms to free myself or my brethren from bondage."

"Yet that may well not be the meaning that others have carried from your message, for I know that there are people abroad in this land who would quote you back to me as a man who stands deep in the thrall of slavery and yet who refuses the power of arms."

"I am, Mr Cuffay, opposed to the use of arms so those that say this of me, are correct."

"Then how would you have your freedom?"

"In the ways that I have taken it."

"And how would you have the freedom of your brothers and sisters?"

"By similar means."

"And is that not insurrection?"

"Call it what you may, Mr Cuffay."

"But do you not see, Douglass, that the loss of one slave here or there may be tolerated as the vagaries of business, much like the death of a cow or pig, but that a general call for all slaves to set themselves free cannot come but at the overthrow of the slaveholders and their world and that they will not tolerate that?"

"I care not either way for their toleration. I will have my freedom and the freedom of my brothers and sisters."

"You may not care one way or the other, but I suspect most strongly that their intolerance will care for you. And then how will you act? When the slavers' guns are raised to the foreheads of your brethren and you could strike them down? Will you not act then?" And now Cuffay's voice dropped to a quietness that was almost a hiss. "When he has his gun at your wife's neck and by that power will take both you and her back into bondage and the power of liberation lies in your hand, where will be then the Christian morality of your friends who will never face that choice and so can urge with ease the path of brotherly love?"

He had come to stand close to me now, looking up at me, and yet despite the smallness of his stature it was I who felt dwarfed, for I could see that he held the power of truth at this moment. The silence between us grew deeper and more profound as we looked into one another's faces and though I longed to look away I felt I could not, for Cuffay's eyes, formerly so bright and edged with an ease and laughter, were now like chips of slate; hard and unyielding as he held me still with his question.

Then the gangling man broke the moment.

"Indeed, Mr Douglass, you must see that they will give up little or nothing unless their hand is forced."

"Who, sir, are 'they'?" I asked, glad of the chance to turn aside and gladder still to turn my confusion into anger. "My friends, who paid for my passage here when I was threatened with re-capture by the agents of Thomas Auld? The good people of Ireland and Scotland, who put their hands into their pockets to raise the money to maintain the cause of the end of slavery? Are they the people you would dispossess? People who have done nothing but good, are they to be punished in a court presided over by you?"

"'They', Mr Douglass, 'they' are the ones who live by work of others and yet refuse even the right of suffrage from the major-ity. 'They' are the ones who have become rich through the pov-erty of others. 'They' are the people who have driven thousands into the slavery of manufactory life while they live at their ease in the sweet air of the country."

"That song again! I have seen no-one in this country who has been forced to work in the ways that my enslaved brethren are forced, seen no-one who is owned as property by another, no-one who can be sold as a chattel at the whim of another. You, sir, preach of slavery yet you know nothing of it and will never know anything of it by virtue of the hue of your skin. You are, Mr Cuffay", I said, turning to the latter again, "entirely correct when you say that there are white men abroad in this land who know nothing of our life."

"And you are correct, Douglass, when you say that there are no slaves in an American sense in this land. But yet I believe that Julian speaks through analogy and metaphor and that when he refers to slaves, he does not mean slaves in an American sense, but in the sense that people here are enslaved by their fear of destitution if they do not work. Slaves come in many forms, but yet they are still slaves."

"But they are free to come and go, to leave one employer and take their work to another. They are not circumscribed in the ways that my brethren face. No-one here patrols the streets en-suring that the poor are in their houses and not abroad at night;

no-one here can slay a man or woman with impunity for the crime of disobedience."

"I agree, and I am sure that Julian also is agreed on that."

"Indeed, Mr Douglass, I am. For I did not and never have said or written anywhere that the slavery in America and the slavery here are of the same exact dimensions. But you are incorrect to say that people here may come and go as they please for all the employers together decide upon a wage for a job and none will pay more than that agreed price. So, to go from one to another brings no advantage."

"But still the choice is there."

"A choice like offering a condemned man which prison cell in which he would choose to serve his sentence."

"No, sir, not at all a choice of that sort. A choice which gives some control over one's life, instead of the total command the master has over the slave."

"If it is so, that the master has complete command then how is it that you set yourself free from him?" Again, Cuffay's quietly insistent voice cut across the white man's stridency.

"I do not mean, Mr Cuffay, that he has ownership of mind as well as body."

"Yet you used the words, 'total command' and they seem to me to be a part of your argument."

"They are a part of my argument, sir, as far they may make my case plain; that the bondage of my brethren is of a kind altogether different from any situation that may obtain in this country."

"To which I would say, Mr Douglass, "interrupted the white man, "and have said often and loudly to all who would listen that there is an analogy to be drawn between the lives of the poor here and the lives of the slaves in America."

"To which I would answer that you can only speak such nonsense from sheer ignorance of the lives of the slaves!"

"And are you so knowledgeable of the lives of those who labour in the mills of Lancashire or the manufactories of Birmingham that you can utterly deny the connection? I can only assume that Mr Sturge's great friend Richard Cadbury has taken you on a tour of his places, and from this you can speak with great authority on the lives of the English poor."

"I have not yet been to Birmingham, but when I do so in the next few weeks I shall ask to visit these places of which you speak, in order to pull down utterly your argument."

"Very good, and I shall be most interested to hear Cadbury's answer and also to hear of your observations."

"If we meet again, Mr Cuffay."

"Yes, of course, Mr Douglass, I have kept you too long from your business. Yet I would hope that we will meet again. Indeed I do. Come again whenever you will, my door is always open to you. Julian, will you walk Mr Douglass some of the way to his lodgings."

"I can find my own way, Mr Cuffay."

"I am quite sure you can, but this is not always a good neighbourhood for black men to walk alone through."

"But, Mr Cuffay, I have never encountered the slightest element of prejudice against my skin the whole time I have been in this country."

"Indeed, Mr Douglass, then how came your coat to be torn?"

"That was a mistake, I heard one of the ruffians say so."

"Then they must have mistaken you for another black man. Indeed, they must have done so." He paused a moment. "Yet indulge me, and let Julian be your guide through these streets. I promise you he will not speak further of the matters we have discussed, but will be but your guide and friend until you part. Julian?"

"Indeed, Mr Douglass, it will be my honour."

So I left Cuffay's shop, eager to be back at my lodgings, for what had begun as the briefest visit had ended in a discussion which had lasted by my calculations several hours. It was with great surprise, then, that when we emerged into the street it was still light and there was still some considerable bustle abroad.

Indeed, when I arrived at my lodgings - the tall man having walked with me to the corner of the street but no further - I discovered that in total my talk with Cuffay could not have lasted more than an hour.

Yet he has left my mind in a turmoil.

<hr>

DOUGLASS'S LETTER TO ANNA
JUNE 14, 1846

My dearest Anna,

What excellent news it is that we have had, that Garrison's journey to this country is now all arranged and that he will depart from Boston within the month. His fire will lend great strength to our cause here. For, even though we have made advances in winning the minds and pockets of many of the very best people in the land and especially in London, we do need his guiding hand through the shallows and rapids of the movements here. He has always been the great friend that I could trust with my being and now I feel somewhat the need for his assistance, that so many call upon me for my allegiance or my voice.

Garrison's great advantage is that he knows the movement in all its complex features; who is with, who is not. I fear that my own newness could lead to my being drawn in directions not wholly helpful to the cause of the abolition of bondage. That this happens is as a result of my callowness rather than by reason of any conspiracy on my part.

Thompson and I have parted company for a while, and he has returned to Scotland to continue the campaign against the Free Church while I remain here in London. Yesterday I dined with Henry Vincent, who wished to be remembered to Garrison with his great good wishes and intimations of his pleasure at the news of Garrison's definite plans to visit me. He told me, further, of the plans he and others have been laying for the formation of an organisation in Britain that will tread towards the end of slavery along definite "Garrisonian" lines. So, the man becomes a movement!

Your
Frederick

————

DOUGLASS'S DIARY
JUNE 18, 1846

This last week I have felt caught within the greatest confusion. For since my conversation with Cuffay and his companion, I have been moved to question much that I previously held obvious and dear. Not from having been questioned by another on the matters, for that has happened often, but rather because of the manner in which Cuffay asked his questions. It felt at moments almost as though he knew my doubts and held them up before me.

Then today came a note from him, inviting me to some celebration to which he is travelling out in the country north of London next week. He writes that he has companions he would wish me to meet.

All the while, I feel that I cannot discuss my meeting with this man for it is clear that there are many in the cause of abolition who regard him as a pariah, utterly removed from the sphere of their friends and allies by virtue of his attacks on men such as Sturge. So, I must choose either to have no more association with him even by note or to arrive at some means by which I may conceal our meetings.

————

DOUGLASS'S NOTE TO CUFFAY
JUNE 19, 1846

Mr Cuffay,
I will be glad to accompany you this coming Saturday, June 22.

Frederick Douglass

DOUGLASS'S NOTE TO JOSEPH STURGE
JUNE 19, 1846

My dear Mr Sturge,

I fear I must decline your invitation to dine this coming Saturday, for I have been invited to watch a performance of Shakespeare's "A Midsummer Night's Dream" and, having never seen the great poet's work on a stage before, I am loath to miss the opportunity. I would hope, though, that we will be able to meet and talk informally again before June 27.

Yours sincerely,
Frederick Douglass

GARRISON'S LETTER TO DOUGLASS
RECEIVED, JUNE 21, 1846

My dear Frederick,

I write to tell you of my immediate plans.

After I received Thompson's letter, officially inviting me to visit Britain, I set about making arrangements and will depart from Boston within the next two weeks. The ship from Halifax, and I will travel from there by virtue of the crossing being so much shorter, will deliver me to Liverpool on or about August 1.

Frederick, I would wish to meet with you as soon thereafter as possible. We have been greatly heartened here by your letters, both those that come directly and also those which pass first through the hands of your sister Harriet, but a letter is no match for actual keeping of company.

I am also, I must tell you, greatly relieved that the campaign against the Free Church has gone so well and that Buffum is now happy with the progress we have made. It is most important that we maintain our unity in the struggle, for divisions can only weaken us.

We must also keep our eyes firmly upon the goal we wish to achieve, never allowing ourselves to be distracted from what it is we most desire.

I look forward to our reunion.

Your friend,
William L. Garrison

DOUGLASS'S LETTER TO ANNA
JUNE 23, 1846

My dearest Anna,

Yesterday being midsummer's day, I travelled with some friends to watch what is perhaps a supremely English event. For I went to watch a game of cricket. This is a traditional village game which has been played here for many years, but in the last few years has become more popular with the city and town dwellers as a pastime. It is a summer game, and is very keenly followed by people of all sorts and classes.

I attended a celebration of the mid-summer and so involved not merely the game, which lasted much of the day for cricket often takes long periods of time to finish, but also many other activities and gatherings.

I travelled out with my friends by rail to a town called Watford, and then from thence on to the village of Heronsgate where the celebrations were being held. Although it had rained for much of the previous week, and indeed has rained more in the summer here than I ever remember at home in either Maryland or New York, the day dawned beautiful and stayed so all the longest day through. In consequence, I think, the celebration was attended by even more people than the organisers themselves expected and I was astonished to see such a large gathering.

The village of Heronsgate itself is delightful relief after the hurly-burly of London. Its roads and lanes are clean and tidy, and the air is sweet after the endless eddies of smells and stenches which I have come to think of as being the smell of London. As a consequence, the few inhabitants of the village themselves are a stark contrast to the pallor of so many of those with whom we travelled out. Indeed, many of the latter seemed to see the day as a holiday from the grimness and grime and often expressed their envy of those who lived here.

After speeches from the organisers, the crowd settled itself around the edges of the playing field and the game commenced. I was fortunate indeed to have a gentleman seated next to me who took it upon himself to explain to me not merely the purpose and rules (or rather "laws") of the game but also its place within English life. The former of these elements, I do not pretend to grasp even remotely for much of what the gentleman remarked as important seemed to me to be a nothing, and only the faintest connection was made within my mind to anything of which I have experience - and that was to the game of baseball which is becoming similarly popular among the working populations of our own country.

Yet it is but the faintest connection, for what seems to characterise cricket more than anything is the players' reluctance to win unless they can do so by means which are obviously fair and seen to be fair. They dismiss themselves from the game, they applaud the efforts of their opponents; in short they play with a clear sense that being gentlemen is more important than being victors.

This idea of the gentleman's game has even more importance to their conception of their activities when one realises that the virtues of playing extend beyond the boundaries of the playing field and into social life. Cricket draws together players from all levels beneath its rules (the "laws"), to which all are equally subject. The gentleman, when overturned by a social inferior, is expected to depart without protest just as much as is the servant dismissed by his master. The rubrics of wealth, power and station are set aside when the players cross over the rope which marks the playing field and they come together under laws which determine the conduct of all. So, the lowest and the highest may stand shoulder to shoulder for a while and are thus reminded that albeit there is great distance between them for the rest of their lives, they are still all players of the English game together. The hope is, that this notion will instil throughout the social body the ideas of fairness and honesty, and of playing to the rules.

It was indeed an idyllic vision into which it was hard not to fall, as we sat beneath the elms trees planted around the village green watching the players all in white. The village church stood at the far end of the green, and all were drawn together. I feel as though I have learned more about the English character from watching the easy spectacles of this one day than I have done from weeks and even months of observation of the more serious enterprises of these people.

By the late afternoon, the game was concluded to the satisfaction of both players and spectators and after a few more speeches from our organisers, the grass was cleared and a small stage erected. For the second half of the day's main entertainments was to be a performance of a play by William Shakespeare, and what should it be but the most apt piece, "A Midsummer Night's Dream". Although it is not a work I have ever read and I did find the language difficult, and despite my general objections to the practise of theater generally, I must say that I found the spectacle of a group of simple people taking upon themselves the labor of part-learning and rehearsal in order to stage a performance for the pleasure of their friends, most inspiring. The stage itself, as the evening wore on towards darkness, was lit with a few well-placed torches and the magical qualities of the play became evident before us.

As we wound our way back through the darkness of the lanes to the rail station at Watford, where the train especially hired for the day still waited on us, I felt most at home here. For I know that when this darkness turns to light, the friendship of those in my company will not turn to revulsion at the sight of the color of my skin. I would urge you, my dearest Anna, to take advantage of the most generous efforts of my friends here and overcome your objections to crossing the ocean to be here at my side.

Your
Frederick

It does not suit me at this moment that my friends at home in America should know that I have sat much in the company of Fergus O'Connor and Ernest Jones, and so I have kept that intelligence from my letters. But I would keep my own record of the events that day, that I may look back on them in years to come and remind myself that I have seen a glimpse, a merest glimpse of what the world might be.

Having agreed to accompany Cuffay on his outing, I arranged to meet with him at the corner of the Strand on which stands the "Crown and Anchor" Inn as this is a place of which he is very fond, he told me by return. This struck me as most strange for I did not think of Cuffay as a man overly fond of the literary types who had frequented his place in the past nor of the gentlemen who had founded the Whittington Club in recent years.

When we met, I asked him whence came his attraction to this spot. To which he replied that this was the very place in which the first Charter meeting had been held and thereafter the first version of the Charter written. Indeed, he remembered that night almost ten years ago with great emotion for there were gathered then, he said, upward of four thousand ordinary men and women come to claim their rights as citizens and that their ordinary eloquence in the absence of any great leaders who had since appeared was what he remembered mostly.

It was extraordinary to me that such a mighty event had happened in a place I knew so well and had visited on numerous occasions in the company of many who had never remarked this historical moment. When I said this to Mr Cuffay, he remarked that there are many histories competing with each other for possession of the past and he was not in the least surprised that men who thought themselves important should pass over events at which they had not been present as though they had not happened.

At which his wife, who had come along with him, struck him a sharp but seemingly playful blow with the basket she carried, and remarked that some important men had best bestir themselves lest they miss the train.

My surprise at Cuffay's tale, which even now I am not sure I entirely believe, was compounded still further when we arrived at Euston station, for here stood a train filled with people all going to the same destination as ourselves. In all, there must have been perhaps four hundred souls assembled for Cuffay's outing and all, he said, invited by Feargus O'Connor to come and watch the cricket. At this I was most annoyed and told Cuffay that if he had told me that I was to go with him to an event planned by such a notorious individual as O'Connor then I would most surely have refused.

"You know Feargus O'Connor well, then, Douglass?"

"I have not made his acquaintance in person, but I have heard a great deal of him"

"I see."

"What do you see?"

For an answer he turned away abruptly and beckoned a man standing close by to join us. "This is Frederick Douglass, Will, of whom members of the Free Church of Scotland speak so well in their journals. Mr Douglass, this is Will who had a great knowledge of what goes on within church circles from his reading of newspapers."

"Indeed, Mr Douglass," said the young man, "then from my readings I would hold you to be a scoundrel and a fraud".

I was about to protest, when he continued.

"But I know the authors of such written opinions to be scoundrels and frauds themselves and would see their foes as my friends. I am glad indeed to make your acquaintance."

"And I yours."

Turning again to Cuffay, I saw that I was too late for he had walked away and was climbing into the train. He was about to close the door when I reached him and laid my hand upon his arm.

"But Sturge and others like him are not scoundrels!"

"Neither is O'Connor."

I hesitated a moment longer, but then as the train began to move I swung myself up by the door and into the carriage.

"You are right. I will not judge the man until I am in a position to make my own judgement. I have long prided myself on the independence of my opinion and I can see that, however briefly, I had lost my grasp on that for a moment. Please forgive me."

"You owe me no apology."

For the rest of the journey, first through the northern edge of London and then out into the countryside, I talked with other passengers in the carriage, several of them being very interested in meeting me for they had heard, they said, of the famous American black man come to castigate the allies of the man-stealers in this country. Once again, I was forcibly struck by the total absence of prejudice towards my skin among these people, among whom I sat and talked without ceasing until we arrived at our destination. From the rail station to the village of Heronsgate, for that was our intended point, was a brisk walk of perhaps an hour.

The appearance of the village itself is most remarkable, for it stands within the grounds of an old estate and is comprised entirely of new buildings, some of which seemed but very recently completed. At the centre of the village, on a platform of wood so newly cut that I could smell the resins, stood a large man who looked, with his ample frame and side-whiskers, the epitome of an English gentleman. As soon as he opened his mouth to greet us, though, this idea withdrew for he had a strong Irish accent and a decidedly ungentlemanly manner, for he was bluff and friendly with all on a large scale. He welcomed us, he said, to the first celebration of the completion of the Chartist Land League estate on which as soon as possible the first pioneers would take up residence to demonstrate that there are other ways to live beyond the fear of poverty and destitution, beyond the destruction of the family by demands of the almighty guinea and its terrible logic.

What better way to celebrate the conclusion of the first stage of the great scheme, he said, than by a festival at the midsummer. The bricklayers and the carpenters who had labored so long and hard this spring to have the cottages finished invited us all to a cricket match, to be played on a field they had marked out at the edge of the settlement. At this proposal there was laughter and agreement in equal measure.

We then followed O'Connor, for this is who I took the speaker to be, through the street to the field. Each of the houses, while small by the standards of some, was a good deal larger than slave quarters and was large enough to accommodate a family. They were also, as far as I could tell, of a very sturdy construction which was greatly superior to much of the poor housing I had seen in London. That it was also a good deal cleaner than London was not surprising, given the absence of occupants, but even so the lightness this effected was very welcome.

After we were all gathered at the field, O'Connor and another man made speeches of welcome again and invited us all to be seated to watch the game. Then the two teams, dressed in their work clothes, stepped out from the crowd and very soon the game was begun. Never having this sport played before, nor anything akin to it, I soon lost concentration and began to look around at the crowd.

Whilst they watched the cricket with some interest, many were also taking the opportunity to relax and stretch out in the sunshine, for it was now become a gloriously sunny day and the sky was blue without the wash of smoke and soot I had come to accept as a normality in the city. This easy relaxation, punctuated with laughter and applause, settled slowly over us all until after about an hour, the players called for drinks. At which, a cow was led out by a man carrying a milking stool and he took up a place at the edge of the field where he began to send spurts of fresh milk into the cups produced for the players. Who, when all cups were filled, raised their drinks to the health of the cow, who they loudly announced for all to hear, was named Rebecca. At which intelligence, everyone applauded and cheered.

When this break in play was ended, and the game about to recommence, I took the chance to turn to Cuffay who was seated a few feet away and to ask who was the Rebecca of whom everyone was so proud and fond? At which he smiled, and replied that she was not a woman of whom Joseph Sturge, or indeed Henry Vincent these days, would approve. But he would say no more of the identity of this woman of whom they were all so pleased to hear, but said merely that she was a reminder to all here present that subordination would not be forever our lot.

From his expression, I knew that his use of the word "our" was a challenge to me but I forbore to respond and he continued, saying,

"Here comes O'Connor himself, with his glass of milk in his hand, to join us. Mr O'Connor, what a fine day and what a fine setting for your triumph. This is Mr Douglass, of whom you may have heard."

The large man planted his feet firmly, held out his meaty hand to me, and shook hands.

"A friend of liberty is a friend of mine."

Then he turned to Cuffay, taking him by the arm and leading him a few paces distant. Where they stood, in intense discussion, for several minutes until O'Connor strode off without even a parting gesture. Cuffay shrugged and then turned back to me, seating himself again beside me.

"So, Douglass, how will you explain your day in the country with us ruffians to your friends in London?"

"I have not felt the need to explain myself to any man this several years, Mr Cuffay, and even if there are men in London to whom I am beholden, that does not mean they own me. I think both they and I are sensible of that."

"Indeed, you may be right. But I do think that they will not be altogether happy at the company you keep."

"Again, Mr Cuffay, I feel you are more sensitive to these matters than I. For I have often told my friends here in England that I would speak on any platform which was dedicated to the overthrow of slavery in my country, no matter who else stood on that stage beside me, and on no occasion has anyone save yourself balked at this condition."

"You hear me wrong, Douglass, if you think it is I who balks. My meaning is that there are many active in the cause of the end of American slavery who are a little chary of any parallel being drawn between the condition of the slaves in your country and the condition of workers here."

"And I would be one of them, Mr Cuffay. You know my thoughts on those who seek to see the condition of working people here as the same as my sisters and brothers in America."

"Mark me, Douglass, I say any parallel. Not that the two situations are entirely the same but that there can be seen connections of some sort between the two. Certainly, there is no slavery of force in this country. Yet there is slavery to money. These people you see around you. If they do not work, they do not eat. And be assured that they do not choose the wages for which they work, for if they did they would ask a little more for labouring the hours that they do. Ask any one of them, go on and ask if any one of them has their needs met by the money they earn."

"I am sure that I agree with you, Mr Cuffay, but I would still hold firm to my conviction that there is a world of difference between selling the hours of one's day to another and being bought and sold one's self."

"And there is a world of difference between the world you have inhabited since you came to this country, and the world many of those around you now live in during the days of the week. I wanted you to come here today because of one thing and one thing only. To accept a challenge from me, to come with me into the sinks of London for a day and at the end tell me whether you think the people that you meet deserve the lives they live."

"I accept of course, and without hesitation. But I do not understand why today had to be the preface to such a challenge."

"Because I wanted you to see, before entering the world I will show you, that people do not choose to live there but are compelled. You see around you now a crowd who would live here in these conditions if they could, but that choice is not available."

"Why not? Surely, Mr O'Connor's project is to make such a life the property of these people?"

"Let me ask you a question in reply. If runaway slaves set up a community and declared themselves free, how would the slaveholders respond?"

"They would hunt them down, but I do not see .."

But Cuffay was distracted by a great cheer from the playing field, and we both turned to look. A tall young man was standing at the centre of the field, apparently reciting a poem for the few snatches we could hear contained both rhyme and rhythm. Yet for want of hearing all that was being said, we both rose and walked nearer, as did many another of our assembly. Before we were arrived, though, those ahead of us broke into loud applause and cheers and many stepped forward to clap the man upon the back. O'Connor himself came to the young man's side and, raising their clasped hands above their joint heads, cried "Mr Jones, Mr Ernest Jones; a friend indeed." To which the crowd applauded still louder.

By the time we were re-settled around the edge of the field, Cuffay had moved off to talk with other people and for the rest of the afternoon as I sat enjoying the warmth of the sun on my face and the sounds of the simple pleasures of those around me, he wandered restlessly through the assembly pausing to talk intently to various individuals. Every time I looked up I could see him, apparently oblivious to the events of the game through his attention to another set of tasks.

Mr Ernest Jones came and sat beside me, after asking permission from myself. In an accent very different from any of the others I heard that day he said that he thought that this occasion pointed to the future, to a world where leisure and not toil was the most important. He said that he hoped we would both remember this day in the years to come, for he knew that the path to the future would be crowded with obstacles. Then, with a sudden tear in his eye, the young man jumped up and disappeared into the crowd.

At length the game concluded and Cuffay returned, carrying a small basket of food. As he seated himself beside me, his wife - who had left us almost as soon as we were arrived at the village - re-appeared to join us and almost mockingly complimented her husband on his industry. He laughed and asked whether or no I wished to stay for the play that was to be staged by a group of the assembly. When I discovered that it was a Shakespeare play, I heartily assented and said that I much admired his work and would be happy to see a production. I hoped, I said laughingly, that it would be "A Midsummer Night's Dream" for that would be the play for this night. To which Cuffay answered that there were some in the crowd who would agree with that.

While I tried to fathom this remark, I watched the stage being prepared for the performance. It was of the simplest order, just a raised platform supported by trestles and a curtain at the back. On which the small group performed most admirably and I found myself thoroughly absorbed by their playing and their production of the language, which I have always found difficult to read but here the spoken version was very easy to follow.

At the end, we clapped and cheered the players as darkness settled over all. One by one the torches which had lit the performance were extinguished until we were all standing in the darkness, seemingly unwilling to leave. Until Cuffay's voice boomed out that it was time to depart, time to return to London. As we walked through the darkness of the lanes, I was still under the thrall of the day's spectacles and resisted all attempts by Cuffay to draw me into conversation and was happy to sit in silence on the train all the way back to London.

When we parted, it was very late and Cuffay left me with words to the effect that I should remember our agreement. To which I made a perhaps somewhat sharp response that I would and then entered crossly into my lodgings, reflecting that the man was incapable of stepping aside from his path for even one moment.

He had gone a few steps away and I was in the process of unlocking the door of my lodgings when he returned swiftly and suddenly to my side. With a few muttered words to the effect that he thought I might find these useful, he pressed into my hand a number of sheets of paper and then hurried off. When I was in my room and with the candle lit, I looked at the sheets and discovered that, contrary to all my expectation, they were a series of essays by a Reverend James Pycroft on the Englishness of cricket. It was in reading these, as I sat on the edge of my bed, that I came to see the importance of the place the game occupies in the minds of some of the English, for the good cleric refers to the playing field as "a sphere of wholesome discipline and good order" and goes on to consider the game as a desirable metaphor for the state of English society. In these essays there are no rebellious cows, nor indeed even a workman, present. The game of cricket on the village green comes to the centre of an image of a world in which all are equal under the rules of the game. Yet I could not understand why Cuffay, of all people, had been so insistent to press these essays into my hand.

Still pondering this problem, I took myself at last to my bed. I slept extremely well, partly from tiredness after the gentle but extended exertions of the day, but also by virtue of the pleasant dreams which filled my sleep. I dreamt of my mother for the first time in many years, of her brief and rare visits to my grandmother's house. Here every gesture seemed to me a measure of the degree to which she wished protect me from the world I would enter once I was no longer an infant. The final moments of the dream, though, from which I woke almost immediately, were her parting from me. She stood at the doorway of my grandmother's shack, telling me that she would return as soon as she could. Then she walked away, never looking back as though she knew that one glance would render her incapable of departure. And I was rooted to the spot, no matter how much I wished to run after her.

<hr>

DOUGLASS'S NOTE TO CUFFAY
JUNE 24, 1846

Mr Cuffay,

I am pleased to accept your invitation to go with you into the streets of London. Yet I do not understand why you refer to this *invitation* as a *challenge*. A challenge to what, and to whom?

Sincerely yours,
Frederick Douglass

<hr>

DOUGLASS'S DIARY
JUNE 25, 1846

I am just now returned from my journey into the streets of London with Cuffay, and though my hands are still shaking I must write down my emotions at what I have seen. For my understandings of the world, the views that I have held close to since my escape from slavery and more especially since I took up the cause of my brothers and sisters in bondage, have been shaken to the core.

This is how it came out. Cuffay met with me at the corner of the Strand and Arundel Street, at the door of the "Crown and Anchor". From here he led me and north and east, through a maze of streets into which I had not previously ventured, each more narrow and gloomier than the last. Until at last we came to a door at the side of a tall brick building which overshadowed the whole of the tiny street in which it stood. In all of the face of the building this door was the only break. No windows were in evidence anywhere in the grim surface. He knocked upon the door and then beckoned me to come and stand with him across the street, where we both affected no interest in the door until it was opened and a man who, from his manner, clearly knew Cuffay beckoned us inside.

We stepped through into a deep gloom where what little air there was swirled with dust. Cuffay introduced me to the man.

"This is Jeremiah. He risks much for you today, Mr Douglass, and so I would exhort you if asked to deny all knowledge of him."

The man shook me briefly by the hand and then led us into the interior by way of a series of stairs and passages until we were arrived at a small window overlooking a very large room. Here, were a huge number of people of all ages coming and going in a frenzy of incomprehensible activity. I could make no sense of what they were about and all appeared before me as pandemonium. I looked at Cuffay questioningly, but he merely indicated that I should watch.

After a while, the chaos began to resolve itself into a complex pattern of movement, because I saw the same activities constantly repeated by some within the overall random rush. There were a number of men and women who were engaged in a rhythm of movement from one place to another along the long benches which stretched across the room, before returning to what now appeared to me as the start of the line. In a few minutes longer, I could see that each performed the same series of actions as they progressed and that all of the movements together kept them always bent over the benches, so that they shuffled along. Overlaid onto this pattern of movement was what seemed like the chaos of the children, who darted back and forth from under the benches to the corners of the room and then back again. Their movements were, to me, utterly incomprehensible. The more I watched, the more oppressive the whole scene became, for the room seemed to me to bear down upon not only those in it but also upon myself as a mere watcher. I felt as though I were gazing into a small pit of hell, for even in all the years that I had been a slave I had not once seen a place like this, where the air was choked with dust and all the people present seemed imprisoned by themselves.

For I had also noticed as I looked in upon them that there were none present who took the place of overseers. No whips fell across their backs if they faltered and no authorities paced the spaces between the benches. Yet in this absence they worked with a furious intensity that was alien to me as an ex-slave, for whenever the master or his presence was absent from the field or room in which we worked, we seized the moment to cease our labour. For us, this was some small recompense for the theft of our lives. These people, though, seemed trapped in this place of their own free will. None stood in the room to drive them on, and no-one stopped them from fleeing this hell-hole and yet they worked, worked at a speed that seemed to grow ever faster as I watched.

Then, suddenly, all stopped and they rushed out as swiftly as they could. In seconds the room was deserted. Quite literally, the dust began to settle, and as it did I became in the silence more aware of the loud ticking of a clock. It occurred to me that the time for lunch had come, and that it was the clock which acted as overseer here. Or at least it was the clock which commanded the time in which these people would work, but still I could not divine why it was that, without the human presence to urge them on, still they labored as fast as they could. And why they chose to remain within such conditions. Then, almost as soon as they had departed and these few poor thoughts occurred to me, they rushed back in again and began again the wild dance of their work. After a few minutes the air was again clogged with dust and the noise rose back to an almost deafening level, so that the sound of the clock was entirely smothered. I was again lost to any world I knew.

After a few seconds of this, Cuffay tapped me on the shoulder and gestured that I should come with him and we hurried quietly and carefully from the building. As we reached the door through which we had entered, I turned to thank Jeremiah for his assistance but he was already closing the door behind us and Cuffay had gripped my sleeve to pull me away. He half-ran, half-dragged me away from the street and did not speak until we were returned to the main thoroughfare.

"I apologise for the haste and almost roughness with which we left Jeremiah, Douglass, but we could not run the risk of placing him in peril of losing his employment."

"To free a man from such an awful place would seem to me the greatest kind, Mr Cuffay."

"Indeed, sir? And then what would he do for employment in this city? When all the employers of the area would know within the day that he was not a man to be safely employed, for he allowed the likes of yourself and myself to trespass in his employer's works? Would you have him starve in his freedom?"

"He would have his liberty, which is sacred to all men, and I am sure that he would rather not starve."

"What makes you so very sure, Mr Douglass? Remember, Jeremiah is only employed by the manufactory owner, he is not the property of that man and so when the working day is done and Jeremiah is paid for his work, he is of no more concern to that man. Indeed, I am quite sure that his employer does not even know his face but merely recognises him as a name and number in a ledger, easily replaced and even preferably replaced should he seem a trouble of any sort. Why, Mr Douglass, do you think I labour at the trade of tailor? Because there are none within this city who will employ me for any other work, and precious few who will employ my services as a tailor. There are many times when I live only by the labour of my wife, who is a little more removed from my infamy and can go abroad under her maiden name."

"But then surely he could leave this city and seek employment elsewhere?"

"It is true, Mr Douglass, that not all the towns of England are as riddled with the ills of the manufactory plague as is London, but the problem is always that if he does not work, Jeremiah does not eat. And London, for all its ills, pays better wages than almost anywhere else. So, stink and rot as it may, at least it does not starve its people."

"Stink and rot, indeed! Now, sir, you go too far. Indeed it is not the most wholesome place that I have ever lived but it does not stink or rot!"

At this Cuffay made no answer, but merely led me further through the maze of small streets into which we had now passed. I had now no idea where we were, other than that we were moving eastwards. It was a sobering experience, for the further we went away from my now familiar haunts, the more drab and awful the place became. The houses became smaller, more crushed in upon each other and in time, I began to agree with Cuffay that there was indeed a stink to the place. And it was unmistakably the stink of human filth that pervaded the air ever more strongly.

At length, Cuffay turned in under a low archway and led me through into a courtyard surrounded on all sides by houses, in the middle of which was a huge pile of rubbish piled high against the sides of a series of small huts or sheds. Here the smell, by dint of being trapped within the ambit of the houses, became even stronger and almost unbearable. My horror rose still higher when I saw not only that the mounds were alive with rats feeding on the rubbish but that they squabbled most violently over the excrement which seemed to ooze from beneath the doors of the sheds. These were, it was now clear to me, the toilet facilities for all the houses I could see. I turned away with revulsion.

"Good God, Mr Cuffay, these people are animals, to live in such conditions!"

He looked at me a long while, standing very still even while all around us the courtyard heaved with activity and movement.

"It is true that they live like animals, Douglass, but that is not the same as being animals themselves. I understand that there are many in America who would see you as an animal, by virtue of the colour of your skin. I am surprised that you would so easily make a judgement of others, which placed upon yourself you would so strongly protest."

He took the hand of a passing man, who seemed almost indifferent to our presence but stopped under his touch.

"Why is it, Mr Douglass, that you assume that these people choose to live like this when you would protest that all of those of your brethren who live under slavery in America, do so under silent protest?"

"Because, sir, they live in slavery!"

"And these people live in utter freedom, choosing to be like this? Think that, Douglass, and I have nothing more to say to you. When we first met, you called me your brother of skin. If that is true, then it is my misfortune. I would plunge my hands and face into bleach, rather than be thought brother to one who can hate so much whilst demanding that others should love him."

He strode off, out of the courtyard and disappeared from my sight. As he did, it seemed to me that the one hold I had on this place that helped me to navigate my way through it, was snatched away and I was left abandoned in this unutterable place. I rushed from the awfulness of that place and out into the street, hoping to call Cuffay back but he had long vanished from sight. I was alone and with little idea of how to make my way back to my familiar surroundings. I was still more unsettled by the thought that I was expected at dinner at the house of Joseph Sturge and that I had no idea of how to make my way from here to that place.

For the first time since departing from home, I lost my sense of myself, leaning there against a wall and trying to catch my breath. I was also most intensely angry with Cuffay, for having abandoned me in this way and resolved there and then that I would have nothing more to do with him, when I was approached by a man who looked extremely poor. His clothing, quite literally, was in rags. I took him for a beggar and felt in my pocket for some small change, so thoroughly destitute did he seem to me. I held out a farthing to him.

"You would hire me?"

"No, sir, I would help you."

"You would buy my service?"

"No, sir, I would give you money to buy yourself food."

"And will that help me?"

"I would have thought that food would be of assistance to one who seems so hungry, yes."

"And will you come back tomorrow and give me another farthing?"

"I do not understand."

"I will be hungry again tomorrow. Will you come back again and give me more money, that I will not be hungry then?"

"If we meet again tomorrow, I will give you another farthing, yes."

"And if I bring my friends who are as hungry and in need as myself, will you also give them a farthing?"

"I regret, sir, that I have but a little money. Certainly insufficient for such a purpose."

"Indeed, Mr Douglass, I had heard that your intentions were not matched by your abilities."

"How do you know my name, sir?"

"I know you."

"What is your name, sir? I would know your name as you know mine."

"My name, Mr Douglass. I am Rebecca."

By now I was entirely convinced that the man was mad. Maddened perhaps by poverty and by the drink I could smell on his breath, but still nevertheless mad and I turned away to leave him where he was. When the name "Rebecca" reminded me that I had heard this name before. I turned back. He stood there still, with a smile on his face.

"You called yourself Rebecca."

"I am Rebecca."

"Rebecca was the wife of Isaac, mother of the Hebrews. I do not understand you, sir."

"I am not that Rebecca. I am the Rebecca of whom you have heard tell more recently than your mother's bedside fairy tales."

"The cow!" I remembered now that the cow acclaimed at Heronsgate had been called Rebecca by the cricket players and that the crowd had cheered for being named thus.

"The cow is named after myself and my brethren. My brothers and sisters who fought for their freedom because they knew the master's promises were lies. They named the cow for those of us who claimed our right to walk the roads without paying for the privilege of passing through some charlatan's toll booth; we roamed the highways in our hundreds to show that was had been ours since the mists of time would remain ours, no matter what the masters might say. They named the cow for those of us who rotted in the jails for five years as a gesture of remembrance, of a hope deferred if you will."

He swayed slightly on his heels, as though he were drunk, and then lifted his head until he was gazing up at the sky before continuing in a lilting tone. "The Hosts of Rebecca are dispersed, but they are not entirely gone away. Just as the tribes of Israel were scattered, so too are we. Just as the Temple was brought low, so too are we." The tears were now beginning to run down his face, his voice cracked and faltered.

I stepped close to give the figure comfort but before I could do so, Cuffay appeared from a doorway a few yards off where he had clearly been standing hidden and interposed himself between myself and the other.

"No, Mr Douglass. You are of the opinion that such as my friend here are animals are you not? This man drinks, and you are for temperance are you not? He is the product of his own weakness, is he not? He was "a man of violence" and you are a good Christian who does not believe in the necessity of such actions, are you not?"

And he turned away with his arm around the man's shoulders and led him off. When they were some distance off, Cuffay turned again and gestured.

"That way, Mr Douglass. That way back to your friends who do not smell, who do not drink, who do not shit. That way to those who have never lifted a hand in anger or frustration. That way to the men who always think they know best what is good for others."

Then he turned again and strode off, still leading the distraught man. I stood stock still, watching, until they were lost in the crowd. At which point I, too, felt lost. I was, in a literal sense. But I also felt that I had lost my grasp on some of the certainties of my life under the impact of Cuffay's questionings and exhortations.

I still feel that I am lost, for I feel that I have little or no answer to many of the mass of questions asked of me by Cuffay.

DOUGLASS'S LETTER TO ANNA
JUNE 26, 1846

My dearest Anna,

Our work here proceeds from strength to ever greater strength. Whenever we hold a meeting in London, it is crowded to the doors with sympathisers and supporters, and of these two groups the latter grows larger by the day. By which I mean that there are ever more people prepared to give of both their time and their money to our cause.

With this London tide moving on a crest, I leave tomorrow for Birmingham. A more industrial place than here, I have been invited by both the Sturge brothers and also by the local business man, Richard Cadbury, to address the annual meeting of the Anti-Slavery Society there. It is a mighty chance for us to extend our influence to an area not previously affected by our arguments.

I shall begin, I know, by calling on the memory of brother Charles Torrey, of whose death I have just been informed. His murder by the state of Maryland is a crime against all mankind. What can the continued imprisonment, for the crime of aiding his enslaved brethren to freedom, of a man so ill that the regime seemed almost designed to kill, what can it be called save murder? He was slain, as Our Lord was slain, for imitating HIM who came to open the prison doors to them that were bound.

Though I never met him in person, though I might have done for it was through Baltimore that I fled north, I have been in company with many who did and all spoke of the selflessness of the man. Heaven send that we are all so dedicated when we are called to service.

After Birmingham, I shall conduct a brief tour of the north-west of England before returning to London in time for the World's Temperance Convention, at which I have also been asked to speak. We are reaching into corners we never dreamed possible, and I intend to denounce those of the temperance persuasion who have travelled from the slave states to this meeting, for their refusal to be seated in the same room as our enslaved brothers and sisters. To them, it seems, the evil of a black skin is more profound than the evils of drink.

Your,
Frederick

DOUGLAS'S NOTE TO CUFFAY
JUNE 26, 1846

Mr Cuffay,

I would speak with you again and I would hope that we can have this conversation in terms more civil than those on which we parted last. I am at your disposal.

Frederick Douglass

DOUGLAS'S NOTE TO CUFFAY
JUNE 27, 1846

Mr Cuffay,

I am sorry, sir, that you returned my last note unopened and unanswered. I leave now for Birmingham and the north, and will not return to London for several weeks. I shall try to speak with you again on my return.

Frederick Douglass

DOUGLASS'S LETTER TO ANNA
JULY 2, 1846

My dearest Anna,

I travelled to Birmingham in company with Joseph Sturge, for whom I have developed a great liking and he, it seems, for me. We disagree on so little, that I find we can make great progress in our discussions.

We were met at Birmingham by not only Richard Cadbury, come with a delegation of workers from one of his manufactories to greet my arrival, but also by the surprise of James Buffum's presence on the platform as well. I had not expected to be reunited with him until I reached Newcastle, and so it was both an honor and a pleasure to be greeted from the train in such a fashion.

The meeting was, once again, a great success and was filled with the best and most respectable citizens of the city. They took very well to my remembrance of Charles Torrey and took up a collection for his family. They also took very well to my description of the Americans as great professors of freedom; great professors of their freedom to oppress their black brethren. Finally, they took extremely well to my argument that the influence of British opinion upon America, owing to the identity of language, religion and habits of thought, was greater than that of any other part of the world, and that therefore the greater the weight of British opinion expressed against slavery, the faster slavery would be brought down.

At the end of the meeting, Mr Cadbury approached and congratulated me on the concision and appropriate limitations of my speech. Indeed, he continued by telling me that he had heard altogether too many lectures recently in which the speaker rambled from one unrelated topic to another so that by the end one felt that everything and nothing had been said. We were joined by Buffum, who also congratulated me on the accuracy of my attacks. "Better one accurate ball from a musket than grape from a cannon pointed in the wrong direction", said a voice. This proved to be Edmund, Joseph Sturge's brother. Despite the war-like tone of his analogy, we were all agreed on the substance of his notion.

We had retired to Mr Cadbury's house, and were seated in his drawing room at our ease and talking of the progress of the cause of the abolition of slavery, when Buffum started and, apologising for not having delivered this before, handed me a letter. In which was an invitation from the Scottish branch of the Anti-Slavery Society to become an agent for them and offering me a small but adequate salary. This was a great relief to me, for it means that I will not have to worry constantly about an income from the sales of copies of the "Narrative". Although these go well, and cover my expenses at all points, this is not the same as an assured payment. It may also mean that I can begin to plan the finances for your own crossing of the Atlantic.

I was, I told Buffum there and then, happy to accept this offer. The evening concluded with another round of good wishes and congratulations, before I retired to my bed for the night, well pleased indeed with the day's work.

The next morning, Mr Cadbury invited me to visit one of his manufactories and the attached village in which the workers employed therein live. This was of great interest to me, for I began to see that it is possible for a master to have the care of his employers uppermost in his mind even when he does not own them body and soul. Indeed, Mr Cadbury's treatment of his workers is a great deal better than that I have seen visited upon many slaves in America, even though he does not have the living welfare of his employees as his direct interest, for their are not his property and any one may easily be replaced from the great fund of labor that I have seen on every street of this city.

From now until the end of the month, Buffum has arranged a tour of the north of England for me ending in what we plan to be a great rally in Newcastle-upon-Tyne, after which I shall return to London for the World's Temperance Convention.

The news that Garrison will be with us at the end of the month has put even greater vigor into the hearts of all who are already invested in our cause, for they know - we have told them - that his presence and his power as a speaker will carry still more before us.

Your
Frederick

━━━━━

PART TEN

THE STORY OF EAMONN
MACDONAGH, CONTINUED

The village was divided between those who were gone and those who climbed over the wall to visit me. Though I was lonely for company I came to prefer the absent ones, for those who remained asked so many questions to which I had no answers. What is to become of us, why did this happen, how did this happen. At first I tried to answer them, when they came climbing but too often my answers seemed to sink into them and disappear. I watched my words blow through the air towards them and melt away into their faces. Having no effect, because the questions continued to pour. There came a time when I began to prefer the occasions when just the words blew over the wall and they stayed in their beds because I could flick the words away. You cannot flick your mother, your friends, their wives, and their children, away.

They would leave me at times, sometimes for nearly a week, leave me to my business. Then they would return, with their questions. Always the same questions. What is to become of us, why did this happen, how did this happen. My silence made no difference. I would turn away and look out towards the sea, but the words just crowded behind my back.

How – this was easy. The blight. Yet even this simple answer did not satisfy.

Why – harder. Because we depended too much on the potato. But why? Because there was no other source of food. But why? Because, because.

What – I do not know. That answer, though, just angered them. Then why, they would answer me. Then how, they answer me.

So it went, our dialogue.

Until my mother climbed over the wall, with tears in her eyes. Eamonn, Eamonn, she said. Eamonn why are you still here? Can't you see?

> See what?
> That it's done.
> No.
> Yes, Eamonn. It's done. The world is an empty
> place and you are all that's left in it.
> Then it's been pointless.
> No, not that. We have appreciated your com-
> pany. It's lonely here. Watching the world drain
> of people is a lonely business.
> But there are so many, so many of you there.
> I know they are here but I can't see them, can't hear them.
> What use is knowledge that you can't taste, can't touch?
> What should I do?
> Go.

Her tears started down my face. I knew they were her tears, for there were none left in my own dried and hollowed body.

> Why?
> Because you're done here. We are grateful that you stayed
> when all the rest couldn't wait to rush to the boats. Frankly,
> though, we need to sleep and you're keeping us awake
> rattling around out there. The others think that you should
> just climb over the wall and join us. But you were my first
> child. I wanted more for you than I wanted for the others.
> I know that was wrong. I could see in their faces that they
> knew you were special to me. I want more for you than this.
> How?
> I will make it happen for you.

Three days later, the carter on his way from Clifden to Galway found me at the crossroads, where the lane up from the village crosses the main road and then wanders away into the bog. He says that he almost just drove on by, he was so used to passing bodies. Ones lying down and dead, and the ones still standing but already dead. He was lifting his whip to twitch the horses when he noticed.

How can a man with no feet stand up?

———

PART ELEVEN

My dearest Anna,

As is ever the case on this anniversary, my thoughts turn to home, to the country of my birth. In the nearly eleven months I have spent in Ireland, Scotland and England, the contrasts between republican slavery and monarchical freedom have become ever clearer to me. With one extremely brief exception, an incident so trivial it seems barely worth the mention, I have not encountered in my whole time here any prejudice directed towards me on account on the color of my skin. There are, to be sure, many people who have disagreed with the tenor of my arguments and the tone of my speeches. Yet they have restricted their disagreements to those elements of my presence; at no time have they complained that a black man has no right to make such arguments or to tell such stories because his skin is black. Nowhere has a door been closed in my face, or a railway carriage been forbidden to me, with that phrase that rings every day in the ears of black men and women in the United States; "niggers are not allowed".

I turn to this reflection on this day, of course, because such differences cast a long shadow across the face of American freedom. Or rather, across American professions to freedom. For no matter how American liberty proclaims itself in constitutional statements, a word goes unspoken even though its presence is all-important. When American politicians say that "all men are created equal", they mean "all white men"; when they talk of justice for all, they mean justice for all whites. And so it goes.

That is the great advantage that falls to the friends of freedom and liberty in this country; that when they proclaim freedom and liberty they extend those rights to all people, white and black, British and American. These lovers of republican freedoms are the people who sympathize with Louis Kossuth and Mazzini, and with the oppressed and enslaved, of every color and nation, the world over. They constitute the democratic element in British politics, and our own republican government could learn much from these subjects of a crown.

Such thoughts come easily to me today, but they are mixed with a growing regret which has been with me a good deal these last few weeks, as I have come closer to the first anniversary of my arrival here. This regret rests on the knowledge that I may not now return home to the bosom of my family without placing myself in the greatest danger of the loss of my liberty. Such is the state of American freedom today, that it poses sharp questions to men whose only crime is that they have taken the words of American freedom to be literal whilst possessing a great barrier to those sentiments; a black skin.

American freedom asks that I choose between my family and my liberty, for with the "notoriety" I am told now surrounds my name and writings in the United States, the possibility of returning to my former protective obscurity is impossible. In the turmoil this presents to me, I would know from you what you would have me do.

There are friends here who would pay for your passage and also that of the children, so that you might come to live here in this country with me. I know that this is an idea you have rejected before, but I would ask you in my hour of despair whether or not you might reconsider. I say this not to guide you to one answer or another, for I would also have you know that if it is your wish that I return then I will do so in the knowledge that we are strong enough in each other to withstand all tribulations such an act might bring.

Tell me, then, my dear wife what course of action you would see taken by

Your
Frederick

My dearest Harriet,

I would know from your own pen, rather than from the rumors that reach me here, if indeed it is not safe for my return. For the intelligence I have received comes only from our good friends within the cause and I feel they cannot tell entirely what is the life of the black man and woman in America. Do they exaggerate the perils? Or do I enlarge the chances of my going now unnoticed? Are there strangers loitering past the house, looking for signs of my return, or is the house unrecognised as the abode of the family of that "wicked runaway"?

Speak just what you think, dear sister, in the knowledge that only my eyes will see your candor.

Your loving brother
Frederick

DOUGLASS'S LETTER TO ANNA
JULY 11, 1846

My dearest Anna,

I am now arrived in Newcastle-upon-Tyne, from where I will stage many forays to other towns in the north of England and the south of Scotland, in furtherance of the cause. This is an excellent base from which to make these expeditions, for it stands near the center of the region and has good transport in all directions.

I have been offered lodgings in the house of those excellent friends of the cause, the Richardsons. This household of the Friends, consisting of Henry and his wife, and his sister Ellen, has made me immensely welcome since my arrival. I had almost forgotten what it was to sleep within a home and not to have search for the rooms of the house in a different place every morning! Henry's business and Miss Ellen's teaching keep them both from the house for long periods during the day, and so it is Mrs Henry Richardson who has most constantly kept my company these last two days since my arrival. Her simple homeliness has been a welcome contrast to the whirl of these last few months, and we have already spent considerable periods of time simply sitting in the garden of the house and discussing horticulture. This is a subject on which she knows a great deal and has been hard at work educating me out of my complete ignorance, such I may now tell the difference between a delphinium and a dahlia.

These few days have served in me very good stead, for I now feel utterly recovered from the profound tiredness which was coming over me in waves in the last few weeks. There was so much to be done, and I felt as though my chance of doing it all was retreating away ever faster. Now, I begin to feel as if I may be able to meet the demands of the coming summer weeks.

Miss Ellen informed me at breakfast this morning that her teaching responsibilities will be at an end at the end of the week, and that she has planned a number of trips to local places so that my recovery from what she terms my "exhaustion" may be completed. In the meantime, she has instructed me with an ironic earnestness to continue my education at the hands of her sister-in-law.

Even if these few days were not so designedly therapeutic, I would still be very happy to be spending my time in the company of such intelligent and unprejudiced people, whose closeness to God is not in the least tinged with the hypocritical piety I have long come to associate with "God-fearing" southerners in our own country, whose acquaintance with the bible seems to have as its only purpose the justification of enslavement. These Friends, though, turn not exclusively to the pages of the Good Book for the justification of their ideas and activities but apply their hearts and their minds to the establishment of what is moral. So, we do not debate references to chapter and verse but what is good in human conduct.

We have little disagreement on these matters, and I find my

faith in Christian folk somewhat restored by the example of the members of this remarkable family. When I said so to Mrs Henry this lunchtime, she replied that I would do better to visit their very good friend and companion, Miss Elizabeth Pease, who was at present in Darlington visiting her father from her home in Edinburgh. As I have heard much mention of this lady and her reputation of a friend to all that is good and honorable, I said that I would be very happy if a visit to her house might be arranged.

Tomorrow, Mrs Henry tells me, my education in horticulture will continue with a visit beyond the wall that divides the garden of the house between the area I have already explored in her company and what she laughingly terms "her arboretum".

I must, I think, in conclusion ask that you forgive me for the rather fevered tone of my last letter. I was more tired than I cared to believe and I have come to recognise that such fatigue endured in isolation can create phantasms in the mind much larger than they would seem in the gentle light of company and closeness to those I hold dearest in my heart. I only wish that these words could be addressed directly to you, rather than having to endure the knowledge that they will pass through the hands of an interlocutor, even if she be one as sympathetic and kind as my sister Harriet. Once more, dearest Anna, I would urge you to learn your letters, that we may speak directly to one another even though separated by an ocean.

Your
Frederick

DOUGLASS'S LETTER TO ANNA
JULY 15, 1846

My dearest Anna,

I am this very hour returned from a visit to the beach at South Shields with my good and excellent friends, the Richardsons, and I knew that the instant I returned I must write and tell you what they have proposed. For I would know your thoughts on their suggestion.

But first let me tell you how this came about, for then you may forgive my delaying such momentous news- at least momentous to myself and my beloved family, whatever others may think - rather than speaking all at once. With Miss Ellen's teaching duties concluded for the summer, Mr Henry decided that we would all benefit from a trip to the sea, saying that he always found that nothing was better for any feelings he might have of tiredness or slight illness. So it was that early this morning we loaded ourselves into a phaeton and left for the sea. The journey itself was entirely uneventful, and we were quickly arrived. The beach looks out towards the north sea and tide was very well withdrawn and I could see that the major attraction of this place was that at such times as this, there was a huge expanse of level and smooth sand on which to walk, or ride, in order to take the air.

The air itself was, even though it is the middle of summer here, chilly. Mr Henry's word for it, though, was 'bracing'. Nevertheless, I retreated into my top coat. What a sight we must have made for all the other people on the beach that morning, and there were several groups engaging in the same sort of activity as ourselves. A prosperous couple, clearly expecting their first child soon, and their sister, in company with a black man several years their junior, all walking and talking as though they were all of a piece. In America this would have been foolhardy on their part and simply foolish on mine, to believe that we could somehow invent a colour-blind republic of four and then parade its existence in a public place. Yet, no-one passing us remarked on our company. Not even when, in a fit of laughing at one of her brother's jokes, Miss Ellen took a hold of my arm to steady herself.

Indeed, she did not immediately release her hold and continued to hold me by her side as we walked along. For several moments I could think of nothing but the hand of this white woman upon my sleeve, holding my arm in a gesture of friendliness not extended in this way to me by a white woman since I was a child. So it was that I initially did not hear the first part of the conversation that she had begun with her brother and her sister-in-law.

"But does this happen very much in America, Frederick?"

"I am sorry, Miss Ellen, I was somewhat distracted by my thoughts. Does what happen very much?"

"My brother tells me that he has intelligence from our friends there that many men have begun to sell their own children."

"It is a trade which has been going on for many years now. What Mr Henry may have heard is that the trade has in recent times become rather more extensive, though I could not say for sure. It is not something that slavers have been much prepared to broadcast. I think that perhaps what has rather happened is that our friends have become prepared to talk about it openly. They have come to see it as slavery's dirty secret rather than their own."

"What has wrought that change?"

Henry coughed very loudly and turned our attention to a number of the seabirds walking at the water's edge, saying that they were a migrant bird from the south that came to roost here in the summer, before leaving again at the beginning of autumn, finding the climate here too cold for their liking. He proposed that we walk a little closer, that we might try and see their plumage. After several minutes, we gave up on the effort and resumed our aimless wandering.

Mrs Henry asked if it were true that Garrison was planning to come to England and I replied that we were looking forward to his arrival every day.

"He is the most experienced speaker of the cause and can rouse even the most apathetic audience through his pictures of the condition of slavery and his use of the bible to show what an unchristianness the owning of slaves is."

"How did you come to his acquaintance?"

"When the cause first took me up, he was at the convention

in New Bedford where I made my first public address. It was he and Wendell Phillips who drew me in completely and I have not regretted a moment since, whatever the dangers to which it has exposed me. Indeed, when I first considered the possibility of writing my *Narrative*, it was with the two of them that I discussed it. Once, of course, I had talked with my family."

"I have not yet had the chance to read your story, I regret to say, for it has become most difficult to lay hold of it."

"That, Miss Ellen, is as true for myself as it is for you! But I am glad of such difficulty, for it means that even those who cannot hear me speak wish to know my story and buy the book in order so to do."

"I am looking forward to the opportunity that tomorrow will present. But what did your family say on the matter of the publication?"

"They were afraid for me, of course. But also agreed that it would be the very best contribution that I could make to the freedom of our brothers and sisters still held in bondage."

"You still have ..?"

"Only my sister Harriet and I are free."

"What wicked people!"

"More inured to the state of things as they are than actively wicked, I fear."

"Why so?"

"Because the openly wicked are engaged in actions against which we can argue and agitate. They have chosen their route, and can sometimes be persuaded from that path. Indeed, there are several now active and thorough in the cause who were formerly owners and whippers of other humans, who now speak with great thunder and horrible experience of the awful effects of slavery upon those who enslave Those more passive are accustomed to see the world in which they live as the only possible world. To challenge that is to turn their own existence upside down. My father's wife was such a woman."

"Your father's wife?"

Again, Mr Henry interrupted the conversation to remark that he thought the tide might be turning and we should consider whether or not we would have time to complete our walk as we intended, or should we consider turning for the carriage now? He asked his sister's opinion for, he said, she came here at least every month and therefore might know the motions of the tide better than the rest of us. She replied, almost shortly, that it seemed to her that there was plenty of time to reach the picnic spot before the tide came in and then we might return along the higher path. Then she turned back to me.

"Your father's wife?", she asked again.

Again, Mr Henry attempted to intervene, but she turned upon him.

"Henry, I am talking with our guest and it is most rude that you continually interpose yourself between us."

She turned back to me, but over her head, Mr Henry looked at me with an expression that I could not misconstrue after all my years and training in the arts of slavery's dissembling. I did not know, though, how I should proceed. On the one hand, I had my truth and would speak it. Had spoken it many times before and had come to see it Thomas Auld's shame and not my own. On the other, I was being directed to keep some part of my truth from these two women. If it had been another man, who had not shown me the kindness and hospitality that Henry Richardson had, I would have had no hesitation but to speak. But he had shown himself a good friend to the cause, and most welcoming to myself.

Thus caught, I stood in silence.

"Frederick?"

"Mr Douglass."

"I am in some difficulty, Miss Ellen, for your brother .."

"My brother? Henry?"

"Ellen, there are some things, some matters, some aspects .."

"Henry, I will decide for myself what I can and cannot know."

"Ellen!"

"Henry."

She took a firm hold on her brother's sleeve and marched him away from myself and her sister-in-law, until they were at a point sufficiently distant from us that we could not hear what intervened. Mrs Henry and I stood in an embarrassed silence, until she spoke.

"They are often so, for Ellen is very wilful. Especially with her brother, for Henry must go about a great deal more than she or I and therefore has a clearer sense of what will go. Ellen, though I love her dearly, does seem to me to be more the child."

"Children's eyes, though, are often the clearest when it comes to spying out some of the twisted ways in our world. It was from other children that I began to learn to read and write, for they could not see where was the harm in sharing their knowledge with a playmate. Until their parents beat "sense" into them."

The other two now returned, Henry rather red in the face but seemingly more quiescent than before. His sister, though, had a strong glow in her cheeks and fire in her eyes.

"Frederick, my brother agrees with me that it would be very rude if he should interrupt our conversation again. I have assured him that I have a very clear sense of what is improper and that he need have no fear that our continued intercourse will take any path other than one utterly seemly for that between adult friends. So."

She took my arm again and, turning her back to her brother, asked me a third time.

"Your father's wife? What is the meaning of this convolution?"

I felt constrained to release her hold from my arm, for I now felt most uncomfortable. I turned to face her, that her brother might hear all that was said.

"My father, Thomas Auld, was my mother's master. It was his wife's misfortune that she should see every day the resemblance of her husband both within the house and also playing in the slave quarters without."

Her silence was most profound. She turned to look out towards the sea and as she did I saw the glitter of a tear at the corner of her eye. She looked back to me.

"I see I must apologise for the intrusive rudeness of my questions. Something from which my dear brother sought to protect me. I am sorry, Frederick, and I apologise to you also, my dear brother."

She held out her hands, one to each of us. We took them and the three of us stood conjoined for a moment. This assembly was dispersed by Mrs Henry's stepping up to join us, saying how pleased she was that all was now resolved and for the best.

"Not resolved, my dearest sister, for we still face the intractable fact that Frederick is regarded by his own father as a piece of property rather than as his child."

"Miss Ellen, I would much rather that we spoke of other matters more directly related to the cause of the end of slavery."

"But what could be more directly related to the matter than your own present personal condition, for is not that the product of this vileness?"

"I do not think, however, that my circumstances are of great import upon the more general argument against bondage. Garrison is as well capable of making that argument as I am, indeed oftentimes I think he is better at it. My best contribution .."

"Is your story. The story of the slave who has taken his freedom and become a man."

"Exactly."

"But is not the fact that your parentage is as much a part of your story as any other part?"

"Yes, and I have never denied that that is the case. Indeed, my 'Narrative' begins by identifying that man as my father. It is a source of constant sorrow to me that I carry his mark in my flesh. But these are not the circumstances to which I now refer."

"What then?"

"My present condition, madam, is that I feel suspended between two possible courses of action both of which are heavily imbued with consequential pain. I can return home, and face the prospect of being at any time seized by bounty hunters employed by my own father. Or I can remain here, separated from my family."

"Will your wife ...?"

"Anna has chosen to remain in the United States, come what may. It is her home, the place she knows and she feels that she would be uneasy here."

"But .."

"There are no buts that can change my state, Miss Ellen. I have considered the position in every way I can, and am now only concerned that the distractions of these matters may affect my ability to speak and agitate for the cause. When I first came here, I did think that the joys of liberty and freedom from the fear that holds every ex-slave's heart would outweigh the pain of separation. And so it was for a while, but now the distance from home, from my loved ones, bears down more heavily upon me every day. That is my burden to carry, I know that, but my concern is that such thoughts distract me from what must be done here."

"What if you were free?"

"I am free, madam, I took my freedom and no-one will take its essence from me again. This chattel became a man the day he overthrew the slave breaker's whip, and I did that for myself."

"I did not mean that, sir, and I hope you will forgive any form of words which might have lead you think any differently from my meaning. What if you were, were. Henry what is the word ..?"

We all, each in turn, returned her questioning gaze answerless, for we did not understand the question. We needs must have the word of the question before the question itself be understood. Then she answered herself.

"Manumitted. That is the word, is it not?"

"I will not give my approval to the system of bondage, madam, by engaging in its trades. That is the message I have learned most clearly at the side of Garrison. No union with these people, be that political union or a bond made in trade. I have taken my body from them. I have no need to buy it back again. And every slave who works to buy himself from their grasp is not only perpetuating the world of bondage by not rebelling against it, but is also enslaving himself not only to his master but also to himself. Any slave who would have should take it, not sweat his life away earning that which is already his. I would not, by being drawn into their world, give these people the relief of being able to think that their trade is anything but the most vile business the planet knows. 'The Lord sayeth, he who touches pitch shall be defiled.'"

"And if I were to choose to defile myself in your cause?"

"I do not understand."

"I understand that you will have nothing to do with these people, and I see the goodness in your argument. But what if I were to take on the burden of touching pitch?"

"I do not understand."

"What if I were to raise the money to make a legal fiction of the already existing truth of your liberty?"

"I cannot see the purpose in this, madam."

"It will give you the choice, to remain here or return home to your family. As you will."

"But Garrison."

"Mr Garrison will never face the same choice as you have before you now. I am sure, I know that he is a brave and noble man in the cause of the abolition of slavery. Yet he could on any day choose to turn aside. He may come and go in ways that are simply not there for you. Ways that I would be honoured to make possible."

I knew not what to say at this juncture. Part of my life wanted to scream, No, no compromise with the man-stealers! Yet, another part wanted to say, Yes, give me the power to return home to my beloved family without having the fear of being taken up at any time and thrust back into the clutches of Thomas Auld. I excused myself and walked away along the beach to be alone with my thoughts. Even after several minutes of contemplation, I was still so confused that I would have made no sense with any words I might have offered. I returned to their company, saying that I needed time to think and would prefer that we discussed this matter no further. They accepted, and we continued on our way.

But now, I sit alone at their house again, and I would know your thoughts on this matter. Can I let another sin on my behalf, that a good may come of it? Or is this but a mere temptation, sent to try my will by holding out the promise of a false freedom to pull me back into the orbit of these thieves?

I would beg, also, that at this time you discuss only among the closest members of our family, for whatever other confusion is set before me I do see the logic to Miss Ellen's argument that this is a matter that only members of our race will fully understand.

But I must know your answers as soon as you can come to them, for Garrison arrives here in a very few weeks.

Your,
Frederick

DOUGLASS'S LETTER TO ANNA
JULY 19, 1846

My dearest Anna,

The confusions of my last letter have been still further strengthened these last two days, and I now find myself within a whirl of thoughts and ideas to none of which I have what I think to be sufficient answer. My hosts, I think, misinterpreted my silence as hostility after we returned from South Shields - when in fact it was confusion - and suggested that I might like to take a visit to Darlington, in order to meet the famous Miss Elizabeth Pease.

Thinking it would be best to be alone with my thoughts for a while, I agreed and they sent word in order to facilitate my departure. Miss Pease replied by return that she would be most pleased to have my company, having heard a great deal of my activities from her friends and correspondents. I had the journey from Newcastle to her home town to consider what this might mean.

On my arrival, though, I discovered that there was no ulterior intention to her words, but simply a statement in support of the fact that she has now become an almost complete invalid and must rely for her information about the world on the good offices of her friends, who either come to visit regularly or who write even more frequently. Yet this is become no impediment to her knowledge of the doings of the world, as I discovered during our first conversation. She tested me - there is no other word for it - on my activities since I had arrived in England, and was required by her to answer a number of very searching questions about my opinions. Not just of ideas and movements in general, but very specifically of individuals and their movements, thoughts and actions. All this was conducted without very much ceremony, for when I arrived at her very modest little house the door was standing ajar and even when I knocked on the lintel, no-one came to usher me in. I knocked again, and the only answer I had was a voice calling from within that I should enter.

I did, and identified the way to the voice. I found Miss Pease sitting in a small room which, by virtue of the fact that there were several opened windows which looked out over a very formally organised garden, seemed an extremely airy and light place. Yet there was a strangeness to the light which I could not immediately identify, and did not have the moment to then, for my attention was caught by a welcoming voice near at hand. Miss Pease herself was seated at an angle to one set of the windows and as soon as my eyes rested on her, I knew the strangeness. For these windows were set in the wall in such a way that someone seated, as she was, could look out into the garden without stooping or bending.

"Mr Douglass, what a great pleasure and indeed honour it is to make your acquaintance. You must forgive me for not rising to greet you, but the pain it would cause me would not be matched by your sense of any fulfilled decorum. Besides, I have never been troubled by such considerations before and see no reason why I should be so troubled now. Have a seat. Miss Richardson tells me you and she have had a dispute of some sort."

Even accustomed as I have become during my year in this country, to the forthrightness of many British people, I was a little taken aback by Miss Pease's directness.

"I am not sure that dispute is the correct word, Miss Pease. But that is not why I am here. I have come to make the acquaintance of one of the most renowned friends of the enslaved this country has ever had the privilege to be mother to."

"Pretty words. Everyone who speaks of you, says you have the power of words. And they say truly. Yet I have listened to many in my time who spoke prettily and who spoke of nothing of any consequence at the same time. Dispute or not, tell me what has passed between you."

"We discussed my freedom and my bondage."

"A riddler, I see."

"No, madam, a contradiction posed for all black men who would have their freedom and would take that freedom by their own hand. That we are free by our own action and yet still bound to slavery by the laws of the United States."

"Indeed, I had not realised that only black *men* were moved in this way."

A brief silence, and then.

"I apologise for my vehemence, madam."

"Oh, do not apologise. For it is very rare that the public platform comes directly to my house. It is much more usual that I have to be content with insipid reports in newspapers of the doings of the world. It is really very *invigorating*."

"I have apologised, madam, and I would be grateful if you did not continue to mock me in this fashion."

"I must, then, also make my apologies. It is so seldom that I have visitors who are not friends accustomed to my manner that I sometimes forget that not everyone finds this to their liking. I am sorry, Mr Douglass, but my awareness of mortality makes me brusque."

"I will not make another apology, then, for we will begin another cycle. To the matter. Miss Richardson offered to purchase my freedom from Mr Thomas Auld and I replied, perhaps with too little consideration for her kind attentions and too much sensitivity to my situation, that I did not need the assistance of anyone else to obtain something I already had; to whit, my liberty."

"That is very close to her version of the events, with the simple exception that she felt that she did not then know how to make amends for what she thought of as her insensitivity to you. She says you have been very quiet, even withdrawn, since this conversation."

"Indeed, I have, madam. But not from any anger towards her."

"Then why sir?"

"Because I do not know what answer to make to her proposal. For there is nothing I would rather have than the liberty to be re-united with my family. Yet we cannot, will not, engage in a trade with the man stealers. Everything for which we have contested would lose its moral ground in such an exchange."

"I, we."

"I do not understand your meaning."

"When you spoke of your desire, you said "I", but when you spoke of morality, you said "we"."

"I did?"

"You did."

"Something Miss Ellen said touched me more deeply than I care to admit. That this was a choice which Garrison would never have to face."

"But is that not the case?"

"Of course it is, but you cannot know the esteem in which I hold him."

"Tell me, then, that you may convince .. me .. of the case."

"More than any other in the cause, Garrison was the one who took me up and showed me that this work was that for which I had been born. Other people are good and noble in the cause, but he is the one who both knows the strategy and the tactics for victory and also has the utterly unshakeable faith and belief in what it is that we are doing. Some call him a fanatic, but if he is then he is a fanatic for the good of mankind."

"He is a good man, no-one disputes that. At least none of my acquaintance. But that is not, I think, the matter. You are worried by your friend's response to the decision you might take."

"I would be worried, were he just my friend. But he is more than that, he is my example."

"In all things?"

"In all that matters."

"Why?"

"Exactly because he can turn away. I cannot, for my black skin marks me out whether I will have it so or not. But he could refrain from the cause. I honor him for the fact that he never does."

"Never?"

"Not once in all the time that I have known him."

"Then he is indeed a most remarkable man. Yet that in itself does not turn aside the fact that any time he could."

"But he will not! I know that he will not."

"I wish that I had a companion or friend who had such faith in my steadfastness."

"I hear nothing but good of you, madam."

"People find it very difficult to speak ill of an invalid, no matter their true thoughts. Yet I do think you exaggerate, in my case if not in that of Mr Garrison."

"I accept that it will, in the end, be time that makes that judgement. Yet I do have faith in the man."

"Is that the matter, though? Is it not rather that you face a situation which is not to be judged on personal faith or probity but on the material facts of the world in which we live. You would be the one of the very last, I think, to deny that colour prejudice does exist in the world we occupy whether we would have matters that way or not. It is that which precedes any consideration about the people involved. Whatever fellow feeling Garrison may have with the slave, he can never himself be a slave. He has sympathy, I grant, but he cannot have empathy. That is the gulf over which he cannot reach. You are as near and yet as distant as Thomas Fuller's Welshmen, who live on mountains 'whose hanging tops come so close together that shepherds on the tops of several hills may audibly talk together, yet will it be a day's journey for their bodies to meet, so vast is the hollowness of the valleys betwixt them.'"

She touched her fingers to the volume in her lap, from which protruded a letter which she seemed to be using as a bookmark.

I sat in silence for several minutes, so struck was I by the image she had employed. I tried to find refutation of the argument in my memories of meetings and of travelling with Garrison, but the more I considered our history in the light of this quotation, the more I seemed to see its truth. I remembered moments when we had spoken one to the other, when the bulk of the meaning was clear but small parts remained obscured. I remembered an occasion when, on walking in the streets of an Ohio town in the early evening I had become agitated by what I took to be the obvious signs of hostility all about us, but to which he was oblivious until the moment we were assaulted. However I would have it differently, our past history did now seem to be a tale of distant closeness.

So agitated was I by this thought, that I excused myself and requested the opportunity to take a walk in the garden. Here, I hoped to find some way of calming my agitation. Instead, what

I seemed to see was a harmony born of the juxtaposition of dissimilars; soft silver-grey foliage beneath the sharpness of deepest purple flowers, darkest green waxy leaves behind a froth of white blossom. This nature seemed to underpin her argument; that it was the difference between the two which made them complement each other.

The confusion must have been written large in my face by the time I returned to the house, for as I entered Miss Pease held out her hand to me with such a look of profound concern that I was much moved and at the same time worried for her welfare. I took her hand and sat beside her.

"All I would have you do, Mr Douglass, is be sure that you act in the clearest light and understanding. We can do no more than be sure of ourselves and speak our truths, no matter how they are received. I have lost more than one friend by that course, but I have always the consolation that I have not lied to preserve a false friendship. Hold your course and your true friends will return to your side, in good time."

We sat now some time in silence, for I knew that she was right, no matter how I might rebel against the idea. And that I must therefore choose a course of action with which I would feel truth. There we sat for some time, this elderly white woman and I, hand in hand. Here, I felt, was a closeness which came from having her urge upon me the importance of seeing the distant between us and yet not allowing that to become a gulf we could not cross.

Then, after several minutes, she spoke again and as she did so released her hold upon my hand.

"For example, I understand that several of my former friends in the cause of abolition with whom I argued some years ago, are now returning to my side in the company of yourself and your good friend William Garrison."

"I am entirely at a loss to understand what you mean, madam."

"I mean the formation of the Anti-Slavery League."

"I know of no such formation."

"But the date and place for the foundation meeting is set. I have a letter here, somewhere, from my old friends Thompson, Vincent and Lovett which tells me of these developments."

"I say again, madam, that I know nothing of this. I would, therefore, be very grateful for sight of this letter."

She set down the book she had upon her lap and, reaching round to her small desk which was covered with letters and other articles of correspondence, retrieved an envelope addressed to her and containing what seemed to be a proclamation with a smaller sheet of paper attached. She passed both to me. The larger sheet was indeed a poster advertising a public meeting, called for the "Crown and Anchor", and announcing that at this meeting a new organisation in the cause of abolition, to be called the Anti-Slavery League, would be founded. Below this was a list of speakers invited, a list which included both Garrison's and my own. So shocked was I by this, that I would have been able barely to understand the letter even if it had not been written in Henry Vincent's spidery hand. Yet Miss Pease seemed almost unaware of what was passing through my mind, for she continued to talk to me even as I tried to read the note.

"I made myself extremely unpopular with many people when I complained to any who would listen that the old British and Foreign Anti-Slavery Society made no reference in its name or its activities to the slavery of working people at home whilst at the same time casting a long gaze across the Atlantic Ocean. Now it seems some people are coming around to my opinion that we would do well to take note of the Lord Jesus Christ's injunction that we would do well to remove the plank from our own eye before addressing the problem of the mote in another's."

"I do not think of the bondage of my brothers and sisters as a mote, madam. To me it is a little more than that."

"I was not referring to you, Mr Douglass. I meant those who so vigorously attacked me for the suggestion that the word "chartist" appear in the name of the old organisation, both for consistency and also to persuade the working people of this country that they would do well to have some interest in the cause; it being theirs as well as the domain of the well-to-do with a need to salve their consciences."

"Yet I cannot agree, madam, that the condition of the English working class is at all akin to that of the enslaved in the Southern states. The slave cannot choose to come and go, but must be always at his master's whim, to be fed or no, to be beaten or no. The worker here is not the factory owner's property, to be bought and sold as a chattel whenever he will."

"I do not doubt a difference in conditions. It would be foolish indeed to say that both live lives of the same ilk; although it is the kind of foolishness into which some would enter. It is not condition which is at issue here, but position. Both the slave and the worker must work, and in doing so they give over the fruits of their labour to another."

"But .."

"Give me no buts for a moment, Mr Douglass, for that is the fundamental. That is what the slave in America and the worker here share. They have a common interest which lies beneath all differences, a commonality which tells me that, no matter what aid they may receive from other quarters, they must themselves grasp for liberty. As the poet said "Who would be free, themselves must strike the blow". With that in mind, we can look past the differences to make common cause against a foe with two faces but one head."

It was clear that this speech had quite exhausted her, for Miss Pease - who had half-risen from her seat in her vehemence - now sank back onto the cushions which half-filled her chair and lay there with all her concentration on catching her breath again.

I, on the other hand, now had a mass of thoughts whirling through my mind. Even while I could see the truth in her assertion that I alone could choose my path and even while I knew that she was right to argue this was not a situation which Garrison would ever face and that therefore his advice was useful but not crucial, I could not help but think that I barely, if at all, knew this woman while Garrison had been my friend, companion and comrade for several years and that together we had endured assault and abuse. Yet, now, there was the matter of this change of strategy and tactic, this plan to form a new party, to which I had not been made privy. Clearly, there were some in the cause who did not feel as scrupulous as I about the need for discussion and consultation. For the briefest moment, I confess, I wondered whether or not the decision to make such a move were not an entirely "white" compact. A thought I dismissed as unworthy.

I was caught back to the immediate situation by Miss Pease's request that I lend her my arm, that she might take a short walk in the garden, that she might benefit from the freshness of the air. As we wandered, there seemed a reluctance between us both to renew the conversation and so we walked in silence. Whether it was the fact that we were the only souls in the garden and this was itself a private place, I do not know, but I felt the awkwardness of walking in the company of a white woman recede, until we seemed two friends beyond colour enjoying a stroll. She remarked on the way in which plants with the same colouration but very different foliage had been set together to produce an interest, and I replied that this was a quality of the garden I had entirely missed during my earlier turn.

"Nature has much to teach us, Mr Douglass, if only we know how to look."

"That is, Miss Pease, not a form of argument with which I have much sympathy for I have heard too many times at home the use of such analogies to justify the continued enslavement of my people."

"And I have heard many such here, used to underpin the continued theft of life and its joys from working people. But it is not nature which is at fault, rather the manner in which we look and take understanding from what we perceive."

I could not but agree with this point, and so we continued to walk in the quiet peacefulness of the garden.

Yet now that I am sat in my room in the late afternoon, I cannot avoid the whirl of confusion that this meeting has set in train in my mind. I would have wished to have told you of my decisions, rather than merely have visited my uncertainties upon you.

I am, though, still

Your
Frederick

DOUGLASS'S LETTER TO HARRIET
JULY 21, 1846

My dear Harriet,

Surely, your letter could not have come at a worse time for me, for I remain caught within a network of confusions in relation to my position here. And now this! I know that, as your brother, I cannot forbid this marriage but I would ask, nay urge, that you reconsider. Not merely for my part or that of my family, but for your own welfare. I know nothing of this man you say intends to make you his wife, and from your previous silence about him I can only infer that you know very little of him.

Even if my position here were not so desperate, Haughton having failed to send me any profits from the sale of the *Narrative*, I would be loath indeed to finance the purchase of a wedding dress for my sister, my beloved sister, to be married to a man I have never met and of whose prospects and future plans I know nothing.

Frederick

My dearest Anna,

On reflection I regret most sincerely the tone I adopted in my letter to sister Harriet yesterday and if it were not already mailed, I would have it back. Tell her that she must blame my tone upon my present agitations here, and that I regret my harsh words. Please, also, give her the attached monies.

This last comes as a loan from Miss Richardson, for I am now returned to Newcastle. When I explained my difficulties, and my regret at the words I had used to my faithful sister, she advanced me the money I have enclosed with this, saying that she would not have my commitment to the cause give me any private anguish. I knew, though, from the way in which she said this and from the look with which she favored me, that she did mean only this present matter. I avoided, though, any reference to our previous conversation, saying that until I knew your mind on the subject I could say nothing.

I would, then, urge you again to speak your mind, that I may know what you would have me do.

Your
Frederick

My dearest Anna,

We have had a series of the very finest meetings here in Newcastle these last three afternoons and evenings. Each afternoon I have addressed a different circle of the city's women, urging that they use all their influence and effort to keep the question of the abolition of slavery before the attention of their husbands, who are among the most influential in all the city. Each time I have stressed the unchristian nature of slavery, and drawn the analogy between Pharaoh and the Jews, and the slaveholders and our people. And then at night, I have spoken to crowds which have grown bigger each night, to argue that slavery is an abomination against the brothers and sisters of my audience across the ocean.

Miss Richardson has come with me to all six occasions, and quizzes me at length after each about the forms of words I have employed. She is a very fine auditor, for her praise is not for itself and her criticisms are always designed to give greater strength to my next effort. No subject is banned from our debates, and so I have discussed my two dilemmas with her even though she acknowledges herself to be the cause of one of them. She says I should set that consideration aside, and debate the philosophy of the matter with her. She has a very fine mind and I find myself drawn into a democracy of the intellect with her. So intent are our debates, that on two occasions now I have not noticed when she has taken my arm when we have been walking, so intent on the argument have I been. Only afterwards have I realised that this has happened, and seen how easily I overleap one of the petty hurdles of colour prejudice in the land of the free!

I also feel forearmed for the arrival of Garrison, whose ship's arrival is announced for the next few days. Geography demands that, once I have concluded my business here, I will travel south to Sheffield and meet him there within the next week. In the mean time, Thompson and Vincent are announced as coming from Glasgow in time for the last great assembly in Newcastle, the day after tomorrow.

Every day, meanwhile, I wait on news from you that will tell your mind on the matter that has been at the very front of my thinking this last three weeks. Even though I know by the time you receive this, I will have your reply, I cannot forebear but to ask you once more to tell me what you would have me do.

Your
Frederick

Whatever the problems I may be encountering myself, I know also how important it is that I continue with my work. I cannot allow the circumstances which assail my own life to distract from the larger tasks which present themselves to me. I am, at least as much as I am my own man, in the palm of history.

After the successes of the first series of meetings here in Newcastle, I was anxious for the arrival of Thompson and Vincent, that we might press home the advantage we had gained over the friends of the man-stealers. I was also, though, anxious on account of their appearance for other reasons; namely, that I wondered how they or I might raise the subject of the planned new association for the cause, of which none has seen fit to tell me even though my presence at the forthcoming founding meeting is already advertised.

I had hoped to question them both at the earliest opportunity, but the circumstances of their arrival made that impossible, for the local friends had arranged that they be met with some pomp when they disembarked from the train. They had come from Glasgow, via Edinburgh, and as a consequence both were tired and a little shaken. They bore up well, though, in the face of the gathering in the station that they were expected to address and were then carried directly to a meeting with the city mayor. With his chains of office, about which Thompson was later rather witty, and his officious manner, he kept us for some time in the entrance hall of the city chambers but after Vincent and Thompson had made their replies, a smaller party was invited to the mayor's parlour for sherry or tea or coffee - all of which I declined by virtue of various and different convictions.

So it was, then, that it was not until almost the very minute before the three of us were to be announced onto the stage of that evening's meeting that I had the chance to ask them both what was afoot, and why it was that no-one had seen fit to invite my opinions on the matters at hand. They both showed surprise - whether feigned or not I cannot tell - that I had been kept in ignorance of developments, but both also said that that moment was not the time to have the discussion. Then, as Vincent proceeded us onto the stage, George Thompson leaned close and hissed that honesty in the cause is a mutual affair and that it would be well that I did not ride too high on the hobby-horse of my feigned offence at the activities of others.

What exactly he might mean by this I cannot tell, but I know now that I must be careful these next few days, that I do not assume that they know one thing when it might be entirely another that they hold against me. Indeed, it may be that they know nothing, and all this is a white sham to keep me in my place. All may be resolved by Garrison's arrival. That is my hope

DOUGLASS'S LETTER TO ANNA
JULY 28, 1846

My dearest Anna,

We have had the finest meeting here in Newcastle yet, at which both of our recent arrivals spoke with great vigor even despite the rigors of their journey here. With Vincent before and Thompson after, I felt my speech flanked by two of the greatest friends of our enslaved brethren in this country.

Knowing as they did that this was to be the last of our meetings here for some time, the audience made sterling efforts to fill the collection plates that were passed, that we might be given a good sending off. They also approved a motion from the chairman that as many copies as could be spared of my *Narrative*' be sent to the city as soon as possible, that our message might be carried even into the homes of those who could not be present that night. With a great roar and much applause, the meeting ended.

We leave tomorrow, to make our way to Sheffield, for news of Garrison's imminent arrival has now reached us. With that mighty sword of the cause of the abolition of slavery to hand, we shall cut a swathe through the south of England and sweep away any still-remaining opposition or indifference.

Your,
Frederick

DOUGLASS'S LETTER TO HARRIET
JULY 28, 1846 (ATTACHED TO THE PREVIOUS)

My dearest sister,

I would take this opportunity to apologise for the tone of my last letter to you in the most heartfelt fashion, for it was my last intention to seem to be either ungrateful for your efforts or unmindful of your needs. I was more than a little taken down by the timing of your letter, that is all, and responded in a manner I now can see was unfriendly.

Nevertheless, the substance of my argument remains the same, that I cannot approve a union with a man of whom I know nothing and of whom you yourself seem to know very little. I stand ready and indeed even willing to be persuaded otherwise, but until that happens I cannot give my consent to your marriage.

Your loving brother,
Frederick

DOUGLASS'S LETTER TO ANNA
JULY 29, 1846

Harriet,

be sure that this letter does not pass into the hands of any of Garrison's lieutenants for the time being. Indeed, it would be as well to deny its existence until such time as I indicate otherwise.

My dearest Anna,

As soon as we had stepped down from the platform, I demanded of Vincent and Thompson that they tell me what was afoot, that a challenge to the established ranks of the friends of the cause in this country was to be mounted, and to be mounted without any discussion with myself. The former replied that this had been under debate for some considerable time now, and that in one way my presence in the country at this time was not relevant to that discussion. This was, he said, a matter of strategy as much as anything that was being reviewed by people long in the cause.

Nevertheless, I replied, I did feel that as a member of the enslaved race who was present in the country, who has given up his family life and home for the cause, I could have been consulted on this strategy. For it revealed itself to me, and I thought to many others, as tactic rather than as strategy and that therefore it would be as well to have considered how such changes of direction might impact upon the public perception of ourselves. To which Vincent replied that he cared not a fig for how the public perceived us, only that we were successful in our endeavor.

To which I answered that I thought part of our success rested on our ability to command the support of the public. Without them at our side, we were not powerful enough to put aside slavery. Vincent said he thought they were ever behind us, and that we should be leading them on into pathways they had not yet seen as part of the route they must tread. Our job is as much the education of our support as the winning of their support.

With which I concurred, saying that this was one of the major reasons for my authoring the Narrative.

At which point Thompson interjected that he would be most interested to hear what other motives I had had in its writing. The insolence of his tone was unmistakable, especially as this was his first contribution to our discussion. I said that the desire to prove myself to be who I was, was also a part of my reasons, for so many had suggested that I was other than what I claimed.

"Indeed, sir, I cannot imagine why that might be," Thompson continued.

"I am not sure why you have chosen to adopt this manner

with me, Mr Thompson, for I have always considered you a friend since our first meeting. If anything has happened to alter your view since we last parted on good terms, I would be grateful if you would say what it was."

"It is just that I find your demands that others be open and honest in all things a little, how shall I put it, a little ironic."

"If you have something to say to me, sir, I would prefer that you say it directly instead of hedging it around with cryptic remarks."

"I, and several others, have had conversations with James Buffum."

"Concerning what?"

"Concerning your claim to have been in Scotland at a time when Buffum is quite clear that you were not!"

"I had private business, sir, that I needed to conclude."

"Hah!"

"Do you not believe me?"

"Whether I believe you or not is an irrelevancy!"

"I take that comment very ill, sir."

"I do not care how you take it. For I will not be judged by someone whose own criteria would show himself to be lacking. You have the gall, Douglass, to accuse us of not having been open with you!"

"Gentlemen, gentlemen, I do not care one jot who has been open or closed with whom. All I care is that we make the best moves we can to build a movement capable of inflicting the death-blow to slavery. Slavery of all kinds, Mr Douglass. I know that you and I will disagree as to the nature of political slavery in this country, but if through drawing a number of movements together we can construct a solid wall against slavery then what can be your objection?"

"My objection, sir, is to the manner in which this has been done!"

"What matter the means when the end is so good?"

"The matter is the insult I feel that has been done to my race."

"Your ego, more likely!"

"Thompson, you and I have been friends in the cause of the overthrow of injustice for many years now, so hear me carefully. Just as I do not care who has wronged in one direction, I do not care who has wronged in the other. But I do know that neither you nor I will ever know how it is to feel the gaze of another fall upon us as though we were no more than a beast, a piece of property to be set against a balance sheet and nothing more. Some small sense of that has come to us from Mr Douglass's writings and speeches. Only some small sense, but it would be as well that we take notice of that and be sure we are scrupulous in our dealings with him, that we do not replicate the attitude of the slaver. I would ask that you both consider for a moment that you may in some small part be wrong and that the other may have some right about him."

Before Vincent's quiet reason, the squall that had blown up between myself and Thompson was calmed. I knew there was considerable rightness in what he said. Then he continued.

"Mr Douglass, we have acted in the way we thought right. I accept without reserve that the manner of our action may have caused you some sense of ill-feeling but that was not our intent. What was, was the consideration of how best we might further the cause of the end of slavery in the Americas, and we considered that this was best achieved through the connection of the condition of the American slaves to analogous conditions here, that we might draw in all who would see the end of brutality and injustice to a great and overarching cause, and that to achieve that end we have set out to construct a new party that pulls all these threads together. We have done this because it has become clear to us that the old organisations here have moved to become a block to this and we have therefore no option but to go past them."

"But I can see no analogy between what I have seen here and what I know to be the condition of the slaves at home. The slave is a chattel, the workman is free to come and go."

"We are not arguing a concurrence in all things between the two, but rather that there are analogies, points of contact where one condition may shed light upon the other."

"I disagree!"

"Douglass," Thompson took me by the elbow. I shrugged his hand away with some force but he took me by the arm again until I turned to look him in the eye. "First, I would make an apology for my earlier tone. As ever, Henry's good sense has reminded me of the proportions of our debate. Let me ask you a question. Were you ever beaten?"

"You know I was! What point is there to this?"

He pushed a piece of paper, a piece of newspaper, into my hand.

It told the story of a private soldier, John Frederick White, who had been flogged to death while serving in the British army. The account made much of the petty nature of the man's offences, when compared with the irreversible punishment inflicted upon him. He waited in silence while I read the piece and then, when I looked up, said,

"You see?"

"I see that this man was wrongly flogged to death, and I know that whoever beat him in such a fashion deserves to have the mighty hand of the law fall upon him. What I do not see is what this case has to do with the cause of the abolition of slavery in the United States of America."

"It is analogy we seek, Douglass, analogies that may bring those who are of one cause into alliance with those who are of a different, but analogous, cause. So that, together, they may strike a harder blow than they may strike separately."

"The force of a blow is irrelevant, unless it be well-directed."

"We feel that we cannot fail to strike home, with such a large target in view."

"The large target of man's injustice to man?"

"Exactly so!"

"A target I think more resilient than you, clearly."

"Why so?"

"Because I do not think, on the basis of my own experience, that something so long-lasting, so rooted in the human soul, is so easily pulled up as by an alliance between those who hate chattel slavery in my country and those who abhor the flogging of soldiers in this."

"It is a step on the road."

"So is the bringing-down of one form of injustice in one place at one time!"

We would have continued thus, I am sure, for the rest of the night had not our friends in the north of England come to take us to the reception organised to bid us farewell. For the rest of the evening, I was distracted by the demands of a social gathering and then, later, by thinking over how it was that I was to take my farewell from the Richardsons, who have been such good friends.

Late in the evening, I found myself seated alone in a small carriage with Miss Ellen, for her brother and sister-in-law had excused themselves earlier. We rode in silence through the now-darkened streets, for I was near-overwhelmed with a great mixture of feelings: from anger with several people I considered my friends, and with myself for having given up the hostage to Buffum by staging such a transparent fraud in Ireland; from sadness that I was about to leave the company of people whom I had come very quickly to think of as my close and dear friends. This, and a great deal more, was passing through my thoughts with such intensity that I did not, at first, hear Miss Ellen speak to me.

"You must excuse me, Miss Ellen. I am much distracted this evening."

"On what grounds, Frederick? Please do not feel that you must keep anything from me, unless you wish so to do."

"There is a dispute with the cause at the moment, concerning the best strategy to carry our arguments forward."

"Between which arguments?"

"Between those who would concentrate on the one injustice of chattel slavery and those who would broaden the cause to include every form of wrong that mankind ever invented."

"Indeed? Do the latter faction argue so foolishly?"

Her question was asked at a quiet volume but nevertheless I could detect within her voice a tone which demanded that I consider my formulation again.

"Perhaps not quite so, but they would have an alliance made between all who would in some way show an opposition to a range of injustices which they think of as connected by what they term analogy. Which I cannot see."

"Because your own condition blinds you?"

"No, madam!"

She looked at me across the carriage. I could see her face, yet could not clearly fix her expression. Yet her silence told me what look was upon her face more clearly than if we had stood in the street in the middle of a sunny day.

"No, madam, I think not. I have merely argued that the differences are greater than the connections between the condition of slavery and the conditions of injustice endured by free men."

"Why do you think I have never married?"

Her question so entirely surprised me, that I had no answer.

"Is it because I am so plain, or indeed even repulsive, that no man would think of having me?"

"Indeed not!"

"I thank you for your vehemence. So then, tell me what you think."

"I do not know."

"Because by marriage I would become my husband's chattel. That is the law in this country. So, I do not know to what supposed parallels between slaves and free men you may have objection, but I do know that my own adherence to the cause of the abolition of slavery has its roots in the same ground which has kept me a spinster. For my love of my liberty is greater than my fear of a childless old age."

I did not know what to say to this, so I sat in silence until she asked another question.

"Do you suppose the life led by private soldiers in the British army is so agreeable to them that they stay within the discipline of their own free will?"

"I do not understand the purpose of your question."

"It is simple enough."

I felt now as I supposed many of her pupils must have felt when placed under a withering inspection of their insufficiencies of knowledge.

"I have no real knowledge of life within the British army, Miss Ellen. You know that as well as I and therefore should understand why I cannot answer."

"Then why do you presume to know that there are no parallels between your life and that of John Frederick White?"

"Who is he?"

But as soon as I asked, I remembered the name.

"Was he free to come and go as he pleased, to work when he chose and then move off to another employment when he tired of soldiering? Tell me, Frederick, in what ways other than in name was he a free man?"

"I do not know!"

"Then why do you resist with such insistence those who do? Those who know both circumstances and can see the link between them, the thread which ties them into the greater bundle of wrong? I fear, Frederick, that this weakness flows from one of your strengths."

"I fail to understand your meaning."

"I mean that your belief in your own rightness, which has been such a tower to you in the years of slavery's darkness, may now be blinding you to the rightness of other people. George Thompson may not know how the lash of slavery feels on his own back, but I think he may know that one lash feels very much the same as another. I fear that your awareness of your own position may have blinded you to the need for sympathy for that of other poor suffering souls. There, I have said it."

She now sank back into her seat, as though exhausted or perhaps relieved of a great burden. I did not know what to say, for I think I knew at that moment in my heart that she was right. Not that my determination to free our suffering brothers and sisters from bondage has ever wavered, but that this imperative had blinded me to the suffering all around me.

"But the doctrine I learned from the very first moment I came within the circles of the cause was that slavery was the greatest evil of my country and that it must be purged in order that the country might show itself to be the home of civilisation that it claimed. I learned that at the hand of Garrison and Phillips, and now it seems that one of these two has turned aside from that."

"No! As I understand the matter, all that Garrison would argue is that for the cause to grow here in Britain it must have a connection which reaches into the lives of those less affected by the purely moral argument. Nothing more than that. He will not say, as I understand it, that slavery is in any way decreased as an evil by this move, that it does not remain the main target. Simply, that we need to gather in all the forces that we can muster to strike a mighty blow."

"Then why has no-one said this to me before? I admit, that half my suspicion flows from the fact that I discovered this move by accident, when shown a letter by your good friend Miss Pease, who was most taken aback that I knew nothing of what was proposed. Why was this discussion kept from me?"

"I cannot tell."

And, it seems, no other here can, or will, tell why this was. I must wait for Garrison's arrival to know the roots of this concealment. Yet I cannot forbear from the thought that part of the difficulty he and his lieutenants have had with this decision is that they cannot think of me as their equal in these tactical and strategic discussions. I am a man who can tell a story, and tell that story of bondage and escape to good effect, but that the philosophy of the cause is beyond me. They would have me tell the facts of my life, but would reserve the thinking for their white selves.

Your,
Frederick

My dear sister Harriet,
I must urge that you employ the same caution with this document as with its predecessor. When there is a moment of quiet here, I will write to your good self further on the matters which pertain directly to ourselves.

Your brother,
Frederick.

DOUGLASS'S LETTER TO ANNA
AUGUST 2, 1846

My dearest Anna,
The journey from Newcastle to Sheffield was a silent undertaking, for I knew that there was little point in raising the matters closest to my heart with either Vincent or Thompson, for even if they were disposed to a discussion with me, their knowledge of the roots of the matter was so slender that I would learn nothing of great import from them. After they had peremptorily deposited me at the hotel here, they continued on their way to London, to make preparations for the meetings there.

So it was that it was a great relief to move from their silent company to the silent isolation of this hotel room, where I will wait for Garrison's arrival. An event which is scheduled for the near future, for his ship was announced at Liverpool yesterday. If I know one thing about that man, even despite the confusions into which my consideration of him has been thrown these last few days, then I know that he will not idle on the triviality of renewing acquaintances along the way even with his closest British friends but he will strike to the heart of the matter as he sees it. So it is that I expect him at any moment.

It is a great irony that even as I wrote those words, there was a knock upon the door, which announced his arrival. The boy sent up from the desk was barely into his announcement, when he was brushed aside and there in the doorway stood William Lloyd Garrison.

As he stood there, with his hand outstretched and looking as he ever did with his tie pulled loose from the collar, the sweat glistening on his bald forehead on even the coldest day from the heat of the brain beneath the skin and his eyes burning out from behind the tiny lenses of his spectacles, I forgave him everything. Forgave the year-long silence, forgave what seemed to me as subterfuge. For what I remembered was that day in Nantucket five years hence almost to the day when this man stood before me with his hand outstretched just as he stood now, saying that he had heard many speeches against slavery but none as directly moving as that which I had just delivered. Though it was the first time that I had ever done such in public, I knew then when he asked if I would be prepared to come into the cause that my life until then had been leading to that moment; and I know now that my life since has taken its main purpose and meaning from this man. It was his example that persuaded me that there were white men who would take the plight of the enslaved into their own free hearts and give up their lives for the end of bondage.

We stood, clasping hands, for several moments together and looking into each other's eyes. His gaze melted my doubts.

He let the silence last but a few moments, though, before he began with a procession of questions about how matters had progressed in the time that I had been here. He had had, he said, reports from numerous people but wished to know from me what my exact thoughts were. When I reminded him that my letters to yourself had been passed along to be used by the cause in whatever fashion they saw fit, he looked at me directly and asked if these letters told the whole of the story. I felt then as a child caught out in a lie of omission by a parent, and thanked my mother's memory that she had given me skin which does not easily show a blush.

I replied, though, that I had been perturbed by the proposal to found a new organisation to express the cause here in Britain when at my arrival I had been directed into the company of the existing parties. To which he replied by way of the arguments that I have already half-accepted; that the need was for a broad party, which drew in all those who had an interest in wrongs both connected to and analogous with slavery. All this said almost in the manner of delivering a public address, with much gesturing of the hands. I made no argument here, but straightaway asked why no-one had spoken with me over these proposals.

Again, he took me by the arm and looked me in the face. He said that there were those who had expressed the opinion that I was not wholly in the camp of the cause. I replied quite hotly that as far as I was aware there were no others in this country who could count themselves as ever having been in the camp of bondage in quite the manner I had been. I asked, further, the names of those who had shown so little trust in me that they would say such things in private letters to others but never express such feelings to my face. He said he could not tell me. I replied that the truth was, that he would not tell for whatever reasons he might have. He said he was no tittle-tattle, to which I replied - this time rather hotly - that even if that were the case, and I did believe that it was, that it did seem nevertheless that he had acquired the habit of listening to such.

He had no argument to this and we stood for a moment looking into each other's faces and there was a moment here when I thought that our friendship might be about to founder on the rocks of a white man's propensity to listen to other white strangers before he would hear his black companions. Yet then, he drew his breath deep and admitted that it would have been better had he asked my version of the rumors before springing to conclusions. Having said which, he asked if there were any substance to the noises he had heard that I was not wholly within the camp but had been distracted. I asked if he had any reason other than the gossip to believe that this was the case. To which he replied that he had not; indeed he was encouraged beyond his expectations by what had transpired during my time here in Britain so that he began to think even that the tide of public opinion might be turning in its majority to our side.

He was, he said, enormously pleased and proud by what I had done during my tour. He gripped me by the shoulders, and I felt for the briefest moment as though I were within the grasp of the father that I never had and now beyond the reach of the father who has denied me all my life. But then this epiphany faded, for Garrison released me and tried to turn the conversation into a new path, to whit whether or no I would speak at the founding meeting in London. To which I replied as I stepped back that I would, that Miss Richardson and Miss Pease had together convinced me that this was the right strategy and that I would concur.

He seemed, I have to say, a little taken aback at this but recovered to say that he was glad that whatever barriers had been raised between us were now set aside.

And so it is, for it is his existence, his presence, which I can see I have needed at my side to remind myself of what is important and what is not. People may quarrel, misunderstand one another and become suspicious of one another's motives in action; but they must continue despite all this to act in the cause which they think right, or they are lost.

We leave directly for London.

Your,
Frederick

My dearest Anna,

I am returned to London. Four days in the company of that bright flame and I am quickened. To be here with Garrison is to be drawn into the company of perhaps the very best men and women in Britain; those who would call themselves his friends and companions. We stopped on the way from Sheffield to London, so that I might fulfil an engagement to speak in Newcastle-under-Lyme which I had made some time since. Despite being with me, Garrison forbore to speak on this occasion but merely sat quiet at the back of the hall, saying he wished only to listen.

It was a strange occasion for me, to take the stage as the centre of the evening while elsewhere in the hall he sat unremarked and indeed almost unnoticed. I could not prevent myself, even as I spoke, from glancing repeatedly to where he sat at the rear of the chapel half-lost in the gloom beneath the choir and organ balcony. He sat intently throughout the evening, showing no signs of approbation or displeasure at any point but only at the end of night when we were retired to the house of our hosts, he clapped me upon the back and said that I had done a thoroughly good job.

We departed by rail for London early the next morning and we were both engrossed in our own affairs for much of the journey. He in the unceasing writing of letters - I do not know how he can achieve this in the rattling and bumping atmosphere, but he does and has done as long as we have known each other - and I in reading a novel. I know that this is a rare event for me, but this came to my hands recommended most highly by one of our hosts who the previous day had told me that I might find this work by one of my countrymen at least diverting on the tedious journey we were embarked upon. My preparations for the coming Temperance Convention in London being completed, I was happy to take this chance at a break from my normal routines and spent the day reading in this "narrative of a four months' residence among the natives of a valley of the Marquesas Islands" which Miss Ellen has given to me, saying how much she has enjoyed it. Though it is mostly fanciful stuff, the sort of travel writing designed to assuage a reader's feelings that they might need actually to visit a place themselves whilst granting them knowledge of the place in the much cheaper form of a hard cover, the author does seem to understand that the line between civilisation and savagery is drawn not by the color of the skin but by the behavior of its inhabitant. I was also interested to note that we are very much of an age with each other, and have resolved that I should keep an eye for any further works this promising start produces, though I cannot see what he might do after this tale.

This fiction kept me amused and even interested until the very outskirts of London and though it is very rare indeed for me to spend a day in the reading of novels, I did not feel that my time had been wasted.

When we emerged from the train, there was a small crowd there to welcome us upon our various returns to the great city, at the heart of which stood George Thompson. I forgave him much of what he had said directly to me, and also what I suspected he had said in letters to the man by my side, when I saw the expressions of clear and definite friendship exchanged between himself and Garrison. I was reminded that these two had stood shoulder to shoulder in the cause for over a dozen years, and that without them there would have been no mechanisms for the safe passage of my brothers and sisters out of bondage and on to a place of safety. Thompson made a very fine little public speech of welcome to Garrison and reminded also those present that London was very fortunate to have myself back walking its streets.

We grasped each other by the hand as soon as ever we had the chance and resolved to be as brothers in the cause of the end of injustice. Then he led the two of us away to a waiting carriage and on to his house. When, in the course of the journey, I raised again the subject of my recent anger and disagreement with him, he replied that it was forgotten already on his part and that now all were resolved to work hand in hand to bring down slavery, it should become an incident of the past, trivial as all the other ancient disputes.

His house is most pleasant, and we were all soon installed there. Dinner was an extremely convivial affair, and drew in several friends of the cause from other parts of the city, some of whom I had not yet had the opportunity to meet. After which, I was very glad to retire to my bed and I slept soundly despite being back in the bustle of London.

Yesterday morning, we were all awake early to make our final preparations for the Temperance convention and then left to walk to Covent Garden. Along the way, we had reason on several occasions to stop and speak with small groups of bystanders who were curious to know why such a small procession was proceeding through the streets at such an early hour. I have to say that I was both surprised and a little shocked to discover that many of these London workers had not heard of the convention and indeed when its purpose was explained seemed rather unsympathetic to the mission of temperance. One, indeed, wagged a fist in our general direction saying that if we had to work all hours such as he did, we too might feel the need to seek consolation in strong drink. I remarked to Thompson that this reminded me of those of my brothers and sisters on Thomas Auld's plantation who took solace in regular Sunday drinking bouts, to which he replied that the two cases were so very different that there was no useful comparison to be made. Which I found a little odd, but had no time to pursue with him because the next minute we were arrived at the hall and within minutes were being seated among all the other delegates.

And what a magnificent assembly it was, of supporters of the temperance pledge from all around the globe! I saw my old companion from Ireland, Father Theobald Mathew, seated among a crowd of his supporters, and many another friend of the mission. The event began with all the usual messages of welcome, one from her majesty the queen, and the exchange of greetings between all the delegations. Then began the speeches and I must admit that, it being a warm and even stuffy room and myself being more than a little tired from the travelling I had done recently, I began to nod. When suddenly I was returned to full consciousness by the eruption of Garrison out of the seat next to me, demanding that he be allowed to respond to the previous speaker. I was half brushed aside as Garrison hurried past me and moved down through the hall towards the dais mounted on the stage. As soon as he began to speak I gathered that one of the American delegates, Edward Kirk, had made some comment in his speech that Garrison had interpreted as being pro-slavery and was now being excoriated extempore. It was Garrison at his best, speaking off the cuff and with great and focused indignation; to any who had not seen him before it would have been the most extravagant sight. He would have carried all before him, had not certain members of the other American delegation made such a determined attempt to interrupt and throw down his speech, claiming that this was nothing to do with the main business of the day or indeed of the convention. I could see, in their protests, the strategy of prevailing by insisting on the separation of matters more honestly linked together and I rose, asking that I be allowed to speak in support of Garrison. There was a deal of disturbance at this point, from members of that delegation from which Kirk had emerged, and also in opposition to them from our friends in the hall. At length, I was called to the dais and given five minutes to address the assembly. I began simply and straightforwardly by thanking for having allowed me into the hall and then, turning towards that delegation, I continued by saying that it was greater courtesy than I had come to expect at home, where not only where people of my color not allowed to enter meetings of the American Temperance movement but their parades were

often attacked by gangs of whites who would prefer to see the Negro reduced to the state of an animal by strong drink than that they be allowed to join in with the mission to end such abuse of God-given bodies. I finished by saying that I for one was glad that the absence of color prejudice on this side of the Atlantic had allowed me to sign the pledge and before stepping down, gestured my thanks to Father Theobald Mathew in his seat in an upper gallery. There was great applause as I returned to my seat, which overwhelmed the abuse and gestures from the American delegates, but then the chairman of the convention moved a motion that Mr Kirk be requested to withdraw his statement and that Mr Garrison be requested to make no further outbursts. Kirk accepted immediately, knowing that this bound no other member of that insolent delegation but that it would silence Garrison. Who also read the motion in this way, and said that he was withdrawing forthwith from the convention, and he swept out of the hall to the clear delight of American delegates.

Our small group was now in some confusion as to our future procedures, and this prevented us from making any properly useful contribution for the rest of the day. Not that we would have especially wished so to do, for after this engagement the convention subsided into what I can only describe as sententious torpor thereafter.

I walked home with Thompson, with whom I now feel entirely reconciled, but when we arrived we discovered that Garrison had returned in a state of considerable agitation and had then left, saying that he was going to visit old companions in the town of Gravesend and would return presently.

I would rather that he had remained here, for I have not yet had the opportunity to discuss with him Miss Richardson's offer which, in the absence of any objection from yourself, I have decided to accept. Yet I would know his mind on this before I am entirely settled. I cannot tell how he will react, and know that it is this which keeps me awake until this hour, waiting on his return.

Your,
Frederick

My dear Phillips,

This is the first occasion I have had to write to you since arriving and even though it is not the most propitious circumstances I have nevertheless taken the chance. I am seated on a railroad train, in company with Douglass, on the way to London; where we will begin the public excoriation of the slavers and their friends within the Temperance movement.

Douglass is, I think, wholly returned to our camp. I am confident of this not only because we had an opportunity to speak long and hard to each other when we first met and also because I have had the chance to hear him on a platform. Only this previous evening, I heard him lecture on slavery in a small town close by the homes of our old friends the Wedgewoods. It was no small revelation to hear and see what bounds he has made since we last shared a stage together. His speech made such an impression that I find I can recall whole portions verbatim even the next day. It was strong stuff indeed!

He began by describing the differences between slavery and other forces which are sometimes given the same name, and I knew by that that he still had our discussion in his mind. His arguments, though, were none with which I would disagree, for he emphasised the gap of cruelty which extends between chattel slavery and other systems of oppression, and on that we are agreed. But then he moved into two passages of the most outstanding rhetoric both of which I will reproduce below for you, to see the ground he has made as a speaker:

"Cruelty marks every part of the system. The slave cannot be held as a slave without cruelty. Men don't go into slavery naturally - they don't go into slavery at the bidding of their fellow men - they don't bow down their necks to the yoke merely be being entreated to do so - the whip must be there - the chain must be there - the gag must be there - the thumb screw must be there", each of these phrases was accompanied by a great gesturing with the relevant implement and then he paused a long while until all were rapt for his next words, "the fear of death must be there, in order to induce the slave to go to the field and labor for another man without wages."

He then concluded by saying,

"I wish the slave owners to know that one of their slaves has broken loose from chains, and is going the length and breadth of England, spreading before the people of England the damning deeds, that are perpetrated under the veil of slavery. I want them to know that one who has broken through the dark incrustation of slavery, is lifting the veil by which the abominations of the slave system in the United States has been so long hidden from the Christian world".

All this made a great impact upon the audience, who were moved in great ways by his words and passed all manner of resolutions of support that would have had greater force had we already founded the new Anti-Slavery League as a conduit for their energies. That will come.

It is, though, in the position of a speaker that we need to hold Frederick. He needs to recognise that his greatest use to the cause is as a teller of his story, as a mover of people's hearts, while others of us move their heads and their pockets. Indeed, it is as a teller of his story that he has done extraordinary work and he has entirely vindicated the decision - if we can call that which was largely compelled by necessity a decision - to send him here. Whatever other criticisms our friends in the cause here have of him, they are all united in the opinion that he has already done great work in winning the minds of the British public to our side; I have every confidence that the history of his own people and also that of ours will remember him for this if nothing else.

Yet I do wish that we had chosen his travelling companion with greater consideration, for Buffum does not now seem to me to have been much of a match for Frederick's strength of will. He seems not to have been able to curb any of his more extravagant excesses and, whilst nothing public of any note has happened to harm our cause - indeed, Frederick has been scrupulous in his behavior on every count that matters - there are rumors, hints and words whispered behind hands that leave me a little uneasy. Nothing definite occurs to me, but I am left with the sense that the man here is not the man I came to know in New Bedford. He seems to have an independence which I know I should applaud were it not that I feel a kind of father's love for him, and feel that ambivalence that afflicts every parent when a child ceases to be wholly within the grasp.

Yet we will talk on these matters when we have time to ourselves. At the moment, we are both engrossed in our work and we both know that our arrival in London will only signify a greater increase in the level of activity. We plan, as an interlude before the work of founding the new Anti-Slavery League, to attend the Temperance convention. Frederick has taken the pledge and is now wholly within this camp as well. I feel sure that all will be settled within days and look forward to that day when I can write this as definite news rather than as informed speculation.

Yours, to the'end,
Wm. Garrison

GARRISON'S LETTER TO HELEN
AUGUST 9, 1846

My dearest,

A week here, and still no letter from you!

That week has been filled with activity - preparation for the formation of the Anti-Slavery League tomorrow evening, visiting a number of old friends to convince them of the rightness of this move, and attending the Temperance convention. This latter, I admit and I am sure you will hear, was not my best performance, for I lost my temper and instead of holding the line against the disgraceful behavior of Kirk and others, I allowed myself to be provoked into walking out of the convention. I was so angry that I took myself off to Gravesend to visit Mrs Thompson and the children, for she has left George alone in the city for the summer. I fear that my precipitous departure - I walked straight from the Covent Garden hall to the railroad station - left George alone also. Alone with Frederick Douglass, with whom George has been jousting during much of this year about the former's supposed sympathies with the Catholic Irish; sympathies that extend, the rumors say, beyond a human fellow-feeling for those suffering privation and even starvation, towards advocating some version of Irish independence. I wish I knew more of this situation, for it is clear from the brief conversations we have had that George is much exercised by what he sees as Douglass's meddling in a British affair.

Even though it has been but a week, I already have felt the need to retreat from this maelstrom of clashing egos and knew that Mrs Thompson would be the ideal person in your absence. The depths of her calmness - for she is never shaken from her stance, no matter what the circumstance - is an example to us all of how we might live our lives. We were walking upon the promenade within a very few minutes of my breathless arrival, for she was only perturbed that there was no lunch for me to take because of my unexpected and unannounced appearance and she wished to remove me from the house until such could be prepared. She finds great solace in the movement of the tides and breezes, and within a very short period of being returned to her company, I found myself calmer than I have been than the last time she and I walked thus - more than eleven years hence!

I spent a gloriously quiet time in the company of herself and the children, having sent word that I would return to London today, to complete the preparations for tomorrow. Even now, as I sit on the train returning there and thinking of you, I can feel the tension returning to me; for not only must tomorrow go well if we are to progress with our mission here, but I have word that Douglass waits to speak to me on my immediate return on a matter that cannot wait.

Yours ever,
WLG

<hr />

DOUGLASS'S LETTER TO ANNA
AUGUST 9, 1846

My dearest Anna,

Though it is extremely late in the evening, I know that I will not sleep until I have written to you and told what has happened. For my path, it seems to me, is now clear before me even though it may seem almost entirely obscured to another looking at my actions from without. This may be ever thus, that we cannot know the workings of another person's mind but becomes still more the case when I know that the majority of spectators are white men and women who have no conception of what it is to be black in their world and neither do they have any wish to make the leap that might give them the smallest insight.

When Garrison did not straightaway return from his visit to Mrs Thompson at Gravesend, I sent word that I wished to speak with him on his return on a matter of some importance to both of us. I did this to be sure that we would have the chance to talk together even in spite of the rush of the next few days. So it was that when I had the news at Thompson's house of his train, I left for the station and was standing on the platform to greet him. We shared a few pleasantries, but I said that I wished us to be in a congenial setting before I turned to the matter uppermost in my mind. So it was that we sat in silence in the carriage from the station to Thompson's house, and in silence from there to the top of Hampstead Heath. For I wished that our conversation be had in private and in a place where we would have no interruption.

That is how I came to be seated on a park bench at the side

of a white man, looking out over one of the very greatest cities in the world, and with him waiting on my opening word. The clearer this reflection became to me, the less I felt inclined to begin, for I was caught in a reverie about the distance I have travelled in the last few years. From chattel, nay beast of burden whipped to its labor by the lash of Edward Covey, to the companion of the finest men and women of our times. I felt as though my world had been turned right way up for the first time in my life, and that now I could approach a station in life with which I would be happy. Yet I also knew that, this moment could dash all that away, for if Garrison withheld his approval of the scheme proposed by Miss Richardson, I would have to choose to tread my own path. Thereby, possibly, losing the love of this man who I had come to regard, I realised, almost as a father; certainly as the father of my present intellect. As all this passed through my mind, I became aware that Garrison was waiting for me to speak and that we had been sat for some considerable time now in silence.

Yet somehow I could not bring myself to bring the quietude which had descended between us. There have been so few moments of this sort these last few years, and especially since my arrival in these islands, that I wished to hold the moment longer. I wished to savor the pleasure of simply being seated at this man's side. Yes, because he is white and I am black and in the world in which we both live this is a fact which carries a burden but also because the fact that I regard him as my friend is a marker of how far in this world I have travelled. As you can see, my thoughts had now begun to repeat themselves and it was this that gave me the impulse to begin to speak.

I told him of my loneliness here, and of the conversations that I had had with Miss Richardson, and of her offer. He sat in silence throughout all this, and then continued to sit beside without speaking or indeed moving for several minutes more. I did not know what to make of this, for I had expected a response of some sort. Indeed, I began to think that this silence betrayed some kind of contempt towards me, that he did not even feel the need to respond. I could not look round at him, but sat there staring out over the city. I could feel the anger growing within me, that he did not even feel the need to argue with me, or even indeed to abuse me for a decision of which I knew he would disapprove. At length, this anger grew to the point where I turned abruptly towards him and was about to demand an answer when I saw his face. He seemed, somehow, to have aged years in the few minutes since I had finished speaking. I could also see that there were tears started out upon his cheeks, and that they were moving slowly and unheeded down his face.

I was struck dumb by this spectacle, dumb and frozen in place. I could not reach out to him, nor could I speak. I realised that it was not contempt or lack of feeling which had produced his silence, but rather a profound sorrow at what I had said. I was about to attempt to take back what I had said, to try and set it aside, so thoroughly returned to my heart was he at that moment. Yet before I could speak, without looking towards me, he spoke.

"It is true, then, that the river between the races is swift and treacherous to the extent that neither side can make a crossing. Perhaps it were better not even to have attempted such."

"What can you mean by that, Garrison? I have spoken to you in this fashion because you are so close to my heart. As far as ever is possible, I do not even think of you as a white man, but simply as a man. And I hoped that you had similar thoughts about myself."

"I did, Frederick, and I still do. Which is why this comes as the shock I confess it is. I see now that I could see nothing of your heart and I can only think that this is so from the color of our skins."

"How so, sir? Is it not more reasonable to suppose that it comes from the lack of communication between us these last few months. We were, in America, accustomed to telling each other our thoughts face to face or by letter all but every day. Yet these last months we have been far apart, not simply by the fact of the Atlantic ocean between us but also because neither of us have reached out to the other across its waves. I account myself as guilty in this respect as any other, but would now make amends for this as quickly as I ever can."

"But why this absence of communication? Do you not think it speaks of something more?"

"I cannot speak for you, Garrison, but I know that on my part the failing was largely caused by the whirl of events since I arrived in this country. I felt almost as though I were being born again."

He winced at this, it seemed to me.

"And so, Garrison, William, my good friend. My dearest companion and friend. Forgive me my silences, and talk with me now as we have done before. Tell me your opinion of this scheme Miss Richardson has prepared."

Again, he sat in silence but this time without the tears. I knew that, having asked, I must now needs wait on his opinion. Eventually, he slowly turned towards me and spoke almost in a whisper.

"I cannot give my sanction to such a scheme, Frederick. It flies in the face of everything I have believed and argued these last twenty years. It is a compact with the devil that you are suggesting."

"I do not think of it so. It is no compact at all, for I reject Thomas Auld's right to my body, but a stratagem to set me free all the better to assault our foes."

"He who touches pitch, is thereby defiled. Is that not the argument of the Good Lord? Would you seek to set yourself above Him?"

"No, William, I would not and I am shocked that you would think so."

"Then how can you justify this?"

"I can only by seeing that it is Miss Richardson's choice to take upon herself the burden, the odor, of being the one who is defiled. I see that as her choice, as her chosen sacrifice for the greater good of our mutual cause."

"But what will our enemies say?"

"When have you ever before taken note of them?"

He paused again.

"We are not, you are not, touched by the filth of slavery in any part of this arrangement. I see great good light in Miss Richardson, William, that she is prepared to enter this sordid world to do us good, when she knows exactly that we cannot do this."

"But Frederick, Frederick. Can you not see how we will be harmed by this?"

"I can. Yet I can also see how I will be aided."

Now, he spoke very softly and deliberately.

"So that is your motive. I had hoped that we had all moved beyond that. I had hoped that we were engaged in this crusade because we sought the downfall of slavery and the end of the bondage of fellows. But I see that that is not the case."

"You can say that, sir, because you have the luxury of being able to speak so! You will never have to face the choice that stands before me now. Do you think that this is an easy move for me, to hold myself still under the thrall of the man from whom I fled when I claimed my rights of freedom as a human being? Perhaps you were right, after all, when you said that the gulf of race lies between us. But it is not a gulf of my making! I can see into the world of the white man, because that has been the condition of my existence since the day of my birth. But I see, sir, that you are not prepared even to make the smallest effort to see into my world. I can see that you have no conception of what it means to be black in a white world - that is hardly a surprise - but what cuts me is that you seem to have no wish, no desire, even to take the tiniest step into blackness. I had thought, sir, that it was a fellow-feeling which had brought you into the cause, a wish to see your brothers and sisters free from bondage. But I see that that is not the case. I can only presume some more private and selfish motive then, is what drives you."

By now both of us had risen to our feet and we were standing squarely before each other. I had never before seen such anger in his face, and even though I knew my words were the direct cause, I could not stop myself now.

"What is it that drives you so, that you must always be of our cause whilst at the same time refusing to stand at our side? I thought that I knew the answer to this. I though I knew you, but now I see that I do not. What dark motive is it that compels you so?"

"I am aghast that you could speak so, Frederick, for I had thought these many years that my actions alone would speak loud enough for me, that I would not face this questioning. I see that it is not so, but I have no answer for you. I look within myself and all I see is the wish to be of assistance to the cause that I see as the greatest movement of our times. I have no dark motive."

Yet even as he spoke these words, he turned his face away from me and I could see that a carelessly thrown dart had been the most accurate of all. I had struck a target at which I knew, even as I found the mark, I would rather have not even essayed. And I thought, for the briefest moment, that I could snatch back those words. Yet I could see on his averted face the impossibility of this. I wished to reach out and place my hand on his shoulder, to assure him that my words were not meant; but I could not, for within my heart I knew that in some obscure sense they were, that his own words on the distance between the races were now reflected back to him and that he should see that the gap was at least as much of his making as of mine. I could not look at him any longer, and turned away.

So it was that we stood there in the early afternoon, side by side but no longer together, looking out over London towards the river Thames. What I could not see at that moment, can not see now as I write, and wonder if I will ever be able to understand, is whether or not this separation is solely between myself and Garrison or whether it is a single marker of a much larger separation. I have hoped, these last five years, that we could o'erstep the institutions of slavery by the good will and good works of those people on both sides of the racial division. But perhaps it cannot be, perhaps there is too much bad blood between us for any one friendship to overcome.

Then again, perhaps it is only by fumbling our way forward, making mistakes but being willing to acknowledge that that is what we are about, that we will make any progress. Perhaps that history which lies between us can only be set aside through generous effort on both sides.

He turned at last towards me and, because I could not look him in the face, spoke to my cheek.

"You are right, Frederick. Perhaps there are motives in my actions which lie beyond the gaze of the daylight mind. I would have you see, though, that even if they are present, they are as nothing compared to my conscious purposes. I have chosen to set aside the fellowship of my own race. My own family, my own flesh and my own blood, are as nothing to me compared to the purpose I have in bringing down the man-stealers. I have lost the number of the family occasions which have been disrupted and ended by some casual word in which was reflected some relative's contempt for what they call my madness. I see it not as a madness, though, but as the only hope for my race. For if we cannot set aside the wrongs we are doing to your people, then surely history and God will wreak upon us some terrible revenge.

In that belief, I have been willing to take on the name of madman or fool. For those insults are as pinpricks beside the guilt I should feel if I faltered in this purpose: but it cuts me when you also turn upon me. I had thought we were companions in a great cause, but now I can see that there has lain between us this abyss which I could not before see. That is my foolishness, and I would have you forgive me for it and mark it down as no more than that."

Turning, I took his proffered hand and wordlessly nodded my assent. For I knew, even before it was mentioned, what play our enemies would have of any sign of a dispute within our ranks.

"We will speak no more of this until we are through the public formation of the new Anti-Slavery League and it is well established. We are friends again and perhaps this dispute, if and when we can resolve it, will make our friendship stronger. That is a conversation, though, we need to postpone until the urgent business is behind us. The two of us, together, on a platform will put many of our opponents into confusion and the cause will take great strength from public unity.

This other matter we need not consider as a public concern and let us keep it as a private affair until we have had the time to discuss it thoroughly between us. We will, we must, find the time during our tour of the west of England. For now, though, we will wait."

This said, the two of us embraced and walked down from the heath together in great conversation concerning the matter and the manner of our speeches for tomorrow night.

I will write as soon as ever I can, with news of that event and also with intelligence concerning every other subject of concern to us both.

Your,
Frederick

DOUGLASS'S LETTER TO ANNA
AUGUST 11, 1846

My dearest Anna,

The breach seems healed and I am glad that it is so, for it enabled last night to be the success that it deserved and needed to be. We met in company with many of the great luminaries of the cause of the abolition of slavery on both sides of the Atlantic to begin anew the great work. It was agreed by all that a new party was needed, a party which openly eschewed the taking of money from the friends of slavery even by the most circuitous route - and at the same time motions of censure were passed against the Church of Scotland, the British and Foreign Anti-Slavery Society, and the World's Temperance Convention for their close and distant associations with the man stealers. It was further agreed that the new party would cast the lens of its attention over the many forms of injustice that have parallels and analogies with the chattel slavery of America, and would organise them also.

So, you see, we have a compromise in which all have given and gained. I hope with my heart that this will carry us all to the end we seek.

It was with both trepidation and satisfaction that I found myself seated among such a company. Here was Garrison, restored as my companion; there, James Buffum generously agreeing that my strategy of direct offensive against the mealy mouths of the Church of Scotland has gone well in our favor. Here was William Lovett, the old champion of change through moral argument and friend of the cause of universal brotherhood; there, George Thompson, opponent of all that can be termed oppressive. Here was Henry Vincent, the old warrior; here, by his side, was Henry Wright; there, newly arrived from Dublin with copies of my *Narrative*, James Haughton. This last plans to remain in London at least two weeks, to arrange for the publication of a new edition of the *Narrative* produced in London. He was so generous and excited that I instantly forgave him all the problems I have had with obtaining as many copies of the book as I have needed at times.

We all missed certain friends, and noted our greetings to them on this notable day. We wrote a letter to Wendell Phillips, which everyone signed, and another to Elizabeth Pease who we hear has fallen seriously ill with a congestion of the heart.

We concluded, after the tasks of publicity for the public meeting to announce the formation of the League one week hence, with a humorous motion that we sing songs and celebrate our progress, to which all heartily assented.

This next week, I can see, will be a whirl of business for this is the great moment when we may take the step from a few voices scattered and crying in a wilderness to a gathered force which can speak in mighty tones and be heard far and wide. It was a source of great consolation to me, after my recent doubts, to see so many white men utterly committed to the cause of the end of the bondage of our brothers and sisters.

I write this now, that you will not be disappointed if you hear no word from me for a while. As soon as ever the business of next week is concluded, I will write and you will certainly have heard from me before I depart for the tour of the West Country which begins in two weeks.

Your,
Frederick

GARRISONS'S LETTER TO PHILLIPS
AUGUST 11, 1846

My dear Wendell,
As well the public letter of greeting to which this is attached, I thought it would be useful for you to know how matters stand here. We are all reconciled into a single force now, but the route to this has been a hard way. I can see now that we had made too many assumptions about Douglass and that had we trusted him in the same way that we drew other confederates into our strategy, we would have won him easily to our side. I must tell you that we had a very stiff encounter, during which some harsh words were spoken on both sides. The upshot is, though, that he is returned to our camp with renewed vigor. He goes abroad, telling all that he meets that the course we have determined is the right one and we, equally well, have agreed that his plan of campaign against the Church of Scotland was the correct route to take. We are reunited and united. I am glad of it, not merely because it makes the tasks before us easier to fulfil but also be-

cause I realise that I have a father's affection for him.

Ever yours,
Garrison

Dear Helen,

  This is a beautiful morning, and I lack nothing to complete my enjoyment but your own dear presence, and that of the children. O that I could embrace you all, and bestow upon you as many kisses as my affection would prompt! But here I am, - the wide ocean rolling between us, and my work but just begun. It was my hope to be able to leave for home in the steamer of Oct. 4th; but it seems, now, impracticable for me to get away before the 19th. Henry C. Wright is also so circumstanced, that he will not be able to leave till that time. This will make the delay of a fortnight, which will be very long to you, and also to me; but yet it is only a fortnight, and it is better that we should consent to this temporary separation, than that my mission should be left in an imperfect state. It bids fair to be serviceable to an extent surpassing my most sanguine expectations. We have formed an Anti-Slavery League for all England, and last evening held a public meeting, which was fully attended by a most intelligent, respectable and enthusiastic assembly. I would have readily given several guineas, if you and the Boston friends could have been spectators. It was a real old organized anti-slavery meeting, such as was never held before in this metropolis. George Thompson was in the chair, and made a brief but earnest speech, in which he referred to me in a very kind and complimentary manner. Henry C. Wright made the opening speech, and it was a "scorcher", and received great applause. I followed him - and on rising, was received by the assembly with a tempest of applause, they rising from their seats and cheering loudly. I made a long speech which elicited the strongest marks of approbation. Douglass was received in a similar manner, and made one of his very best efforts. I never saw an audience more delighted. Henry Vincent made the closing speech, which was eloquently uttered, and warmly cheered. James Haughton, at the commencement, presented a resolution, welcoming us all to England, &c. &c. Rev. Mr. Edward Kirk, of Boston, was in the meeting, but he found the atmosphere too warm for him at last, and left the room. We began at half past 6, P.M., and did not adjourn until 12 o'clock, very few having left at that late hour. Every thing was encouraging to the highest degree.

Dearest, you have my heart. I shall think of you in the din of public excitement and the silence of privacy. My health is excellent, as I trust yours is. Love to all the dear friends without specification.

Write by every steamer.

Yours ever,
W.L.G.

DOUGLASS'S LETTER TO ANNA
AUGUST 18, 1846

My dearest Anna,

This week of hard work is done, and its fruits mark the labor as well expended. For the public meeting yesterday evening was a great success in its object of founding a new Anti-Slavery League here in Britain. Tomorrow I have one more meeting to attend before taking a few days' vacation in Southend, in the company of George Thompson, and his wife and children. After which, I shall turn my face westwards though I shall not travel as far in that direction as I would wish.

Your,
Frederick

DOUGLASS'S DIARY
AUGUST 18, 1846

I find myself now thrown into the uttermost confusion by the last twenty-four hours. The meeting, once it began, was, to be sure, a great success. All was achieved that had been planned the week before and the Anti-Slavery League was put in train. I suppose that history may honor those of us present last night as the founders of a new era.

But I find myself, now, afloat on a sea of whiteness and alone in this room, having to consider at what cost I have purchased this place in history. For I did last night, something which I had sworn to myself I would never do. I passed one of my own race by, one of my own brothers. Turned my back upon him and walked away.

When we arrived at the "Crown and Anchor", there was already at the door a number of our men who were there, Garrison told me, to act as stewards for the meeting. I was a little surprised by this, never having encountering such a procedure before, but I bowed before the superior experience of our friends here and went on into the room. It is a large, long and narrow room at the rear of the inn which was at this point very thinly populated by early arrivals. Those one or two I knew I greeted and was warmly received by them in turn. I continued to the front of the room and took my seat between George Thompson and Henry Wright. The latter was to begin the meeting and the former to chair it, as we had agreed the previous week, and both were very solicitous of my welfare. All the enmity between myself and Thompson seemed entirely wiped away, and I am sure that this is due to Garrison's intervention after our conversation of a few days ago.

We sat, talking in a very general fashion as the room began to fill up, and my small fears on entering about the possible size of the audience began to evaporate. Just as I was thoroughly relaxed and even looking forward to the start of the occasion, my attention was caught by what seemed to be a very intense discussion taking place at the entrance to the room, between the stewards I had seen earlier and a number of people none of whom I recognised. Even as I began to watch what had been intense discussion, clearly became vehement and the volume of the debate increased noticeably. Yet from where I was seated I could not hear what was being said and so rose from my seat and, stepping down from the platform, began to walk to the back of the room. As I did so, I was somewhat aware that Thompson, also, had risen and was gesturing to the stewards. By the time I reached them, one of the men had turned towards me and indicated that there was nothing to concern me taking place.

"I will be the judge of that, sir", I replied, and made as though to step past him.

At the very same time as this was happening, the people at the door made a concerted effort to enter the room and the man before me, distracted from the rear, was unable to prevent my stepping past him and directly into the path of those attempting to push into the room. I found myself face to face with a man I seemed to recognise but could not remember. He was a small red-headed fellow with an air of profound poverty about him, for his clothes were worn and patched and he himself was pale and very thin. He clearly knew me, for he essayed a greeting in the few seconds we were before each other, before he was pushed away and back towards the door of the room by the stewards who had now re-organised themselves. All this occurred in the strangest quiet as both sides strove with main force to achieve their end.

Yet when it was clear that they were to be denied the room, the red-headed man began to whisper urgently to those close around him with the result that he was suddenly lifted onto their shoulders, so that all within the room could see him over the heads of the stewards. At which point he called out as loudly as he could,

"We are here in the memory of Rebecca, the memory of Rebecca! We are here…"

But at that moment he was knocked down again by a forward surge of the stewards, who now succeeded in repelling the crowd out through the door and then quickly closed it against them. But not before I remembered that I had seen the red-headed man in the company of William Cuffay in the East End, that day before I departed for Birmingham and then the north of England.

I had, though, no time to reflect on the meaning of these events, for I was taken by the elbow by George Thompson who urged me to return to the dais as swiftly as I might, that the meeting could begin and thus the disturbance would be put from the audience's minds. Whether it was despite, or because, of the disturbance, I felt the power of inspiration move within me on this occasion and the word flowed from my lips with a vigor and a power I had not previously thought I held within myself. Speeches came from many lips and the meeting was in full progress by the time I was invited to the platform.

Yet even as I made my way to the lectern from which I planned to begin, the Reverend Edward Kirk, well known to many of us in the room from previous clashes, began an impromptu contribution from the floor which was cunningly designed to sound - to any naifs present - as though it were commendatory of our actions in separating from the old organisations. Indeed, the cunning of the man might well have swayed some of the less wary in the room had he not let his guard down when, by force of custom and habit, he referred to me as "that colored man" and revealed by his words and his tones, his genuine feelings of prejudice and dislike for all of my hue. At once, an outcry began in the room as several who had been unwilling just to shout him down for fear of seeming undemocratic, took the chance to demand that he return to his seat and be silent. Which he refused, and attempted to continue; at which the turmoil grew greater, until with a great gesture of outrage, he swept from the hall, taking in his wake one or two who had not seen through his charade. He departed to the sounds of great applause for his departure and so it was only with some gesture and effort that I was able to commence my own contribution. I thanked the reverend doctor for his introduction, which much amused many of those remaining in the room, and then made my speech as we had agreed.

I took my seat when I was finished, to applause and foot stamping, and a clap on the back from Garrison. So it was that it was some minutes before the next speech could begin. This prolonged and repeated applause, in tandem with the many motions and resolutions we made, kept the meeting going for close to six hours and it was nearly midnight before we were concluded and even then we stood in little groups discussing how matters stood, and seemed unwilling to leave the scene of this triumph.

At last, however, I and a few of those left at the very end stepped out into the street and were preparing to move off, when we encountered a small group of those who had attempted to enter the meeting several hours before, still standing on the sidewalk without. Although they had made no further attempt to enter again after the stewards had so thoroughly expelled them, neither had they departed entirely. Some half a dozen remained and, when they moved towards us, the stewards again stepped forward whilst some of our British friends suggested that we move off in the opposite direction. Which I would have done, had I not caught sight of Cuffay in the group. As our eyes met, he called out in a loud voice, "Remember this place, remember what has happened here before. Do not forget the ghosts of those still present here." And those around him joined in, calling out "Remember, remember". I stepped towards him until only the stewards were between us, at which point somehow everyone else became still, so that the two of us might speak even though still held apart by the linked arms of the stewards.

"Remember what?"

"Remember the drawing and signing of the Charter within these very walls"

"The Charter?"

"The Charter by which working men and women of this country claimed their rights. Rights of which they have been stripped these many years, the loss of which has reduced them to the very edge of slavery. Whatever you may think, Mr Douglass, the analogy is all too clear to anyone here who must live by the power of their arms alone."

"You are mistaken, Mr Cuffay. I am now persuaded that the end of chattel slavery in my country is best pursued through a great alliance of all those who wish to set aside oppression of all sorts."

"Then I welcome you back."

"I have never been absent."

"That is not my memory of our last meeting. It seemed to me then that you had thrown in your lot with those who would, in their own interest, see a grave division between the slavery of the Americas and the slavery here in England."

"Then you were mistaken."

"Easily said, harder to do."

"Meaning?"

"Meaning that when my friends and I attempted to enter this meeting, we were prevented from doing so. Prevented from entering the room where three of us here present now drafted and signed the first Charter. Prevented from entering the house which was always the centre of our business! Prevented, and you, Mr Douglass, did nothing to protect our right to speak."

"You have no right to speak at any of our meetings, Cuffay!" This interjection came from Henry Vincent, who now stood at my elbow and gripped me by the arm.

"That's a strange song for you to sing, Henry," Cuffay replied, "for I can remember many occasions in the past when I defended your right to speak before meetings, even though I knew what would come out of your mouth would be nonsense of the worst Liberal kind."

My expression must have betrayed my confusion at this point, for Cuffay returned his gaze to me again.

"Yes, Mr Douglass, Henry Vincent and I are old friends. We stood together in the early days of the Charter, though Henry has other interests now. Has he never mentioned me to you before?"

Much of this little speech induced rough laughter among Cuffay's confederates, and a look from Vincent that I could not ignore.

"Yes, Henry, I have met Mr Cuffay before."

"And not mentioned it?"

"I have not yet felt the need to account for all my movements to anyone here in this country. I came here a free man and remain here so." The arrogance I heard in Vincent's tone had already produced an anger in me I could not suppress in my voice.

"I did not mean .."

"Mean what, Henry?" Cuffay was now clearly enjoying the situation.

"I was not talking to you!"

"True, but I was talking to you. We could, of course, have had this conversation earlier but these fellows prevented it." And he patted one of the stewards on the shoulder.

I was now most struck by the man's fearlessness. Even despite his small size, which was emphasised by the very bulk of the stewards, he seemed to have a presence which lifted him above those around him.

"Mr Douglass. All we wished was that we might debate the relationship between slavery in the Americas and slavery here. All we wished was to applaud the decision of our friends within the abolitionist movement to recognise such a connection, and then to debate further what might be done to bring both evils to an end."

"You wished to disrupt our meeting with your incendiary talk!" Vincent interrupted again, and again tried to pull me away.

"Incendiary! Incendiary! What, when the employers of this country call upon the military to drive workers protesting peacefully from the streets with the flats of swords. When men and women are beaten within their own homes for discussing a combination of their interests, and are then put out into the street because the house in which they live is owned by the man who also steals their labour from them every day and who then robs them of their employment as well. When none within the halls and corridors of the respectable will hear us speak, but all continue with the praise of the world we live in, telling us that matters are all well. Is it incendiary then to say if we cannot raise a hearing one way then other methods may be needed? Is it incendiary to argue that it is not enough to show that we are suffering patiently, but that we need to consider the means by which that suffering may be ended? Incendiary, Henry Vincent? Have you forgotten that you yourself spent some time in prison for arguing this, for arguing that the Charter be heard."

But even as Cuffay was speaking, Vincent and the others were leading me away, saying that we must go, that we could not afford to wait any longer, that the man was unhinged by the years of poverty and deprivation he had suffered, that they felt sorry for him but there was nothing to be done, that to be associated with him would damage our cause in the eyes of those who mattered, that the Chartists were a spent force, that, that, that…

I could bear it no longer, but pulled away and turned back. When I was within a few yards of Cuffay, who was still standing calmly and watching us, I called out,

"I wish to devote myself to the bringing-down of one form of injustice, that is all."

He replied, "Who are you, Frederick Douglass, to say that one injustice is more important than another, for the simple reason that it was done to you?"

Then he turned away and walked off into the night.

PART TWELVE

I got new feet in Dublin. Beautiful new feet, with carved toenails and even an arch across the instep. So well made that at a glance it was hard to tell if I had my trousers pulled down. With the trousers up, of course, the straps made everything clear.

The man who made them for me, asked what size they should be. Here's your chance, he said, to have feet the size you've always wanted. I just showed him my boots. To give him his due, though, he made me a spare pair as well.

It's hard, he said, learning to walk on them. And I've had several clients who've broken their new feet. So.

He was right. I couldn't tell that my boot was touching the ground until it moved against my calf. People stared at me in the street. Though it was hard to tell whether that was because of my awkward walk or because I had the smell of the west on me, the smell of famine and death. All the people in Dublin looked so fat to me, even the thinnest of them.

The ship to England was crowded, packed tight with desperation and relief. When I crossed the water, I knew all I had to do was wait. He would find me.

In London, I faded into the crowds. So many street shows for people to watch, one Irishman swinging his legs a little stiffly as he walked was hardly worth a second glance. I walked and I waited. I sat in parks and watched my compatriots drift from elation to relief, on into resignation and beyond to despair. Their lives were thrown into a new set of scales; those who found work had some little money but had to endure the abuse, those who didn't were abused as beggars but could walk away whenever it became unbearable.

I sat, and I strolled, and I waited. I watched and was not seen by any who passed me.

Then, one evening, as I stood in a doorway the voice of the Pole whispered behind me. I stepped back a little into the darkness.

Quietly, my friend. You must make less noise,
lest we are overheard and noticed.
Strangest thing that I have learned. That there are
versions of invisibility. There is that which is so far
away that it is not seen. And there is that which is
close by, and yet still goes unseen. A man with no feet
clicking his way along the road. They see my absent
feet. From the ankles up, though, I am vanished.
I still have my feet, though. So make less
noise for my sake, if not your own.
Yours is yet another species of invisibility. You are there,
people see you and what you do, but as soon as you
move beyond their sight they forget your presence.
That day in Ballinasloe?
Indeed. It was a good day's work.
It is good to know you think so. The primary
purpose was amply fulfilled, but it is the spectator
you brought there that day of whom I wish to speak
now. His cause prospers, I hear. I wish him well,
though he does seem, how shall I say it …
Naïve?
No, not so much naïve as too optimistic.
Why so?
I think he will find all too soon that he has reached the
limits of his persuasion. That he has persuaded those
able and even ready to be persuaded. Then comes the
problem. What happens when he makes his argu-
ment, knowing it to be good, sees it acknowledged to

be such by his listeners and then has them brush it
aside as irrelevant or as of no interest to them.
Of no concern, surely?
No, no, my old friend. No interest. Not a source of
interest, of income. He will face, soon enough, the brute
reality that there are some who would rather make
money than be upright men. Indeed, there are some
who believe that their making of money is proof itself
of their moral status. They are a part of the problem.
And the other part?
Those who do not care one way or the other. Those
who have no concern in the matter because the matter is not immediately before them. Fortunately, the
solution is simple and singular to both cases.
What would you propose?
That we make him a proposal. His skill in speaking. Our, how shall I say, expertise in other
matters. Together, a formidable combination.
I think that he already holds you in some horror, for what he has already seen you do and the
pleasure you seemed to take in the doing.
True enough. He has rebuffed my approaches previously.
Then how can I speak …?
Because I think that he will find you more
persuasive. I certainly hope so.
Why so?
I have no fears for you. You are too far down our path
to go back. But once he has heard the words, they cannot be unheard. He will not know it, for I would have
him make a free choice, but if he rejects our offer…
…your offer…
…my offer… if he rejects my offer then I would have
to see that as a rejection of myself as well. That I cannot have. He has seen my face and could identify me,

and even I cannot forever walk unseen through the
streets. If he does not accept our proposal, then …

and at this moment the Pole put his hand on his cloak, at the
very place where I knew the pistol to be

You would not!
I would. Ours is a cold world, where cold deeds
are necessary. That is why I have a cold heart.
There comes a time for all men when they must
choose, to be with us or to be against us.
How is it, though, that you are the one who
can choose when it is the time for others?
I have earned the right, I think.
You must, though, let me speak with him first.

But before I spoke to Douglass, I spoke with another man. An
Irish man stopped me in the street near to Paddington Station,
recognised me for one of the people he said and asked if I had
business in the west. Of England, that is. He seemed entirely
unconcerned that those passing by could overhear our words,
and spoke almost as though he wished his acts to be both public and transparent. Much surprised by this, I replied that indeed I did. He asked if he might prevail upon me for some assistance to the cause. O'Connor's cause, I replied. Yours also, my
friend, he said, for O'Connor's cause is the cause of all working people. And I said I would do as he requested, because he
did not glance down at the sound of my feet before asking, and
nor did he enquire if I was capable of the walk through the
trees that would be required to fulfil the mission with which
he charged me. He saw me simply as a man who might do what
was needed.

That was how it was that I missed Douglass in Bristol, for instead of crossing that city I stayed at the station and travelled
on to Exeter, knowing that Douglass would be there shortly
after me. Knowing, also, that another would follow both of us
to the west.

PART THIRTEEN

PART ONE

GARRISON'S LETTER TO HENRY WRIGHT
AUGUST 26, 1846 (AN EXTRACT)

My dear Henry,

...We have accordingly decided on having such a meeting on Friday evening, in the largest and the best public room in Exeter...

...we are to meet with a select number of friends at Bishop's residence, tomorrow (Thursday) evening. Thus, you see, our way is fully prepared before us...

GARRISON'S LETTER TO HELEN
SEPTEMBER 3, 1846 (AN EXTRACT)

My dear Helen,

...From Bristol, we went to Exeter, where we met with a cheering reception, and had a large and glorious meeting. I left Frederick there, to give another lecture. ...

GARRISON'S LETTER TO RICHARD D. WEBB
SEPTEMBER 5,1846 (AN EXTRACT)

My dear Webb,

...Since I parted from him at Exeter, he has had an enthusiastic public meeting at that place ...an anti-slavery league has been formed, auxiliary to the London League, under very cheering auspices. Our friend Francis Bishop, at Exeter, is an admirable co-worker, and spared no pains to make our visit an eminently successful one...

...I have this glorious scene here, it is Daguerreotyped in my heart...

AUGUST 27, 1846

BRISTOL TEMPLE MEADS STATION, EARLY MORNING

Two men are standing side by side, having risen from their seats at the announcement of the train to Exeter. They seem barely to acknowledge each other's existence, but whether this is by reason of disaffection or familiarity, it is impossible to tell at this point. Whereas in many others places elsewhere in Britain, their presence would have attracted some attention, here no-one remarks it. There has been, after all, a presence of Black people in Bristol for the best part of 250 years and they have become part of the place. Rooted in, as much part of the scenery as the white facades of the houses in Clifton which look down over the city.

When the train arrives, they climb aboard and sit opposite each other in a carriage in which only one other is present. There is a perfunctory exchange of greetings between this pair and the third passenger, after which a silence settles as all return to their own thoughts and activities. Frederick Douglass begins to write letters, using a small travelling case so dextrously that it is clear he is well-versed in the art of using travelling time for other purposes besides getting from one place to another. William Garrison reads through a bundle of letters and newspapers, at times underlining passages or making clippings which are inserted into a folder on the seat beside him. The third, after reading from his book for some time, sets the book aside in favour of watching his fellow passengers in what is initially a reasonably surreptitious fashion. As the journey continues, though, he becomes more open and obvious in his gaze.

Until.

"Gentlemen, at the cost of seeming intrusive, I must enquire. Are you both Americans?"

"Both of us, yes."

"I thought that it must be so. You have that air."

"Which air is that, sir?"

"The air of busy boldness. It is most unusual."

"We are both busy men, sir. Mr Douglass here and I are engaged in the great task of winning over British public opinion on the question of slavery."

"I am not sure that I understand."

"We are touring Britain together, speaking at public meetings and trying as best we may to change the generality of opinion with regard to slavery in our country."

"It is an unusual tactic."

"How so?"

"I would have thought that there were very few blacks who would advocate their own enslavement."

"You misunderstand me, sir. We are for the abolition of slavery. Mr Douglass here himself escaped slavery."

"Indeed, and where was he in bondage?"

"I was held in the state of Maryland. I am able, and indeed accustomed, to answering for myself."

"My apologies, Mr Douglass. I meant nothing by continuing my conversation only with your colleague. I thought that you were still engaged in your reading."

"Granted, sir. It is just that I am a little sore on that point."

There was a brief but awkward pause.

"And you are going to Exeter?"

"Yes."

"Not a town known for its forward thinking, I would have thought."

"We have friends there, and anyway we are used to entering the lions' den, are we not, Frederick?"

"Indeed."

Another brief and awkward pause, this time almost a silence, settled between them and Douglass turned his head to watch the north Somerset coastline slipping by. Then the train stopped at Weston-super-Mare and the Englishman alighted, but not before he had ascertained that a meeting was planned for Bridgewater in the nearest future and he promised to attend.

Barely an hour and a half later, the train was approaching Exeter by way of the long curve of the Exe valley. As the train entered the station, the Douglass and Garrison - who had not spoken since the departure of their fellow passenger - prepared to disembark and became busily absorbed in their preparations. Then the train was slowing to the platform and moving in under the green and cream canopy. They stepped down, to be greeted by a small man dressed in clerical black, who shook both of them firmly by the hand and then led them to the exit.

Once outside Francis Bishop led them, by way of a narrow and steep path, to the road in which he lived. Where they could take tea before walking into the city centre to meet some of the more influential supporters of the cause in the city. They were still a minority, he said, but he was confident that the impact of the two visitors would change that. All this in a slightly breathless tone, for the path was indeed a steep climb and Francis Bishop was sweating and almost gasping by the time they emerged onto the new north road and turned for the short walk to his house.

Here, he led them inside, calling to his wife to come and meet his old friend William Garrison and his companion Mr Frederick Douglass. On seeing that Mrs Bishop was heavily pregnant, Garrison and Douglass both insisted that she return at once to her seat. Which she did willingly enough, even while all the time calling to the maid to bring tea for the visitors. The four of them sat in the Bishops' parlour drinking tea and talking of the journey from Bristol; how dull the Somerset levels were, even though the train was now a deal quicker than it had been.

Then Mrs Bishop seemed to recall her duties as a hostess and called the maid to show the visitors the rooms in which they would sleep while staying here. The maid, a local girl, led the two men up the stairs even though she could barely keep her eyes from them; they being the first Americans she had ever seen, she said. Said she would bring hot water up for both, as soon as it were boiled. And within a few minutes she was knocking on Garrison's door with a large enamel jug, for which he thanked her. Then he was knocking on Douglass's door, to offer the water to him before he took his own share.

Douglass accepted the offered jug but was stayed from turning into the room immediately by Garrison's hand on his arm. Douglass looked down at the hand and then up at the man's face. They looked at each other a long while, and then Douglass turned back into the room. Yet left the door open, so that Garrison could follow to collect the jug for his half of the hot water. Poured the water, and then turned back again onto the landing to hand the jug to the other man before closing the door so that he might wash. Garrison in turn closed his door.

Some time later, the three men appeared from the front door of the small limestone house. Being at the middle of a row of similar buildings, and being the house of the warden of the whole group, this door stood at the T of the paths leading both to the other houses and also down to the road itself. There were small lawns on either side, made only of grass, and these ended at a low wall separating the gardens from the road. At the point where the path passed through the wall, there was a large archway also made of the limestone through which the men stepped and turned towards the city centre. On seeing a large, even imposing church building to their right, Douglass asked if this was the cathedral of which he had heard so much - to which Bishop replied with some amusement that it was not and indeed it was not even one of the more auspicious churches of the city.

"No," he continued, "that is but the St David's parish church which is occupied by a good son of the Church of England. You know the type, Garrison, too holy to consider saving the souls of any but the most respectable sinners. When I asked if he would consider sponsoring our meeting here, I asked only out of sport to hear the exact tone of his reply - which was that he must consider the whole of his parish and that it would not do if he were seen to be in support of any minority interest which might adversely affect the well-being of any other of his parishioners. When I suggested that he ask his parishioners what they thought, ask them I said in the manner that the Society of Friends enquire of their brothers and sisters what the feeling of the whole community is, he turned a quite delightful shade of purple."

"No, Mr Douglass," he said turning again to the other man, "the cathedral is in the centre of the city but we can take a small detour on the way to Mr Sercombe's offices if you wish. I am sure that Mr Sercombe will sympathise with the cause of a small delay when he hears of it."

Having so concluded, the three continued into the city centre along that rarity in this city, a level road of some extent. After making their way past a number of new commercial buildings and then through a tatter of medieval houses, they emerged from a narrow alleyway onto the cathedral green. This was very much more to Douglass's imaginings and at his urging they spent some time walking around and admiring the building from the outside. He said that he wished to return, if it were possible, to examine the interior. At the look of some surprise on Mr Bishop's face. He replied that this was not because he felt any great sympathy with the theology of Anglicanism but rather because he wished to see how men in virtual slavery could still devote their time to the construction of such magnificence, despite using such rudimentary tools. It was, he said, as much a monument to the creativity of its builders as a hymn of praise to God.

But let us proceed with our immediate business, which way must we go? Bishop directed the two men down a long, narrow and steep street towards the river. The street, indeed, descended at such a steep angle that when they looked up they could see over the roofs of the houses, out over the river and up towards the first great sweep of the moors to the north of the city. Dartmoor, sir, said Bishop, seeing where Douglass's gaze had come to rest but we must turn down this way. As he led them into a narrow and enclosed side street, he continued by commiserating that neither of the visitors would be present long enough to be able to take a journey out onto the moor. It is a mighty combination, he said, of wildness and the evidence of human habitation clinging to its face. Douglass cast a final glance in that direction before following the other two men along what was no more than a lane running down towards the river.

Mr Sercombe's offices are at the riverside, on the old quays. Even though the trade has long since died back from its bustle of years gone by, he likes to maintain the family traditions rather than following the other rising men of commerce up into the city centre. He says he cannot abide being in a place where he is surrounded by such folk, even if they are all engaged in the same practices. Here we are.

The three emerged from the cobbled lane onto the old quayside. The buildings here were in a state of some disrepair even though it was clear that a considerable degree of business was still conducted on both sides of the water. The largest of the buildings, and the only one showing any signs of recent paintwork, announced itself as the offices of John Clampitt Sercombe, seedsman and hop merchant; also, vice consul for the kingdoms of Spain and Prussia. At the doorway stood two men so deep in debate that they did not notice the appearance of the trio onto the quayside. Indeed, they seemed to be disputing rather than simply speaking and then one of them concluded with an angry gesture of the hand and turned aside.

To see, directly before him, the two Americans and Bishop approaching. His demeanour changed momentarily and, before the other man, could move, he had stepped forward and held out his hand. Ignoring Bishop, he introduced himself to Garrison and Douglass as William Wilkinson and said he was extremely glad to make their acquaintance. It is an excellent day for this city that you have come to denounce the evils of slavery here, an excellent day indeed. You have done great work denouncing the hypocrisy of those churchified men who seem so pious and yet have their hands in the slavers' purse. I look forward with great anticipation to hearing your speeches, and would be glad if you have the time to entertain both of you to lunch. Yet before they could reply on their own behalf, Bishop interjected to say that the visitors were on a tight schedule and all was already arranged.

Indeed, sir, Wilkinson replied and then strode off with the barest gesture of farewell to the two Americans and none at all for the other two. Bishop and Sercombe, for it was he who was the man left standing at the door of the offices, covered any difficulty with ease and led the two indoors. To a well-appointed large office looking out over the river where several other men were seated, all of whom rose when the party entered and introductions were made all round. They were, in total, a good number of the supporters of the cause drawn from the city's businessmen and clergy. Soon, tea and coffee were served and the group settled into a conviviality which was both pleasant and brisk. For when the introductions and the arrangements for the evening were agreed, Sercombe and several of the others indicated that they must be about their business. It was agreed that all present here would also be present that evening, and would bring with them such guests as had already been agreed.

Thus it was that, by lunchtime, the two Americans found themselves at their leisure for a few brief hours. They chose, almost wordlessly, to set off into the city in different directions.

Frederick Douglass hurried to take shelter in a doorway from the sudden squalls of rain blowing across the cathedral green. Once he had wiped the rain from his face, he looked about and found that he was leaning against the entry door to the local circulating library. Even as he realised this, the door opened and an elderly gentleman emerged, who seemed a little startled to encounter Douglass standing so close against the door. Sufficiently so, that he retreated half a step back into the building, all the while looking up at the tall black man.

My apologies, sir, if I have startled you by standing so close in to the door, Douglass said, but as you can see the rain has come on suddenly and I took advantage of this doorway as shelter.

Are you lost, young man? The elderly man replied.

Not at all, sir, Douglass replied. I was on my way to admire the interior of the cathedral when I was caught by this shower and took shelter here. And, now that the rain has passed, I shall continue on my way.

Without further pause, he stepped out from the doorway and hurried to the nearest path across the green to the main entrance of the cathedral building, which was at the west end of the structure. The old man stood and watched him go, before returning into the library from which he had appeared moments earlier with all the signs of departure about him.

Douglass, meanwhile, reached the main huge wooden doors of the cathedral and without a moment's hesitation opened the smaller door cut into the large panel and stepped inside.

The green was now entirely deserted.

As he entered, he was visibly moved by the glorious and sweeping capture of space defined by the arched and fluted columns rising in parallel down the centre of the building. This central space was filled with rows of pews and was lit both by numerous quantities of candles in stands around the base of each of the pillars and also by the stained glass windows above.

Beyond this area, though, the side passages of the cathedral were darker, almost gloomy even despite the fact that it was daylight outside. He stood awhile, at a point which gave him a direct line of vision right down the centre of the main aisle of the building and on into the choir stalls and the great brass and gold altar beyond that.

Even though his own patterns of belief were solidly within the traditions of Protestantism and dissent, he felt that this really was a place both of beauty and also gentle faith. Here and there, individuals knelt in the pews engaged in private prayer. The whole place had a feeling of antique and preserved peace and contemplation, which he inhaled slowly along with the more unfamiliar scents of melting wax and incense. Once he felt as though his heartbeat had slowed and his breathing was appropriately paced to the building and its air of quietness, he began to walk about so as to have a better sense of the place. The complexity of such religious buildings fascinated him, for he had been educated to see one's relationship to God as a simple and direct affair. Yet here, the architecture implied that this was a more complex structure containing small private places as well as the large and open public arenas. Private chapels each with their own aura, some of which seemed neglected almost to the point of disuse and others which clearly received daily attention. The same, he began to notice, was true of the monuments which clustered along the outer walls of the building. Not only were some positioned beneath windows whilst others stood in deep gloom, but the styles of construction were a history of monumental masonry over perhaps 600 years. Some were great ornate structures, with statues of Indians and soldiers supporting a canopy and all surrounding an elaborate account of the great man's works and deeds. Others were simple brass or marble tablets, with a brief account of the name and family of the body nearby. Some were simply factual, whilst others told in prose and poetry of the emotional damage inflicted by the loss of the person commemorated.

Further, some were clearly undusted and unpolished, whilst others showed the signs of constant attention. He read the names of strangers who came from towns and villages of which he had never heard as he strolled on until one simple marble slab caught his eye. It told of a woman who had died near Exeter, which was in itself not extraordinary but what was, was that the plaque described her as being "of the island of St. Christopher". A few steps further, and another memorialised a wife whose husband was "of the island of Barbadoes". A little further again, and a large stone commemorated at great length and with considerable verbosity a soldier who had died "of Yellow Fever at St. Domingo". Yet another remembered a mother whose son was "of St Elizabeth's in Jamaica". All these people, save the last, had died at least 50 years before.

Douglass had seen before how the great facades of many towns in this country were erected on monies from the slave trade but previously this had been in the cities known for their participation in the business of stealing and selling human flesh: London, Liverpool, Bristol. He remembered how, just two days earlier, the hands of one of his hosts in that last town had shaken as he gestured at the great sweep of white houses in Clifton and had enumerated how the builders and owners of nearly all the properties had made their money from the trade.

Yet this was different, this was not a town where the connections were clear. There were no large public buildings named after slavers and their families. This was a town at the edge of British wealth. It had been, he understood from his hosts, a much more powerful town in the past but had been retreating for the last 100 years at least. Yet even here, the connections reached. Even here, in this provincial town, there were links out to the world. Men from this town had fought against the slave revolutionaries in St. Domingo, against the men whose names and doings he had heard whispered by American slaves as a message of hope and promise to one another. Women from this town had married and given birth to men who had become planters in the islands of the Caribbean, men who had bought and sold his brothers and sisters in skin.

He turned away, feeling as though the whole place were a sham. A disguise of piety stretched over the crimes of theft and murder, cruelty and indifference. He remembered how, earlier in the day he had described this place as a monument to the men who had built it; now, he saw it as a charnel-house, haunted by the ghosts of the men and women who had died building it. Haunted by the ghosts of the men and women far away worked or beaten to death by the men and women who came home again to be buried in this place, or who had their bones shipped home to be placed beneath the flagstones. Men and women washed their gold in the Atlantic waves and then brought it here to raise monuments in the memory of their own devotion to Christian works.

He almost ran from the place, through the great doors and out onto the large paved area before the building. He stood there, panting and swaying. He half-turned, caught sight of the place again out of the corner of his eye and nearly fainted. He sat down on the low wall which stood alongside the steps leading up and away, and found that his face was washed with a clod sweat. A man, dressed in a long black cassock, emerged from the doors out of which he had run and approached him.

Are you sick, he asked? Douglass looked up at the man, and found that he could not speak, so constricted was his throat. He lowered his head, to try and ease the swaying sensation he felt. Young man, you seem most distressed, the man continued. What ails you? Douglass looked up again, and saw the man before him as some dark angel sent to taunt him. You, sir, he cried as he leapt to his feet, you are what ails me! You and all your kind!

Then he ran, away across the green, leaving the deacon watching in amazement at the sight of a black man running through the streets of Exeter.

A group of local men stood at the far end of the pier, on the river side, watching a huge barge making its way slowly past the treacherous curve of Ball Hill's muddy heave. The barge's skipper knew enough to trade the difficulties of the low tide now for the advantage of later having the rising tide at his back once he was through the narrowness of the entrance and into the main channel of the river. Bastards, one of the men muttered. Right enough, one of the others agreed and lifted his chin to bellow the same insult out across the water. In vain, for no-one on the barge took any notice, even if they heard. Yet if the men's looks in that direction were baleful, they were nothing compared to the open hatred they turned towards a number of smaller boats entering the dock through the channel below them.

Why don't you fuck off, one of them shouted down. To which the men in the boats below made no reply, but rowed steadily on past the pier and towards the beach. The effect of this was not to deflect the abuse, but to strengthen the feelings among the men above. Arh, one of them shouted down, fuck off you bastards.

Whether or not one of the men in the boats below actually did mutter that they were coming not to fuck off but to fuck their women, the men later claimed that this is what they heard. Almost instantly, one of them had picked up a stone and flung it down into one of the boats, striking a seated man squarely on the back of the head. The latter slumped forward, splashing those around him with blood and they started up, making the boat rock and sway. Above, on the pier, one of the local men had unbuttoned his fly and began to urinate down on another boatload. Another stone thumped into a body. The already swaying boat began to rock more violently and, to a fierce delight, a couple of its passengers fell out into the water. By now, the first boat had reached the shore and several of the men aboard scrambled out and began to run up the beach towards the pier.

The group above threw a few more stones, and then began to run before those coming from the beach reached them. The urinator was slowest, trying as he was to button himself as he ran, and one of the passengers caught him by the collar and pulled him to the ground. On seeing this, two of his companions turned back while another one ran on into a public house which stood some way off at the edge of the clustered cottages. By the time the two reached their friend, he was on the ground and his pursuer was aiming kicks at him. They bundled the attacker backwards and pulled their friend to his feet. But by then more of the boat's passengers were up and out onto the ground above the beach and the three found themselves surrounded.

Blows and kicks were aimed at the three from all sides. One of them slipped, and took a nailed boot in the face. He screamed and tried to roll away, but another boot caught him on the back of the head stunning him. Even as the other two tried to pull him up, they too were knocked onto the ground and the kicks began to fly. At the very moment when the three were entirely trapped, a glass shattered. A crowd of men rushed out of the public house and began to run to their rescue. The men from the boat now retreated a few steps and regrouped to defend themselves.

But the men from the public house did not rush to the attack, but rather stood a little off and began to pelt the men with glasses they had brought out with them for the purpose. Although they were for a time successful in fending off the missiles, a few from each volley got through to inflict deep cuts to hands and faces, and the men from the boats began to retreat still further. This provoked another hail of glass, and they broke and ran for the boats.

By now, the whole area was in uproar, with men and women emerging from the sheds, shops and houses of the immediate vicinity to discover what was happening. When word spread that men from the town were fighting them from across the river, many of these spectators hurried forward to join in. Within a very few minutes, two of the boats had been swamped and men from them were swimming away as best they could. Those who tried to wade ashore found themselves kicked at and stamped on until they fell back into the water. Seeing that the attack was not ceasing, the men still in the boats made a rush for the shore by driving their crews to a frenzy of rowing, then jumped and swarmed ashore. They drove the local people back up the beach a little way, but they still faced the hail of glass from the pier above. This determined them to charge the pier, where they again managed to drive the crowd back. They had size - for most of them were sturdy and strong men who made their living through furious physical labour - and organisation in their favour and soon had driven the crowd off.

The thirty or so who had been the heroes of this advance recognised the public house as the source of much of their travail and began to smash the windows and force the door. At which point a company of the local police materialised, along with several militia, and ordered the men to cease. Their protests were ignored, and they were turned back towards the boats. The senior officer among the police, having forced the men back, told them that they were not welcome here. To which one replied that he had noticed.

Which got him arrested, and taken off to the town jail. Despite the protests of the others, the officer told them that he intended to charge this one with disorderly conduct and then advised, no, instructed the rest of them to return to their camp on the other side of the river.

The news that one of the navvies was detained in the town jail inflamed rather than quietened the resentment now simmering among the local people. One of the original group, with blood still clotted in his hair and streaked over his face, began to gather a party of his friends and relatives to accompany him to the jail. As they walked through the streets, telling whosoever they met what had happened and where they were going, and soon many others joined them until there was a considerable party assembled. Which was told, when it arrived at the jail door, that they were to disperse. They replied by shouting that the constable should bring out the navvy for the kind of treatment he would understand, deserved.

The constable's reply, which was to remind them of the riot act and to shut the door in their faces, at first heightened the anger of the crowd and they began to bang on the door and to shout at the windows. The constable, though, was a cunning judge and guessed that silence would absorb the resentment of this crowd rather better than response. So he left the door shut. After a while, people began to drift away until only a small knot was left standing there.

<hr>

AUGUST 27, EVENING
AT FRANCIS BISHOP'S HOUSE

By seven o'clock, a group of the city's most prominent Liberals was assembled in Francis Bishop's library. The room itself was already quite small, and was rendered smaller still by the bookshelves which covered every wall. The men present all knew each other well, from years of worshipping and politicking together, and had little to speak with each other of any great substance and so the conversation consisted of pleasantries and immediate small matters. That is, until the two visitors from America entered the room in company with Francis Bishop. Then, all changed as the two were greeted and welcomed to the city. With much shaking of hands and placing of other hands on shoulders, they made their way into the heart of the room.

Where, once Bishop had summoned a silence, John Sercombe, city councillor, made a short speech of praise and welcome which concluded by reminding everyone present of the public gathering the following evening. After which, the gathering divided into two smaller groups each assembled around one of the visitors. This enabled the local dignitaries to make their acquaintance and allowed the visitors to engage in the more private part of their business; namely, the raising of funds by private donation. At one point, John Sercombe found himself stood by the side of Frederick Douglass.

A very fine assembly, Mr Douglass, he said. All the people one would expect and a few more besides. We are honoured to have both yourself and Mr Garrison here in our city. Many visitors are tempted all too easily to pass us by because we are perceived as being at the edge of the known world.

But is not Cornwall further west still from here, and with even fewer towns of any size?, asked Douglass.

Indeed, sir, and I am surprised that your tour does not take you there, said Sercombe.

We did not feel the need on this visit, for we are wholly assured of the support of the people of Cornwall who have been staunchly against slavery since the days of Wesley's mission, Douglass informed him.

Wesley, yes, said Sercombe with less enthusiasm in his voice than he had previously displayed.

Whatever one may think of the man's theology, Douglass continued, it cannot be denied that he did great works in the cause of my people.

But Sercombe's attention was already drifting and Douglass, annoyed by this, determined to recapture the man's attention.

He did so by enquiring as to the whereabouts of the man, was his name Wilkinson, that he and Garrison had encountered earlier that day. He was surprised not to see him here, when he had expressed such clear support for the cause of the abolition of slavery and when Sercombe himself had asserted that all such men in the city were present. The effect of the words was exactly as Douglass had hoped, for Sercombe instantly turned back to him with his attention entirely focused. We did not think it appropriate to invite him here this evening, he said rather sharply. But why ever not?, continued Douglass. He seemed to me entirely the sort of man whom we should welcome into the embrace of the cause for the favour he shows us now and the support he might offer later.

We were trying to protect you, Sercombe said, now looking directly at Douglass. Protect me from what?, the latter asked. From the man's reputation. His reputation? And your stated convictions. My convictions? Your teetotalism; the man is a wine and spirits merchant. He supplies most of the city's public houses with their liquor. We cannot prevent him from attending the public gathering tomorrow, but we thought that you would rather not have to endure his company this evening.

With this, Sercombe turned aside and pursued a conversation with Garrison. The others in the room had clearly caught some element of the exchange between the two men because, after a brief lull in which no-one spoke to him, Douglass then found himself surrounded by several men all too eager and willing to engage him in conversation about his life in America, about the status of the tour thus far, his plans for the immediate future. Anything, indeed, except the present circumstances.

In a short while, the evening began to break up as several of the guests had business to attend first thing in the morning and others indicated that they were unaccustomed to be abroad in the city this late at night even without the events in Exmouth. Which led to a brief exchange of information, Douglass and Garrison having heard nothing of the recent disturbances in that town which were the result of tensions between local men who thought themselves robbed of work by the appearance of the great gangs of navvies working on the railway line. Not to mention the more general disturbance these people brought with them, with their heavy drinking and their loose behaviour. And then that damned man, O'Connor, seeking to come here and ferment still more trouble.

Feargus O'Connor?, asked Douglass.

The very same. Have you heard of the scoundrel?

A question Douglass felt unable to answer in the present company, but he was saved the difficulty by Garrison asking what business O'Connor had here in this town. He proposes to hold a mass meeting of the navvies working on the railway line to

Plymouth, was the reply, to discuss their supposed grievances and also no doubt to agitate for his own extreme opinions. That man should still be in the jail for his past actions, not allowed to wander the country arguing revolution and riot.

The discussion was becoming heated, until Bishop interjected that he had heard that the madman was busy raising monies for the construction of communal villages for his followers, in which free love was practised and drunkenness was rife. There was much head-shaking and snorting at this, in the midst of which Douglass excused himself.

Lying on his bed, he found it impossible at first to sleep. The city was all around him but it lay in such complete silence that Douglass felt as though he could hear his heart beat and that every small movement he made on the bed echoed like a mighty crash. The darkness, also, was such that he could see nothing.

It was this latter, in the end, which overcame his tension. Unable to focus his attention upon any element of the room, his mind began to drift. When at last he dozed, he dreamed of cricket matches, cows and a large man with an Irish accent standing in the middle of a crowd and sharing a vision with the people all around him.

AUGUST 28
FRANCIS BISHOP'S HOUSE JUST BEFORE DAWN

Frederick Douglass has been awake for some time already, woken by his dreams, and sits before a window. Looking out into the darkness, he is remembering the night in Baltimore when he was finally ready to run. With all the preparations made, he had slipped out of the house before any of the white people were awake and had hurried through the streets to meet Anna Murray. This free black woman was ready to risk her liberty for the love of himself.

He wonders why this memory has come to him now, this memory of the time in his life when he took the step from resisting slavery to breaking its bonds. He cannot understand it, but nevertheless the conviction remains within him untouched that this was one of the most important moments in his life. For, without that step into danger, nothing else since would have been possible.

———

PART TWO

AUGUST 28, EXETER IN THE LATE MORNING

William Garrison and Frederick Douglass were making their way back into the centre of the city from visiting the catacombs built into the steep slope running up from the river to the remnants of the old Roman walls which once marked out this far extent of the hand of the Empire. When they reached the graveyard which was tucked into this corner of the city the two men, panting and even sweating a little from the exertions of the climb, turned and looked back out over the river and towards the west.

The Romans knew what they were about, said Garrison, when they stopped their march west at this point. See how the river makes a natural boundary, a place where they could say to the people beyond 'this side is our dominion and if you make no incursion to this bank then we will not cross into your territory'. The Celts beyond must have thought that a fair exchange.

Perhaps, replied Douglass, if they understood what was being shouted at them across the water. Yet do you not think that we might be imposing our own sense of the land onto history. We think the Romans stopped here because we see no good evidence that they proceeded no further. Yet perhaps they failed in their attempt and the people of the west expunged the signs of the violation of their lands.

An idle speculation, said Garrison, by which I mean no insult to you but merely that we might engage in such fantastical thinking about any subject. Though I cannot see the point of it.

My point is only that those who have won the battles of the past have written the history of that past. We do not know if we will succeed in our efforts in the future and I have a premonition that if we do not, history will not treat us kindly, no matter what we might want today. All I mean is that I think we would do well to see the possibility of more than one version of the past as the necessary condition of more than one version of the present.

We have our truth, replied Garrison, I do not see why we should need more.

Douglass's answer was cut short by the appearance at the far end of the graveyard of Francis Bishop, come to collect them for the next part of their day. He had arranged, he said, a boat trip for them down to the little village of Topsham which had been the Roman port for the city. They could return by way of the Topsham road, originally a Roman road, in time for the evening meeting. He hoped this was agreeable to them, which it was.

The three men left the graveyard, pausing only while Douglass halted briefly and attempted to decipher the very worn inscription on one stone, and then redescended to the river bank by way of a narrow street less steep than the climb through the catacombs. Here, the boat Bishop had arranged stood ready and in a very few minutes the three men were being rowed swiftly downstream. Bishop explained that haste had been in order for it was only when the tide was full that it was possible to take this route. Then there was nothing more to discuss and they could spend the journey looking at the poor houses clustered along the bank at this point, which gradually gave way to fields too wet even for the poorest dwelling to be erected. Then they were passing through thick reed beds which at this time of year towered overhead. Yet, no matter how narrow the channel became, the boatmen seemed to find his way through almost without effort. This, Douglass thought, was the key to success in a trade and journey of this sort; to have the correct guide to lead one through the difficulties.

At one point the channel divided and although the right-hand route headed towards a sharp bend over which a low bridge passed, the boatman steered that way. When asked why, he replied that the other channel narrowed very quickly until it became impassable just out of sight from where they now were.

After the bridge, under which they passed with heads lowered, the river began to widen a little and the view off to the west where the ground stood lower opened out. But then, just as it seemed to be developing into a really wide stream, the reed beds closed in again and even moved out into the water. Now, they had to cut back and forth seeking a passage through the always narrowing channels. Yet still the boatman seemed unerring in his judgement and within a few minutes they emerged again.

To see, ahead of them on the shore, the small town reaching right down to the water's edge. For the most part, the land lay low and the houses stood but a few feet clear of the water. At the very centre of the town, though, a church stood on a high piece of ground protected from the river by a tall wall into which a flight of steps were set. At the foot of the steps there was a slipway, and it was towards this that the boatman headed. He put them ashore without a word, accepted his payment from Francis Bishop and rowed away downstream. When Douglass asked why this was, Bishop replied that the man would have to return to the city through the canal because the tide had turned and the channel down which they had come would now be nothing but mud. The canal, he continued, was the reason that Topsham had fallen into quietude from the busy place it once had been; it had drawn away those ships which previously had not been able to reach up to the city due to the narrowness of the river and which had therefore been obliged to use this port as an access to the city. Now, though, Bishop continued all that has changed and this has become a very quiet place indeed.

Bishop led the way up the steep steps from the slipway and directly into the churchyard, where he hurried ahead saying that he wished to find the vicar of this place who he wished to introduce. Thus left alone for some time, Garrison took up his seat on the wall looking out over the river while Douglass wandered the paths of the yard, idly examining the stones.

So it was that when Bishop returned, Douglass was crouched out of sight peering at a part of the graveyard wall. The other three men struck up a conversation which developed so swiftly that not for several minutes did they think to interrupt themselves to seek out Douglass. When they did, he was still intently examining the stones of the wall which divided the yard from the road and supported the greater height of the graveyard. So intently, indeed, that he seemed not to hear their approach until they were upon him. Then he started up and, brushing the crumbs of earth from his trousers, shook hands with the vicar and was drawn into the discussion. Yet even though he more than maintained his end of the debate, Douglass seemed to Garrison - who knew him a great deal better than the other two - to be much distracted.

The others not seeming to notice, though, Garrison said nothing. The rest of the afternoon passed well and the men parted at the vicar's door with protestations of good faith and resolutions to meet again if the chance arose.

Yet as soon as they were out of the door and walking along the main street of the little town, Garrison turned to Douglass and asked the matter of his distraction. This question, though, instead of eliciting the response expected, seemed to deepen Douglass's confusion still more and he turned away, saying that he must return to the graveyard again, that he would follow them shortly. With that, he turned away and hurried off back the way that they had come.

Garrison and Bishop were at a loss as to a response to this, and stood for several moments in the street questioning each other as to an appropriate reaction. In the end, Bishop's wish to respect Douglass's need for solitude overcame Garrison's determination to know what was the matter, and the two set off slowly along the road back to Exeter. Even at the slow pace they adopted, though, they were long returned to Bishop's house on the far side of the city before Douglass reappeared and retired directly to his room.

So it was that they did not see the mud stains on the knees of his trousers and the badly removed grime which covered his hands. By the time he entered Bishop's library a little while later, he had changed his clothes ready for the evening and washed his hands so thoroughly that only a broken nail remained as sign of his activities. The maid had been persuaded to take his clothes and clean them directly, and had also been sworn to secrecy with a bribe and a smile.

Thus readied, the men left the house and began to walk along Queen Street to the Subscription Rooms, where the evening's meeting was to take place.

━━━━

AUGUST 28,

A TOPSHAM GRAVEYARD

Frederick Douglass, once he had parted from his two companions, retraced his steps as swiftly as he could without running to the graveyard positioned so that the spirits of those who lay within its walls might look out over the expanse of the river, the low fields on the far bank and then on towards the Haldon hills rising as the horizon. Once through the gate, though, he stopped and seemed almost unwilling to continue, almost at a loss as to what he should do next.

He wandered here and there among the stones, stooping to examine many and, again, if we were able to draw nearer we would have heard him muttering the dates of the burials as marked on the stones. At first he moved quickly but as the dates moved further back into the eighteenth century he became gradually more deliberate. Not least because, by the middle-point of the previous century, more and more of the stones were now laid flat and he had to stoop lower still to read them. The arrangement of the yard made his movement easier, for it was clear that - with a very few exceptions related to family connection of one sort or another - the people interred here had been buried in more or less chronological fashion. So, a man buried on May 12th 1742 lay next to another who had died four days later but was also in the company of his widow, who had survived him by several years. All were laid extremely close together, as though those who had been responsible for the size and organisation of the yard had known that it would have to serve for many years.

By now, he had reached the 1720s and was moving very slowly. His lips audibly shaped the dates;

June 14

June 9

May 28

May 12

Then he found that for which he was searching.

A narrow strip of empty ground, bordered by stones dated May 12th and April 29th. He stepped back, as though to be sure that there truly was a space rather than one he imagined, one that he willed into being.

Between the two stones, there was a strip of grass perhaps no more than a foot wider than the space between all the other stones. Wide enough, though, to have become a pathway from one line of graves to that beyond. And used as such, it was clear, for the grass was worn down and flattened. Indeed, it did seem no more than a path of convenience. Except that there was no other such in any of the other rows of graves. Only here, between April 29th and May 12th, 1722.

Douglass walked away, came back again to look as though wishing to confirm utterly that what he had seen was there. Twice more he made this short journey, until it was clear to him that there did seem to be an unexplained space between two of the graves. Unexplained, for there was no sign of a stone. Nothing distinguished the grass over this place from that of the paths which it connected.

This confirmed, he turned and walked again to the place by the wall where he had been bending down earlier. Again, he had to kneel to see what he had found before. To read what was there. For, at the level of the grass and indeed descending below into the earth, there was an unusually smooth part of the graveyard wall onto which some words had been scratched. Slowly, and with great difficulty, he read again the words he could see:

remember, Good Lord, my brother James
taken from me by the white man's deeds
buried here May 4th 1722 anno domini after

To read any more, he realised, he would have to scrape away the grass and the earth and looked around for a tool, an implement of any sort. He had to go all the way to the side of the church itself before he found anything at all, and even then all he could discover was a piece of roof tile. Which served as a crude spade, to dig away at the ground. He was lucky, he knew, that no-one had passed by and seen him for he was now behaving in such an odd fashion that he would surely attract attention to himself. Yet he did not care.

He set to work with the tile, scraping out the earth from its juncture with the wall and beginning to dig down. It became clear very quickly that there was more lettering below the level of the grass. A few minutes' digging revealed a little more. But a little more that made Douglass sit back on his heels with an expression of surprise, even shock, upon his face.

he took his own life in despair

There he sat for some time, staring down at the words uncovered. Then he set too again, pausing only when he jagged and broke a nail against the stone in his hurry to see what else lay concealed. It took perhaps half an hour before he had cleared away enough soil to be sure that he could read all that was written there. All of it in the tiniest cramped lettering carved into the stone with some crude implement, a nail perhaps or a blade.

at our continued imprisonment in this town
after our homeward ship was forced
into this harbour for repairs
all of our suspicions at the long delay seemed justified
by the captain's indifference to my brother's
agitation and eventual fate

but I see now that the man was sim-
ply that and nothing more
indifferent to us by virtue of the colour of our skin
so it is that it falls to me to sail home with
the mask of stoicism set tight
after leaving this monument to my lost brother
buried here by white men without even
a stone to mark his place

───────

Oblivious to the blood still oozing from his shattered nail, Frederick Douglass sat on his heels in the graveyard and wept.

When his tears were over, he pushed the earth back into place with his boot and trod it back until all the lettering was concealed. Still there, but now hidden from the casual gaze of any who might enter the yard to look out over the river or to lay flowers on the grave of a lost relative.

Then he strode off along the road back to Exeter, back to Francis Bishop's house, back to the meeting he must address that evening and soon.

───────

PART THREE

...On Friday and Saturday crowded audiences were addressed at the Subscription Rooms in this city by Mr William Lloyd Garrison, a native of America, and Frederick Douglass, an escaped slave, on the best means of eradicating American slavery. The freed bondman made a great impression, from the powers of most moving and persuasive eloquence which he displayed, and the conscientious truth manifested in their affecting story. Considering that he is yet a young man, and has already remained twenty-one years in slavery and ignorance, his talents and acquired knowledge indicate his mental powers to be great...

...some slight interruption took place, in consequence of a gentleman wishing to address the meeting: he had attempted to speak before Mr Douglass began, but the meeting being impatient to hear Mr Douglass, the chairman decided against him...

Sercombe was on his feet, raising his hands for silence even though there was little enough noise in the room before. He welcomed all those present, saying that he was delighted to see such a good turn-out of the town's quality. Exeter was honoured, he said, to have such guests as they had this evening. Agreement was rumbled on several sides. For here, he continued in a slightly louder voice, here in their company, were the great voices which had been raised so long and so loud in the cause of the end of American slavery, William Lloyd Garrison,

313

editor of the *Liberator* newspaper. Here, also, was Frederick Douglass, author of his own life story and fugitive from bondage. The two men together and in their different ways, knew what a wickedness is American slavery and we people of this city should be glad in our hearts and minds to have such men among us. There was much applause, after which Sercombe invited Mr William Lloyd Garrison to have his say.

As the White American rose to his feet, so too did the Irish man standing half in the shadows at the back of the hall. But before he had even a moment to clarify what he intended, the porter's hand descended firmly on his shoulder and propelled back into his seat all the while warning him in a growl that if he moved again from his chair he would be put out.

So Eamonn MacDonagh sat and listened. Listened to Mr William Lloyd Garrison's denunciation of the trade in human flesh that continued still in the United States of America. Listened to his call for the British people to take up the cause of the abolition of the slave trade. And heard not a word of it, for the words broke over him like waves over a rock. They did soak in, but they did not wear away any of the hard surface. For the skin of this man did not resemble the flesh, the skin, of other men. For though it had a waxy sheen, there was no candle softness about it. All the tallow, all the fat, had been melted away, leaving only a hardness behind.

When Mr William Lloyd Garrison was finished and had sat down to great applause, and Sercombe introduced Frederick Douglass, and Frederick Douglass rose to speak and began by saying that he was delighted to be here in Britain for in his time here he had never once felt prejudice directed towards him on account of the colour of his skin, it was then that the Irish man leapt again to his feet and this time cried out,

And what about prejudice directed against a man on account of the tone of his voice?

What of those who would throw a man down by reason of his birthplace?

Sercombe half-rose to his feet but the porter was already at the man's back, grasping him by the collar. Seeing this treatment being administered to a man he thought a gentleman, no matter what his present state, William Wilkinson got to his feet and called out that the porter let the gentleman go. The porter, surprised by this, let go of Eamonn MacDonagh's coat. He took the opportunity of stepping further away, and continued his argument concerning the prejudice against Irish voices.

But he was drowned out by the angry voices of the audience, who had not come tonight to hear these ravings, but the planned and considered speeches of two men who knew their business well and spoke of a cause close to their hearts. Sercombe banged on the top table with the flat of his hand, until some order was restored. Even Wilkinson paused in his flow in response to this unexpected assertion of authority by Sercombe, whom he had come to regard as a reed in the winds of opinion.

Sercombe looked directly at the Irishman the whole time he spoke as he called for a vote on whether the audience would hear this heckler or Frederick Douglass. The Irishman attempted to object to being so called, but he was shouted down by those nearest him. He did not even stop to hear the outcome of the vote, but strode from the room, brushing aside the porter's grasp. As he slammed the door behind him, he heard a wave of applause and then a single voice speaking into the silence which followed.

———

For whatever reason, Douglass spoke well that night. Perhaps the interruption, rather than throwing him from his stride, briefly dammed the flood of his rhetoric which, when released, flowed all the more strongly. Those who would know, though, most especially Garrison, remembered the speech that night as one of his finest. Not one of his most influential, or even directed to one of his largest audiences. Simply, one of the best in form, sentiment and delivery. Of course, all three grounds, an auditor such as Garrison would be biased in certain ways.

Douglass made all the usual gestures, all the practices of the art which he had studied so carefully for the previous few years then refined and honed during his months in Britain and Ireland. He showed the chains. He paused for what seemed to the audience an immensely long time with the slaver's whip in his hand. Held it out so that they might see the blood crusted and hardened into the thongs. He called out the indignities of segregation in America, and compared them to his free passage into this hall. He named the names and titles of those hypocrites who called themselves Christian but nevertheless had a pocket filled with the man stealer's money. He told the truths of the life of the slave, with its physical and mental tortures. Told his own life, with the beatings and the insults, and at every turn insisted on its veracity by naming those who had committed the crimes against his person. Then he moved on, to argue that he relied not only on the truth of his account but also on his reliance on the great principles of justice, love and mercy. He asked if these might not be wielded by Englishman on behalf of American slaves, wielded to bring moral and religious influence to bear against American slavery.

He sat down to great, even thunderous, applause and the pencils of the journalists scratched away as they framed their assertions that Exeter had never seen a black man of this ilk before and very few white men either.

What followed was motions of thanks to the speakers, all passed, and another motion to found an Exeter branch of the Anti-Slavery League under the chairmanship of John Sercombe and with Francis Bishop as secretary received easy assent. The speakers then rose to make their thanks to the audience for their attendance and their attention.

As they moved through the hall towards the door, shaking hands and pausing for brief discussions, the two Americans became separated. Garrison was deep in conversation with a man to whom Sercombe had led him, while Douglass was some way to the door when he was obliged to halt his progress as an elderly couple made their way into the aisle before him. Standing thus still, he was suddenly aware of a presence very close to him and of a voice he vaguely recognised whispering urgently.

"How very interesting that you neglected to mention how you took your own freedom through a raised fist in the face of that monster Covey. Very interesting indeed."

Then the man had elegantly manoeuvred his way past the elderly couple and to the door. Where he turned and looked back at Douglass before stepping out into the now gathering gloom beyond.

The vague picture which had been formed in his mind by the sound of the voice became clear, sharp and reflected in the features before him. He tried to push his way through the crowd as quickly as he could, to follow the man, but by the time he reached the outer door, the man was across the road and walking briskly towards the garden gates. Then, strangely it seemed to Douglass, he paused and looked back. He looked as he had when Douglass had first seen him in Ireland, standing there with his cloak tossed open and back off his chest, so that he seemed much larger than he actually was. He stood there a moment, between the gates that stood slightly ajar.

Making several apologies, Douglass pushed his way through the last remnants of the crowd and then ran across the road towards the gate. He was about to enter the gardens when he was grabbed around the neck from behind.

So shocked was Douglass at being assailed from another direction that before he could resist, he was pulled off his feet and onto the ground. His attacker had a firm grip around his throat with one arm and with the other grasped the wrist of the hand with which Douglass was trying to throw him off. Before his head was finally forced down, though, Douglass saw the man he had been following stop, turn, look back to what was happening in the road. Douglass's assailant began shouting that he was not done yet, he was not done, that the other must wait a little longer.

A faint and unwanted memory from slavery stirred in him then, and he remembered that an assault could be halted by an obvious gesture of surrender. He let himself go limp and sank beneath his attacker's weight, to lie with his face pressed to the gravel. Panic rose in him briefly when he realised that the man who was now sprawled across his back did not understand the gesture and seemed to be still intent on choking him. All the while his attacker was shouting that the other must wait.

Though he could not see what happened next, Douglass remembered the words for many years after.

"I will wait one minute more. He could not wait to follow me, like the lamb called by its master. He knows what is coming."

"No, no! I have not had a chance."

Douglass was about to renew his resistance when the man suddenly released his hold and stood up. As Douglass lay there the exchange continued.

"We agreed that you would speak to him before now."

"I had another mission. Some of my people needed my assistance with another matter."

"We, you and I, had an agreement."

"And I have begun to think that this is not the moment. This is not yet the moment. I do not deny that it may come but not yet."

"One minute."

Douglass looked up now, to see his assailant step towards the other until the two men were almost pressed against each other. It was, it seemed to him, a gesture filled with both love and opposition.

They stood there a while and then suddenly, the shorter man turned and began to stride away.

At the edge of the park's deepening darkness, he turned and drew a pistol from his pocket and fired it before vanishing into the trees. The bullet struck Douglass's attacker, who fell to the ground. Douglass ran forward but before he reached him, the man was sitting up and looking around.

Both men were surprised; Eamonn MacDonagh, because he was still alive; Douglass, by the identity of his assailant when he realised that it was the Irishman from the hall. For this was not the man he had been when these two had last met. There was a brief and absurd moment as the two looked at each other. Then Douglass held out his hand, all the while very deliberately avoiding eye contact with the other, and demanded to know what he was about.

Yes, sir, I demand to know, he said, for the Irishman was looking around.

"My bag."

Douglass, too surprised by this to wonder how it was that the man was not dying or at the very least bleeding, found and brought him the bag.

From which the Irishman pulled a foot. Douglass stepped back a moment and watched in brief amazement as the man pulled off his boot and unstrapped his foot from his leg. The toes and much of the front part of the foot was shattered, and the man poured the tinkling pieces out of his boot. Then strapped on the new foot and pulled the ruined boot back on.

The Irishman began to talk almost before he was back on his feet. He began to apologise, profusely and earnestly, for his actions. Not, he said, not his actions in the hall for those he believed had been a right and proper protest. Against the actions of the English in Ireland and also against the actions of the English here in England towards the Irish who had come here in a desperate search for work, for all hope of work and livelihood at home was now quite gone.

No, he said, he apologised for having thrown Douglass to the ground in such a manner but that he could not think of another way to prevent the ambush. He hoped that he would be forgiven and then the Irishman paused in the flow of his words and held out his hand, Frederick Douglass took it and then, looking straight into the other man's eyes, nodded. Only then did he realise whose hand it was he held, for he was so very changed from their previous meetings. He was, he realised, holding the hand of Eamonn MacDonagh.

"Come with me", the Irishman said and almost laughed, "though I'll need your help. I've mastered walking on the level, but where we're going I'll need your help."

Then the two set off together through the streets of Exeter.

———

PART FOUR

THE RAILWAY LINE WORKINGS BETWEEN EXETER AND DAWLISH

He had always lived and worked near water, thought Kevin Donnellan, as he stood looking out over the estuary. Coming here was meant to be the great escape; from the cold, the damp, from the starvation he could see stalking the lanes when all that others saw was a few rotten spuds. From the water that ran through every corner of his life. All the other kids have loved being out on the bog for cutting the turf in late summer, but he had hated the squelch of the brown water between his toes. Hated walking to school through the great deep puddles which filled and blocked every path. Remembered, and hated still more, the day when his father had announced that school was over and that it was time for Kevin to start work with him.

Hated that day not for the memory of his father's words, but for the cold wetness that had slapped its way into every corner of his body as the small boat rode over the waves. Hated the memory of his father's laughter when Kevin had puked his guts over the side of the boat, for they had not that day even left the shelter of the bay. After that, he went fishing with his father every day except Sunday and had therefore come to love churchgoing as the fine alternative to being soaked wet and freezing cold even on the warmest day. Loved the unintelligible mutterings of the priest and had mouthed unknowingly the responses; it was the mystery of the words, the movements, the rhythms that he wished for all week long because the pointlessness of it all released him from worrying about the dreadful concentration of the fishing.

He was, he thought, lost in that when the boat overturned and suddenly the taste of salt water replaced the thin whiteness of the bread in his mouth. Spluttering and gasping, he had struggled out from under the sail and pulled himself back along the mast until he could reach up and grab the gunwale. But then, in pulling to haul himself out of the water, he had turned the boat full over and thrown himself back into the darkness of the water. He had come up again, first, under the boat and into the foul darkness roofed by wood and floored by water. Ducking down to pull himself out into the daylight again had called up all his strength, for the fear of being completely under the water terrified him. With eyes and mouth clamped shut, he had pulled himself by touch alone out and up into the air until he was able to look around.

By the time the other boats reached him, he knew his father was gone. And was ashamed that the fear had been so big in him that he had forgotten utterly the man's existence until he felt himself safe from drowning. For all he knew, in his thrashing he might have kicked his father's clutching hands loose from a handhold on the boat.

For days after, whenever he tried to sleep, that thought came to him through his dreams. He could see himself pushing his father's head under the water, pushing down hard as a way of levering himself up and out. Could see himself kicking the desperate man's clutching hands loose from his legs, so that he might climb up onto the overturned boat, kicking into his face to break the grip. And every time he dreamed these dreams he would wake, not screaming but with an awful coldness creeping through him. A coldness that told him he was cursed if he stayed here. Cursed so that none of the other fishermen would sail with him.

All that was left to him was to leave. This, he could not tell to his mother, for he knew that his departure would throw the family into a poverty that would make their present destitution seem luxury. He had seen what had happened to other families where the man had died or run. The lunacy of hedgerow wandering was there only for the luckiest in that circumstance. The only thing that held him was the knowledge that without him the potatoes would lie unlifted and would then rot in the ground. The thought that that, at least, would bring death swiftly through starvation gave him no comfort. So he waited and watched, watched the tops of the plants and waited for the signs that he could go into the field with the spade.

He had found a few leaves blackening, but they had been picked off and the earth pushed higher round the plants. And he watched.

One morning he and his mother had walked to the allotment as usual, to look at the plants and they had agreed that it was time. He had worked digging all morning in the soft early autumnal light and had filled baskets, pausing only occasionally to look out over the bay towards the open sea. With enough lifted, he carried them back to the pit by the house. Where he buried them and pulled layers of cut top turf over to keep out the light and stop the potatoes greening.

The next day he went again, to carry on digging. Every day for a week, excluding the Sunday morning, Kevin laboured lifting potatoes from the dark peaty soil and then carrying them in great baskets to the pits he had dug weeks before in preparation for this moment. Every evening he piled the potatoes into the holes and then carefully covered them with dry soil and turf. So that, after eight days, he had lifted the whole harvest. Now, in the knowledge that he had done all he could - bar staying here and that was impossible, he knew - he was ready to depart. He found that, now, he could not look his mother in the eye when she asked if he wanted more tea but merely nudged his mug with a finger.

Kevin lay awake that night while the rest of the family slept, preparing himself to leave but held to the mattress by some force he could not wholly comprehend. Then he pushed himself through the thumping of his heart and the dryness in his mouth to pull himself as quietly as he could to his feet. There was no difficulty in leaving now, for he had nothing to gather up, nothing to take with him that he was not wearing at that moment when he stood in the utter darkness of the cottage.

The disorientation of the darkness was such that he began to sway, almost to stumble, almost to faint, and he turned to the door before he was overwhelmed.

Outside, the darkness was less deep, less profound and anyway he knew his way from the door to the lane so well he could have walked there with his eyes shut. That thought, indeed, made him close his eyes and he began to step, slowly and carefully, towards the gap in the hedge with his chosen blindness preventing him from seeing his home for the last time.

By dawn, he was some ten miles away and walking along the rough road that wound its way across and through the bogs towards the east. The daylight, and then the sun, came up before him, so that he felt as if he were walking into a new life. That lengthened his stride, lifted him even though his stomach began to slop and gurgle from the absence of even the thinness of breakfast. All day he walked, knowing that he had to be as far away as he could this day if he was not to be overhauled by his mother's entreaties and pleas. As he walked the sun moved from his face to his right side, from the hills and heather before him to the flashes of the sea to the south.

When he came to the turning where the road ran down to Bun na hAbhann, he stopped and looked down the road towards the tiny port remembering the times he had walked here with his father carrying baskets of dried fish to sell to the factor there.

This was a rare event, only happening when there was enough fish caught to spare for a trade, and Kevin had every one of those days in his mind as he pecked at the loose stones of the road with his boot. He knew, also and in another part of his brain, why he could not take the next step along the way; because this was as far as he had ever been from his home, from the cottage where he had been born, from his world. He had almost, he thought, expected the ground to cry out that he should go no further.

Once he took another step along this road, he knew, he could not go back again. So he waited for courage to come to him. He waited in vain. He felt as though he could not go on without some sign from beyond himself that he should continue. It did not come. He knelt on the stones and prayed to God for guidance. None came. In that moment, slowly and reluctantly, he began to think that the only source of strength for himself was himself.

He began to walk again.

━━━━━━━━

It had took him a week of walking to reach Galway, a week of eating whatever he could find and of chewing grass and heather stalks when there was nothing else, of drinking water from streams when he could and from bog pools more often, of sleeping under whatever poor shelter he could find. Once or twice, passing carts gave him a ride for a few miles but every time he found himself unable to hold much conversation. For the first time in his life of long conversations and open expression, he began to hold matters within himself. The further he went from his home, the more secure he made his memories within himself.

He avoided cottages and houses, even when he was offered shelter, and preferred his own silent company. Thinking back to that time, he could remember nothing of his thoughts and had only the vaguest recollection of anything he had seen or heard. He felt as though those seven days had become a barrier between himself and the past, almost a time in which he had remade himself and his world.

Then, one Tuesday morning, he found himself standing before a bridge. Off to his right there was a huddle of old cottages which seemed to have turned their backs on the world across the river, and beyond them the sea glittered and danced under the clear autumn sunlight. Across the bridge he could see the place a passer-by had told him was called Spanish Arch, where the Spainies had come for many years to do business with the

Irish behind the backs of the English. Beyond the cluster of buildings, the town itself was gathered along the harbourside and up towards a large low hill.

Kevin hesitated at the bridge, though, because this felt like another step that could not be retraced. Across this bridge was not-home, was the other bank of the Corrib river. Home was where your feet were planted firm and solid on the ground, while over there the earth moved faster and it was harder to keep a balance.

So it was that, when he lifted his foot to step onto the bridge, he did so with a care that verged on fear. A fear that the great blocks of the bridge would fall beneath his foot's touch into the fast water below with a great crash. He let his weight come down and the bridge held. With a great out-breath, he hurried across.

Galway was, by a long mile, the biggest town, the only city, he had ever been in. Its cobbled streets, its houses built right next to each other, its dozens of shops all crowded close, were wonders. As was the good piece of land right in the city centre that seemed to be used only for growing flowers and a few trees surrounded by lawn grass. A terrible waste of good land, he thought, as he walked past. As many people as there were, though, Kevin thought that there should be more, for he had seen as many as Clifden the once or twice he had been with his father.

He kept walking.

It wasn't until he was out beyond Galway city a good way and onto the road that ran straight to Dublin that he noticed it first. As he passed a field of potatoes that stood still unlifted, and he thought it strange for the autumn was now well on. Ah, but then, he thought, it always happens a bit and he walked on.

That had been near the crest of a small hill, where a light breeze stirred the air. When he walked down into the little valley beyond, where the air was still and damp even in the early afternoon, it was much stronger. It sent a small shudder through him, and now he hurried, to be away from it as fast as he might. But the faster he walked, the stronger it became until he came to a clutch of cottages all grouped close by the road, with a small track running in off the main road.

He turned off into the little yard between the cottages, and as soon as ever he was in that space it caught him like a slap in the face. With a hand up to his mouth and nose, he moved closer to the great pit at one end of the yard.

The turf had been pulled back at one side, so that what was beneath could be seen. The pit itself was filled with a thick black, reeking stew.

Kevin stepped back quickly, to stop the stench from turning his gagging into vomit. Stepped back and turned to knock at the door of one of the cottages. No answer. He tried another. The same. The entire little village was deserted. It was the stench that had driven the people away.

It had been versions of the same story all the way to Ballinasloe. Villages, single cottages, emptied of the people. Everywhere, the clinging smell until Kevin thought it was soaking into his skin and that if ever he got away from here and met strangers, they would know where he was from by the smell of him. The stink of the rotting potatoes had completely replaced the smell of peat smoke, not only because it was so strong but in the many miles he had walked since Galway city, he could remember seeing only a handful of smoking chimneys. Rotting potatoes were replacing living people.

Ballinasloe was different. There were still people here. This was the town at the edge of the west, the edge of the east. It had always been, in Kevin's mind, a town more like Samarkhand than Galway for it was the place where the bigness of the rest of Ireland began. The place of the town in the world was confirmed for him by two things as he walked past the great horse fair ground and then on into the main street. No one stared at him, no-one registered him as the outsider, the stranger passing through their small universe.

And, he saw his first black man. Standing at a corner, in conversation with a man who was clearly a westie. Kevin stood, a distance off, looking at the black man. He was young, certainly less than thirty, but he had an air of self-assurance and confidence about him that set him aside from all those around him.

There was a moment when Kevin wanted to cross the road, to touch him, to rub his skin to see that it was as real as his own. He was prevented from this by the appearance through the crowd of a man before whom all parted; he heard someone mutter that it was the English land agent. Even though he had not seen this man before, Kevin had seen his type and was filled with a silent anger.

Then all that was shattered by an explosion right beside him. The noise was so appallingly loud that he was stunned by it. It was all the thunderclaps that he had ever heard rolled into one, and it sent him staggering back. Staggering into a man who pushed him and began to run, but not before Kevin had seen his face. Seen the harelip that was not the most unfamiliar part of that face. For, for all that this man had the same features as any other, there were so different in their shaping and coloration that Kevin knew in an instant that the man was not Irish nor English.

Then the man was gone.

In that moment Kevin knew he had to be away too, away from Ballinasloe before anyone remembered that he was a stranger here.

Someone no other had seen before.

Another guiltiness came to rest on his shoulders. A feeling that, somehow, whatever he did or didn't do, would bring a blame to rest at his door. A blame that, even if no other placed it there, would haunt him at the edge of every thought, every breath. A blame that would wake him in the night with dreams of his mother lying dead and cold in that village where he had first realised what he had done when he had buried the potato harvest. He had not saved his family, but condemned them. His flight had been the boot swung at the chair beneath the roped man, not the chair as he had intended.

Only one place to go then. The English wouldn't import food to Ireland, but they would export men. Kevin met a Mayo man on the road, who was going to England and said that he would be happy to have Kevin walk with him. You have a darkness in you, the man from Mayo said, but then so do we all now.

Yet others, it seemed could not see the mark upon him and took him into their company. The man from Westport he had met on the boat, who had taken Kevin in and made him part of the navvy company he was taking to England.

Kevin knew that the man's interest was in his size and strength, for at his age he was a good deal larger than many and though still really a boy he had the muscles of a man accustomed to the hard labour of boat and field. Yet he had feared, the first time he lifted a pick, that he would strike another with it; had known, when the first dynamite stick he had lit and then turned to scurry clear, that the flying rocks would strike someone down. That none of this happened meant only, to Kevin, that it had not happened yet.

His life in the camps was regulated in such a way that he could surrender any need for larger thoughts to the simple business of work. Six days a week work, and then watching while the others strode off into the night come Saturday. He would lie in his tent, or wander the workings. Anything which didn't require that he speak too much or share his life at all beyond the simplicities with others.

Then the gang leader had told them all they were being hired for a new job. The rates were agreed and the job would last perhaps two years. They all accepted, and then headed south. To the camp all ready for them in the woods between the great sweep of the estuary and the hills rising behind them. Yet the first Saturday when Kevin had set off for his walk, he had met an Englishman under the trees who had said that it weren't wise to wander too far round here.

Then, come a payday they were short. When the gang leader was approached he shook his head, so a group of them went to the foreman's office. Camp security, he said. For their own protection. Too many people round here disliking, hating even, Irish on their doorsteps. And when they asked why they were the ones who paid, the foreman had said they didn't have to stay, they were free to go back to Ireland any time they chose.

It got worse. The newspapers the foreman brought, and gave the men who could read well, talked of the scandal of the sink of licence in the woods, by which they knew was meant their camp. They asked the foreman where such stories were born, but he swore he did not know. And he tightened the security, which cost more money.

But though the foreman could control what went out of the camp, he needed to bring in supplies, food and equipment and of course more men. Who came with stories, and other newspapers. The *Northern Star* told how everywhere foreman and owners were using all manner of trickery and lies to take money from working men's pockets.

Kevin's sober wanderings had given him a knowledge of the camp and its place that showed all the ways in and out, until he could almost walk straight out and back in again without even being missed. He listened to the talk, the grumblings, the loud voices urging action of one sort or another that were swiftly stifled, but he did not feel part of it. All he wanted was to work himself until the tiredness numbed him to a good sleep.

But as the spring turned to summer, this became ever harder. Partly from the light evenings and mornings, but more from the talk. There was a small Dublin jackeen who was ever trying to organise collections for the folks at home, but none believed the money would ever arrive for sure didn't they all know what a jackeen was like. But the man's stories grew steadily worse, until words like starvation, corpses in the street, eviction, poor house buzzed in Kevin's ears like wasps. Slowly, more and more men got stung.

They made a collection that the jackeen was to take. But the foreman found out, called it a collection for a combination, warned them that such was illegal and that he would put them all out on the road, and confiscated the money. The wasps buzzed a different note as the man strode off down the muddy path between the tents.

The jackeen had been at Kevin's side a few days later, asking did he know such and such a place on the river bank. He did. Would he collect a little something for the jackeen from there? Kevin thought a while. He would.

So here he was, standing by water again. Standing like a fool, waiting on something to happen.

When a man appeared beside him in the darkness, so quiet and soft that Kevin hadn't heard him come up until he was right at his side. A man who asked if he had a friend from Dublin, to which he replied that he did. This is for him, the man said, and passed Kevin a bundle of what seemed to be leaflets or posters. There was something about the man, something in the way he spoke English. For he spoke it as Kevin himself did, with the Connemara accent but before Kevin could ask, he was gone again. As quietly as he had come, though he walked strangely, almost as if his feet were not his own.

The posters said that Feargus O'Connor was coming, to speak to them.

AUGUST 28TH, THE SAME

The foreman tore down as many as he could find, saying that if he found out who was to blame for this he was out of the camp immediately. All those who knew, shook their heads. All those who didn't, shook their heads as well. Sure, blame's an interesting word now isn't it, muttered the little jackeen.

They worked all day as usual, if anything better for their concentration, every man's thinking, was sharp and focussed. The posters, it seemed, had had the same effect as a crystal dropped into a solution at just the right moment. Suddenly, everything formed around it. Suddenly, the name Feargus O'Connor shaped everything: the anger about money, the fear about home. It all came together.

The foreman, though, couldn't understand why, when he had asked them to finish late so that they might have the ground cleared and ready for some more blasting in the morning, they had all agreed. They, too, wanted the ground cleared. They were in no hurry.

They finished in the mid-evening. The men trusted with the dynamite went up to lay the charges for the next day but left them unfused, and then all the men walked back to the camp to eat. Sitting at long trestles pulled out into the late light, they ate and then sat there. None moved. The foreman came through with bottles, setting them on the tables and thanking the men for the day's good effort. But the bottles stood untouched. The foreman urged them to drink. The jackeen reached over and pushed the cork back into the bottle nearest him. The foreman stepped forward. The jackeen stood up. He reached barely to the foreman's chin. The foreman told him to sit down and drink.

Saying he would do as he wished, the jackeen turned into Malachy Joyce. And Malachy Joyce turned to the men sat all around him to say,

Brothers, we have a man to meet. He's expecting us up by the tower on the hill. The brothers from further down the line will meet us there.

Then he turned to the foreman and, as every man in the camp got to his feet, Malachy asked the foreman to step aside and picked up one of the lanterns from the trestle.

As they walked up through the trees towards the ridge where the tower stood that could be seen for miles in all directions, Malachy said that they should gather any dry wood they could find. When they reached the open ground before the tower, the wood was piled. Kevin, at Malachy's suggestion, coiled a length of fuse he had brought with him into the side of one of the heaps and Malachy gave him the lantern.

The men from Newton Abbott, and from still further down the line, began arriving soon after. There they stood, hundreds of them, mingling in with each other and talking about which camp they were in and the conditions there, and what had happened these last weeks and how the notices for this meeting had been spread, until they were all drawn into one crowd. Men from different camps discovered that they came from villages close together, had common relatives.

All the while, Kevin noticed, Malachy was shifting from one foot to the other and looking off into the trees where a path wound up from the road below. The more the buzz among the men grew, the more Malachy looked back and forth. Then, just as Kevin was about to go over, a man came up the track and walked over to Malachy. They shook hands.

Brothers, Malachy shouted, brothers.

A silence ran through the men and they turned to look at Feargus O'Connor. He was not much to look at, Kevin though, but then he began to speak.

Malachy nodded to him and for a moment Kevin didn't know why.

Then he pulled the candle from the lantern and lit the fuse.

―――――

AUGUST 28,

THE ROAD FROM EXETER TO EXMOUTH, LATE IN THE EVENING

It had grown steadily more gloomy as Frederick Douglass and the Irishman walked away from the city centre and then out of the city completely on to the road which ran first straight as the Roman foundations on which it was laid, and then began its serpentine wind between the fields beyond that small town. They crossed a river that, from its size, Douglass guessed was a tributary of the estuary that he thought was now somehow off to his right. Then they seemed to be veering away from the river and off into the countryside.

333

All the while, the Irishman talked quietly, almost beneath his breath, of the events that had struck his life in the last year. Talking of what had happened, what he had seen, since their paths had last crossed.

He had reached a point twice already in his rambling account, but then had each time returned to the beginning and started over. Douglass was beginning to fear that he had been taken away not by a man in need of his company, but by a lunatic. The further they walked in the gloom which swirled into a darkness in the deeper, narrower parts of the lane, the more this feeling grew within him until he had come close to the point where he was considering turning back. Turning back now, while he was still sure of the path back to his lodgings.

Then they came out of the lane's dimness to a place where the banks lowered and Douglass could see that the land fell away towards the river, which shone a faint and occasional silver. Beyond, he could see hills turning a deep cobalt blue as the sun went down behind them, throwing its last great traces up into the empty sky above as golden pink flashes. Douglass stopped a moment, to watch this sunset but the Irishman's hand dickered at his arm. Urging him to come, to move on, to get there. They walked again to the accompaniment of the Irishman's muttering voice but now Douglass was distracted, half because he now knew the story being told and half because he had become intrigued by the way the road, now running parallel to the river, rose and fell against the land's independent rising and falling in such a way that his view of the landscape away to the west was constantly changing and revealing a series of complex arrangements of water, land and sky. At one time, the river was invisible and the land and sky darkened together. Then the river came back into view as the land fell away, and the water reflected back the dying sunlight.

And then, and then.

The river and the hills disappeared as the hedge became suddenly, abruptly, higher. Now, Eamonn MacDonagh has stopped talking. The sunset is complete and only the thinnest light is left in the sky. Here, in the darkness of a Devon lane, an Irish hunger artist is lowered from the back of a young black American and pulls at his sleeve.

Douglass can see, even through the gathering darkness, that MacDonagh has an expression of urgency about him. This is the place, he says, this is the place and he proceeds to hobble ahead.

Douglass follows him and together the two men climb over the gate into the orchard. In under the trees, the darkness is more profound but in such a way that when light does penetrate it seems strangely more illuminating. The moon's obliqueness shows Douglass where the trees stand, so that he can follow MacDonagh. The dew, thick on the long grass underfoot, soaks his trousers up to the knees. Then he is lost in a darkness that fills the space between the ground and the lower branches of an especially large tree. It is such a size that, in the darkness, he has walked right in under its branches until they have cut off all the light. MacDonagh grips his wrist, almost as if he knew this would happen.

Help me, he says, help me up and then follow me.

And, as Douglass pushes, he pulls himself up into the branches, before reaching back to offer Douglass a hand. By now, Douglass feels that he has gone so far down this road that he may as well see it to the end. So he climbs up after the older man.

Once up into the bowl of branches, it is difficult for the two men to climb beside each other for the space is cramped. So MacDonagh climbs up first and then Douglass follows. Douglass knows his head is above the top of the higher branches because what moonlight there is, now returns. With the darkness below so thick, he now feels as though he is hanging in mid-air. Slowly, he realises that the land falls away before him in such a way that from this height it seems as though he is suspended above the great sweep of the estuary. The water glitters under the moonlight, in a steady arc from right to left that ends where the lights of a small town intermingle with moonlight reflecting off the sea. Directly before him, the hills even at the distance of several miles rear up again as a great bank of heavy black-purple which ends in the definite but irregular line of an horizon of blue deep enough almost to be black.

The effort of climbing the tree has made Douglass's heart pound, and the sudden view has made him bite back his breath at its unexpectedness. Then, suddenly, he has to gasp for breath as his head swims a little. And he becomes all the more aware that the older man beside him is breathing easily, calmly, as he stands among the branches gazing out over the river.

His breathing settles again until he, too, is calm and still. They stand there, in silence, holding tightly to the branches and looking out over the river. An unlikely trust begins to grow in that silent darkness. Unlikely, because neither of the two men would have chosen, would have predicted, this moment. Yet both of them feel, know even, that they are in the right place and at the right time. Both of them feel, even know, that this absurd moment makes sense.

MacDonagh points upstream, towards a house Douglass can just see in the gloom, standing on a spit of land between the two rivers.

"They tell me that it is called Riversmeet House," MacDonagh says, "because the man who built the house thought that was where the two rivers meet. He thought that he could stroll to the bottom of his garden, and look down on his mastery of the world. But the currents flow deeper than that, and do not merge until further downstream."

His arm sweeps down the river, drawing Douglass's gaze to a point directly before them.

"There", he says, "that's where the rivers meet when the tides are gone out."

Then, at this moment of calmness, as they turn to look out across the water, the flames spring up on the hills they are facing.

From this distance all that they can see are the fires across the river. Huge beacons blazing up at the crest of the hills, above the tree line. As one huge bonfire roars up, peaks and begins to die back again, another springs up. Then another. Another. The fires move along the horizon.

For as long as the fires burn, the two stand in the tree and watch. Then darkness falls back again.

Eamonn MacDonagh knows that it is the Irish navvies, gathered to stake a claim on what is theirs. And he knows that the power they hold in their hands could be greater than the one he knows how to wield. The rich and the powerful call Eamonn's work terrorism, but it is the power within these working men that strikes the real terror. He knows this, even as he knows he cannot be a part of this coming power. He has trod too far down his own path to turn back now, even though he knows that turning might be the best. While he is on this side of the rivers, the navvies are standing together on the other bank to hear the words of Fergus O'Connor, calling the rich and the powerful to account and calling on the navvies to become a part of the accounting.

Frederick Douglass cannot tell what has lit these fires, but he can tell that the force behind them is greater than any he has yet seen moving in the world.

They watch, even after the fires have ceased to burn.

Neither of them speaks as they climb back down from the pear tree, walk away through the orchard, part at the gateway and then turn in opposite directions. Neither of them will come here again. Neither of them will ever mention this moment to another person. Both of them, though, will carry its memory through the rest of his days.

Eamonn MacDonagh will remain in England for a few years yet. He will, however, find the smaller towns too exposed. He will think himself too obvious, as he moves around the streets on his false legs and so he will move first to Manchester and then London. In a few years, he will make a bomb and plant it against the wall of a prison and thereby help several of his comrades escape. I do not know if he died in the blast or returned again to the west, for he disappears entirely from view hereafter. Within a few years of this happening, though, W B Yeats will write a poem in which another MacDonagh appears as an ambiguous presence.

———

On December 5th 1846, Hugh Auld, to whom his father Thomas had transferred his title on Frederick Douglass, accepted a payment of $710.96 and signed the papers relinquishing his claim on Douglass's life. Very soon thereafter, the title was passed to Douglass by his English friends. He will live until nearly the end of the century, and in that time he will become the greatest Black man of his era. He will return to England again, first in 1859 and then again with his second wife Julia in the 1890s, but on neither occasion will he visit the South West. He will see the end of slavery and its rebirth in segregation. He will die, of a heart attack, in 1895 the day after delivering his final speech in which he called for women's suffrage and having to walk home because he could not find a carriage to carry him across the white man's city.`

———

Out in the garden at night, standing in under the last of the pear trees, I rest my hand on the trunk and look out to the west. I can understand some, even most, of this story. What happens next, though, is unclear. So I stand, watching for the fires to leap up again, brilliant against the trees.

ABOUT THE AUTHOR

Richard Bradbury lives and writes in Devon. His play, Become a Man, was performed as part of the London bicenntenial of the abolition of slavery commemorations. He is currently completing a companion novel to Riversmeet, The Last Painting.

ABOUT THE MUSWELL PRESS

The Muswell Press is a newly established independent press run as a co-operative. We aim to publish quality books that engage with the world – fiction, art, childrens' literature or non fiction. 'Riversmeet' is our third publication, timed for the 200th commemorations of the abolition of slavery. More books are in development. Please see www.muswellpress.co.uk

ALREADY PUBLISHED

Out of Time is a passionate and violent parallel world that mirrors our own and shows that, for all our hopes and expectations, fate has its own plans.

"Time is not what it seems. It lets two worlds share it, perhaps more than two. An infinite number..."

Joe Harding is locked out of his house and chased out of town by a band of citizens determined to kill him.

He must learn to survive in a parallel time zone, torn between finding a way back to his own world and choosing a future amongst a youthful dissident community in which he discovers shelter and love

James Boswell: Unofficial War Artist was published by The Muswell Press on 9th November 2006. It features drawings and paintings taken from the archives of Tate Britain, The British Museum and The Imperial War Museum. The text is by William Feaver. Most of these works have never been seen by the public and form a unique record of the soldier's life in World War 2. They are of particular contemporary interest as Boswell was stationed in Iraq in 1942/43 where he drew extensively.